Ring

Alex Gerlis is the author of the acclaimed Spies series of four Second World War espionage thrillers which are noted for their detailed research and intricate plots and feature two great adversaries: the British spymaster Edgar and his Soviet counterpart Viktor. The television/film rights for *The Best of Our Spies* have been bought by a major production company.

Born in Lincolnshire, Alex was a BBC journalist for nearly 30 years. He lives in west London with his wife and family and three black cats, a breed which makes cameo appearances in his books. He's a lifelong supporter of Grimsby Town, which has provided some preparation for the highs and lows of writing novels. When asked if he has worked in the field of espionage he declines to answer in the hope some people may think he has.

Also by Alex Gerlis

Spy Masters

The Best of Our Spies
The Swiss Spy
Vienna Spies
The Berlin Spies

The Richard Prince Thrillers

Prince of Spies
Sea of Spies
Ring of Spies
End of Spies

ALEX GERLIS

RING OF SPIES

10 CANELO

First published in the the United Kingdom in 2020 by Canelo

This edition published in the United Kingdom in 2021 by Canelo

Canelo Digital Publishing Limited
31 Helen Road
Oxford OX2 0DF
United Kingdom

A CIP catalogue record for this book is available from the British Library.

Print ISBN 978 1 80032 220 2
Ebook ISBN 978 1 78863 873 9

Look for more great books at www.canelo.co

Printed and bound in Great Britain by Clays Ltd, Elcograf S.p.A.

Characters

Richard Prince British intelligence agent, detective superintendent

Tom Gilbey Senior MI6 officer, London

Hon. Hugh Harper Senior MI5 officer, London

Sir Roland Pearson Downing Street intelligence adviser

Lance King MI5 officer, London

Hanne Jakobsen Danish prisoner (and British agent), Ravensbrück

Second Lieutenant Andrew Reeves South Staffordshire Regiment

Franz Rauter RSHA officer, Berlin

The Colonel Deputy director at Latchmere House

White MI5 interrogator at Latchmere House

Bartholomew MI5 Disciple

Major Olszewski Polish intelligence officer

Hood MI5 officer at Huntercombe

Flying Officer Ted Palmer RAF pilot

Helmut Krüger Abwehr officer

Otto Prager Abwehr officer

Jim Maslin Agent Donne (John Morton)

Agent Milton Nazi agent in the UK

Brigadier Oakley Directorate of Military Intelligence

Jan Dabrowski Agent Dryden – Nazi agent in the UK

Agent Shelley Nazi agent in the UK

Agent Keats Nazi agent in the UK

Agent Byron Nazi agent in the UK

SS-Brigadeführe Walter Schellenberg Head of the RSHA

Hauptsturmführer Klaus Böhme Aide to Schellenberg

Field Marshal Wilhelm Keitel Head of the OKW

General Alfred Jodl Chief of Staff of the OKW

General Heinz Guderian Chief of Staff of the OKH

Spencer Steward at Hugh Harper's club

Joseph Jenkins Office of Strategic Services liaison officer

Major Mark B. Fine US Army 7th Armored Division

Audrey Former MI5 officer

Arthur Chapman-Collins Former Treasury civil servant, British Nazi

Lenny Fenton British fascist in Bermondsey

Sid McConnell British fascist in Bermondsey

Vince Curtis British fascist in Brixton Prison

Len Warder at Brixton Prison

Lieutenant General Cunnington British Army General Staff

Lieutenant Nate Markham US 9th Armored Division

Paulette Dubois French resistance fighter

Tom Bennet MI9 officer

Podpolkovnik Iosif Leonid Gurevich NKGB officer

Sturmbannführer Alfred Strasser SS officer

Boris Novikov NKVD officer at Ravensbrück

Hauptsturmführer Reeder SS officer at Ravensbrück

Heinrich Mohr Gestapo officer, Rostock

Myrtle Friend of Arthur Chapman-Collins

Mr Ridgeway Man at art gallery

Prologue

Cambridge, October 1933

'Well I never, fancy bumping into you!'

He'd been struggling to attach his bicycle to the railings in the howling wind and near-horizontal rain, weather more like the deck of a ship in a storm than a cobbled street in Cambridge in early autumn. When he turned round to see who'd spoken, the man was standing just beyond the immediate glare of a street lamp, not quite in the shadows but close enough to them to be unrecognisable.

'I'm sorry, were you talking to me?'

When the man stepped forward, the yellow light revealed him to be fair-skinned, perhaps in his forties, the fashionably wide brim of his trilby tilted downwards and the collar of his coat turned up. For the life of him he couldn't place the man.

'We met at the Fitzwilliam drinks in the summer; you may recall some dreadful classics bore introduced us. I do hope he's not a chum of yours.'

He'd managed to secure his bicycle now and turned round to face the man properly. He was still none the wiser.

'I'm shocking with names and I...' He was aware that his stammer was more pronounced, as it always was when flustered like this.

'Don't worry, so am I. It's Arthur: I seem to remember you were about to be interviewed for a job at Gonville and Caius, weren't you – tutor in medieval literature, I think?'

'Yes... that's right.'

'And did you get it?'

'I'm afraid not, no...'

'I say, shall we go into that pub for a drink – out of the rain, eh?'

Arthur clutched his elbow and steered him across the road. They bought their drinks at the bar and then Arthur said to follow him. They ended up in a narrow alcove tucked under the stairs at the back of the pub.

'Good to be out of the storm, eh? Cheers!'

Even without the hat, he still couldn't recognise the man. He'd normally remember either a face or a name, if not both, but this man was to all intents and purposes a complete stranger. He recalled the drinks party at Fitzwilliam, of course, but was sure he'd not met the man there, let alone discussed the job at Caius with him.

'I'm sorry to hear you didn't get the job.'

'So am I. I had thought I—'

'I hear a chap called Goldstein got it.'

'Goldman, actually, but yes...'

'Still, I imagine you can now push on with your doctorate – how's that going, by the way?'

'Slowly, but—'

'I also heard,' Arthur dropped his voice and leaned closer over the narrow table between them, the smell of warm bitter on his breath, 'that you had a bit of bad luck with that grant you were hoping to get?'

'The Sawston Award? Yes...'

'A Professor Mendel made the decision, I understand?'

'Amongst others, yes...' He stopped and stared down at his half-pint of mild, which he'd barely touched. He was racking his brain for some memory of having met Arthur but still drew a blank. Yet this stranger sitting opposite knew an awful lot about him. It wasn't as if he'd exactly publicised his failure to get the job at Caius, and the outcome of the Sawston Award hadn't even been officially announced yet.

'Both Jews, you realise?'

'I beg your pardon?'

'Goldman and Mendel – they're both Jews.' There was a glint in Arthur's eyes, as if he was excited.

'I assume so.'

'And are you happy about it?'

'Well of course not! I was the best-qualified person by a mile for the Caius job, and my paper for the Sawston Award was first class, but Professor Mendel treated me as if I was a primary school pupil. I'm sorry, but I'm angry, as you can see…'

Arthur leaned back, still smiling, and said nothing for a while, allowing the younger man opposite to talk at length, going red in the face as he did so, his voice stuttering as he became more angry.

'Of course I know Goldman and Mendel are both Jews… I'd not felt able to mention that to anyone, not until now… Obviously I'm not prejudiced, but… I don't need anyone to tell me about Jews and what they could get up to – I'm an expert in medieval literature, after all, especially German medieval literature, and even legends have some basis in fact…'

When he finished, he looked as if he was about to cry yet at the same time relieved to have unburdened himself. He muttered an apology as he drank his beer, and Arthur told him not to worry, of course he understood – in fact he'd also been the victim of Jews, as had so many people he knew.

'Between you and me, I've heard that a wealthy relative of Goldman's had promised money to the college funds.'

'How do you know that?'

'Let's just say that people I know are very well aware of these matters. Tell me, how much was the Sawston Award worth?'

'One hundred and fifty pounds – it would have meant I could concentrate on my doctorate for an entire academic year and not have to take on anything else, like working in the library and writing essays for barely literate but very wealthy undergrads on closed scholarships.'

Arthur stood up. He was not a particularly imposing figure, but he looked confident – the kind of person who usually got his way. 'There are some like-minded people I think you ought to meet. Could you come down to London for dinner one night next month?'

He said it depended on the day, but possibly, yes…

'I'll write to you at Jesus. Meanwhile, this will help with your expenses. Best not open it until you're back in your rooms.'

–

The man left the pub without waiting for him. He finished his drink, composed himself and went back to his rooms. It was only later on, when the poetry of von Eschenbach became a bit too much that he remembered the envelope the man had given him.

For the next hour he stared at its contents scattered across his narrow bed.

White ten pound notes: ten of them.

One hundred pounds.

Chapter 1

'Is anyone else alive?'

None of those gathered around him replied. The room was dark and damp, with the smell of earth and disinfectant hanging heavy in the air. There were four or five others there: a couple of medics, an officer from Divisional Intelligence and another officer from Corps Headquarters, the ones who were supposed to have rescued them. None of them looked directly at him.

Second Lieutenant Andrew Reeves of the South Staffordshire Regiment was slumped on the floor, clutching a flask of water tightly with both hands to stop its contents spilling out. A doctor had already taken a quick look at him and said he was fine and told the medics to dress his wounds. In truth Reeves looked dreadful: his face and hands were filthy, he hadn't shaved for days and his eyes were bloodshot. The parts of his face not covered in oil and soot were deathly white.

'So all the others are dead – I'm the only one left?'

'No, of course not, Reeves. Look, we just need to debrief you, then you can have a hot meal and a rest. I bet you're looking forward to that, eh?' It was the officer from Corps Headquarters doing his best to sound jolly while trying to muffle a hacking cough. Somewhere in the distance came the sound of artillery fire, and Reeves jumped at the sound.

'What about my platoon? Last time I counted them, there were still a dozen alive.'

'I fear it may be fewer than that now.'

Second Lieutenant Reeves nodded as if he was expecting as much. 'And B Company? I assumed command of it when Captain Hall was killed: there were ninety men when I took over.'

The officer from Divisional Intelligence shook his head. 'Perhaps a dozen were evacuated. Look, how about you have that nice hot meal first and then a rest, and we can ask you a few questions afterwards?'

'And the rest of the brigade?'

'We're still working that out. We know the 1st Airlanding Brigade sent in two and a half thousand men, and we estimate fewer than five hundred have been evacuated. But that doesn't mean the rest are dead by any means. The majority would have been taken prisoner.'

No one said anything for a while. The screams of the wounded from down the corridor seemed to be getting closer.

'It was a bloodbath, you know... a fucking bloodbath.'

The shocked silence in the room was interrupted by a rolling *crump-crump* of artillery fire.

'We understand that, Andrew, we—'

'Well you don't, actually. If you weren't there, you won't understand.'

Reeves looked at the two officers accusingly, as if they were to blame. Then he hauled himself up from the floor and moved slowly to a chair. He was tall, well over six foot, and when he stood under the single light, it was clear he was younger than he looked hunched in the shadows: probably still in his early twenties. He sat up straight and ran his hand though his hair.

'It felt... it felt like half the fucking German army were there waiting for us. We were told we'd be catching them by surprise. Instead they caught *us* by surprise.'

One of the officers asked the medics to leave, and the two men drew up chairs in front of Reeves. One of them patted his knee.

'Obviously the operation didn't go quite to plan, Andrew, and I think—'

'Didn't go quite to plan? You don't need to tell me, I was there! And I'll tell you something else, sir…' The 'sir' had a hint of sarcasm to it.

'What's that, Andrew?'

'They were expecting us, sir. The fucking Germans were expecting us. They knew we were coming.'

—

A fortnight earlier, he'd been at the battalion's final briefing, given by a colonel from Corps Headquarters. The tension in the room was palpable. Faces seemed to be drained of colour.

'This is an ambitious and extremely well-planned operation that aims to invade the Netherlands through Belgium and then, using a combination of land and airborne forces – and not forgetting air support, of course – capture a corridor of land over key rivers and canals, enabling us to advance north-west to the German border, thus outflanking the Nazis.'

The colonel looked rather pleased with himself. 'Along with four parachute brigades, your 1st Airlanding Brigade will be part of the 1st Airborne Division. Other units will advance by land across the border and through Eindhoven, while airborne units will seek to capture and establish bridgeheads, in particular here and here – the Meuse at Grave and the Waal at Nijmegen.'

He had paused to sip from his glass of water and attempted a joke about it being too early in the morning for whisky. Only one or two people in the room bothered to laugh with him.

'The objective of the 1st Airborne will be the town of Arnhem. We aim to capture and secure these two bridges over the Rhine: the railway bridge here – to the west of the town – and the main road bridge here through the centre. The town itself is located on the north bank of the river, so we will drop the majority of our forces around there. The idea is that once we have secured these crossings, our forces moving up from Eindhoven will be able to continue their advance towards Germany.'

Their commanding officer had then taken over. He didn't speak with quite the same degree of confidence as the colonel. 'The 2nd Battalion the South Staffs will be landed here, around Landing Zone S: the Airlanding Brigade's job is to secure the drop and landing zones around Arnhem so the parachute brigades have a clear run to the two bridges.'

He'd stood for a while staring at the map, a look of mild incredulity on his face, as if he didn't quite believe what he was looking at. The room had become restless during the silence, before someone said they'd better get a move on, they had a busy few days ahead.

—

Months later, Andrew Reeves was very clear in his mind that his life was now in two quite distinct parts: before Arnhem and after Arnhem. The nine days in between had been no kind of life at all.

It wasn't as if things had gone terribly wrong at first. The South Staffs had landed in their gliders close to LZS – Landing Zone S – and had made their positions secure around Wolfheze. The parachute brigades had arrived in the various drop and landing zones and made their way to the bridges. He was commanding a platoon of twenty-seven men, part of B Company, which had landed with a hundred and forty men in total.

But within hours it became clear that Arnhem was far better defended than they'd been expecting. The railway bridge in the west of the town was blown up before the 2nd Parachute Battalion could reach it, and by the time the Paras got to the northern end of the main road bridge across the Rhine, the Germans were well entrenched on its southern side.

The fighting became increasingly bitter. On the third night – it could have been the fourth morning – Reeves had found Captain Hall, his company commander. 'There was an intelligence briefing for the company and battalion commanders,'

Hall said as they crouched close to each other in a ditch by the side of a road. He had a nasty gash down the side of his face and gripped Reeves's wrist as he spoke. His breath reeked of tobacco. 'The Germans have got their best battlefield commander in western Europe – Field Marshal Model – based in the town; they've got artillery, and they've got the 9th and 10th Panzer Divisions here too. Imagine, Andrew: we were told this was a well-planned operation and what do we find? Two bloody Panzer divisions and a fucking field marshal!'

Reeves replied that if this was a well-planned operation he'd hate to see what a bad one looked like, and Hall had laughed slightly manically. The captain had started to stand up and Reeves had to pull him down and warn him to be careful.

Soon after that, the battalion had retreated to a perimeter around Oosterbeek. Slowly the number of men in his platoon diminished. By the fifth day, he was down to a dozen, and the battalion was so badly hit he took over B Company when Captain Hall was one of a dozen men killed when a shell demolished their bunker.

When the Paras holding the northern end of the bridge were overwhelmed, it was decided to evacuate what was left of the 1st Airborne Division. All Reeves could do was attempt to keep as many of his men alive as possible. For five days he had no sleep, crawling through their defences to say an encouraging word here or give an instruction there, often to men quite a few years older than him.

Eventually an order worked its way up from headquarters. On the night of 25–26 September they were to evacuate the town, crossing to the south bank of the Rhine by boat.

When a Polish unit rescued them a few miles south of the Rhine, Reeves thought he was hallucinating. He was dizzy and felt nauseous but was sure he could see children singing and dancing in the distant fields, some of which appeared to be bathed in sunshine, others in the depths of winter.

When he arrived at the British base in Nijmegen, he was so delirious he thought he was in England, and remained that way until the tablets they gave him took effect. Within minutes he knew where he was, and the utter horror of what he'd been through was sharper than any hallucination, more dreadful than any nightmare. He wished he'd not taken the tablets. For the past nine days he'd been closer to death than life.

And the worse part of it was his utter conviction that the Germans had known they were coming.

They'd been expected.

Chapter 2

Berlin, August–October 1939

'They sent me to Jesus, you know.'

The man in the hospital bed seemed to be close to death, his breathing increasingly laboured, and even in the dim light of the curtained side room he appeared colourless.

His visitor always assumed Helmut Krüger was a lapsed Roman Catholic, but then there was nothing like imminent death to concentrate the mind. He edged his chair closer to the bed and tentatively placed his hand on Krüger's arm.

'You'll be at peace, Helmut.' Taking on something of a religious role felt awkward, as did the physical contact. 'You'll be with Jesus soon.' He hoped that might give him the comfort he clearly sought.

The man in the bed turned his head towards him, and although his eyes were more closed than open, his face creased into a smile. 'I don't mean that Jesus!'

–

That morning, Franz Rauter had been summoned to his boss's office on the top floor of Tirpitzufer. Otto Prager had been with the Abwehr since it started in 1920 and spoke slowly in his very proper Hanoverian accent.

'Your colleague Helmut Krüger – how long have you shared an office with him?'

'Perhaps five years, Herr Prager, maybe a couple of years after I joined the service.'

'And do you consider him to be a friend?'

'I'd hesitate to say "friend", sir, but we were certainly friendly, if you understand what I mean.'

'I do understand, but do you trust him?'

'Certainly, no question of that.'

Otto Prager nodded his head and said nothing for a while, deep in thought. Then he stood up, walked over to the door and opened it, peering up and down the corridor before closing it again. 'Good – and the feeling would appear to be mutual; he certainly trusts you. What do you know about his condition?'

'He hasn't been at work for a few weeks now and your memo last week said he'd been admitted to the Charité.'

'I went to visit him last night and I'm sorry to say he has deteriorated rapidly. He is very near the end of his days, I'm afraid.'

'Poor Helmut.'

'Indeed poor Helmut. He's a very private person, isn't he? I suspect he was probably embarrassed to discuss his condition with anyone. Tell me, Rauter, did he ever mention to you an agent of his with the code name Milton?'

'Once or twice in passing, sir, never any details; just that he expected that one day he'd be one of the Abwehr's top sources. All I know is that Milton is English and Helmut recruited him there.'

'When I saw Helmut last night, we agreed he would have to hand over his agents. It was a very difficult conversation. As you well know, Rauter, no intelligence officer likes to give up his agents, and for poor Krüger, doing so is an admission that his end must be near. We discussed the matter and he insisted he wanted you to take Milton. I'll stay involved in the case and I'll be the only person other than you to know his true identity. You should go and see Helmut today.'

'I'll go after work, sir.'

'I wouldn't leave it that long, Rauter. You should go now.'

He left his office almost immediately, walking across Potsdamer Platz and up Hermann Göring Strasse before stopping in a bar he knew on Schiffbauer for a couple of glasses of schnapps to calm his nerves. He hated hospitals and he was genuinely sad that Helmut Krüger was dying.

He went into the Charité hospital through the main entrance on Luisenstrasse, but it took another fifteen minutes walking through the vast complex of buildings to find the correct ward. Herr Krüger, the ward sister told him, had been moved to a side room that morning. A Herr Prager had paid for it.

And once Krüger had assured his visitor he didn't mean 'that Jesus', he opened his eyes and with some effort moved into something closer to a sitting position. 'In 1934, I was sent to Cambridge, in England – have you heard of it, Franz?'

'Yes, of course, Helmut – it has a famous university.'

'In fact it was Otto Prager's idea. He'd heard about language courses that were held there over the summer holidays. Herr Prager had picked up that the Soviets were active in recruiting students there – upper-class Marxists, he called them. His view was that if there was what he described as an undercurrent of Marxism at the university and being a communist was fashionable, then it was possible that there'd be some kind of reaction to that. What he meant was that there could well be a group of students who disapproved of communism to the extent that they could be possible recruits for us.'

'You mean fascists?'

'No. I think in truth Herr Prager disapproves of fascists as much as he disapproves of communists: his view has always been that extremists make bad spies. But he felt nevertheless that there would be people who could be attracted by the conservatism and sense of order that Germany offered. He told me to enrol on a course and keep my eyes and ears open. I might find a suitable candidate or two, but in any case it would be a good opportunity to improve my English, which would help the service too.

He also gave me the names of three or four people to approach if I got the opportunity. They'd been identified as people who could be sympathetic to helping Germany: potential agents.'

'Identified by whom?'

'By a trusted and sympathetic British person, as I understand it, who performed that role for us – talent spotting I think they call it, looking for British citizens who could be persuaded to work for us. Franz, you'll need to come closer, I can't speak too loudly – and perhaps you could pass me some water?'

Rauter allowed him a few moments to regain his composure.

'I travelled to Cambridge in July 1934. It was such an extraordinary contrast to Berlin. As you know, the Nazis had been in power for a year by then: you'd already joined the Abwehr, hadn't you?'

Rauter nodded.

'Well you don't need telling what the atmosphere was like here: much as it is now but without the pessimism and the gloom – and the bombs, of course. But Cambridge was so peaceful: the sun always seemed to shine, and after my classes in the morning I'd go on bicycle rides and explore the city and the villages and countryside around it. Quite a number of students stayed in the city during the summer, usually those who needed to study or work. And that's how I met Milton – he was one of the names on the list, you see. Maybe you could open the curtain, Franz? I don't know why it's so dark in here.'

He closed his eyes for a few moments and lay back on the pillow. 'My course was at Jesus College, hence my earlier reference. We chose that college because two of the names on the list were at Jesus – Milton was a student there. Also it was near Trinity College and Herr Prager thought I might have some luck there; a tutor at that college was also on the list. However, Milton was the only one I was able to find. He must have been twenty-seven or twenty-eight then and was studying for a doctorate in medieval literature. He was very brilliant but rather shy, and he spoke with a stammer that he was obviously very self-conscious about. He spent most of his time in the college library, and that's how I was able to get to know him. He wanted to improve his German, which is how our friendship grew: I would talk to him in English and he would correct me and then respond in German, which I would correct in turn.

'To be honest, at first I wasn't too sure about him as a potential agent. He didn't appear to be too interested in politics, and when I felt able to ask about Marxism at the university, he seemed unaware of it. I assumed his name was on the list in error, but as I got to know him better, I could see why he was a potential agent.

'The important thing to remember with the British is the extent to which social class matters to them. Everyone seems to be aware of their standing in society, and I would say that Milton came from the lower middle class, which is apparently a very uncomfortable place to be – certainly at Cambridge, where most people were of a much higher social standing than him. At least that was how he saw it, and I certainly detected a degree of resentment in him. I think he felt he didn't fit in, and as a consequence I would say he was something of a loner. As you know, Franz, people who feel they don't fit into a society tend to make good agents against it – they have few qualms about betraying it because they'll feel it has in some way betrayed them.

'It was also clear he disliked Jews: he seemed to resent them in general and certainly blamed them for some setbacks he'd received. The previous year he'd been on the shortlist for a post as a tutor at one of the colleges, but the job went to a Jew, and he also said a Jewish professor had been on the panel that failed to award him a grant he'd been expecting. If you could pass me more water, Franz, please… thank you.'

After sipping from his glass, Helmut Krüger sank back on the pillow and closed his eyes. When he resumed talking, they remained closed. 'In contrast, Milton was certainly a great admirer of Germany: not so much what was happening here at the time, although he did admire our sense of order and purpose. But he had a more romantic notion of Germany, which seemed to have its roots in medieval times and especially in Middle High German literature. Is that something you are familiar with, Franz?'

'I'm afraid it isn't, Helmut.'

'Don't be too afraid: it's very intense and extremely complex; I don't recommend it. I had to read it so as to be able to affect an interest: poets such as Heinrich Frauenlob, Wolfram von Eschenbach and Walther von der Vogelweide, and mystical writers such as Johannes Tauler and Meister Eckhart. Milton was fascinated by them and I was able to use that fascination as a way of drawing him into our world. Of course, it took time, but Herr Prager was very good at showing me how to handle him. He said it was like an angler trying to catch a fish: once you have the hook in its mouth, then as long as you're patient, it's just a matter of time before you can reel it in.

'When I returned to Berlin, we contacted a professor of medieval literature at the Ludwig Maximilian University in Munich and arranged for Milton to study there in the summer of 1935, which we funded. By the end of that summer, he was our agent, even if he didn't fully realise it at the time. We instructed him to join the British Army in late 1937, I think it was – possibly early in 1938, I get confused. By the time he realised he was an Abwehr agent, it was too late. Franz, please could you ask the nurse if I could have some painkillers?'

The nurse sent him out of the room while she dealt with the patient, and then told him he'd have to leave.

'He's very ill.'

'I know... but another fifteen minutes?'

'No more than five.'

When he returned to the room, Krüger looked paler than before and his breathing was even more laboured.

'Remind me what day it is, Franz?'

'Wednesday, Helmut.'

'I doubt I'll live to see this weekend. I hope not, my pain is too great. I never imagined… Come closer, Franz. My belief is that as the war goes on, you'll be able to trust fewer and fewer people, and more to the point, fewer and fewer people will trust you: the Nazis have never liked the Abwehr. Otto Prager you can trust, but how long he'll survive, who knows? Likewise Admiral Canaris and General Oster; they're professional intelligence men and not Nazi Party members, but they're at the top of the organisation so you'll have less to do with them. But whatever you do, don't share information about Milton with anyone. Set up a ring of agents around him, and above all, don't be rushed. He's not very senior at the moment; give him time, allow him to get promoted, and when we finally need him, then he'll be in a position to provide invaluable intelligence, as opposed to merely useful intelligence. Have you got that, Franz?'

Krüger had gripped Rauter's wrist with his bony and surprisingly strong fingers, his eyes now wide open and more alive than they had been.

Rauter said he had.

'Protect him as a source. Take time before you reel him in. If you listen to some people in this city, we'll have conquered Europe within months and the British will cave in, but I'm not so sure: this war could last years, and the effectiveness of our intelligence operation will lie in our ability to keep our sources going, rather than using them all up at once. Once Milton starts supplying intelligence, he may only last months, so you mustn't rush him.'

Rauter started to speak, but the nurse came in and stood with her arms folded in the open doorway.

'It's been more than five minutes.'

When Rauter turned round to say goodbye, Krüger's eyes were closed once more.

—

Helmut Krüger had hoped he'd be dead before the weekend, but he hung on until the Monday. One month later – in the middle of September and a fortnight after the start of the war – Otto Prager disappeared from his office on the top floor of Tirpitzufer.

For a day or two no one said anything, but then a meeting was called for all the officers in the unit Prager had headed. The new boss talked at length about the need to ensure their expense claims were properly filled in before mentioning briefly that Otto Prager had retired. One of Franz Rauter's colleagues said he was surprised there'd been no mention of it before, not least from Herr Prager himself.

The new boss – who looked and sounded more like an accountant than someone who worked for an intelligence service – said this was something he wouldn't know about, and in any case, the meeting was over.

The following week there was another meeting, one that began with a sombre announcement: Herr Prager had sadly died the previous evening, apparently of a heart attack. He'd given many years' valuable service to the Abwehr and please could everyone stand in silence for one minute, which in the event barely lasted thirty seconds.

Chapter 3

'How was your Christmas, Prince?'

'It was fine, thank you, sir – it seems so long ago.'

'I imagine Henry enjoyed it?'

Another of the awkward silences that had punctuated their conversation followed.

'Caught any murderers recently?'

Richard Prince looked up at his dining companion, unsure whether this was a serious question. He decided to give him the benefit of the doubt: there was no reason to fall out on what he'd been assured was a purely social occasion.

'I'm afraid not, sir. I rejoined the force last June, and since then the good people of Lincolnshire have been particularly law-abiding: predominantly minor crimes these days.'

'Maybe that's down to your reputation, Prince, the criminal fraternity of Lincolnshire not wanting to risk being caught and all that.'

'Quite possibly, sir.'

They were upstairs at Simpson's in the Strand, their table in the West Room overlooking the Strand itself, the grime-streaked roofs of red double-decker buses passing silently just feet below them.

'So you'd like the skate to start?'

'Yes please, sir.'

'Good choice: I think I'll go for the crab – and for main course? This place isn't what it was before the war, but it's still decent enough. I could weep when I look at this menu, though: before the war, their roast beef from the carving trolley was quite the best in London. Now… I think I'll go for *les pieds de boeuf*: ox feet done with carrots and onions – it's carrots with everything these days, isn't it? And what do you fancy? The *bitock de boeuf* isn't bad: fried minced beef steak served in a cream sauce.'

'That will be fine for me, thank you, sir.'

'No more Nazi spies?' Tom Gilbey had waited until their starter had arrived.

The younger man laughed. 'None who've made themselves known to us, sir. I think one was probably enough.'

'When I asked earlier if you'd caught any murderers, you replied you were "afraid not": I'm curious as to what you meant by that?'

'Simply a figure of speech, sir.'

'Really, Prince?' Gilbey leaned back and watched as the sommelier topped up their wine glasses, then glanced at his dining companion trying to work out whether to believe him. 'Because you see, Prince, if I was the cynical type, I would say that wasn't so much a figure of speech as an expression of your true feelings.'

'I'm not sure what you mean, sir: you do rather sound like one of those shrinks you tried to persuade me to see last time I returned from Germany.'

'What I mean, Prince, is that you sound bored. What kind of cases are you working on these days? Burglaries, missing tractors, behaviour likely to cause a breach of the peace – maybe a bit of black-market racketeering as a treat, that kind of thing? Nothing quite as challenging as a clandestine mission inside occupied Europe, is it?'

'No, sir, but not quite as dangerous either. And at least these days I get to sleep peacefully in my own bed every night knowing my son's in the next room.'

They watched as a man and woman at a nearby table got up and prepared to leave. He was considerably older than her and glanced nervously around the room.

'He's probably hoping no one here recognises him, eh? Don't come to Simpson's if you're having an affair would be my advice.'

'Could be his daughter, sir.'

'Ever the detective eh? Have you ever considered you might be wasting your talents, Prince?'

Prince didn't reply, but shot a suspicious look at Gilbey as he carried on eating.

'You were our best agent, there's no question about that. Between the end of 1942 and last February, you spent a total of twelve months operating in enemy territory, which is a remarkable feat. Both your missions were a considerable success and contributed significantly to what we can now safely assume is an inevitable Allied victory.'

Prince pushed a boiled potato around his plate, carefully steering it clear of the bright yellow mustard. 'But at some considerable personal cost, sir.'

'Of course, but look around here: everyone in this dining room would have made sacrifices during the war – all of us.'

Prince put down his cutlery, placing it across his plate as if to indicate he'd finished, even though there was still plenty of food on it. 'Are you trying to cajole me into rejoining the Service?'

'No, Prince – I told you, I wanted to catch up, see how you are, and also tell you that at long last we expect Turkey to join our side any day now, and thank you once again for your part in bringing that about.'

'So this is a purely social occasion?'

Tom Gilbey signalled for the sommelier to refill their glasses, then ordered another bottle. 'You're a football fan, aren't you, Prince?'

'I am sir: Nottingham Forest.'

'Aren't they the oldest club in the world?'

'I think you may be confusing them with Notts County, sir. Such a mistake would be regarded as a capital offence in Nottingham. County are the oldest professional club in the world, perhaps their only claim to fame. Have you brought me down to London for a chat about football?'

Tom Gilbey responded with a non-committal shrug.

'I imagine if there was any news on Hanne, you'd have told me by now, sir?'

'Nothing, I'm afraid, Prince. One has to take the view that no news is good news, though I do realise that must be awfully hard to accept. We'll keep looking for her. We have agents and contacts throughout occupied Europe, as you know. Sooner or later we're bound to find out what the Nazis have done with her.'

The sommelier brought the new bottle to the table, complimenting Gilbey once more on his impeccable taste and pouring some for him to try before decanting the rest into the carafe. The whole process took twice as long as it should have done.

'This Château Haut-Brion is wonderful, don't you agree?' Gilbey said when the man had gone. 'Despite my family's now sadly distant connection with the gin trade, I still regard wine as a more... interesting drink. They manage to keep a decent cellar here even if they've had to convert half of it into an air-raid shelter.'

'Do pardon my confusion, sir, but am I here to talk about wine or football?'

Gilbey studied his glass carefully, holding it up and slowly turning it to catch the light.

'As I understand it, football players are transferred from one club to another, and money is involved, which seems rather mercenary. Do you care for some more potatoes, Prince?'

They watched the waiter nervously spoon potatoes onto their plates.

'I suppose selling a player from one club to another makes things rather commercial, but at least it's clear-cut, eh? Club

A wants a player and club B agrees to sell him. I mention this, Prince, as a way of telling you that another organisation is interested in your services.'

Prince finished chewing his beef and sipped from his wine. 'And they're prepared to pay a fee for me?'

'Not exactly,' said Gilbey, relieved that his companion's initial reaction hadn't been one of outright hostility. 'Not cash, at any rate. But certainly I'd expect something in return.'

'And is this as a secret agent?'

'A little quieter, if you please, Prince. No, not as such – well, at least not in the way you've worked as an agent for us. This won't involve operating in enemy territory or even going overseas. It will entail you working on a mission within this country and the role will be something between that of a police detective and a secret agent.'

'Is that as much as you can tell me, sir? Not even the organisation?'

'It's as much as I can tell you until I know you're amenable to the idea. You'll still be required to work clandestinely, and there'll inevitably be an element of danger.'

In spite of himself, Prince couldn't avoid looking interested. It was apparent to anyone watching the pair: the younger man now appeared more relaxed, with the trace of a smile on his face, unbuttoning his jacket and raising his glass to his companion as he drank from it.

'And you say all within this country, sir?'

Gilbey nodded. 'It sounds as if you're not averse to the idea.'

'I hope you understand that it's not as if I'm unwilling to serve. When we last met, back in September I think it was, you said that I'd always regard myself as a secret agent, that it would always be the most fulfilling and absorbing thing I'd ever done. I may have been rather dismissive of that at the time, but I have to acknowledge you were correct, sir. Not a day goes by when I don't compare the rather routine nature of what I do now with the... well, excitement, there's no other word for it, of operating in enemy territory. I'd go on another mission for you at the drop of a hat, sir, but you understand about my son. I'm all he has now and I owe it to him not to put myself in such danger again, so I had rather reconciled myself to investigating burglaries and the like. But if this job is in this country, then I'd certainly like to find out more.'

Tom Gilbey didn't reply, but leaned to his right, looking beyond Prince to get someone's attention, beckoning them over with his hand. Within moments a well-built man appeared by their table.

'Ah, Hugh... why don't you pull up that chair and join us? I take it you've eaten?'

The other man nodded, smiling at Prince briefly, not taking his eyes off him as he sat down.

'Have a glass of wine. Have I ever mentioned their Château Haut-Brion?'

'Frequently, Tom.'

'Hugh, this is Richard Prince, whom we discussed. Prince, this is my colleague Hugh Harper. Indeed, the Honourable Hugh Harper.'

'Please, Tom, really...'

'Hugh and I were at school together. In fact we were in the same year—'

'I doubt Mr Prince is interested in our schooldays.'

'Hugh, I mentioned to Richard the possibility of him coming to work for you, and he expressed some interest.'

Hugh Harper shifted his chair closer to the table and leaned towards Prince, patting him on the forearm.

'Well that's splendid news. Let me tell you a bit about our outfit. Whereas Tom's lot look after our intelligence activities beyond these shores, my organisation – some know it best as MI5 – fulfils a counter-intelligence role within the United Kingdom. In a nutshell, and in the context of the war, we have primary responsibility for catching Nazi spies. You could say...' he leaned back and glanced at Gilbey, 'that the operation you

24

assisted with so ably in 1942 should have been under the aegis of my organisation. There are occasions when my colleagues in MI6 take a very generous view of their brief and extend their activities well beyond their remit, but one is prepared to regard that as all water under the bridge, eh? Tom has been most decent in recommending you for this particular role.'

–

After their lunch, the three men walked along the Strand until they came to a taxi rank close to the Savoy. Gilbey and Harper waved Prince off as he headed back to King's Cross. They looked like parents putting on a show of good cheer as they saw their offspring off for another term at boarding school. Once the tail lights had faded in the gathering afternoon dusk, the two men continued along the Strand in the direction of Trafalgar Square.

'He seems like a good sort, Tom. I actually rather liked him.'

'You sound surprised, Hugh.'

'Only because you described him as chippy: "typical grammar school", you said. "Only just middle class" was another phrase you used. I found him perfectly likeable.'

'You've always had the habit of being rather selective in remembering what one has said. I may well have described Prince thus, but I also said he's one of the most resourceful and courageous agents we've used. He's been in and out of Nazi Germany three times in total, and operated in Denmark, Czechoslovakia and Turkey. On his first mission he escaped from Denmark to Sweden and back here, and on the last one he managed to get from Turkey into Czechoslovakia and then from Prague to Munich before catching a flight to Switzerland, would you believe. Both of his missions were considerable successes in terms of the intelligence he gathered.'

'So you keep telling me, Tom, but then it is out of character for you to recommend him to us, unless of course you think you owe us.'

'If it was up to me, Hugh, I'd have sent him on another mission long ago. But there's his son, you remember I told you?'

'Wife died, you said.'

'His wife and daughter were killed in a road accident in 1940. His son, Henry, was just a year old; he was at home at the time. There was a disaster when Prince was on his mission to Denmark. Young Henry was being cared for by Prince's sister-in-law, who brought him down to London with her to stay with a friend for a few days. Henry was the only one who survived an air raid and was taken to hospital unable to say who he was. To cut a rather long and terribly unfortunate story short, the matron at the hospital quite improperly allowed him to be adopted, and we completely lost track of the poor little chap. Prince was devastated, of course, when he got back here. We pretty much turned the country upside down looking for the boy. We still hadn't found him by the time Prince returned from his Turkish mission, but then he took matters into his own hands. To this day I've no idea how he tracked the child down, but I've no doubt he broke a few laws in the process. Hence his reluctance to leave this country for the time being, and one can hardly blame him.'

'And I thought it was a case of you doing the right thing by passing him on to us.'

'Perish the thought.'

They'd passed Northumberland Avenue and Gilbey was guiding Harper across Whitehall.

'I say, why are we heading this way?'

'Meeting with an old school chum of ours, Hugh.'

'Hang on, Tom: please promise me we're not meeting Roly. I beg of you... The last time I crossed swords with him, I thought he was going to put me in detention. Remember that sickening sense one had at school when we were sent to the prefects' room?'

'Come on, Hugh, it will be like a school reunion.'

'Exactly – and just as ghastly. You seem to have set me up.'

The prime minister's intelligence adviser seemed to fill most of his office deep inside Downing Street, leaning back in his chair and smiling with just a modicum of grace as Gilbey and Harper entered. His hands were intertwined high up on his chest and he appeared to be impervious to the high temperature in the room. The window overlooking an internal courtyard was shut fast, a dirty net curtain not quite covering it. Two chairs had been arranged in front of his desk and he indicated that they should sit.

Despite a somewhat aloof and fussy manner and the appearance of a well-fed but nonetheless put-upon bank manager, Sir Roland Pearson was not to be underestimated. He knew everyone who mattered in the various intelligence agencies, and his network of contacts ensured he was one of the few people with a broad appreciation of what was going on: an 'overview' was the word the Americans used. He was the gatekeeper – another word the Americans used – between Churchill and his intelligence agencies, and he also had the ability to distil and edit intelligence exactly as the prime minister wanted it. 'Roly,' people would observe, in a resigned but resentful way, 'has Winston's ear.'

Sir Roland had been at school with both Gilbey and Harper, though a few years above them. Despite this, his manner was that of a schoolmaster rather than a former fellow pupil.

'Family well, Hugh?'

Hugh replied that they were, thank you very much.

'And your brother… Charles?'

'I think you may mean Christopher. He was in your year.'

'Of course he was. Mentioned in dispatches in Normandy, I see.'

'Yes, thank you, Roly. Chris is now the hero of the family.'

'Good show. No doubt they'll put his name on that board at school, eh? Those names of former pupils who fought in the

Great War, they used to move me to tears – when no one was watching, of course.'

'He's not dead, Roly, not yet at any rate.'

'You heard Osbourne was killed at Arromanches? Legs blown off apparently. Poor chap used to get terribly homesick at school. Christ knows how he must have felt.'

The three of them nodded gravely and shook their heads in unison, a silence following.

'I understand you met Tom's protégé Prince today, eh?'

'I did.'

'And you liked him, did you? Think he can be of assistance to you on this operation?'

'I very much hope so, Roly. I thought I was there to say yes or no to him. Didn't realise this needed your approval.'

'Everything needs my approval. When I heard about your little problem, it was me who suggested to Tom that Prince would be just the man to sort it out for you.'

'I'm terribly grateful, Roly.'

'Normally an agent of Prince's calibre would be operating inside enemy territory, but I recognise the urgency of this case. He comes at a price, though, I need you to understand that.'

'I wondered if there'd be a catch.'

'I want to make it very clear that Prince needs to know everything. You're to hold nothing back from him.'

'I'm not sure what you mean by everything, Roly. Surely not *everything*?'

'The word does not have multiple definitions, Hugh.'

'I mean, it could be taken to include the Ultra intercepts!' Hugh Harper laughed at the very notion that Prince could be privy to Ultra.

'Actually, it does.'

'Come off it, Roly: Ultra is called Ultra for a very good reason, because it's even more secret than "Most Secret". Do you realise how restricted the list is of people who have access to it? There are generals and admirals who aren't on the list. It's strictly need-to-know, and even then—'

'I really don't need a tutorial on who has access to Ultra!' Sir Roland Pearson was clearly angry; his face coloured and he banged his desktop. 'I have oversight of that list and I want Prince on it if he undertakes this mission!'

Gilbey leaned forward, his manner more conciliatory. 'Perhaps I can reassure you, Hugh, how utterly trustworthy Prince is. He was arrested by the Gestapo in Copenhagen and didn't utter a word, then went to Berlin in December '42 and came out with first-class intelligence. He returned the following month and produced more first-class material from inside the Nazi rocket factory before he was arrested and sent to a concentration camp, and still he managed to maintain his cover. Then he escaped back to Denmark, where despite being ill with typhus he managed to contact our most secret source in Copenhagen and with his help get over to Sweden. I can tell you one thing: had there been any question mark over Prince, that source in Copenhagen would have been betrayed, there's no question about that. Both his missions have produced intelligence that has already been of considerable help to us.'

'So,' said Sir Roland, looming across his desk in the manner of a headmaster disciplining a pupil, 'you give him everything, even Ultra. Understand?'

'With respect, Roly, my understanding was that Winston himself has to authorise access to Ultra.'

'With respect, Hugh,' said Sir Roland, 'he has.'

Chapter 4

England, March 1944

'The eyes give it away. You can't control them, they always betray you.'

It was Bartholomew speaking, the leader of the Disciples, the name by which MI5's team of followers and watchers had become known.

'An innocent person's eyes will show a mixture of surprise and annoyance at being stopped. More than anything else, they'll look confused. But a guilty person's will show fear and almost resignation – momentarily at least – as if they expected to be stopped.'

And when they stopped the man they'd been following across London since a quarter to eleven that morning, his pale blue eyes flashed that mixture of fear and understanding that Bartholomew was carefully looking out for.

Guilty.

After he was arrested, they took him straight to Latchmere House in south-west London. The large Victorian building overlooking Ham Common was MI5's main interrogation centre and the first port of call for suspected German spies, the place where they aimed to turn them into double agents.

The prisoner was interrogated by a Mr White, a tall, formally dressed Yorkshireman; seemingly languid, he was possessed of a stamina that enabled him to conduct sessions that often lasted twelve hours or more. All the while he'd sit motionless in a heavy three-piece suit, unbothered by the temperature in the room, his voice never betraying any emotion or giving any clues to the person on the other side of the table.

The interrogation lasted four days, with just a few hours' sleep allowed here and there, the occasional meals sparse and increasingly unpalatable. On the fifth day they left him in his cell all day – a tactic that had been known to unnerve prisoners to the extent that they suddenly became more voluble when the questioning resumed.

The interrogation recommenced on the sixth day but was as fruitless as the previous five, so at 9.30 that evening, White sent the prisoner back to his cell and climbed from the basement to the top-floor office occupied by the Colonel.

The Colonel, the deputy director at the centre, devoted some time to ensuring the curtains were properly closed and fussing with his fountain pen before joining White at the table.

'I understand he's not budging?'

'No, sir. He's sticking to his story.'

'Which is…?'

'That he's a Polish refugee called Jan Dabrowski from Poznań who was working in France when the Germans invaded Poland and made his way over here. He claims to have been working at an engineering factory in Salford called Maddocks Brothers Engineering that was destroyed in an air raid. He was off shift when the raid happened and naturally all records at the factory have been destroyed. Two nights later, his lodging house was bombed out. That was in the middle of January, some two months ago. Since then he's been moving around the country looking for work, which he says is the reason he was in London.'

'And do you believe him, White?'

'Of course not, sir.'

'The bombing of the factory and the lodging house… that all happened, I presume?'

'Yes, sir, obviously that was the first thing we established.'

'Rather too convenient, eh?'

'Of course, but he's a professional: keeping his story simple and consistent and not volunteering unnecessary information. If we assume he is indeed this Agent Dryden we've been watching out for, then the Germans have considerably improved the standard of their agents and the way they've prepared them. Up to late last year, the ones they sent over were second rate, but not any longer.'

'Unless of course his story is true: maybe he isn't a spy after all?'

'That's always possible, sir, but he behaved exactly as the intercept told us he would, and I'd remind you that intercept was from the same source that identified the two other agents, Shelley and Keats.'

'And a lot of use they were to us.'

'I know, sir but we had to leave it to the police to arrest Keats, and they didn't send enough men. As you know, he managed to throw himself in front of a train before they could apprehend him. That was in November last year, and the following month we tracked down Shelley, dead in that boarding house in Coventry. The post-mortem said he'd been dead for at least a fortnight and that cause of death was a heart attack. The landlady said he'd paid cash up front for the room and when she hadn't seen him for a while she'd thought he'd gone away for a few days.'

'Probably scared to death, literally. And there was nothing in his room, was there?'

'No, sir, same as with Keats and with Dabrowski if he is Agent Dryden. Nothing to give them away, decent identities, plausible cover stories.'

'You brought in that chap from Polish intelligence to interrogate him in Polish, is that correct?'

'Indeed, sir, Major Olszewski.'

'And what does he say?'

'That Dabrowski is undoubtedly Polish, though whether he may have some ethnic German background, he's not sure. He said he stuck to his story and seemed to be very comfortable talking about Poznań. Olszewski asked him which football team he supported, and said he had to sit through a long history lesson on Warta Poznań. Apparently they won the Polish League a few years ago and Dabrowski insisted on recalling all the results from that season.'

'So he believes him?'

'Major Olszewski was there to assess whether Dabrowski is a Pole from Poznań rather than whether he's a spy. But he did say something very interesting in that respect. Poznań is close to the German border and has a large ethnically German population. When he asked Dabrowski about his background, he insisted his family were ethnic Poles. However, he says that at one point he referred to Poznań as Posen, before quickly correcting himself.'

'And the significance of that…?'

'Posen is the German name for Poznań. Olszewski is adamant that an ethnic Pole would never use it. He believes it was a slip-up on Dabrowski's part.'

The Colonel looked up at the ceiling, contemplating what to do next. 'Is that really the best we've got against him: using the German word for Poznań?'

'That and the fact that he did what the intercept told us he'd do, sir.'

The Colonel drummed his fingers impatiently on the table. 'I don't know, I really—'

'How about if we were to consider this a case of the last resort, sir?'

The Colonel shook his head. 'You know how reluctant we are to go down that path; we're not the bloody Germans after all, are we? Our guidelines are perfectly clear: we only deem a case to be of the last resort and act accordingly if we believe there is an imminent threat to life. Sir Roland Pearson has to sign it off, and he'll only do so if a case meets these strict criteria, and even then he's reluctant. Give Dabrowski one more go and take Olszewski in with you.'

'And then what, sir?'

The Colonel shrugged. 'Then we'll see.'

They woke Jan Dabrowski at five the following morning. This time they took him to a different room, one with the clinical appearance of a medical room of sorts, with a more menacing air to it. White instructed the guards who'd brought him in to remain, both standing behind him as he sat handcuffed to an uncomfortable chair.

'Eight days ago, Mr Dabrowski, you arrived in London. By an unnecessarily long and indirect route you made your way to Kentish Town station and from there walked to Warden Road, arriving there at noon. You remained outside the Admiral Napier public house for nearly an hour, apparently waiting for someone. At one o'clock you hurriedly left the area and returned to Kentish Town station, where you hailed a taxi and asked it to take you to Flask Walk, just behind Hampstead Underground station. You remained there for another hour or so before attempting to hail another taxi, at which point you were detained.'

White looked carefully at the Pole. 'And here we are, Mr Dabrowski. We've had nothing approaching a reasonable explanation for your movements, or why you went to the Admiral Napier.'

'I told you. Since I lost my job and my room in Manchester, I've been travelling the country looking for work. In Birmingham I met a man who told me he knew an Irishman in London called Michael who's always looking for labourers and pays well, and that I could find him outside the Admiral Napier pub in Kentish Town most days at twelve noon. I went there but didn't see him.'

'Really, Mr Dabrowski, is that the best you can do? Every other Irishman is called Michael as far as I'm aware. And then despite being down on your luck, you decide you can afford to take a taxi to Hampstead – which you could have walked to – and unaccountably wait behind the station there for another hour. Why?'

'I've told you, I realised I may have got confused and thought the man in Birmingham said something about Hampstead station.'

'And the taxi fare, how come you could afford that?'

'The man in Birmingham lent me money. In any case, what have I done wrong? I've not broken any law, have I?'

White looked at him long and hard. There was no question the man's journey to Hampstead lacked subtlety and had aroused suspicion, but his behaviour in the interrogation had been impeccable and he'd stuck to his story. He waited a while before responding. 'We had very specific information that a German spy using the code name Dryden would travel that day to Kentish Town and then to the Admiral Napier. Our information is that once your contact was satisfied you'd not been followed and it was safe to do so, he'd approach you. No doubt there'd have been an agreed form of words; we all know how it works.

'When he – or indeed she – didn't appear, you went to the fall-back location, where there was also no sign of your contact. Our information was that if you had not been approached by then, you were to abort the mission, which is when we decided it would be nice for you to come and have a chat with us.'

Dabrowski shrugged, a 'what can I say?' gesture.

'You are Agent Dryden, aren't you?'

The Pole shook his head and looked suitably confused.

'How did you get here, Dabrowski – to this country? There's no record of anyone of your name entering in 1939 as you claim you did.'

'It was chaos when I arrived. I'd be surprised if there was a record.'

'Who is your contact here? Tell us that and everything about your mission and we'll take the view that you've been cooperative. That can literally be the difference between life and death. Make sure he understands that, Major.'

Major Olszewski spoke in Polish, Dabrowski shaking his head all the while. Afterwards, though, White and Olszewski agreed they'd noticed a very slight change in his demeanour. His body seemed to tense and then slump, and Bartholomew remarked how he had definitely spotted the flicker of fear in his eyes with which he was so familiar.

—

'And that's it – you all agree?'

They were crowded into the director's surprisingly small office. They'd been joined by Hugh Harper, who ran MI5's section responsible for tracking down German spies, and Lance King, Dabrowski's case officer.

'Yes, sir: I regret to say we aren't going to get any more out of him, not with our current approach, that is.' White, whose demeanour was normally unchanging, now looked uncomfortable. 'I realise I am saying this with the considerable advantage of hindsight, but I can't help thinking we perhaps ought to have let Dabrowski continue from Hampstead. He might well have led us to something.'

'My orders,' said Bartholomew, looking annoyed, 'were to arrest him if and when he left the fall-back rendezvous location.'

'Exactly, Bartholomew, and I'm not blaming you, but we had precious little against him to start with and I can only work with what shreds of evidence we have.'

'I understand you spoke with him, Olszewski?' Hugh Harper looked at the Polish officer. 'What did he say to you when he was offered the opportunity to cooperate in return for his life?'

'Not much, sir. He repeated that he was simply a refugee from Poznań who was looking for work. He said all this talk about an Agent Dryden was completely beyond him, he didn't know what on earth what you were talking about... that it must all be a coincidence. As for the life-or-death option – like a good Pole he said that both are in the hands of God.'

'Well we'll have to see about that,' said Lance King. 'If you chaps couldn't get anything out of him in a week, then I doubt you'll do so if we keep him here any longer. I consider this to be a case of the last resort, I'm afraid.'

The atmosphere in the room chilled as he uttered the words. Everyone knew what he meant. 'I completely concur with that view,' Harper said. 'If we capture a German spy of this calibre and fail to extract useful intelligence from him, we are putting lives at risk, therefore it meets the criteria of a case of the last resort. I'll get it signed off by Sir Roland.'

'You know my view, Hugh.' The director looked uncomfortable. 'I consider information gathered in the manner you're proposing to be unreliable. Under those circumstances people will say anything. It's not the British way of doing things. My interrogators here are the best in the business. If we can give them one more week...'

'A week is out of the question, but don't worry, Pat, we'll not ask you to do the dirty work. We'll move him to Huntercombe.'

–

They'd timed his arrival at Huntercombe for the early hours of the morning, which meant that no more than a handful of people saw Jan Dabrowski.

Huntercombe was the place where Latchmere House's dirty work was carried out. Lance King believed there was a tendency for those at Latchmere House to be a bit too prim and proper, too ready to play by the rules. He didn't think they always displayed the same sense of urgency he found at Huntercombe. Before leaving Latchmere House, King had ensured that any records relating to the Pole's stay there were handed over to him, and he made sure the transfer was accompanied by a minimum of bureaucracy. By the time they arrived at Huntercombe, Dabrowski had become Prisoner 44/1153, and after a quick medical, he was taken to a cell in an isolated block.

Once Lance King was satisfied the prisoner was secure, he went into a basement room, followed by a man who'd silently observed their arrival. He was a short man, not well built but with a tanned complexion and the physique of a boxer.

'That's him, Hood.'

Hood nodded. 'I've read the report.'

'And what do you think?'

'I think he's a class above the others you brought here. You're sure about what you want us to do?'

King nodded. 'And it's been signed off by Downing Street, albeit somewhat reluctantly. He's the third of these agents, Hood, the only one we've caught alive. We have to find out what we can from him. They put White on him at Latchmere and he got nowhere so I'm relying on you.'

'And you're prepared for any possible consequences? There's always a risk involved.'

'I know there is, but you've not let me down yet.'

'There was the Belgian last year, remember.'

'He was a sick man before he came to you. When will you start?'

Hood glanced at his watch – an expensive-looking gold affair. 'I'd propose leaving him there for forty-eight hours. This time tomorrow we'll take him to the farm.'

–

Prisoner 44/1153 was kept isolated in his cell for two days and nights, with no food or water, bright lights blazing away for the first twenty-four hours followed by twenty-four hours of pitch darkness.

At four o'clock in the morning, four men burst into his cell and administered a quick beating-up – nothing too serious but, as Hood liked to put it, something meant to show they were starting as they intended to carry on. The prisoner was then bundled up, handcuffed, strapped and blindfolded before being carried outside and thrown into the back of a van.

Not that Prisoner 44/1153 had the faintest idea of where he was, but Huntercombe was nestled in a fold of the Chilterns Hills, surrounded by fields and hedgerows blossoming with their early spring colours, the trees in competition with each other for the most alluring shade of green or golden brown. The van drove round the countryside for two hours, the prisoner held in position on the floor by the boots of his guards.

When it came to a stop, they were little more than two miles from where they had started. The van parked in a farmyard and the prisoner was carried into what had once been a barn but had now been adapted to Hood's demanding specifications, chief among which was it being quite soundproof.

When he was finally untied and shackled to a chair in a corner of the barn, Prisoner 44/1153's complexion was a deathly white, his face and clothing caked with blood and dried vomit, his face bruised with a nasty cut around his mouth and his eyes wide open with fear.

Hood waited a while for the prisoner to recover his senses and have a good look round. He wouldn't be in any doubt that the barn was a chamber of horrors: there was a table covered with sticks and knives, a machine with wires and clasps attached to it, handcuffs hanging on a wall, and dangling from a roof joist a long rope with a noose at its end.

Hood was sitting in a comfortable chair in front of the prisoner. He poured a glass of water and allowed the man to sip from it.

'Let me make one thing clear: no one knows you're here. Even if you shout at the top of your voice, someone standing on the other side of this wall wouldn't hear you. Had you been more cooperative, we wouldn't need to be going through all this, but it was your choice. More water?'

He allowed the prisoner more than a few sips this time.

'The other thing I want to make clear is that as far as the system is concerned – the police, the courts – you don't exist. There'll be no record of you anywhere. If anyone looks for you, they'll find you've disappeared off the face of the earth.' Hood held a hand up and snapped his fingers, indicating something vanishing into thin air.

'In fact, you may wish to have a look at this. I'll hold it so you can read it.' The prisoner's eyes narrowed as he read what was being held near his face. 'As you can see, it's a notice from the police in Birmingham – that's where you were before you travelled down to London, isn't it? According to this, a Polish national called Jan Dabrowski of no fixed abode was killed in an accident with a goods lorry near Birmingham New Street station on the very same day you were due to travel to London. Conveniently the only witness was a police officer. And there's a nice touch to this: the notice also says that the night before your dreadful accident, you were arrested in the centre of Birmingham for being drunk and disorderly and given a police caution. What that means is that they have a photograph of you – the photograph we took after your arrest. So it will be very straightforward for us to release this and ensure the story appears in various newspapers. I've no doubt your masters will get to see it.

'But there's no need for that, is there? We need you to confirm that you are Agent Dryden. We want you to tell us how you got here, where you've been staying, who your contacts are and who you were due to meet in London last week. Then you'll be spared. You'll be safe in a prison camp until the war ends. We can even give you a new identity.'

Later that evening Hood and King met in the farmhouse next to the barn. Hood confessed that the Pole was the most stubborn prisoner he'd come across. He was saying nothing.

'What did you do to him?' King asked.

'At this stage, not too much. He's suffering as it is. He hasn't eaten for three days now and we've allowed the minimum amount of water. In that time he hasn't washed or been to the toilet and has hardly slept. We gave him a small amount of electricity, just enough to show we're not bluffing.'

'But remember, Hood, it's—'

'It's not torture but the threat of it that will make him talk. Yes, I know that.'

'And if you do have to resort to anything, the bare minimum.'

Over the next two days, the prisoner was roughed up again, handcuffed to the wall, and given small electric shocks. He continued to insist he was Jan Dabrowski from Poznań who'd come to London to meet an Irishman called Michael outside the Admiral Napier in Kentish Town in the hope of getting a job. When Lance King went in to see him, he offered him a deal.

'Forget about everything else we've been asking; all you need to tell us is who you were meeting at the pub and what the meeting was about. That's all. We know the Germans often entrap their agents, maybe by threatening their families. I can promise you if that is the case, we'll do what we can to protect your family.'

The prisoner hesitated for the briefest of moments before shaking his head. He said that if he had anything to tell he would, because this was terrible, but he was Jan Dabrowski from Poznań who…

Lance King decided to return to London, but before he left, he took Hood aside. 'Very well, you can push things a bit further; just make sure he gives us something.'

'Are you sure?'

'Give it a go.'

King drove back to London and met Hugh Harper that afternoon. 'If he's still sticking to his story after Hood has dealt with him, then I'm inclined to believe him. Maybe we can do him for false papers or something and see what happens.'

Hugh Harper nodded slowly, reluctantly agreeing.

'I'll go back there now.'

'Hang on a bit, Lance. Bartholomew's asked to see me. He'll be here any minute.'

--

Bartholomew was breathless when he entered the office.

'When I heard he was still holding out, I spent a sleepless night going over in my mind what happened that day when we followed him and whether we missed anything. I decided to go back to the taxi driver who'd picked him up near Kentish Town station and taken him to Hampstead. I asked him if he could recall anything that would help us. He asked if he was going to be in trouble and I replied of course not, and he said he remembered the man had been writing something during the journey and put a letter inside an envelope. Just before they reached Hampstead, he asked the driver if he had a stamp and he said he didn't so the man gave him the envelope and a ten-shilling note and said that was his to keep if he put a stamp on the letter and posted it as soon as possible.

'The driver said he wouldn't have thought anything of it except that he could have bought over a hundred stamps for ten shillings and frankly he'd have done what the man asked for a shilling.'

'And the letter?'

'He posted it later that afternoon.'

'Where?'

'In Regent Street, not long before we tracked him down that evening.'

'And he didn't think to mention it at the time? He didn't consider a letter he'd been given ten shillings to post might be important? For heaven's—'

'He said he forgot. Of course had he told us that evening, we might have been able to find the bloody letter.'

'I suppose it's too much to ask whether he remembered the address?'

'He says he remembers it was in Chelsea because he wondered whether he should drop it in person on his way home but then decided against it.'

'What a bloody fool! Why on earth didn't he think it was important when you first spoke with him? If it wasn't still in the postbox, we could have turned the sorting office upside down.' Hugh Harper looked furious.

'Did you say Chelsea, Bartholomew?'

'Yes, Mr King.'

'Wasn't that one of the places the radio chaps said the transmissions could have been coming from?'

'You're right, Lance. All the more reason—'

Harper was interrupted by a knock on the door. His secretary said she needed a word and he told her it would have to wait.

'All's not lost, sir,' King said. 'It gives us something to go on with Dabrowski: if we tell him we know about the letter – we can imply we have it – that may break him. I've known that to happen; it shows we're gathering evidence. I'll head back to the farm now.'

The secretary had opened the door again and said she was really most sorry to interrupt, but a gentleman absolutely insisted he needed to talk to Mr King most urgently.

Lance King looked like a beaten man when he returned to the office.

'I'm afraid it's too late, sir. Seems Hood went too far this time.'

43

Chapter 5

England and Belgium, July 1944

It had started as a routine day at RAF West Malling for Flying Officer Ted Palmer. Up at six, breakfast, followed by a pleasant stroll across the airbase to the officers' mess and the morning briefing. There was little cloud – the first thing a pilot always looked out for – and the sun showed promising signs of making an effort that day. There was, however, quite a wind, noticeable enough for young Bolt to comment on as he hurried to walk alongside him.

'Will this be enough to stop us flying, Ted?'

'Don't you want to fly today?'

'Of course I do, but I was just wondering: it does seem quite strong.'

'Should be all right by the time we take off. Don't worry.'

The squadron gathered in the mess and the wing commander himself took the briefing.

'We're down to eleven as Poulsen's had to get his ankle fixed, and in any case two of the Mark 14s need more maintenance. The squadron will split in three: Jonty will lead a section of four to go and help out over Normandy; we'll keep a section here in case any V1s pop over – Flight Lieutenant Rees will look after that; and Bolt and Palmer, you'll have the pleasure of my company. We're going to Belgium.'

–

The wing commander told them it was a reconnaissance flight as much as anything else.

'Unless this damned wind drops, we'll have to take off to the north, and once we get enough height, head east then south-east. Ideally I'd like to cross the coast just south of Margate, get up to twenty thousand feet over the North Sea and cross the Belgian border near Middelkerke – here...' He tapped a point on the map near Ostend. 'Then they want us to drop down over to this area here – west of Aalst – and have a look round. I may take a few snaps while you chaps cover me, but the main aim of our mission is to see where the hell the Luftwaffe is. Apparently they've been mounting some sorties from that area and command wants us to see if we can spot where they're coming from.'

They took off at 10.30, later than the wing commander would have liked, but the wind was still blowing hard from a northerly direction and showed no sign of dropping.

Everything was fine until – in Ted Palmer's opinion – they descended a bit too late approaching Aalst and as a result didn't spot the Messerschmitts until they were swarming around them.

They closed in on Pilot Officer Bolt's Spitfire first, the hunters sensing the weakest of their prey, and within seconds Palmer saw it burst into flames. The wing commander's plane seemed to be getting away, and Palmer had dropped another couple of thousand feet to follow him when he felt a bang coming from his right wing. It wasn't unlike someone throwing a large stone at a moving car, but when he glanced round, he saw the wing tip was missing and the rest of it was beginning to disintegrate.

He made a faultless parachute landing in a ploughed field close to a small forest and had only been hiding there for a few hours when a farmer found him and ordered him politely to follow him, please. Darkness had wrapped itself around the trees.

Fortune, he soon realised, was on his side. He had landed in a Flemish area but the farmer and his family were, they assured him, resistance: Armée Secrète.

A woman arrived very early the next day and carefully checked his papers. Had he perhaps heard of the Comet Line?

The escape network for Allied aircrew.

'We will look after you but it's too dangerous around here – too exposed. We're moving you to Brussels: believe it or not, it's safer there.' She explained that she'd escort him there. He was to do what she said.

The bus from Aalst was crowded and the checks of their papers as they boarded were quite perfunctory. For much of the journey Palmer dozed and coughed as the bus slowly made its way through the Flemish countryside. Brussels began to emerge around them, covered in rain, the passengers joining the bus soaking wet. He was gazing down when he spotted a pair of military boots touching the tips of his shoes. As he slowly looked up, a German soldier was saying something to him in Flemish. He didn't understand a word and a feeling of fear swept over him. The bus seemed to have fallen silent, everyone now staring at him.

The German soldier – an ill-tempered, impatient-looking man in his forties – regarded him so suspiciously Palmer wondered if he'd spotted his RAF flying suit under his overalls. He repeated the word. It sounded like he was saying '*Vuurtje.*' He now looked quite angry, as if Palmer was deliberately disobeying him.

At that moment, a man leaned over holding a lighted match. The soldier continued to look at Palmer as he lit his cigarette, giving the impression he'd not finished with him. At that moment, a couple in front of them got up and made a point of offering their seats to the German.

It was mid morning when the bus stopped by Brussels-North railway station. They walked away from the crowd before the woman spoke, giving him directions. 'Rue Gaucheret: you are looking for number 73. You understand that? Walk past it on the other side of the road and look at the second floor: if there are blue curtains drawn you know it's safe. They'll be waiting for you. When you get there, tell them you've come to collect the medicine.'

—

The woman in the apartment in rue Gaucheret explained that he was now being looked after by the Milices Patriotiques. They were communists, she told him. 'The Armée Secrète, who got you here, are more conservative. We're the main resistance group in this area: the population here is overwhelmingly working class and anti-German.'

Smoke from the woman's cigarette blew towards him as she spoke. She explained that they'd leave soon for a permanent safe house, which was actually an apartment above a café on rue Guido Gezelle run by Rexist collaborators.

'The Rexists are one of the largest groups of pro-Nazi collaborators and the café is frequented by German soldiers, but that means they're less likely to suspect the apartment. Once you're in it, that is.'

It all felt too hurried. Palmer didn't feel it was his place to question the woman; after all, they were the ones rescuing him and he didn't want to appear ungrateful. But he couldn't understand why he couldn't stay there for the time being. Instead she told him to get ready. They were leaving for the safe house now.

They walked briskly through Schaerbeek, Palmer following her at a distance so they did not appear to be together. She assured him that the papers she'd given him were fine: he was a labourer from Charleroi.

But she'd not anticipated a German spot check when they were within sight of the café. She hesitated when they turned the corner and saw it, but it was too late. She got through safely and he was wondering about turning round when one of them saw him.

Moments later, he was forced against the wall, revolvers held to his head, and his clothing was ripped off to reveal his RAF uniform.

For the next few minutes he was the subject of a heated debate in German. It seemed to be about where he should be taken. Eventually the Luftwaffe turned up and were adamant. Any RAF pilots should be taken to the Luftwaffe headquarters: it was essential they were given the opportunity to interrogate him.

The Luftwaffe was based in the Hotel Metropole in the centre of the city, a beautiful Belle Époque building with decor on the ground floor that was almost cathedral-like. He was being treated quite politely, the two officers who'd brought him in speaking to him in English and trying to engage him in a conversation about the merits of the Spitfire Mark 14 versus the Messerschmitt 109.

He was led through a series of corridors and up a flight of stairs, then up another one seemingly going in the opposite direction. Eventually he found himself in what had clearly been a hotel bedroom, its tall windows covered with bars and two comfortable chairs facing each other.

The Luftwaffe officer who carried out the interrogation was pleasant enough. Not what one would call friendly, but not threatening either. He was polite and gave the impression of going through the motions. Palmer was allowed to sit down and given some water while the officer flicked through his notes.

'Very soon you'll be taken to a special prisoner-of-war camp for Allied aircrew... I think you will find it quite amenable... Perhaps to help you as much as us, you could confirm what you were flying and when and where you were shot down.'

They'll be friendly most probably; be prepared for that and don't fall for it... They'll try and lull you into giving them information you aren't required to. Anything to do with your mission is out of the question.

48

Apart from anything else, you don't want to give them details that could help identify anyone who helps you...

Flying Officer Ted Palmer replied with name, rank and serial number. 'I'm sure you'll understand if I'm unable to say anything else.'

The officer nodded as if he had expected that, but looked disappointed nonetheless.

'Can I ask that the Red Cross are informed about me? I wouldn't want my family to worry unduly.'

This went on for a good hour, the Luftwaffe officer looking bored and giving the impression he'd have been shocked had Palmer volunteered any information.

'Yesterday two Spitfire Mark 14s were shot down west of Aalst: there were reports that one pilot may have bailed out. If this was you, it is clearly in your interests to at least let us know.'

Palmer made sure he didn't react. If the officer was talking about only two aircraft being shot down, it sounded as if the wing commander had got away. He said he had no idea where he'd landed, or when.

The Luftwaffe officer closed his file.

'We'll keep you here tonight and you'll be transferred to Dulag Luft in the morning. You were very fortunate indeed that you were brought here: they could easily have taken you to Avenue Louise.'

'What is that?'

Before the German could reply, there was the sound of raised voices in the corridor, followed by a sharp knock at the door. The Luftwaffe officer told Palmer to wait a moment and stood up. Before he could open the door, it burst open and two men in civilian dress marched in. An almighty argument blew up.

As Flying Officer Palmer was handcuffed and marched out of the room, the Luftwaffe officer sidled over to him. 'I'm afraid now you'll find out all about Avenue Louise.'

–

They arrived at a handsome building on a wide boulevard, its front draped in large red flags with black swastikas, the heavily guarded entrance at the top of a flight of stone steps.

The car paused at the front of the building before driving to a rear entrance, where Palmer was hustled out. He was taken to a basement and pushed along a narrow, dimly lit corridor, its floor rough and uneven, the ceiling no more than five and a half feet high, causing him to crouch. He was pulled to a halt outside an iron door, and for the first time he saw who was behind him: a large man whose girth took up the width of the corridor and whose bulk blocked much of its light.

Like many men of that considerable size, his head was small in comparison to the rest of his body, his mouth tiny between the fleshy cheeks and triple chin, his eyes black and beady against his pale skin. He was wearing a black uniform with no markings and carried a small leather truncheon that he used to strike Palmer across his ribs, following up with a kick to propel him into the cell.

The young pilot remained there for what must have been two hours. The cell was pitch black, and the floor was as rough and uneven as that in the corridor outside. Its surface was wet, as were the walls.

His first thought was that the questioning at the Luftwaffe headquarters had been some kind of trick to make him think it was all routine. He began to worry he'd let something slip, some vital piece of information that had aroused the interest of what he could only assume was the Gestapo.

The pain in his ribs eased slightly and he worked out his surroundings. He made out a low bench-cum-bed and sat down, and only then did he realise how terrified he was. His whole body shook violently and he broke into a cold sweat. Try as he might, he could think of no rational reason why the Gestapo would be interested in him. In his confusion, he couldn't work out exactly when he'd been shot down, but it was certainly more than a day ago. They'd probably be telling his parents around now.

Missing in action. Our deepest condolences.

Tears started to flow down his face. The thought of his parents being informed of his possible death was too much. He was still crying when the cell door swung open and two guards hauled him out, roughing him up in the corridor before tying his hands behind his back and blindfolding him.

As he was dragged along the corridor and down a flight of steps, he began to feel dizzy. When they'd beaten him up in the corridor he'd struck his head on the wall, and the blindfold was cutting into the wound. He tried to distract himself by counting the steps, but they were moving him along too fast. When they stopped, he could sense light around him, and he was pushed into a chair, the blindfold now removed.

The two men behind the table in front of him were the same ones who'd come for him at the Luftwaffe headquarters. What languages, they wanted to know, did he speak?

English.

'Any others?'

He shook his head and muttered something about a few words of French. He didn't think his ability to conjugate the verb 'to love' in Latin was what they had in mind. He was feeling overwhelmed now by nausea and his head felt as if it was gripped in a vice. He asked if he could have some water. They replied in German: would he like some water – some food perhaps? He could have a bed to lie on and they could bring a doctor. They wanted him to be well.

He remembered the advice he'd been given. *We've found it's better if prisoners don't let on that they understand German: understanding what they say without them realising it can give you an advantage.*

So he didn't reply and stared blankly at them. More questions in English.

What was his name?

Ted Palmer.

His full name?

Edward Palmer – no middle name.

Spell it.

Where was he based?

Did he work in any other branch of the RAF?

Had he ever been in the British Army?

This went on for an hour, and at the end of it the two men muttered to each other in German, very little of which he could pick up, not least because he was being careful not to look at them. He did hear them both use the word *Warheit* – the truth – more than once, and one of them said *zu jung* – too young – while looking at him. Then they started to gather their papers, both sounding quite angry. One of them said *Zeitverschwendung*, which he remembered was a phrase his German teacher used when he wanted to tell the class they were wasting his time, and as they stood up, he clearly heard them say *Berlin kann es sortieren*.

As he was dragged back to his cell, he worked out what that meant.

Berlin can sort it.

–

Berlin arrived in Brussels the following morning. It came as a relief to Flying Officer Palmer, who'd spent a thoroughly miserable night assuming he was about to be sent to the German capital and wondering how on earth his parents would be coping.

He had no idea what time it was when he was dragged out of his cell. He was taken into a room that was more of an office than the interrogation room he'd been in the previous day. The two Gestapo men were there again, along with a man in what looked like his mid-forties who they appeared to be deferring to. Everything about the man looked expensive: from his tailored suit and silk tie to the complexion and haircut of someone who clearly took care over his appearance. Palmer could smell cologne.

'Our colleague has come from Berlin to talk with you.'

Palmer blinked in amazement. Even with his limited experience of these matters he knew people didn't travel from Berlin to question junior RAF officers. The man looked at him in equal amazement.

'What happened to your head?' His English was very good.

Palmer explained that he'd knocked it against the wall.

'You look terrible. When did you last sleep – or eat?'

He replied that he couldn't remember, but if he was being honest, he didn't feel terribly well. He gave his name, rank and serial number because he couldn't remember if the man had asked him for them yet.

The man from Berlin turned to the Gestapo officers. 'This is ridiculous, absolutely ridiculous,' he snapped in German. 'If I'm to question this man he needs to be in a fit state. Take him away, let him have a shower, give him a meal and clean clothes and then bring him back here.'

When Palmer returned to the office, the man from Berlin was on his own. He'd removed his expensive-looking spectacles to read some notes and looked up as the RAF pilot sat down.

'Your name, please.'

'Edward Palmer.'

'And that is your only name?'

'I'm known as Ted, but… yes: I don't have a middle name if that's what you mean.'

'And your age, please, Palmer.'

He hesitated, unsure as to whether this was information he was supposed to divulge.

'I'm twenty.'

'Date of birth?'

'The sixth of April 1924.'

And so it went on for an hour: questions about where he'd worked before joining the RAF, asking for his date of birth at least half a dozen more times, an offer to be more lenient than he could imagine if he was honest about any other role he'd performed... but no questions about his mission. The man from Berlin had no interest in what he was flying, where he was shot down and how he'd made it to Brussels.

After an hour, there was a knock at the door and an elderly man came in. The man from Berlin said this was a doctor: there would be a brief examination. It was routine: please could Palmer remove his clothes.

All of them.

When the doctor had finished, he briefly addressed the other man in German.

'It is impossible to say, of course, but I would be amazed if this man was over the age of twenty-five. If he was any older than that, there'd be some signs of early ageing, such as lines on the face and increased body fat. I would say in my professional opinion that he's a sexually mature male aged between eighteen and twenty-five.'

'You'd stake your life on that, would you, Doctor?'

'In this building, Herr Rauter, that's not a phrase I'd choose, but I'd certainly stake my professional reputation on it. That cut on his head needs dressing, though.'

–

Matters moved quickly after that. The man from Berlin said there'd be no more questions, and when Palmer asked what it had all been about, the German said it didn't matter, there'd been a misunderstanding. His wound would be attended to and he would be taken to a prisoner-of-war camp.

The man from Berlin – whom Palmer was sure the doctor had addressed as Herr Rauter – nodded at him before shaking his head in disbelief and then leaving the room. Palmer caught a snatch of an angry conversation in the hall, apologetic tones from one of the Gestapo men, the raised voice of Herr Rauter.

'A complete waste of my time... Anyone can see how old he is. In any case, why on earth did you treat him like that if you knew I was interested? Fools.'

When Flying Officer Ted Palmer arrived at Dulag Luft that evening, he was taken to see the senior British officer, a group captain with a nervous twitch and an unlit pipe in his mouth.

He was almost apologetic as he recounted what had happened to him; he thought it was odd but perhaps not that important.

This was not a view shared by the group captain, nor by any of the other senior officers he'd called in to listen to the story.

They all said they'd never heard anything like it.

'And that phrase you used, Palmer... when you finished giving me your account: what was it again?'

'It was as if they thought I was someone else, sir. Heaven knows who, though.'

Chapter 6

Berlin, August 1944

'You can assure us, can you, Rauter, that everything is in order and you're ready to commence when we give you the order to do so?'

The man spoke with one of those complicated southern Austrian accents – Tyrol or Carinthia or somewhere like that – so Franz Rauter leaned forward hoping that would help him understand it better. He replied that he hoped everything was in order but he would need some time to prepare – and have the right people in place.

A summons to meet the three men facing him from the other side of a table in a dimly lit room with the curtains drawn had not, it had to be said, boded well. It had felt like a court of law, but now the three men nodded their heads and muttered, 'Good,' and he should have felt more relaxed.

Except he didn't.

He actually felt a knot tighten in his stomach and his heart beat faster as he realised the enormity of what he was about to do.

A wait of five years was about to come to an end.

–

On most days Franz Rauter walked the mile and a half to work. It was a twenty-five-minute stroll northwards from his apartment on Speyerer Strasse in the Bayerisches Viertel, the

Bavarian quarter of Schöneberg. He'd emerge from the side streets onto Potsdamer Strasse, crossing the Landwehrkanal before reaching his office on Tirpitzufer. When he'd first started to walk to and from work it had been quite a pleasant experience, but now he was aware of the city decaying around him and a general air of menace. He needed too to be alert to new bomb damage – it wasn't uncommon for people to fall into newly formed craters.

On most days he'd leave enough time to stop at the run-down café on the corner of Ludendorff Strasse, though it had to be said there were few places in Berlin these days that didn't have a run-down look about them. But this café had felt run-down even before the war and he felt a vague kind of loyalty to it. It was less crowded than most of the other nearby places, and the proprietor – a large one-armed man – was someone with whom he'd always exchanged knowing looks, though he wasn't sure what it was they were meant to know. Possibly it just meant 'Ah, you're still around.' There was a lot of that these days.

Although the Bayerischer Platz U-Bahn station was just a minute or so from where he lived, he avoided that mode of transport whenever possible. He couldn't imagine a more unpleasant way of travelling, people pressed together as close as lovers, few of his fellow commuters smelling as if they'd washed in recent days. If it was raining or he was in a hurry he'd take the tram, though that too tended to be unfeasibly crowded.

But the main benefit of his twenty-five-minute walk in the morning – and usually the same in reverse in the evening – was that it gave him time to think. And these days he'd reflect with varying degrees of bemusement on the unpredictable way in which life had worked out for him.

For example, he was forty-four years of age and had assumed that by now he'd have been long married, no doubt with children, living in some comfort on the Wannsee or possibly in Charlottenburg. Since his late twenties and throughout his thirties this had been a disappointment to him, and had at times led to bouts of depression, which while not disabling had probably accounted for his being a solitary and reserved person.

It wasn't as if he was an unattractive man. On the contrary, he took care over his appearance. His suits were hand-made by a master tailor on Behrenstrasse before the poor man had been deported. His silk ties and handkerchiefs were from Paris and he had his hair cut every week by the best barber on the Unter den Linden. His 4711 cologne was bought from the original shop in Cologne itself.

Despite this, he lived alone in an apartment in Schöneberg rather than a villa on the Wannsee or one of those fine houses in Charlottenburg. He hadn't – as he reflected at times – even made it to the Kurfürstendamm.

But now he saw how not being married, not having children and living a more modest life had turned to his advantage. He didn't have loved ones to worry about and provide for; concentrating on his own survival was not an act of selfishness, and living where he did meant he led a less conspicuous life.

It was the same with the Nazi Party. All his life he'd eschewed politics. He was from Hamburg, where his schoolteacher father had been a committed socialist and clashed bitterly with his mother's family, who'd enthusiastically embraced far-right politics. He saw how politics caused rifts and decided to remain above it, though his instincts were more in line with liberal traditions. He'd joined the local police and risen through the ranks, eventually becoming a well-regarded detective. Few of his colleagues were surprised when, in 1932, he moved to Berlin to work for the Abwehr – the military intelligence service.

There'd been opportunities to join the Nazi Party; indeed he'd frequently been taken aside and advised that now might be the time. But he'd managed to avoid doing so, and he was by no means alone in that. Many others – even some very senior people – at the Abwehr headquarters on Tirpitzufer remained non-party members.

It was over Christmas in 1943 that he realised he couldn't hold out any longer. The Abwehr was increasingly distrusted in Berlin: its loyalty was frequently questioned and it was beginning to be suspected of undermining Hitler. Franz Rauter spent the few days he had off that Christmas worrying that the Abwehr's days were numbered. His big fear was being conscripted into the army and sent to fight on the Eastern Front, which was tantamount to a death sentence. He decided to reduce the chances of that by applying to join the party: it would be an insurance policy rather than an act of political commitment.

His resolve was strengthened when he was caught unawares by his cleaning lady, who turned up unexpectedly on Christmas Eve – he was sure he'd given her the day off. To his horror, he spotted her tidying his table and looking carefully at the books as she dusted them and placed them in a pile. It could have been his imagination, but he was sure she looked disapprovingly at works by Thomas Mann and Franz Kafka. It wasn't that he was trying to be subversive by reading books by these authors, but they challenged his imagination: they made him think. He wasn't sure his cleaning lady would understand that.

That afternoon he bumped into Frau Oberg, the local Nazi Party *Blockleiter* – block leader – the person most likely to spot anything suspicious and report it. She was a tall, thin woman with piercing eyes, who dressed in widow's black and had a habit of suddenly appearing where one least expected her. Rauter called her – only to himself, of course – *die Hexe*, the witch. And when *die Hexe* emerged in front of him as he turned a corner after his afternoon stroll, she wanted to talk.

How was Herr Rauter?

Had Herr Rauter perhaps heard how both her sons had been promoted?

Did Herr Rauter join her in being grateful every moment of every day for the wisdom with which Herr Hitler was leading Germany?

She moved close to him and peered up into his eyes, searching for any doubt on his part. He assured her he was as grateful as she was for the Führer's... he'd hesitated, searching for a word better than 'wisdom'... *compassion*, and then worried it might sound sarcastic.

'In fact I was meaning to have a word with you, Frau Oberg. I have been intending to apply to join the party for a while now and have been remiss in not doing so. Perhaps you could help?'

She'd appeared at his apartment door later that afternoon with the correct forms to hand and returned with his brand-new Nazi Party membership card – his *Mitgliedskarte* – on New Year's Eve.

With 1944 just minutes away, Franz Rauter shifted his armchair close to his gramophone player and put on a Benny Goodman record, turning the volume down so even someone with their ear pressed to the apartment's door wouldn't hear it. As with his reading, it wasn't that he was trying to be subversive: he knew jazz was banned, but he happened to like it. He leaned back with a large glass of cognac – courtesy of a colleague's recent trip to Paris – in one hand and his *Mitgliedskarte* in the other.

He took some satisfaction from the fact that the records would show he'd joined in 1943.

As 1944 progressed, he realised that joining the party had been a smart move, just as remaining single had. By February, Admiral Canaris and other senior officers of the Abwehr had been replaced, and by July, it had been taken over entirely by the RSHA, the Reich Main Security Office, the organisation responsible for all police and internal security operations, including the Gestapo.

SS-Brigadeführer Walter Friedrich Schellenberg was now in charge, and dozens of Abwehr officers were purged from the organisation. Many of them were like Rauter: senior but still only middle-ranking intelligence officers, the professional heart of the operation.

Some of those who remained were even moved to the RSHA headquarters on Prinz-Albrecht-Strasse, the other side of Saarland Strasse.

If, like Franz Rauter, you remained in the organisation, it was for a good reason. Your loyalty to the regime had never been brought into question – it helped if you were a party member – and most importantly, you had a vital role to play in the Nazi intelligence operation. Perhaps you had an area of expertise or – as in Rauter's case – you controlled a key agent, one who could not be run without your involvement.

That was another area in which Franz Rauter had been smart.

He'd made himself indispensable.

That morning he'd stopped as usual at the run-down café on the corner of Ludendorff Strasse, and was pleased to see that the seat at the end of the bar and against the wall was vacant. The one-armed owner gave him the usual knowing look and without exchanging a word handed him a cup of something that in Rauter's opinion was the closest he was going to get to coffee around Potsdamer Strasse that morning. At least it was hot, and the cup looked like it had been rinsed since the last person had drunk from it. A bun appeared in front of him on a plate, and although it would be hard, with a hint of sawdust, he knew it could be made palatable by dunking it in the hot drink.

He removed a copy of *Der Angriff* from the rack on the wall next to him. Tucked away on an inside page was a short report about 'measures being taken against large-scale criminal activity in Warsaw', which he supposed was one way of describing the uprising. The fact that the report was on an inside page indicated that things weren't going well. All over Europe cities the Nazis had taken for granted were beginning to crumble. He wondered about Brussels and what would happen to the two incompetent Gestapo officers who'd called him there so needlessly. He reckoned they'd escape in time: like rats on a sinking ship the Gestapo were usually the first out. The mischievous part of him hoped not, but then he worried that if they had been captured, they might not keep their mouths shut.

He finished his breakfast and made his way to what had been the Abwehr building on Tirpitzufer but was now merely an outstation of the RSHA. His office was small and overflowing with files, which he had to edge through to get to his desk. At least he now had the office to himself and a reasonable view over the canal. At times it could even be quite peaceful.

But that morning he didn't make it as far as his office. No sooner had he emerged into the corridor than he was intercepted by Kramer, who liked to see himself as some kind of office manager but was probably there to keep an eye on Rauter and his colleagues.

'You're wanted at Prinz-Albrecht-Strasse, now!'

He barked the last word like an instruction on the parade ground. It was accompanied by a toothy yellow smile and a face etched with *schadenfreude*.

'Very well: and does anyone there in particular want me, Herr Kramer?'

Kramer told him he was to report to the front desk. 'And you're to leave now!'

Normally a summons to Prinz-Albrecht-Strasse would be quite ominous, but Rauter was pretty sure as he left Tirpitzufer and walked across Potsdamer Platz and Saarland Strasse into the headquarters of the RSHA that he wasn't being watched. Had he been in trouble, he wouldn't have been left to his own devices like this, though it still didn't mean he had no reason to worry.

He was escorted to an office on an upper floor, the dimly lit one where the three men faced him across a table. He was certain they were all long-standing SD officers, revelling in the fact that the Sicherheitsdienst were now running everything.

The SD was the intelligence arm of the SS though Rauter felt the emphasis was on the SS rather than on intelligence.

The Austrian with the hard-to-understand accent seemed to be in charge. He leaned forward, his head out of the shadow, revealing a long, thin face with a jaw that tapered to a sharp point.

'Agent Milton.'

There was a silence clearly meant as an invitation for Rauter to say something. He knew he had to resist coming across as too clever, but he wasn't in the mood to volunteer any more information than he had to.

'Yes, sir.'

'What of him, Rauter?'

'I have been providing regular reports, as you may be aware. Last September, Admiral Canaris took the view that it was the right time to start using Agent Milton, and I—'

'Admiral Canaris is under arrest, Rauter.'

'But he wasn't in September last year, sir. He and I agreed we would activate Agent Milton and that we needed to send over an agent to liaise between him and his radioman, Agent Byron. As you know, there was an instruction that recruitment of this agent was to be handled by Section 6 of the SD. Unfortunately that has not gone well.'

The three men shifted awkwardly. The Austrian spoke.

'Remind me what happened, please, Rauter.'

Franz Rauter straightened himself in the chair.

'A series of disappointments, sir, I'd be the first to admit that, but—'

'There are no buts.'

'I was simply going to add that none of the three agents we lost was recruited by me. I am on record as having expressed reservations about all of them. As far as we can gather, Agent Keats was killed by a train as he tried to escape from the British police last November. We cannot be sure whether he deliberately threw himself in front of it or if it was an accident.'

'But either way—'

'Either way, he's dead. The following month we lost contact with Agent Shelley. We don't know what happened for sure, but we do know he was found dead in his bedsit in Coventry. The likelihood is that he died of natural causes: one of my reservations about him was that he was clearly not a well man, certainly not well enough to be sent on a mission like that.'

'And Agent Dryden?'

'In March this year, there was a report in a number of British newspapers that a Polish national by the name of Jan Dabrowski was killed in an accident with a lorry near a railway station in Birmingham. Jan Dabrowski was one of Agent Dryden's identities, and the date given was the same one he was due to travel to London. There was a photograph that was unquestionably of Agent Dryden: according to the report, he'd been arrested a day or two before for being drunk. That is certainly feasible: one of the reservations I had about him was his fondness for alcohol.'

'You seem very ready with your reservations about our agents, Rauter. I presume you have none about Agent Milton?'

'No, sir.'

'Of course he doesn't – he recruited him!' said one of the other men.

'To be more accurate, sir, I inherited him. Helmut Krüger recruited him.'

'And what was it that happened in Brussels last month – something to do with Agent Milton?'

'It was a false alarm, sir, quite unnecessary and why on earth the Gestapo there thought—'

'The Gestapo rarely make mistakes, Herr Rauter. And so you are still not in contact with Agent Milton?'

'Since the presumed death of Agent Dryden, it was felt we ought to pause. We don't want to do anything that could alert the British to Agent Milton. As far as we know from Agent Byron, Milton hasn't been compromised.'

'We think,' said the Austrian, 'you have waited far too long to activate Agent Milton. If the military setbacks we're currently experiencing are to be reversed, we need to use all our resources, not least our intelligence agents. If we can even just delay the Allied advance, then who knows, the weapons we are developing could well alter the course of the war. It's one thing having a sleeper agent, but this one could be regarded as comatose. We need to wake him up!' All three men behind the table laughed heartily. 'We cannot afford to have the luxury of an apparently well-placed agent who's not doing anything. You can assure us, can you, Rauter, that everything is in order and you're ready to commence when we give you the order to do so?'

'I think everything is in order, sir, but obviously we need to send over an agent before we activate Milton. We would need to recruit someone.'

'Do you have anyone in mind for that?'

'I wasn't sure I was permitted to have a role in that respect, sir.'

'That attitude, Rauter, is precisely why the Abwehr has been so distrusted.' It was another of the men, a Berliner by the sounds of it. 'Given that you've had so many reservations about the agents we've suggested, perhaps you'd like to recruit this one? You clearly know best.'

'You'd better pull your finger out,' added the Austrian. 'We need to get someone over there very quickly – understand?'

'And be in no doubt, Rauter,' said the Berliner, 'this agent you recruit cannot fail: if he does, the blame will fall squarely on you.'

Chapter 7

Berlin and London, September 1944

Like an uninvited guest at a wedding, Franz Rauter hung around the landing by the staircase on the fourth floor of Prinz-Albrecht-Strasse that Monday morning, 11 September, all the while keeping a watchful eye on the well-guarded door leading to the corridor where SS-Brigadeführer Walter Schellenberg had his office.

Once or twice a guard had come over and pointedly asked if he could help, and Rauter had assured him there was no need to worry, he was waiting for someone. Some of the people hurrying past gave a 'who invited him?' look in his direction. He knew many of them by sight even if they'd struggle to put a name to his face.

He'd been waiting on the landing for an awkward half an hour when the guards at the corridor entrance snapped to attention and the doors swung open. Brigadeführer Walter Schellenberg was at the head of a small entourage, which moved quickly towards the stairs. Franz Rauter hurried across the landing and found himself face to face with the head of the Reich Main Security Office, only just remembering in time to greet him with a *Heil Hitler.*

'Good morning, Brigadeführer. My name is Franz Rauter and I'm based at Tirpitzufer. I'm sorry for approaching you in this manner but I do need to see you as a matter of urgency.'

Schellenberg stopped and looked at him, unsure of what to make of the situation. One of his aides stepped forward as if to move Rauter away, but the Brigadeführer waved him back.

'Rauter, did you say?'

'Yes, sir.'

'What do you want, Rauter?'

'As I say, sir, to see you as a matter of some urgency.'

'I'm sure you're aware there are channels you should be going through. Your head of unit should contact my office and arrange a meeting.'

'I'm afraid there's no time for protocol, sir.'

'Please, Rauter, I'm in a hurry. I have a meeting in the Reich Chancellery and I can't possibly imagine that what you want to see me about can be more important than that!' Schellenberg smiled and the group behind him laughed obediently.

'As it happens, sir, it may well be.'

Walter Schellenberg stepped back to get a better look at this man in a smart civilian suit who was either mad or needed to be listened to.

'Very well, Rauter. I'll be back from the Reich Chancellery at two o'clock and I'll see you then. And I'm sure I don't need to tell you this had better not be a waste of my time.'

—

When SS-Brigadeführer Walter Schellenberg returned to his office just before two o'clock that afternoon, Franz Rauter was sitting patiently in his outer office. Schellenberg was followed in by a young aide-de-camp.

'Tell me, Hauptsturmführer Böhme, what we know about this Franz Rauter?'

'He's a former police officer from Hamburg, sir, where he was very highly regarded. He joined the Abwehr in 1932 and has a good record of recruiting and running agents. There is nothing negative on his file, sir.'

'Well there wouldn't be, would there, Klaus, otherwise he'd have been got rid of like the rest of those traitors at Tirpitzufer. Tell me, is he a party member?'

'Yes, sir.'

'When did he join?'

'Last year, sir.'

'Better late than never, I suppose. What else does his file say?'

'He's regarded as a professional intelligence officer rather than a loyalist to the regime, so he's not one of us, sir.'

'But not one of them either.'

'There is one other matter, sir: last month his work was reviewed by department 6B, who were concerned that he has a well-placed source in England who has not yet been activated as an agent. There was some discussion about who was responsible for sending over a contact. Rauter was instructed to activate this agent.'

'Maybe it's in connection with that. What is the agent's name?'

'Milton.'

–

Since inheriting Agent Milton from Helmut Krüger, Franz Rauter had regarded the Englishman as his insurance policy, not unlike his membership of the Nazi Party. Now he realised he was even more valuable than that. Since the Abwehr had been absorbed into the RSHA and Canaris, Oster and so many other Abwehr officers had been arrested, he saw Agent Milton as a possible reprieve from the death sentence that so many of his former colleagues seemed to face. It was for this reason that he was holding the intelligence he'd just received from Agent Milton tightly to his chest. He knew he'd taken a risk by insisting on seeing Brigadeführer Schellenberg in person, but he wanted to be certain his name was associated with the information he was about to deliver.

He was angry that the message sent by Agent Byron had taken so long to reach him. Byron had transmitted on the Friday evening, but for some unaccountable reason – laziness, no doubt – the message had been waiting for him when he arrived at Tirpitzufer that Monday morning. He should have been contacted over the weekend.

The head of the RSHA was lounging behind his desk. He pointed to a chair and told Hauptsturmführer Böhme to leave. Then he held out a hand in Rauter's direction, the conductor cueing a minor section of his orchestra.

'I have an agent, sir, in England. He—'

'Would this be Agent Milton?'

'Yes, sir. Agent Milton was identified by a sympathetic British national in 1933 and then recruited by an Abwehr officer called Helmut Krüger between 1934 and 1935. We instructed him to join the British Army in 1938. I took him over in 1939 when Herr Krüger died. The plan had always been to do nothing with him for a while, until he reached a position where he could be of most use to us. We instructed him to apply for secondment to his brigade headquarters, and then to brigade intelligence, and from there he went to his divisional headquarters. He applied for a transfer to the Directorate of Military Intelligence at the War Office: this had been our intention for him all along, but the feeling was that it should not be rushed; we wanted his transfers to appear to be part of the normal course of events.

'He was due to start at the War Office in July, but when the Allies were struggling a bit in Normandy, he was sent over there and was wounded in the shoulder, though not too seriously. In August I was instructed to activate him come what may, and was able to recruit and send over a decent contact agent, Agent Donne. Happily this coincided with Agent Milton finally starting work at the War Office.'

'Which is all somewhat interesting, Rauter, but surely—'

'If you please, sir. Milton's first task at the War Office was to work on an Allied plan to invade the Reich through the Netherlands by outflanking our forces. They are going to attempt to do this by a combination of land troops advancing across the Belgian border and heading into the Netherlands through Eindhoven, and large detachments of airborne troops who will... Would it be possible, sir, to go over to your map wall?'

The two men stood in front of a map of northern Europe.

'The terrain in that area is very difficult for land forces: it's marshy, the roads are narrow and the area is crisscrossed by canals and rivers. Their plan is for the parachute divisions – there is some talk as to whether there'll be three or four of them – to capture the bridges over key canals and rivers, specifically here, sir, the Meuse at Grave and the Waal at Nijmegen. Their main objective, though, will be here...'

Rauter glanced over at the Brigadeführer and could see he was now interested – leaning forward, concentrating hard.

'...at Arnhem, and specifically these two bridges over the Rhine: the railway bridge to the west of the town and the main road bridge into the centre. They'll look to land their airborne troops as close as possible to the bridges. Once they've secured them, their armoured divisions and infantry – our intelligence is that this will be led by XXX Corps of the British Army – will advance from behind, across the secured bridgeheads and through the Netherlands.'

Schellenberg stepped back, deep in thought, his hand stroking his chin. 'Do you have any further detail, Rauter?'

'Not yet, sir. The system we're using with Milton is a very secure one, but it does have limitations. We cannot afford to risk him being caught anywhere near a radio transmitter or with any documentation on him. He is alerted through coded telephone calls, and that's how meets are arranged, where the intelligence is passed on to Agent Donne by word of mouth. Donne then takes it to the radioman – an Agent Byron – who transmits it to us. That way Milton will always be clean: they'll never discover incriminating evidence on him or in his apartment. If he's followed and stopped either on his own or with his contact agent, they'll find nothing.'

'Wait here, Rauter.' Brigadeführer Schellenberg went to the door and called his aide over. From what Rauter could gather, he was instructing him to make some urgent calls.

'I don't need to stress to you how important this information is,' he said when he returned. 'It is to be divulged to no one else – you understand? I have no doubt the High Command will want more detail. I want you to move over here – I will find you space on my corridor. The first thing you will do is contact Milton and demand that he provides more information, as much detail as he can. And then I want a thorough report from you, Rauter: the recruitment of Milton, background on him, any corroborating intelligence we have.'

'Of course, sir.'

'One question I do have, Rauter...' Schellenberg was standing in the doorway and Rauter had already got up to leave. 'If I was being very cynical, I'd wonder about such a fortunate coincidence.'

'I'm not sure I follow you, sir?'

'When was it you say you sent over this contact agent?'

'Agent Donne, sir? He arrived in London on the last day of August, I believe.'

'And what... just a week later Agent Milton passes on to him such apparently invaluable intelligence? Wouldn't you say that's quite a coincidence?'

'I saw the recruitment of Agent Donne as a matter of urgency once we knew Milton was about to start work at the War Office, so the timing was deliberate.'

'You don't think some may say it's all rather convenient?'

Rauter didn't reply immediately. 'You may be correct, sir. I accept there's a tendency for some people in my position to be so pleased to get something from their agents that they're not as scientific as they should be in evaluating it. However, my approach is always to be as objective as possible about any intelligence I receive. What I'd say in this case is that it has taken a long time for Agent Milton to start work at the War Office, and once he was at the Directorate of Military Intelligence he was bound to have access to a steady stream of first-class intelligence. I just hope it's not too late, sir.'

'In what respect, Rauter?'

'In respect of helping change the course of the war, in helping to prevent military defeat. If only he'd been there in May and June, we might have had far more reliable intelligence on the Allies' plans for the Normandy invasion.'

'That's true: we may have been less likely to fall for all that disinformation. So are you saying the arrival of Agent Donne and this intelligence about Arnhem is a coincidence or not, then?'

Rauter hesitated before answering. He looked like a man wary of being drawn into a trap. 'I'd prefer, sir, to say that my having recruited a decent contact agent is the key factor here.'

'Let's hope so, Rauter.'

–

SS-Brigadeführer Walter Schellenberg was very strongly of the view that as this was *his* intelligence, the meeting should take place in *his* office. Berlin had become very territorial like that, a degree of importance being attached to where a meeting took place.

However, this was not a view shared by the first person he'd told about it within minutes of his meeting with Rauter. And because that man was none other than Field Marshal Wilhelm Keitel, the meeting later that afternoon took place in Keitel's office. They were in the Bendlerblock, the vast complex set between the Tiergarten and the Landwehrkanal that was the headquarters for various branches of the German armed forces.

Keitel was the head of the OKW, the High Command of the German armed forces. There were just half a dozen men gathered in the soundproofed meeting room adjoining his office. They included his deputy, General Alfred Jodl, and the chief of staff of the OKH – the High Command of the German army – General Heinz Guderian.

They'd waited impatiently as a secretary took an excessive amount of time to draw heavy curtains over the windows and the steel doors to the room were shut. The surface of the table they sat around was covered in maps of Europe. When they were finally ready, Schellenberg carefully repeated what Rauter had told him.

'That's all, Walter?'

'It's quite something, I'd have thought, Wilhelm.'

'There are no documents or photographs – nothing like that?'

Schellenberg looked carefully at Guderian, resisting the temptation to reply that the mail service between London and Berlin wasn't so reliable these days. He settled for shaking his head.

'If we take this intelligence at face value, then it is of enormous significance.' Jodl smiled in Schellenberg's direction. 'To have advance warning of a major Allied attack in an area and a direction we weren't expecting – surely we cannot underestimate its importance.'

'I don't know... On the one hand I agree, but at the same time I worry that this is all a bit too good to be true. After all,' Guderian shifted uncomfortably, 'we should consider whether this could be another of the Allies' deception operations: look at how they tricked us over D-Day! We were made to look utter fools. We far too easily bought into intelligence that informed us the Allies would land in the Pas-de-Calais, and to compound matters, even after they landed in Normandy we chose to believe those same sources that said Normandy was just a feint. We were—'

'We know all this, Heinz, there's nothing to be gained in going over it yet again. We accept mistakes were made, but now we need to...' Keitel hesitated, uncharacteristically unsure of how to continue.

'Your source, Walter, this Agent...'

'Milton.'

'Tell us more about him.'

'I know he was recruited well before the war, and the view seems to have been taken to wait until he reached a more prominent position. I think Rauter's strategy was that because the life span for our agents operating in the United Kingdom is relatively limited, Milton should only be activated at a time when the intelligence he'd provide would be of maximum benefit to us.'

'And this Rauter – can we trust him?' Keitel was nervously fiddling with his spectacles. 'After all, Tirpitzufer is a nest of traitors. Was he close to that bastard Canaris?'

'I'll have him thoroughly checked out.'

'I'd have thought, Walter,' Keitel was gathering up his papers to signal the end of the meeting, 'you'd have been doing that already.'

–

Over the next two days, every aspect of Franz Rauter's life came under scrutiny. Rauter didn't want to make a tense situation worse, but on more than one occasion he felt obliged to point out that while they were putting so much effort into investigating him, they seemed not to be acting on the intelligence he'd provided.

'Surely,' he told Hauptsturmführer Böhme, 'that has to be the priority?'

The Gestapo investigated his private life and searched his apartment on Speyerer Strasse, which he was relaxed about. When the Abwehr had been absorbed into the RSHA in February, he'd decided the time had come to remove the handful of books the regime would disapprove of. They spoke with his neighbours, and with Frau Oberg, the *Blockleiter*, who said she'd never heard anything negative about Herr Rauter.

No one had much to say about the polite, reserved man who was always smartly dressed.

They even discovered that he stopped most mornings at the run-down café on the corner of Ludendorff Strasse, where the one-armed proprietor told them that his customer never spoke much and usually read a copy of *Der Angriff*.

–

'And that's it? They didn't find a framed photograph of Churchill in his apartment, or a hidden transistor? The most they seem to have discovered about him is his fondness for buns.'

They'd reconvened in the secure room next to Keitel's office, and the head of the armed forces was clearly in a sceptical mood.

'My instinct,' said Schellenberg, 'is to trust him. If he's a British agent I suspect we'd have found something on him. To me, the fact that there was nothing in his apartment to show he's an enthusiastic party member is in his favour. For instance, there was no picture of the Führer or any Nazi Party literature. The Gestapo say that if he was working as a double agent he'd have bent over backwards to show how loyal he is. My recommendation is to take this at face value. After all, it's not as if we have much time.'

'I think,' said General Jodl, 'you should get Rauter to send Milton another message asking him to provide more information.'

'That's already happened, Alfred. We're waiting for his reply.'

–

The telephone call for the dry cleaner's came at the usual time on a Tuesday morning.

They are very happy but want more information and detail – as much as you can provide: names of units, start dates, times.

75

He wasn't surprised at the call; he'd been expecting Berlin to respond like this. He was pleased he'd managed to whet their appetite. Had there been no response he'd have been worried.

The day before – the Monday – Brigadier Oakley had called him into his office.

'You've had a chance to look at the file – what do you make of Operation Market Garden?'

He'd replied that it was very impressive but obviously he'd need more time and perhaps more detail, and if—

The brigadier held up his hand for him to stop. 'This is such a big operation that I'm dividing it up. I want you to concentrate on the Arnhem part. And remember what I said last week: your job is to pick holes in it, to be as awkward as possible. Have the cartography chaps in MI4 been helpful?'

He said they had, though he understood some of the maps being drawn up were restricted.

'Bloody fools, not to you they're not. Don't worry. I'll tell Holt you have full clearance.'

He spent that Monday and Tuesday poring over the plans for the assault on Arnhem. He memorised the names of all the units involved and the locations of the different drop zones and landing zones along with the routes they'd be taking from them to the bridges.

Holt in MI4 had clearly been chastened by the repercussions of his failure the previous week to share material with him. He stood at a large table in the centre of Holt's office as map after map was spread out in front of him as if they were delicate textiles for him to admire. After an hour, he left the room with an armful of charts, promising that of course he'd return them at the end of the day.

The maps were in many ways more informative than the file Brigadier Oakley had given him. He was amazed at the detail they contained, much of it no doubt provided by the Dutch Resistance. Some even showed gaps in the hedgerow – the kind of detail aerial reconnaissance photography couldn't provide.

He realised that the most helpful information was the location of the various zones, and he tried to work out how to present that information in a way that made some kind of sense. There were three drop zones, Y, X and K; four landing zones, X, Z, S and L, and one supply zone. Personally he thought they were situated too far from the bridges and too close to the woods to the north and west of Arnhem, but that was the least of his concerns. Eventually he decided he'd recite them as a list, descending from a point north-west of Arnhem to one to the south of it.

He met Jim in St James's Park as planned at a quarter past five that evening. The other man had a certain bounce to his step and seemed quite jolly.

'Do you think I'll be able to pop in for tea?' Jim had been pointing at Buckingham Palace, but he insisted they needed to concentrate. He recited the different zones – DZY, LZS and so on – and then made Jim repeat them a number of times.

'Remember DZY is north-west of the town, you work down from there.'

'Understood.'

'And then you need to remember the name of the units in the 1st Airborne Division. Can you recall them, please?'

'The 1st Airlanding Brigade and the 1st, 2nd, 3rd and 4th Parachute Brigades.'

'Commander?'

'Major General Richard Urquhart I think it is.'

'It's Robert, Robert Urquhart. Let's walk down to the end of that path and we'll go our separate ways, but before that, I think you'd better go over the information once more.'

–

Agent Byron was waiting in the apartment in Shepherd's Bush when Jim Maslin arrived there an hour later. Maslin had spent that time repeating over and over in his mind the information

Agent Milton had made him memorise. Only in his apartment was it safe for him to write it down.

Agent Byron looked at the sheet of paper as if he'd been handed a shopping list. He folded it carefully and slipped it into the seam of his jacket collar.

'You look concerned?' he said.

'I thought we weren't to write anything down… that everything was to be done from memory?'

'You don't need to concern yourself, Jim: the time you were most exposed was when you met Milton. You'd have been stopped long before now if you were under suspicion, and I'm certain no one followed you here. Once I've encoded the message, I'll burn this.'

'And if you get stopped on the way?'

'Don't worry about that either, I won't be. Did Milton say anything else?'

'He said there'll be some more on Thursday. I'm meeting him at Middle Temple, same time.'

'Very well, I'll be here waiting for you. Well done, though. If they're as chuffed with this as they were with the last message, we can consider we're doing a decent job. Now then, if you'll excuse me, I'd better be going. I'm under orders to transmit this as soon as possible.'

—

'You're coming with me, Rauter.'

Brigadeführer Schellenberg had made it sound like Rauter was under arrest. Although nothing would surprise him these days, he did think the timing odd: only a few hours earlier, he'd presented Schellenberg with the latest report from London. As requested, Agent Milton had provided further intelligence, with the promise of more to come. Schellenberg had appeared to be delighted.

'Where to, sir?'

'I have a car waiting.'

Although it was only a short walk from Prinz-Albrecht-Strasse across Potsdamer Platz to the Bendlerblock, they'd travelled in Schellenberg's Daimler and the Brigadeführer had even made an attempt at small talk. 'Do you have enough food coupons, Franz?' It was his way of signalling his approval.

In the secure meeting room they discussed the latest report: the details of the drop zones and the landing zones, the names of the British units involved, Major General Robert Urquhart...

'This is high-quality intelligence, Rauter,' said Field Marshal Keitel.

General Jodl introduced himself and said it was indeed a breath of fresh air to see such good intelligence. 'But can you guarantee that none of the three agents involved has been turned by the British into double agents? They have – I'm afraid it has to be said – an impressive record of doing that. After all, this could be a clever way of getting us to divert our forces north, thus allowing the Allies a clear run further south – say into the Ruhr?'

'No, sir, I can't guarantee it, sir,' said Rauter.

There was clear discomfort in the room at his reply.

'I can only be honest with you. Agent Byron has a code word that he always includes to indicate he's not been compromised, and another one he'd insert if he'd been caught, and there's been no problem there. But no system is perfect, sir: it's always possible that the message could have been altered when it was passed on. It's even possible that one of the agents has been captured and has given away the safety words.'

'You don't sound very confident, Rauter.'

'With the greatest of respect, sir, you didn't ask if I was confident – you asked if I could guarantee that none of them had been caught. It's impossible to guarantee that. But if you're asking me if I think this intelligence is genuine, then my answer would be yes, I believe it is.'

'You'll no doubt be pleased then to learn that you have an ally. You've heard of Field Marshal Model, I presume?'

'Of course, sir, he's in charge of Army Group B?'

Keitel nodded. 'He was delighted when he saw this intelligence. As far as he's concerned, it corroborates what his own intelligence officers have been telling him – that the Allies will launch a major offensive through Nijmegen and Arnhem and that there will be extensive use of airborne troops. Model is convinced your source is accurate and is planning his defence accordingly. In fact, he is going to base himself in Arnhem.'

Franz Rauter found it hard to resist smiling.

'But the question he most wants answered is when the hell this is going to happen.'

'I'm afraid we don't know that yet, sir.'

'Let's hope Agent Milton can come up with a date, eh?'

Chapter 8

London, September 1944

A few days preceding this was the first Monday of September and the first day in his new posting, and it felt very much like the first day of term: that familiar feeling of apprehension and anxiety that had been a constant shadow through his school days and that persisted even now.

He was in the oak-panelled hallway of his small apartment in a modern mansion block in St John's Wood, standing in front of the long mirror and admiring his new uniform – the major's single crown having replaced the captain's three stars that had been on his epaulette for far too long.

He glanced at his watch and realised he had to get a move on, but he needed to calm his nerves. He was only too aware that they'd contact him any day now – he was surprised they'd left it so long.

He went into the kitchen and poured himself a Scotch: if he drank whisky before lunchtime he tried to keep it to a single measure and drink it neat, but his hands were shaking and his breathing was quickening so he made it a double, drinking it swiftly before brushing his teeth one more time and making sure he had a packet of mints in his briefcase.

The number 53 bus took him direct from Abbey Road to his new office in Whitehall. It was a pleasant journey down the west side of Regent's Park, along Baker Street, Oxford Street and Regent Street, through Piccadilly Circus and across Trafalgar Square. His new place of work was on the corner of Horse

Guards Avenue: the magnificent neo-Baroque edifice that was the War Office.

He was escorted to the fifth floor and along a corridor round to the rear of the building, to a room with 'MI18' on the door. Behind it was an outer office with a small stretch of the Thames just visible through the windows, and four secretaries who were all watching him over the top of their spectacles.

One of them eventually asked if she could help, and he explained who he was and who he'd come to see. His stammer, which he'd kept in check until that morning, had returned.

'Brigadier Oakley is waiting for you,' she said, pointing to a half-open door.

–

'Well I've certainly had to wait for you, haven't I?'

The brigadier – a large man whose uniform was at least one size too small – had greeted him formally as he entered the office: an exchange of salutes and formal handshakes. He'd now walked back to his desk and was standing behind it as he looked at an open file on the desktop.

He remained standing in the middle of the office as the brigadier read the file with a mixture of frowns and raised eyebrows. On a trolley next to the desk was an inviting bottle of Dalwhinnie, perhaps his favourite single malt, but he doubted Oakley was likely to offer him a drink at this time of the morning.

'So you're quite the brainbox, eh? A doctorate... in medieval literature! Has that come in useful over the last few years?'

'I haven't actually completed my doctorate, sir. It was taking rather a long time and I'm afraid I got bogged down. I thought if I took a short service commission and went back to it afterwards then things would be easier. Hasn't quite worked out like that, not yet at any rate.'

'I see you joined in early '38: did you see the way things were going?'

'I don't think any of us did, sir.'

'Indeed... So you joined the York and Lancasters... fought in Norway... then Brigade Headquarters in '41 working in the intelligence unit, promoted to captain... Divisional HQ last year, due to come here in July but tied up in France... and of course, Caen. I always said that Monty's plan to take Caen on D-Day itself was completely misguided, but as usual, he wasn't listening to anyone – least of all me. But two months, that was far too long. How was Caen?'

'Bloody, sir.'

'And your shoulder?'

'Bloody, sir.'

'But it works?'

'Oh yes, sir. It was rather painful and messy at the time, but the surgeon fixed it up nicely. I wear the sling every so often to rest it.'

'Says here you're not married.'

'No, sir. The war's rather got in the way, I suppose.'

'I understand, but that arm ought to help, eh? Nothing like an injured officer to attract the ladies. I met my wife when I was on crutches at the end of 1915 after the Battle of Loos. I'm sure that's what attracted her!'

They both laughed, and he shifted round to avoid looking at the whisky.

'Congratulations on your promotion, by the way, quite an important step up from captain to major. Do sit down and I'll tell you about your new job.'

They moved over to a table in a corner of the room, a large map of Europe pinned to the wall above it.

'What do you know about the Directorate of Military Intelligence?'

'That it's part of the War Office, sir.'

'A very important and in my opinion somewhat underrated part of it. Obviously our role is to coordinate all aspects of military intelligence. We're divided into some twenty sections:

these are denoted by numbers, each prefixed by the letters MI, standing for military intelligence. I imagine you know all this, but let me explain a bit about these sections. The two that get all the attention these days are MI5 and MI6, but that's not to say the other sections aren't important in their own right. I have a list here, top secret of course, but have a look. I think we ought to turn the lights on, eh?'

The brigadier placed a chart in front of him and angled it round.

'Too many to go through, but each one is vital, of course. For example, MI4 you'll be working with a lot; they look after maps. We'll also be working very closely with MI17, which is the Director of Military Intelligence's secretariat: that's where I was based until a couple of months ago.

'After D-Day, the director asked me to set up MI18. He worried there'd be a degree of disorganisation and even chaos regarding our advance into Germany. As you know only too well, the advance through France and into Belgium has proved to be most unpredictable, and the rows between us and the Americans and even our own generals not seeing eye to eye has exacerbated the situation. That is to a certain extent inevitable, of course – it's the nature of warfare after all: you can plan to the finest detail, but once the first bullet's fired, all kinds of unforeseen factors come into play. But the director is very concerned that invading Germany itself could be the most hazardous campaign of the war and he wants to ensure the Directorate of Military Intelligence is well prepared for it.

'Our role in MI18 then is to coordinate intelligence relating to the invasion of Germany. You'll be working for me, producing reports on the various Allied plans, checking to see if they clash and looking for any flaws in them. At the very least the director wants to be sure he's not going to be blamed for missing something.'

He kept looking at the list until the brigadier pulled it away. He was confident he'd managed to memorise most of the sections.

'I hope that's all clear? Probably a bit much at the moment, but once you've read yourself in, I'm sure it will all begin to make sense. I'll show you to your new office.'

He followed the brigadier and stood up. They both moved towards the door.

'Best take this with you, Major, your first bit of homework. It's top secret so can't leave the office. Not that we don't trust you, of course, but I'm afraid due to its classification you need to return it to me at the end of the day so I can lock it in my safe.'

He handed him a green folder with *MOST SECRET* stamped on it in red and a white sticker on the front with three words typed on it.

OPERATION MARKET GARDEN

-

His new office turned out to be small, with no windows, clearly once part of a larger room that had been divided up. The walls were an unpleasant shade of light brown and the large desk was bare but for a telephone and an Anglepoise lamp. Pinned to one wall was a faded map of the Indian Empire.

He was soon absorbed in the Operation Market Garden folder, and what he read was extraordinary: it could unquestionably alter the course of the war. Later that morning the brigadier asked to see him.

'What do you make of it?'

'Very ambitious, sir, it's certainly a most bold plan.'

'It is, but your job isn't to sit there and admire the plans but rather to cast a very sceptical eye over them: pick holes, be as critical as possible. If Operation Market Garden goes wrong, we're in serious trouble. I've told Holt in MI4 to let you have access to whatever maps you need – they're just round the corridor.'

By the time he returned the file to the brigadier's safe at the end of his first day, he knew just how important it was. But it was deeply frustrating too. His contact with this Agent Byron had been very intermittent: weeks went by before he heard from him, and the coded messages were always the same: *Are you all right? What is your current role? Be patient; you'll be contacted soon.*

There were times when he wondered whether they'd forgotten about him altogether, and occasionally he'd allow himself the indulgence of letting his mind wander. How would he feel if they had given up on him: would it really be the relief he'd always imagined? The tension he'd experienced since the start of the war never lifted, and the apprehension of waiting for them to contact him and ask him to start providing intelligence was considerable.

One thing he avoided was allowing himself the indulgence of regretting his predicament. Nothing was to be gained from going back on the meeting with the man called Arthur in 1933, or the fateful friendship struck with the German in Cambridge in the summer of 1934. He now knew full well that none of it had been a coincidence, and by the time he went to spend the summer of 1935 at the university in Munich, he'd realised what was happening. When they told him to join the army in 1938, he couldn't refuse. He'd become a German agent and he doubted he could go into a police station and tell them there'd been a terrible misunderstanding and hope they'd understand. The only way to approach matters was to be as professional as possible and so reduce his chances of being caught. Indeed, in the early part of the war he'd even thought he wasn't in a bad position after all: Britain was in a mess, Germany seemed to have a sense of order, and perhaps he could play some part in bringing the two countries together: they should have been on the same side after all.

But now he doubted the Germans would let him go. He knew he was too valuable. He was certain that like a sniper delaying his shot as long as possible, they'd be waiting for the right time. But then what he'd read on his first day with MI18 was so important he was worried it would be too late. There was a way of getting Byron to contact him; it was only to be used in extreme circumstances, but he reckoned this certainly fell into that category. There was a quiet alley off Pall Mall that Byron apparently made a point of visiting every few days: two chalk triangles on the second lamp post and Byron would know to call him.

Two days later at twenty-five to eight in the morning, the telephone rang in his St John's Wood apartment. He waited for it to ring three times, then stop. He felt the usual mixture of fear and excitement and sat down on his bed, all the time keeping an eye on his watch as the second hand swept round. It was always possible it really was a wrong number, which had actually happened a few months ago. But after exactly two and a half minutes, the phone rang once more. He waited until it had rung four times before answering. The sequence of bleeps told him it was from a call box.

Don't say anything – wait for him to speak first.

'A very good morning to you: is that Abbey Road Cleaner's? I left a brown suit with you last Thursday and I wondered if it's ready yet?'

Agent Byron, the man he only knew by his voice.

'I'm terribly sorry, but you appear to have the wrong number. I think you'll find that the dry cleaner's doesn't open until eight o'clock, though.'

'My apologies, I didn't mean to disturb you.'

'It's really no problem.'

They were smart, there could be no question about that. Even the wrong number – that of the dry cleaner's – was only two digits different from his. So much information contained in one apparently innocuous conversation.

This is Agent Byron. A new agent has arrived. You're to meet him tomorrow, Thursday.

His response – about him having called the wrong number – assured Byron that all was well and it would be safe to meet.

At Middle Temple. At a quarter past five.

He made sure to arrive slightly early at the War Office the following day. Not so early that it could arouse attention, but early enough to ensure he'd be able to leave at five o'clock.

He did his best to study and memorise the most salient points in the Operation Market Garden file, testing himself like he used to for vocabulary tests at school. He was able to leave the Directorate of Military Intelligence at five o'clock, walking briskly along the Embankment and under Waterloo Bridge.

–

After meeting with the man called Jim, he was surprised at how calm he felt. He'd expected to feel frightened at the implications of having finally committed an act of espionage – treason, if he was honest with himself – but instead there was a sense of relief that the waiting was over. He could now concentrate on the practicalities of gathering the intelligence and passing it on rather than allowing himself to dwell on how he'd ended up in this predicament in the first place.

He'd told Jim that arranging meetings through Agent Byron was convoluted and potentially risky. He'd only contact him that way in an emergency. Otherwise they'd meet twice a week.

'Do you know St James's Park?'

'You mean the football ground in Newcastle?'

He gave Jim a dirty look and Jim said he was sure he'd find it.

'We'll meet there on Tuesdays from now on and here every Friday. St James's Park is right at the heart of government and there'll be plenty of chaps in uniform strolling around it, but don't worry. It's not far from where I work and I have a perfect excuse for being there, and after all, neither of us will have anything incriminating on us. There's a marble statue of a boy at the southern end of the park, just by Birdcage Walk. Same procedure as today: at a quarter past five you should walk past the statue from the direction of Whitehall. Don't look around for me, but as you pass the statue switch your umbrella from your right hand to your left. When I catch up with you, I'll be giving you directions to Buckingham Palace.'

–

He'd been rather impressed with this Jim. He seemed to be calm, and when he'd asked him to repeat the message to be passed on for Berlin, he'd remembered pretty much every word of it correctly.

Just as he wouldn't expect Jim to ask him any personal questions, nor was it for him to question Jim, but he did wonder about him. For some reason he hadn't expected this agent to be a fellow Englishman.

A traitor.

Just like him.

Chapter 9

Berlin and London, August–September 1944

*Set up a ring of agents around him, and above all, don't be rushed...
Protect him as a source. Take time before you reel him in.*

For five years Helmut Krüger's final words had hung over
Franz Rauter. According to the file, Krüger had been planning
to visit Milton in England in June 1939, but his poor health
had put paid to that. He hadn't been entirely idle, though; even
when the illness that would kill him was beginning to take its
grip, he'd recruited a very good radioman, an Englishman who
lived in Chelsea, in west London. The radioman – code name
Byron – was dedicated to Milton: he'd only receive and transmit
messages in relation to that one agent.

Rauter wondered if Krüger had been too cautious. His own
strategy was to send over an agent to be the link between Byron
and Milton. He knew the wireless operator was often the most
exposed and vulnerable part of the network because of the
possibility that the equipment could give them away. This way
he'd ensure Milton would never be anywhere near the radio
transmitter and nor would the agent who'd make contact with
him. Once Milton was activated, it was this agent who'd carry
the intelligence to and from the radioman.

Rauter had taken the precaution of adding Milton's details to
a central register that held the names of members of the British
military who in case of capture or arrest were of special interest
to various German agencies. Any information relating to this
man was to be passed immediately to Franz Rauter, Abwehr,
Berlin.

He was fortunate in that after Prager's death, Admiral Canaris himself had taken an interest in Milton, and as a professional intelligence officer, the head of the Abwehr had appreciated the need for patience. Every few months Rauter would discuss the case with him.

'He's doing well,' Canaris would say. 'Krüger and Prager recruited a good agent: if only they were still with us. But let's wait, Franz; Milton's getting there but he's not there yet.'

In September 1943, Rauter had asked to see Canaris. He had news, a new posting for Milton. Canaris looked impressed. 'That is a very useful position for us. I think we should pat ourselves on the back, Franz: our patience appears to have paid off. We've been vindicated.'

'We'll now need to send an agent to work with him and the radioman, Byron. Can I go ahead and recruit someone?'

Canaris had looked at him awkwardly. 'The Reich Main Security Office insists on being more involved. They say the Sicherheitsdienst have some good agents we can choose from. I'm afraid we'll have to go along with that.'

'Seriously, sir... the SD?'

'I know what you're thinking, Franz, but I have to be mindful of the way the wind blows in Berlin, which isn't always in the direction we'd like. They want their Foreign Security Service to be given more responsibility and I'm afraid that in this instance I have to go along with it.'

From the moment he first met him, Rauter had had no confidence in the SD's first recruit: a cocky Nazi from West-phalia with a limited attention span who seemed easily bored by the detail of his training. His only merit, as far as Rauter could see, was that he came from a village bordering the German-speaking area of Belgium and could pass as Belgian. He'd been given the code name Keats, and the last they heard of him was that he was killed by a train on a railway track outside London soon after he'd landed in England in the November. He'd never managed to make contact with Agent Byron, the radioman.

If Rauter had reservations about Agent Keats, they were nothing compared to those he had for the SD's next recruit. This man was from Bremerhaven, a teacher of English and fluent in the language but with a heart condition that had kept him out of the army. When Rauter pointed out that this might be an impediment for an agent in enemy territory, he was told not to be so negative and the man was quickly trained – far too quickly in Rauter's opinion – and landed on the Norfolk coast. They knew this because at least Agent Shelley had been in touch with Byron: too many long and barely coded telephone calls in which he recounted how unwell he felt. He reckoned he was suffering from hypothermia after his dinghy journey ashore from the U-boat. They agreed he should follow the protocol for such circumstances. Instead of going straight to London, he was to find a city far away from where he'd landed and do his best to recuperate in an anonymous boarding house. It was weeks before Byron discovered that Shelley had been found dead in his bed.

In March they'd sent over another agent, whom Rauter had to admit appeared promising despite a clear fondness for alcohol and a touching certainty that God would protect him come what may. Agent Dryden was Polish, from a German community near Poznań, with a plausible cover story, and they'd sent him over in February. He'd gone to Manchester to establish his cover, but once he headed for London, everything went wrong. He'd contacted Agent Byron from Birmingham, and despite being given clear instructions as to where to meet him, he'd never turned up at either the rendezvous point or the fallback location. Byron reckoned he'd misunderstood both the time and the locations and had probably been overwhelmed on his first visit to the capital. A week later, a story appeared in a number of British newspapers with his name and photograph and an account of his death following a road accident in Birmingham.

By now the Abwehr no long existed, its functions taken over by the RSHA. Franz Rauter decided to wait: he felt this was a time to keep his head down, and in any case he needed to be sure Milton hadn't been compromised. Although Rauter had few obvious enemies, he didn't have many friends either. Agent Milton, he decided, was a friend he'd never met, his insurance policy. He'd wait.

Then the summons to Prinz-Albrecht-Strasse in the September.

We think you have waited far too long to activate Agent Milton… It's one thing having a sleeper agent, but this one could be regarded as comatose. We need to wake him up!

–

They'd been the stuff of gossip around Berlin for a while now, just over a year in fact. They were the result of a quixotic attempt to form a British unit of the Waffen-SS; similar units already existed for the Dutch, Ukrainians, French and Scandinavians. From what Franz Rauter gathered, the recruitment hadn't gone very well: no more than a few dozen joined up rather than the hoped-for thousands. But a group of those recruits were still together, holed up in a disused school in a bombed-out street in Pankow in the north-eastern part of Berlin.

They had a name – the British Free Corps – and had been recruited from among British prisoners of war: fascists or fascist sympathisers who'd been persuaded that they were on the wrong side and should join in the fight against the real enemy, notably the Jews and the Soviet Union.

Rauter and his colleagues had followed their progress, if that was the right word for it, with wry amusement. Any of them could have told the SS it was a hopeless idea, but for some reason the group was kept together in the hope that its numbers would swell and the dreams of a British unit of the SS could be realised.

The SS officer in charge was surprisingly amenable to Rauter's request that he visit the men to see if any might be suitable for 'other duties', as he termed it. A few days after the meeting in Prinz-Albrecht-Strasse, he turned up at the school in Pankow, dressed in the uniform of an SS officer to keep his cover intact.

There were just thirty-three British men there, and Rauter spent four days going through their files and interviewing them. From early on there was one who stood out, a man in his early thirties with thick blonde hair and a calm manner. His name was John Morton.

'Why did you join the British Free Corps, John?' had been Rauter's first question.

'Because I hate the fucking Jews.' Morton spoke in a pleasant manner, very matter-of-fact, as if he was discussing the weather. 'And not just the fucking Jews: the fucking Russians too and fucking Winston Churchill.'

One of the many things Rauter liked about Morton was that he didn't volunteer too much information; anything he said had to be teased out of him. There was nothing worse than an agent who said too much. Over two long sessions, his life story emerged. In Rauter's opinion, it couldn't have been more ideal.

He'd been born and raised in Leicestershire, an only child who was orphaned by the age of twelve, after which he'd lived in a children's home until he was fourteen. This seemed to have instilled in him a grievance against the British state and left him feeling alienated. He left the home when he was fourteen and started work, moving around the country from factory to farm, drifting from bedsit to boarding house, from north to south.

He'd never married, and in the mid 1930s had joined Oswald Mosley's British Union of Fascists, allowing his membership to lapse just before he signed up to the Middlesex Regiment in the summer of 1939. His war ended when he was taken prisoner at Dunkirk in May 1940, and since then he'd been in a succession of prisoner-of-war camps.

Franz Rauter liked that John Morton had no family in Britain and was familiar with London, having lived there on and off. There was not much that stood out about him; he was the kind of person people wouldn't take much notice of: perfect secret agent material, nothing obviously odd about him but nonetheless something of a loner. He seemed to be someone who got on with what he was told to do, who probably didn't exert himself too much but wasn't a shirker either.

He was physically fit, too – he sailed through a medical – and unlike most of the other British volunteers at Pankow drank little alcohol. How, Rauter asked him on their third meeting, would he feel about returning to England under cover to work for Germany?

Morton hesitated for just the right amount of time before saying he'd be interested in finding out more. This was the correct response as far as Rauter was concerned. What Morton hadn't known was that had he declined the offer, he'd have been handed over to the Gestapo: he knew too much.

Morton proved to be a good student, and in particular he had a very good memory. He was given a new identity – Jim Maslin, same initials as his real name, standard Abwehr operating practice – and a cover story that showed he was exempt from military service due to a nasty and debilitating bout of rheumatic fever.

Towards the end of his training, Rauter had a long chat with him: he wanted to be sure of his motives. 'Do you feel as if we're asking you to be a traitor?'

'I feel the people running Britain are the traitors, not me.'

'But I want to be sure you fully understand the implications of what we're asking you to do – to work against your country.'

'That's assuming I regard it as my country, isn't it? It doesn't feel like my country any more.'

'But you know what will happen if you're caught?'

Morton had shrugged and laughed. 'I won't be caught, will I? There is something I want to ask you, though...'

'Go on, John.'

'I know you said I'd receive all the funds I need while I'm doing this job for you, but when the war's over – one way or the other – it may be difficult for me to settle down. I'll need to be very careful, won't I?'

'I'm not sure what point you're making.'

'I'll need money for when I've finished this job for you. If I know I've got a few bob behind me, I think I'll do a better job.'

That mercenary approach was fine as far as Franz Rauter was concerned. It was agents who were too ideological who bothered him.

–

Jim Maslin – Agent Donne – was landed on the Kent coast and successfully made his way to London, where he arrived on a Thursday, the last day of August.

It turned out Agent Byron had organised everything perfectly, including setting up an interview for him the following day for a job as a porter at St Mary's Hospital in Paddington. Maslin also had his own flat in Shepherd's Bush, a mile and a half west of the hospital. It was a small flat, but well stocked with food and clothes, and most important of all, its own entrance and telephone line.

The key to the flat was hidden exactly as per his instructions, and the morning after he moved in, he went to meet Agent Byron.

Take the number 11 bus from Shepherd's Bush to Dawes Road in Fulham. Get off at the first stop and keep walking until it becomes Fulham Road. Just before the first bus stop on that road, there's a newsagent's. Go in and buy a packet of ten John Player and a box of Swan Vesta matches – but only go in if you think you're safe, that you've not been followed. Then go to the bus stop and get on the first number 14. Go upstairs and sit in an empty part of the bus; it will be quiet at that time of day.

Agent Byron sidled up to him soon after the bus pulled away from the stop. 'Is this seat free?'

'Only if you have a ticket!' *Laugh when you say it; it's meant to sound like a joke.*

'Bus tickets are pretty much all you can buy these days!' Agent Byron seemed older than Maslin had expected. He glanced over: his travelling companion had opened the *Daily Herald* to the sports pages. Everything was fine.

–

Agent Byron's instructions had been clear.

'Your interview at St Mary's is at two o'clock this afternoon. You'll walk into the job: they're desperate these days. As soon as we part after this journey, I'll get a message to Agent Milton: when I hear back from him, I'll be in touch with you.'

He'd started his job at St Mary's on the Monday morning. When he returned to his flat after his shift on the Wednesday, Agent Byron was sitting in the solitary armchair, holding a mug of tea in one hand and a cigarette in the other.

'It's all sorted. Agent Milton is ready to see you. What time does your shift finish tomorrow?'

'Four in the afternoon, same as today.'

'Very well, come over here.' Byron shifted his seat so Maslin could crouch down next to him. He'd opened out an A–Z map of London. 'You're here,' he pointed to St Mary's, 'and this is where he wants to meet you.' He pointed to a spot on the north bank of the River Thames. 'When you leave work tomorrow, walk over to Edgware Road – here – and take the number 6 bus, heading south. Remain on it as far as Fleet Street. If at any stage during the journey you suspect you've been followed, get off the bus and walk around for at least an hour, and only if you're sure you're no longer being followed head back here. But otherwise get off at any stop in Fleet Street and walk to the rendezvous from there. You're meeting Agent Milton at a quarter past five, so there's no need to rush. I'll come here later that evening to retrieve the message he gives you. Have you got all that?'

He made Maslin repeat his instructions, and when he'd finished, he folded up the map. 'And you understand everything about the meeting and what you're to say?'

Maslin nodded. 'I do, though there is one thing... I'm concerned that if it's very busy round there, I may miss Milton. What does he look like?'

Agent Byron laughed as if the question was a preposterous one. 'I have no idea. You see, I've never met him!'

–

For the first time in his life, Jim Maslin found what he was doing to be truly fulfilling. There'd been one or two summers on farms when he'd really enjoyed the work and the lifestyle had been pleasant, but by and large he'd found most of the jobs he'd done and the places he'd lived, along with the people he met, to be a disappointment.

He'd quite liked aspects of being in the army – it was undeniably exciting, and there was a certain degree of comradeship – but he couldn't get it out of his mind that he was on the wrong side. But this opportunity afforded him by the well-dressed man in Berlin was too good to turn down, and in any case, he was no fool. He could only imagine what they'd have done to him had he declined their offer. And it was turning out to be exciting: not only was he on the right side for a change, but he found he was actually very good at what he had to do. He was clearly well suited to a clandestine world: in truth, it was one he'd inhabited for most of his life – always suspicious, never trusting, always moving, always alone.

When his shift finished on the Thursday afternoon, he walked over to Edgware Road and took the number 6 bus as instructed. He left the bus in Fleet Street: it was a minute or so before five and he knew he was too early. The man in Berlin had been quite clear about this.

It's far worse to be early for a meet than late for one, I can't stress this enough. Being early means you hang around, and that attracts attention. And it's hard to avoid looking anxious: you can easily take on the demeanour of someone who's waiting.

He walked up Fleet Street as far as Ludgate Hill and then down Blackfriars to the Victoria Embankment. He remembered working for a week at one of the newspapers on Fleet Street – he seemed to recall it was the *Daily Express*. It had been back-breaking work, carrying stacks of papers up and down stairs.

It was exactly 5.15 when he entered Middle Temple Gardens, vegetable patches obviously now having taken the place of lawns and walkways bordered by well-tended edges, in contrast to many of the surrounding buildings, which were little more than bomb sites. Sitting on a bench in the lee of the ruins of a burnt-out church was a tall man wearing the uniform of an army major. One arm was in a sling and he was leaning back as if deep in thought, enjoying the late-afternoon sun, a cigarette in his mouth and his eyes seemingly closed.

Maslin couldn't be sure this was him, even though Agent Byron's instructions had been to look out for a man in uniform sitting on a bench near the church.

He walked past, taking care not to slow down or look in the man's direction. As he carried on, he transferred his umbrella from his right hand to his left, the sign that as far as he was concerned he could be approached. Another minute and he heard footsteps slowly gaining on him.

'Would you have a light, by any chance? I'm clean out of matches.'

Do make sure you're carrying some!

'Of course: please take the box. I seem to have another one on me.'

'Thank you so much. We could do with more rain, eh?'

So far so good.

Just as Agent Byron looked older than Maslin had expected, Agent Milton appeared younger. For some reason he'd imagined a man in his fifties. He seemed to speak with a stammer, and he'd not been expecting that either. Perhaps the man was nervous.

'Indeed, we're never satisfied, are we?'

The man lit his cigarette and carried on walking. It was a while before he spoke again. 'Let's walk round the gardens and then on to Victoria Embankment. If anyone comes too close, I'll just switch to giving you directions to Cannon Street station: got that?'

It sounded like an order. Maslin said he did.

'When did you arrive here?'

'A couple of days ago.'

'I thought someone was supposed to be here months ago... fucking months ago!'

Maslin was taken aback: even with the stammer, he could tell the man spoke with what was probably a middle-class accent, and this outburst seemed incongruous. Milton looked tense but carried on walking, regaining his composure as he did so. 'I'm sorry, not your fault, of course, but I can't believe how slow they've been. Wondering if they'd forgotten about me has been extremely difficult, I can tell you. I was beginning to think they'd left it almost too bloody late, but as it happens, you've turned up just in time.'

'The man in Berlin said I needed to be sent over here as soon as possible because they were hoping you'd soon have stuff to pass on. Haven't you moved into a new job or something?'

'Keep your voice down, for Christ's sake. You say you were in Berlin?' Milton looked incredulously at his companion. 'What the hell were you doing there?'

'It's a long story.'

'Another time. What should I be calling you, by the way?'

'Jim, I guess.'

'Jim... We had a dog called Jim: golden retriever – used to chew carpets and chase the neighbour's cat: let's hope you're better behaved. I understand the way we do this is I tell you what the message is and you memorise it and eventually it ends up with our friends elsewhere: is that correct?'

Maslin said that as far he was aware that was it.

'Nice and secure, I suppose, though there is scope for a message getting garbled, like Chinese whispers. I'll keep it as simple as possible and you'd better listen very carefully. There's a lot to tell you and every single word is extremely important.'

Chapter 10

London, November 1944

Over the past few days, a noticeable bite to the wind along with a constant damp had descended on the city, working its way into all but the most well-heated premises, of which there were now very few. Regular dustings of snow had turned the pavements slushy and treacherous.

Agent Milton had settled into a routine at the War Office and had managed to dodge any of the blame sweeping around the Directorate of Military Intelligence in the aftermath of Arnhem. 'Defeat' was a word avoided in connection with the operation. The War Office preferred euphemisms such as 'retreat', or 'debacle' if the discussion was particularly acrimonious.

For two or three weeks there'd been an attempt at an inquiry. As far as Agent Milton was concerned, it began on somewhat worrying lines: *Why was Field Marshal Model based in Arnhem? How come the 9th and 10th Panzers were in the town? Why was the railway bridge blown up before the Paras got near it? How come the enemy were able to anticipate the location of so many of the drop and landing zones?*

But soon it was dismissed as a combination of bad luck on the part of the Allies and good luck on the part of the Germans. It was a setback, a mere delay on the road to Allied victory. Everyone seemed happier with muttered conversations in corridors and conspiratorial chats behind closed doors, where blame was apportioned between Montgomery and the Americans.

The directorate dusted itself down, deciding it had played no part whatsoever in the events – another euphemism – at Arnhem. Agent Milton was given a new project: working on more detailed plans for a crossing of the Rhine, one that would hopefully not go wrong.

In the first week of October, Milton had met Donne at Middle Temple and the man he called Jim had a message. 'Our mutual friends say to tell you they're delighted.' They were strolling past the bombed-out church and had paused as an elderly gardener brushed the snow from the path in front of them. 'They say you're to lay low for a while – me too. When they want anything else, Byron will contact us.'

Milton told Jim he quite understood, and when the two men parted outside Temple Underground station, they shook hands as if they'd concluded a business deal.

–

It was seven weeks before he was contacted again. This time the call from a telephone box came at a quarter to seven in the evening – three rings before ending, ringing back after two and a half minutes. The evening calls purported to be to a residential number similar to his.

Meet Agent Donne tomorrow at St James's Park – usual time.

The meeting hadn't started well. As Milton left the War Office and crossed Whitehall, a colleague hurried to catch up and insisted on walking alongside him, chatting as they went under Admiralty Arch and into the Mall. Milton had ignored the first 'Where are you heading?' and when he was asked a second time, he said he'd forgotten something in the office and would have to return there.

When he finally arrived at the park, five minutes late, there was no sign of Agent Donne. The rain, which had been intermittent all day, was now a downpour. When Jim finally turned up – stopping for too long by the statue and looking confused – it was nearly half past five.

'What the hell kept you?'

'And nice to see you too.' Jim was drenched, his cheap raincoat covered in dark patches and water dripping from his nose and chin. 'I told him it was too short notice. I was on a late shift today: due to start at noon and finish at nine. I rang them this morning and said I had a bad toothache and had managed to get a dental appointment at five, so they told me to come in for a nine thirty to four thirty shift and they've only gone and docked my pay.'

'You should have called in sick. Look, we'd better get a move on. I presume you've a message for me?'

Jim slowed down. 'You're to get details of Allied deployments and defences in an area with Malmedy in the north-east corner and Namur in the north-west corner, then follow the River Meuse down to Sedan and back across to the border between Luxembourg and Germany. Apparently if you look at a map it will make sense.'

Milton nodded and repeated the message, then it was Jim's turn to nod. 'They say they want you to pass them on to me on Monday.'

'Monday? That's too soon, it only gives me two days. Tell them I've got the message but can't meet you before next Wednesday. And I don't think we should use either St James's Park or Middle Temple again. Do you know the bandstand in Hyde Park?'

'I'll find it.'

'Not difficult – it's towards the south-east corner. We'd better make it five thirty, though.'

–

Working on new plans for an Allied crossing of the Rhine meant Agent Milton was in and out of the directorate's map department on a daily basis. Holt, the man who ran MI4, was an unpredictable character: officious and awkward one day, the following one friendly to the point of oleaginous with nothing being too much trouble.

That day he was in a helpful mood, keen to tell Milton about a new addition he was hoping to make to his stamp collection. His mind was clearly still on philately when Milton asked – apparently as an afterthought – whether he could perhaps see maps covering the area Jim had described.

'The Ardennes, you mean? Not a hunting ground you've been interested in recently, Major.'

Milton explained he was looking in more detail at the eastern approach routes to the Rhine.

Holt opened the card index on his desk. 'And would you be interested in terrain or position of Allied forces?'

He sounded like a tailor giving a client a choice of material for a suit. Milton said the latter if that was possible, please.

'Mainly US forces there.'

He said that didn't terribly matter.

'Here's the latest American map, Major: plenty on their deployments in the area.'

–

It was raining again when he met Jim near the bandstand in Hyde Park. It was the penultimate day of November and it felt as if it hadn't stopped raining since they'd last met. He had to speak up against the beating of the rain and the whistling of the wind as the two men walked along, shoulder to shoulder.

'You're going to need to pay careful attention, Jim. It's a long list. Starting in the north-east – round Elsenborn – the US 5th Corps… North-east of Dinant, the US 1st Army, then the 2nd US Armored Division just outside Dinant… Have you got all this? The US 101st Airborne Division is in Bastogne and the 4th Armored Division is just south of the town, the 3rd US Army further south in Luxembourg. Christ, if only it would stop raining for half a bloody day… Let's go over it once more, Jim…'

Chapter 11

London, January 1945

'You've been given all the necessary stamps of approval, Prince.'

'Well that's—'

'You need to come to London on Monday morning to meet the chap you'll be working for.'

'Monday? That's—'

'The day after Sunday.'

It was just after six o'clock in the evening and he'd only just returned home from work. He was standing in the hallway in his wet raincoat and was anxious to spend some time with his son before he went to bed. He was not in the mood for a telephone call with Hugh Harper. It was a curt call: no niceties enquiring how he was or pleasantries about the weather or his journey back to Lincoln the previous day.

'What I meant, sir, was that it hardly gives me time to make arrangements. I need to make sure everything is sorted as far as Henry is concerned, and then there's work – I've got a number of cases I—'

'Don't worry about that, Prince. Your chief constable has already been made aware of the situation and will deal with your cases. As far as your domestic arrangements are concerned, you have a nanny, don't you?'

'Yes, sir, but—'

'You have a few days to sort all that out then.'

'So you're the famous Prince we've been hearing all about, eh? Detective Superintendent Richard Prince.'

The man who'd so carefully enunciated Prince's rank and full name had been waiting for him at the entrance of the mews house in London's Mayfair, a narrow building on a cobbled alley set between Brook Street and Grosvenor Street. Now they were in a bright room on the top floor, the sun streaming in through a large slanted window, wide open despite the January chill. The blackout curtains billowed like flags of distress.

Harper had told him to ask for a man called King, and made a laboured joke about a Prince meeting a King. The man had introduced himself as Lance King and said little else as he led Prince up the staircase. He was a tall, round-shouldered man, perhaps in his early forties and thin to the point of looking unwell – an impression enhanced by a pale complexion. Prince's mother would probably have described him as someone who spent too much time indoors.

They sat on a pair of low armchairs, Lance King revealing a pair of scuffed brown brogues as he crossed his legs. 'Just to dispose of any awkwardness, I'm assuming you do know who we are?'

'Mr Gilbey introduced me to a Mr Harper: he said I'd be working for MI5. I know what MI5 is... of course.'

'Of course. First things first: is it going to be Richard, or Prince, or Detective Superintendent Prince?'

'Well, certainly no need for the latter: I'm very happy with Richard.'

'Good, suits me – and you'll call me Lance.' He held his cigarette in front of him as if it were a dart and pointed it in Prince's direction. 'This place, by the way... it's one of the many MI5 outposts. For reasons of security we tend to squirrel ourselves away in various buildings across central London. Hugh Harper has the rather large brief of being responsible for the detection of Nazi spies in this country. I'm one of his case officers. Tell me, Richard, what have they told you about this case?'

'Very little – only that the mission will be in this country, and something about the role being a mix of police detective and intelligence officer.'

Lance King carefully inspected the end of his cigarette, checking if it was still alight, eventually discarding it in an ashtray and lighting a fresh one.

'Since the start of the war, the Abwehr – the German intelligence service – has sent a few dozen agents over to this country. It's difficult to say exactly how many, because of course we don't know about those who've not been captured or who went to ground as soon as they arrived here. But broadly speaking I'd estimate we've captured in excess of seventy German agents operating here. Some sixty of them have been turned into what we call double agents – in other words, we use them to pass false intelligence back to Germany, and of course by its nature that is most helpful to us and unhelpful to them. We used this double agent system to some significant effect with D-Day.

'Some German spies aren't suitable to be used as double agents or refuse to get involved, and in their case they've been tried, found guilty and subsequently executed, as was the case with the spy you caught in Lincolnshire.'

'Wolfgang Scholz.'

'Yes, the late Herr Scholz. There's one further small group: Germans we know about and catch up with but who die before we can do anything useful with them. The spies I'm going to tell you about now are from this group.

'Early in 1940, we became aware of wireless transmissions being made from somewhere in London with a signal strong enough for them to reach an Abwehr receiving station in Cuxhaven in north-west Germany. For us to trace the source of a transmission a number of circumstances need to be in our favour. One of these is the length of the transmission: one that lasts more than three minutes will give us a very reasonable chance of tracing it. Then there's their frequency and pattern. Even a short transmission stands a decent chance of being traced if it is made, for example, every third Wednesday evening between seven fifteen and seven thirty. But these transmissions we picked up were very short: always less than two minutes – not long enough for us to get a fix on them. And nor was there any pattern to them. They'd be made on different days and at varying times and – making it even more difficult for us – often weeks apart. Sometimes the gap between them was as long as two months.

'The transmissions were, as I say, very short and of course heavily coded; likewise the messages from Germany when they switched to receive. Nothing was ever transmitted in clear, but then it would have been most unusual had it been. However, our analysts did pick up two recurrent words, most likely names: Byron and Milton. Because of the pattern in which they're used, we believe Byron refers to the agent transmitting and receiving the messages, while Milton is another agent. Any questions so far?'

'How do they know that Byron and Milton are agents?'

'It's to do with the frequency with which the names occur and their context in the messages. But as I say, the messages were too short, irregular and infrequent for us to trace them. The best our radio detection chaps could do was to say they were probably coming from the centre of London, and more likely to the west than the east, which as you imagine is still a large area. At the same time – and completely unbeknown to the Germans – we are intercepting their most sensitive communications and decoding them—'

'Really! How on earth do we manage to—'

'I'll come to that another time, if you don't mind. In the course of intercepting and analysing many thousands of hours of German transmissions, we also picked up references to Byron and Milton from sources in Berlin we've previously identified as being associated with the Abwehr.

'In November 1943, someone spotted a reference to a Keats in a message to Byron that also mentioned Milton. This was a message from a source whose code we had broken, so our analysts were able to work out much of what it was saying. From what we could gather, an agent with the code name Keats had landed on the east coast of England and made his way to Chelmsford in Essex, from where he was going to travel to London by train. Byron was being instructed to make arrangements to meet him there. We even had a good idea of when he was going to be making his journey, so the local police were instructed to go to the railway station and check all the passengers travelling to London. Unfortunately, Agent Keats realised what was going on and tried to escape by running across the track, straight into the path of a train.

'A few weeks later – December 1943 – another message was intercepted from that same Berlin source, now referring to a Shelley. It appeared this was another agent who'd arrived in England and was making his way to London to be met by Byron, and this time the analysts also picked up something about him meeting Milton. There were two or three intercepts we made where Shelley was mentioned; in one of them there was a reference to him being in Coventry, and then another a few days later suggesting Byron hadn't heard from him. We were obviously worried at this stage – as you know from your experience, we don't like German spies at the best of times, but what we really can't abide are German spies who disappear.'

'And there was no clue as to his identity?'

'Even though they transmit in code, the bloody Germans avoid details like that. We did manage, however, to establish a clear connection between these messages and Byron in London: during the period when Shelley apparently arrived in this country and went missing there was increased traffic between Cuxhaven and Byron transmitting from London. We alerted the local police in Coventry, and a few days later they informed us that a body had been discovered in a boarding house. The papers turned out to be false, so we assumed this was Agent Shelley.'

'Had he been killed?'

'The pathologist said he had died of a heart attack. He was in his early fifties, not the kind of man one would have thought would be sent on a mission like this.'

'So maybe he wasn't Shelley after all?'

'As I say, Richard, his papers were all forgeries, there was no record of the name he was using and the labels on his clothes had all been removed. Now, as you well know, when the Service sends an agent into Nazi-occupied Europe, they go out of their way to ensure their clothing is as inconspicuous as possible, even changing labels and the tailoring as I understand it. The Germans slipped up in this chap's case, he wasn't properly prepared.'

'And did you hear any more from Byron, the radio operator?'

King shook his head. 'No – well not for a while anyway. The Germans must have taken the view that the deaths of Keats and Shelley called for a period of radio silence. However, in March, new transmissions mentioned Byron and Milton along with a new agent. This one was code-named Dryden – I imagine you're seeing a pattern by now. Remember, Berlin is quite unaware of the extent to which we are able to intercept and decode their messages, especially the ones being sent within Germany, which are often in clear. From these transmissions we knew Dryden was already in this country and would be travelling from Birmingham by train to London on a particular date, making his way by a circuitous route to a pub in Kentish Town, where we understood he would be meeting Agent Byron.

'We managed to tail him, but for reasons that are unclear, he aborted the meet outside the pub and went to what must have been a fall-back point in Hampstead. As he left there, we arrested him.'

'Ah – so he's still alive?'

Lance King avoided looking at Prince as he spooned sugar into his teacup and stirred it vigorously.

'If only he were.'

'What happened?'

'An interrogation went wrong.'

'But surely you must have found something out about him?'

'Precious little, I'm afraid. He was very, very good. He claimed he was a Polish refugee who'd come over here after the fall of France, worked in Manchester, where his factory and lodgings were bombed, after which he became an itinerant labourer. He stuck to his story, never wavered from it. You see, he'd been found with nothing incriminating on him and he knew that. Same with the other two: as clean as a whistle. We put some of our best people on him and they couldn't shake him, so finally we got authorisation to be a bit more robust.'

'Do you mean torture?'

'Good heavens, no, absolutely not: we're not the Germans, you know. As I say, something went wrong and Dryden died. We thought we were getting close to Byron and Milton, and instead we're as far away from them as before.'

'And that's it? Not much to go on.'

'There's more, Richard, don't you worry. Once Dryden died, we planted a story about him, along with his photograph, in some newspapers, hoping that might flush out Byron. But more radio silence, this time for the best part of six months. Then, at the end of August, there was a flurry of transmissions in Germany mentioning Milton in particular, and this time the name Donne kept cropping up as well. It soon became apparent that Donne had not only landed in England but had made his way to London and was in contact with both Byron and Milton.

'There were more transmissions by Byron, but again they were very short and there was no pattern as to when they were being sent. But certainly in the first half of September there was a good deal of traffic. It's disappointing that our radio chaps couldn't narrow it down more than they did. At one stage they thought the transmissions were from the Wandsworth area, then they said something about Fulham, but...'

'Could Byron be moving around to make his transmissions?'

'Doubtful: he's going to be using a large and powerful machine and it would be too risky to lug around something as bulky as that. I think we lack a degree of expertise in this area, to be frank. The Germans seem to be much better at it than us; I suppose they get more practice.

'We believe that Donne has been sent to London to act as a go-between, passing on intelligence given to him by Milton to Byron, who then transmits it back to Germany. For the Germans to go to such lengths shows that Milton must be a very highly placed agent. We have very good reason to believe he passed crucial intelligence to the Germans and alerted them to our attack on Arnhem in September, specifically where our landing and drop zones would be and that our objective was the two bridges over the Rhine. One of the early messages used the phrase Operation Market Garden in clear. Very few people were aware of the name of the operation at that stage. And I'm afraid it doesn't end there.'

King got up and paced the room, ending up back by the map. This time he tapped his pencil on southern Belgium.

'The Ardennes: as you know, the Germans took us – more to the point our American friends – by surprise when they launched a major offensive there on 16 December. They did very well at first, moving quickly, capturing fuel supplies and creating a significant bulge eastwards into Belgium. They laid siege to the town of Bastogne, which is of major strategic importance because it's the confluence of all major roads in the area. For a while it looked as if they were going to cause us very significant problems. It's only since the weather's cleared up and we've been able to attack from the air that we've managed to counter their offensive, but it's been a close-run thing.

'The Americans are convinced that the Germans had very good intelligence at the start of their offensive that told them just where the Allied forces were. For some reason they're blaming us, and while we're disputing that we're in any way to blame, we cannot ignore the fact that towards the end of November and during the first week of December there was a lot of radio traffic mentioning Milton again, and we think this was to do with the Ardennes offensive. Hard to be specific, but the timing is difficult to ignore.

'Naturally we're not sharing this with the Americans – we don't want them to think we have a problem – but then we are curious as to why they're blaming us for the intelligence being passed on. We're meeting them tomorrow; all may be revealed then. You're cordially invited.'

King paused as footsteps could be heard approaching the room and the door opened. A large man in a dark three-piece suit came in, mouthing, 'Sorry' as he pulled up a chair close to them.

'Richard, you know Hugh Harper, I believe?'

'Yes, we met last week.' Prince leaned over to shake the older man's hand.

'Welcome on board, Richard: delighted to have you on the team. I take it Lance has given you a thorough briefing?'

'I'm still doing that, sir: quite a lot of ground to cover.'

'It's a complicated business, Prince, and I'm not ashamed to say we've been rather stumped on this one. I don't know quite how much Lance has told you, but confidentially, I fear many of my senior colleagues in MI5 have become rather smug and insist on holding to the view that we have a one hundred per cent success rate in capturing German spies operating in this country. Now of course as the person responsible for this, I ought to be the first to go along with their opinion, but there's always been a worry at the back of my mind. After all, if we aren't aware of a particular spy, then how can we know if we haven't caught him, if you get my meaning?'

Harper paused as he blew noisily into a large handkerchief and wiped his forehead with the back of his hand. 'You'll have to excuse me, Prince, but I'm getting over a beast of a cold. What I'm trying to say is that we're forever patting ourselves on the back and saying, haven't we done well, hoovering up any German spy the minute we get a whiff of them: clever us, silly Germans. But I think the Germans have wised up and their operation has become more sophisticated. I'm of the opinion Milton is a particularly highly placed agent and his handler in Berlin is most astute, hence the idea of sending over a go-between. It's a clever system, rather like the way the resistance cells in France operated – independent of each other so if someone was caught, they wouldn't give the whole game away.

'We cannot prove that someone gave the Germans intelligence about our plans in Arnhem and the Allied dispositions in the Ardennes. Given the increased references to Milton and indeed to Donne that we came across in intercepts – and the fact that Byron was transmitting and receiving around these events – it is reasonable for us to work on the supposition that Milton is providing this intelligence. And there's a big concern we have here. Let's go over to the map, eh?'

Harper slowly got up and led Prince to the map, picking up a ruler from the desk and holding it near Rotterdam.

'The mighty Rhine: Baldwin said it's more our frontier these days than the white cliffs of Dover, and I think he was correct, even if he did say it ten years ago. The Rhine runs from here, where it joins the North Sea at the Hook of Holland, all the way down through the Netherlands and Germany into Switzerland – I'm sure you did all that in geography. The only way the Allies will get into Germany from the west is by crossing it. Arnhem and the Ardennes showed that the Germans are still a force to be reckoned with. Remember, Prince, it's Germany we're invading, not a country like France or Belgium where the native population is well disposed towards us and there are resistance groups to provide us with vital intelligence.

'Meanwhile, the Red Army – which is a formidable fighting force with apparently endless reinforcements – is pushing in from the east. If we don't get into Germany soon, our border with Europe really will be the Rhine.'

Harper stood silently looking at the map, stepping back at one stage and tilting his head as if the Rhine would appear less of an obstacle from another angle.

'The General Staff are very clear about this, Prince: they regard the Rhine as the one major obstacle to us advancing into Germany and bringing this war to an end. However, they're getting very nervous. They subscribe to the view that our Arnhem plans were betrayed to the Germans, and now the Americans are telling them the same was the case with the Ardennes. They've told Churchill they want this sorted before they come up with new plans to cross the Rhine, and naturally Winston is concerned; he didn't envisage the war dragging into 1945 as it is, and—'

'But do our generals know about the possibility that a spy is passing on this intelligence?'

'Good question, Prince, and the answer is not as such, but Churchill's bent his intelligence adviser's ear about it and Sir Roland is insisting we sort it. He is certainly aware of the Milton network – he calls it my little problem, for Christ's sake.'

Harper slowly sat down in the chair behind King's desk and blew his nose again, then helped himself to a cigarette from a wooden box. 'The last thing we want is the end of the war being delayed and us getting the bloody blame for it. I have to be able to look Winston in the eye and tell him we have eliminated any chance of plans to cross the Rhine being betrayed. So that's your mission, Prince: find out who the hell Milton is. Do you smoke?'

Prince said he didn't normally, but yes please, that would be very much appreciated, and he took a cigarette.

'There doesn't seem to be an awful lot to go on, sir.'

Harper and King shook their heads, both men watching him closely.

'May I play devil's advocate for a moment?'

'Go on, Prince.'

'If we accept that this Agent Milton is a traitor who betrayed us over Arnhem and may well do the same over the Rhine crossing – well, to ask an awkward question, does it terribly matter? I mean, the war's as good as won, isn't it? Surely this Milton chap has come into the game too late to do us any serious damage?'

'A reasonable question to ask, Prince. My answer would be that the war is by no means won yet. Any delay could be critical, not least because we can't be sure what Hitler has up his sleeve. They started firing their V2 rockets at us last September, and I can tell you, they're causing more damage than we let on. What we don't want is for Agent Milton's intelligence to help the Germans to the extent that our progress is halted and they have enough time to develop even more dangerous weapons. We hear plenty of rumours about new aircraft and the like. We cannot afford to take our eye off the ball for one minute. We have to treat Milton and the other two agents as being as dangerous now as they would have been in, say, 1940.'

'I understand, sir.'

'Do you have any other thoughts?'

'The code names, sir – there are six of them, aren't there?'

'Correct.'

'And apart from the fact that they're all the names of English poets, could there be any pattern?'

'As you can imagine, we have looked into this.' Lance King was still holding his cigarette like a dart. 'It would be extremely foolish of the Germans to choose code names for their agents that had any kind of discernible pattern to allow them to be linked with actual people. Usually intelligence agencies – our own included – select names or words at random. We did consult a couple of professors at Oxford about the poets, didn't we, sir?'

'Indeed we did. I spent a very agreeable if slightly anachronistic lunch with them at the Randolph. Of course I couldn't let on exactly what it was about, but I did ask them to see if they could deduce any pattern or clues from the use of these names, and in a nutshell the answer was no. Different styles of poetry, Milton and Dryden born in the seventeenth century, Keats, Byron and Shelley in the eighteenth and Donne in the sixteenth.'

Harper stood up and stubbed out his cigarette in an ashtray.

'Get your coat on, Prince; we're going for a drive.'

–

It was a short drive south from Mayfair into a smart residential area with long avenues between squares of Georgian town houses set around well-kept gardens. Hugh Harper had told his driver he'd take his own car, a Rover coupé in British racing green with a black roof and bonnet, which he drove too fast.

'We're in an area called Chelsea; I imagine you've heard of it. Smart housing, some of it converted into flats. To the west of here the housing is not quite as smart and it's a bit more built up but still what they call a desirable area to live in. There's a football team too, so I'm told – odd place for one. Used to be considered a very bohemian area, full of artists and the like, and it still has something of that feel to it. My sister-in-law has a place round the corner; hopefully I'll not bump into her.'

Harper slipped the Rover into gear and drove for a while, at one stage alongside the river, before turning into another square – this one not quite as pristine as the previous ones. He parked at the end of a block and turned off the engine.

'Lance told you about Byron, the agent we presume is the radio operator?'

'He did, yes.'

'Been well-nigh impossible to get a fix on where he is; I'm sure he told you that too. Doesn't help when Lance shouts at the radio detection chaps. They're trying their best. My hunch is that Byron is broadcasting from Chelsea: it's the centre of the area where they think the messages are coming from, but until they get something to actually bite on, they won't commit themselves. But there's another reason why I think he could be around here. Lance told you about Dryden?'

'The Polish chap who came over last June?'

'That's the one, Jan Dabrowski. A catalogue of disasters, I'm afraid. How we were unable to prise anything out of him is beyond me, though one does have to give him a good deal of credit for his courage in sticking to his story. However, I'm of the view that Dabrowski – Dryden – panicked when he got to London and made a mistake, or a series of them more to the point. I think that for some reason when he was waiting outside the pub in Kentish Town for Agent Byron, he thought he was being watched, or that he may have gone to the wrong place. As you know, he then took a taxi to the fall-back meeting point, in Hampstead, after which we arrested him.

'Turns out that the taxi driver who took him to Hampstead forgot to tell us when we first questioned him that his passenger had written a letter during the journey and asked him to post it. He couldn't recall the address, but he did remember it was somewhere in Chelsea.'

Harper opened the car door and gestured that Prince should get out. The two men walked slowly along the street. As they turned the corner, a short man with a slight limp was coming towards them and stopped when he spotted them.

'Ah, Spencer, fancy seeing you off duty! On your way into work?'

'Yes, sir.'

'Jolly good. I may well see you this evening.'

'Indeed, sir, good day, sir.'

Harper waited until the man was out of earshot. 'Spencer's a steward at my club, been there years. Good chap. Odd seeing people away from where you normally do. Anyway, back to Dryden. Christ knows, if I was operating in enemy territory I'm sure I'd be prone to panic – don't know how you've managed it; you must have nerves of solid steel. I think Dryden had Byron's address to use in an absolute emergency and decided to write to him. Madness for him to have the address, of course, but there we are.

'There is one other thing. Lance used a chap called Hood to interrogate Dabrowski. Hood's one of us, but he's not on the books, if you see what I mean. Lance knows I have reservations about us using him, but it's hard to deny that he has on occasions been most effective – though this wasn't one of them. Hood told Lance he'd given Dabrowski a few electric shocks and slapped him around a bit – nothing more than he normally does, but then the Pole collapsed. Hood gave him some smelling salts and says he came round.

'He wasn't making much sense – evidently he was talking Polish half the time, and why we didn't have a Pole there is beyond me – but Hood is convinced he said in English "I have to meet two Englishmen." He repeated the phrase twice and then lost consciousness and died soon after that. Apparently he had a heart attack – another one, would you believe.'

'Did he definitely say two?'

'That's what we were wondering, but Hood's absolutely adamant. So there we are Prince: all you need to do is find two Englishmen.'

Chapter 12

London, January 1945

Agent Milton had never imagined it would end like this. He'd always thought he'd have some kind of warning they were on to him, an inkling at the very least that the net was closing in.

But this was so sudden, and all he could think was how naïve he'd been to think it would be different, as if they'd treat it as a game of cricket rather than the arrest of a traitor.

He'd arranged to meet Agent Donne in Hyde Park, on West Carriage Drive – north side of the Serpentine. For some reason he'd decided that day that it would be safer if he walked south of the park and entered it from the west. He wasn't quite sure why he'd done that, other than to vary his route. He entered the park near the royal palace and strolled through Kensington Gardens towards the rendezvous point. He was close to the lake when he saw them, marching purposefully towards him.

They were about a hundred yards from him and Oakley was pointing towards him with an outstretched arm as if taking aim. As they came closer he heard the brigadier call his name, and then he realised to his utter horror that the familiar-looking man next to Oakley was none other than Major Dorking, the head of security at the Department of Military Intelligence.

He felt his chest tighten and became so light-headed his eyesight didn't seem right, as if bright lights were shining in his face. What made matters infinitely worse was that for the first time, and like an utter fool, he'd concealed a slip of paper inside his hat. Written in closely packed tiny handwriting was a list of

Allied deployments along the Rhine. He knew it was wrong, but it was information he doubted he or Jim would memorise accurately. There was no question they'd discover it when they searched him.

He noticed Major Dorking's hand reach inside his coat pocket, no doubt to remove his pistol, and he wondered whether to hold up his hands. He turned round, and as he suspected, any escape route was blocked: three policemen were walking towards him and he was sure he could see more in the distance.

He was alongside a wet wooden bench and he decided to sit down. He reckoned they'd be less likely to shoot a seated man.

–

'They want the meeting to be in Grosvenor Square, Roly.'

'They must be bloody joking, if you'll pardon my language.'

'They're insisting; they say that as they requested the meeting, they have the right to host it.'

'You'll need to speak up, Hugh, it's a poor line.'

'Is that any better? I said their view is that they called the meeting therefore they should decide where it's being held.'

'First I've heard of that kind of nonsense. I'm not going to their embassy: went there for Christmas drinks and had to stand all evening – and they put ice in the whisky without even asking. Tell them to come to Downing Street – the Americans like coming here: they think they'll bump into Winston.'

'They won't come to Downing Street, Roly, and we're not having them wandering round the MI5 offices.'

'How about my club – or even yours?'

'It's not that kind of meeting. I tell you what: there's a new secure meeting room at the Home Office. I'll get them to come there.'

'Very well, Hugh – and will it be just you and me?'

'I've asked Lance King to come along – he's the case officer on this one – and I want Gilbey's chap, Prince, there too. He's on board now.'

'Very well, but please don't get too worked up about meeting the Americans. Tom and his lot do it all the time. It's just one apparently friendly intelligence agency having a chat with another; it should be fine.'

—

'We didn't realise there'd be four of you.'

The atmosphere had been frosty before the meeting even began. The three Americans had arrived early at the Home Office and hadn't taken kindly to being kept waiting for ten minutes in the chilly reception area before Lance King finally turned up to take them down to the meeting room in the basement.

The leader of their delegation was Joseph Jenkins, an over-weight man in his forties with a severe haircut and a strong Southern accent. He was a senior liaison officer for the Office of Strategic Services in London and seemed to harbour a deep dislike of the British, though Sir Roland Pearson took the view that he was simply one of those people who didn't get on with anyone. It was his nature: highly combative and easily offended. According to his file, he'd been divorced three times, a feat Pearson had never heard of.

Jenkins – who preferred to be called Joseph rather than Joe – was joined by one of the junior OSS liaison officers and a US Army attaché.

'Come on, Joe, it's not a team sport, is it? We don't need to have equal numbers.' Pearson chuckled as Jenkins angrily removed a sheaf of papers from his briefcase. He counted out three copies and tossed them across the table to the Englishmen.

'You may want to read this before we start – two of you will have to share.'

Intelligence Report
Top Secret
Restricted: CATEGORY A

From: Major Mark B. Fine, Acting Head of Divisional Intelligence, Headquarters Company, 7th Armored Division, United States Army

To: Lieutenant General Courtney Hodges, Commander, United States First Army

Through: Major General Robert W. Hasbrouck, 7th Armored Division; Major General Alan W. Jones, 106th Infantry Division

Subject: Issues arising from German offensive in the St Vith area, ongoing from 16 December 1944

Manhay, Belgium, Monday 25 December 1944

I took over as acting divisional intelligence officer, Headquarters Company, on 18 December following the attack on St Vith. The German offensive in the St Vith area began at 5.30 on the morning of 16 December with a strong artillery bombardment followed by units of the 5th Panzer Army advancing towards our positions. The two main units involved were the 18th and 62nd Volksgrenadier Divisions, who advanced towards St Vith through the Schnee Eifel woods, the 18th taking up the northern and centre sectors, the 62nd to the south supported by the 116th Panzer Division.

What is of particular relevance for this report is that while the area contains a number of villages, there was no obvious strategic pattern to which ones the Germans chose to attack and drive through and those they attempted to bypass. They subjected one village to a sustained attack, even though there were no United States forces based there, but entered another apparently oblivious to the fact that it was well defended.

In our sector there were two bridges across the River Our. As the German forces advanced westwards, they concentrated their attempts to cross it on the bridge at Steinebruck, to the south. This bridge was more heavily defended by our forces than that at Schoenberg to the north. The 18th Volksgrenadiers only crossed the bridge at Schoenberg with the assistance of tank units from the 6th Panzer Army that had moved south from their sector.

The German forces continued their advance on St Vith on the main road from the river. Approximately one mile north of this road is the village of Wallerode, outside of which we had located a petrol depot. We were extremely concerned that the Germans would capture this fuel supply intact, thus aiding their advance. Although our engineers had failed to reach the depot in time to destroy it, the German forces didn't approach the depot.

Three miles south of the main road is the site of our former fuel depot north of the village of Schlierbach, which has been closed since early November because the terrain had proved to be too difficult for our tankers to reach it. Despite this, a sizeable unit of the 62nd Volksgrenadiers diverted south from their advance on St Vith to capture the depot.

As per standing orders our troops know it is a priority to take possession where possible of any enemy paperwork they come across, and especially maps. I have been paying particular attention to two maps, one taken from the body of a Hauptsturmführer, or captain, from the 62nd Volksgrenadiers and the other from an abandoned armoured car belonging to the 18th Volksgrenadiers.

Between them these maps give us a detailed and comprehensive picture of the area being attacked by the 5th Panzers. As well as showing roads, villages and bridges, it also covers the terrain and gradients. Along with that was a surprising amount of detail about where they believed our forces were positioned. In our opinion the enemy offensive was based on this data, which would explain, for example, why they made the errors I have detailed above.

I have now had the opportunity to consult the US Army charts in use in November last year showing our deployments in the area. Those charts almost exactly match the out-of-date information on the captured maps.

I have therefore come to the conclusion that the Germans planned the attack using our maps supplied to them in what was most probably an act of espionage.

I am sure you would wish to pass on this information so it can be acted upon as a matter of urgency.

Merry Christmas.

(Major) Mark B. Fine, Headquarters Company, 7th Armored Division

Sir Roland Pearson was the last of the four on his side of the table to finish reading the document. As he did so, he made a 'hmm' sound, raised his eyebrows and nodded, a puzzled look creasing his face. 'That's jolly interesting, Joe, and of course one is grateful for your sharing it with us, but I'm afraid I can't see what it has to do with insisting we meet so urgently.'

'Or indeed,' said Hugh Harper, leaning forward as he spoke, 'quite what the relevance is to us. We are, after all, a counter-intelligence operation. Surely this is a field matter, one for our colleagues in military intelligence?'

Joseph Jenkins said nothing for a while, watching the four men opposite him to see if any of them had other comments to add.

'Major Fine's report about the Germans' maps showing our deployments as of November last year is not an isolated one. We've had similar reports from three other sectors: those attacked by Dietrich's 6th Panzer Army in the north and Brandenberger's 7th in the south, as well as the 5th.

'In some areas the German intelligence was unerringly accurate, but that tended to be in places where our deployments had not altered much since November. In other areas their advance was significantly delayed by a combination of heroic defending by our forces and the Germans relying on what was clearly out-of-date intelligence. This was especially notable around the town of Stavelot. They failed to capture a major fuel depot there and underestimated our strength in that area.'

'Well as I say, Joe, we're obviously—'

'You need to listen carefully, Roland and Hugh and you two guys with no name. We have no doubt that someone supplied the Germans with details of our deployment.'

'It could have been anyone, though, surely?'

'No! This is exactly the point I'm trying to make. It couldn't have been anyone. We've been looking at this very carefully and we've narrowed the information the Germans were relying on to one particular map produced in the middle of November. And before you say that map would have been distributed to our forces in northern Europe and to the British, Canadian, Polish and French armies, and that any of them could be the source for the espionage, let me assure you that is not the case. The map was withdrawn before it was sent out because there was an error in it. The only copies that were distributed were the ones sent to us at the US embassy here in London. The replacement maps were sent a few days later, but due to an administrative oversight, I'm afraid we failed to pass them on to you guys.'

'By "you guys" you mean…?'

'I mean everyone in London on that distribution list: army and RAF headquarters, various intelligence outfits, government departments…'

Lance King muttered something inaudible, Sir Roland Pearson tutted and shook his head and Hugh Harper leaned across the table once more.

'How many people are on that distribution list, Jenkins?'

The American glanced down at a piece of paper pushed in front of him by his assistant. 'We have two distribution lists: one covering us and the Canadians, the other for the British. It's that second list that received the wrong map, the one we're concerned was the basis of intelligence passed to the Germans. That list had thirty-eight names on it.'

'And the maps were all identical?'

'Yes.'

'Which means…?'

'Which means, Roland, that one of your guys here in London gave that information to the Germans. Pass those reports back to me, please.'

Sir Roland stared at Joseph Jenkins as he gathered the papers, indicating the meeting was over. For the first time his angry demeanour had been replaced by the trace of a smile.

'So you have a problem, eh, Roly? You've got a spy somewhere high up here in London. Still,' the Americans were all standing now, Jenkins sounding almost jolly, 'I'm sure Hugh and his pals with no name will find him.'

They'd remained in the room after the Americans had left, Hugh Harper pacing up and down and Prince unsure whether to say anything.

'Winston will be furious, absolutely furious.' Sir Roland Pearson looked shell-shocked.

'Does he need to know?'

'He's the prime minister, for heaven's sake, Hugh: one can hardly keep him in the dark about a matter as serious as this. A bloody traitor...'

'What I meant was does he need to know this level of detail?'

'It's hardly a mere detail; it's far more serious than that. If one accepts that Jenkins, however objectionable he may be, is correct, then we have a traitor in our midst and we need to find him. You can see why they're blaming us, can't you? In any case, keeping it from Winston simply wouldn't work. He's always talking to the Americans. He'd be furious if he found out about this chap through them. In addition, the army are going to be very nervous about planning for a crossing of the Rhine if they know there's a traitor about. You'd better hurry up and find him, hadn't you, Hugh?'

Harper took a while to answer, appearing distracted as he peered at the wall ahead of him. Finally he spoke. 'I must say, what Jenkins told us does rather fit in with what we already know – the concerns we have about Milton, Byron and now Donne. My suspicion is that the spy he is talking about is Milton.'

Sir Roland Pearson stood up and walked over to the door, turning back to the other three before he opened it. 'He said there were thirty-eight names on the British distribution list, didn't he?'

'Yes, but that means thirty-eight offices.' Lance King was tapping his pencil on a blank sheet of paper. 'Would be easier of course if it was sent to thirty-eight named individuals – that way we could investigate each and every one, though even that would be one hell of a job. But far in excess of thirty-eight people will have had access to the map: once it ends up in an office, any number of people with a certain level of security clearance can look at it. I estimate at least a dozen people would be able to see each one.'

'Which is how many – thirty-eight multiplied by twelve?'

'Four hundred and fifty-six, sir.' It was the first time Richard Prince had spoken.

'Always good at maths, were you, Prince? One maths master used to call me a dunce. I'd round it up to five hundred for good luck. Well then, Hugh, there you are: it's a racing certainty Milton will be one of the five hundred or so with access to that map.' Sir Roland was now standing in the open doorway. 'You'd better crack on with it, hadn't you? I'll tell Winston that hopefully you'll have some news for us in – what shall we say, a fortnight?'

'That's a tall order, Roly, all those people...'

'What's the date today?'

'The ninth.'

'End of January then.'

–

'Good heavens, old chap, fancy meeting you here. Are you all right?'

He couldn't work out if Brigadier Oakley was being sarcastic prior to arresting him. He muttered something about feeling queasy – had been all day – and then watched in bemusement as the policemen strolled past with not so much as a glance in his direction.

'Major Dorking and I have a meeting at Kensington Palace, even though much of it's a bomb site these days. Where are you off to?'

Agent Milton stood up, still feeling shaky but relieved beyond measure that he wasn't under arrest. 'To be honest, sir, I find when I feel like this the best thing to do is walk it off. Thought I'd head through the park and then home.'

'Good idea, see you tomorrow.'

The three men bade each other farewell, but moments later the brigadier turned back.

'Should have said, by the way, first-class job you're doing. Well done.'

Chapter 13

St Vith, Belgium, January 1945

The morning of Tuesday 23 January was as still as a silent pond on a summer evening. The sun shone brightly in a clear sky, the air was crisp, and although it was still bitterly cold, it was quite pleasant compared to the dreadful weather the 7th Armored Division had endured since the Germans had launched their offensive six weeks previously.

Major Mark B. Fine ought to have been in a more jubilant mood than he was. The previous evening Major General Hasbrouck had assured him that his confirmation as head of divisional intelligence – and promotion to lieutenant colonel – was a formality. 'Once we're back in St Vith, we'll get it rubber-stamped, don't worry.'

And a month to the very day after the 7th Armored Division and the 106th Infantry Division had retreated from St Vith, they were about to recapture the small Belgian town. But it had been a bloody month, far worse than he could ever have imagined, which explained Major Fine's lack of jubilation.

From St Vith, the division had headed west, crossing the River Salm at Grand-Halleux and basing themselves at Manhay, where they'd waited for a few weeks as the RAF and the American air force brought a halt to the German advance.

But it was while he was based at Manhay that Major Fine's nightmare began. Reports began to emerge of atrocities carried out on American troops by German forces. Intelligence officers from various units were assigned to a special unit set up to investigate these crimes, and Major Fine was one of those involved.

The first massacre – and the worst in terms of numbers – had taken place just outside Malmedy, north of St Vith. On 17 December, units of Lieutenant Colonel Joachim Peiper's 6th SS Panzer Army captured around a hundred and forty troops from an American artillery battalion at the Baugnez crossroads. As far as Fine and his colleagues could ascertain, the prisoners were taken into a field, where early that afternoon the Germans opened fire on them. They were still discovering bodies and trying to work out exactly what had happened, but Major Fine had interviewed some of the survivors and he was in no doubt the men had been murdered in cold blood. He'd helped compile a list of the dead; when he'd last seen it, there were eighty names on it.

He'd visited the field by the Baugnez crossroads when the US forces recaptured the area on 14 January and had seen the corpses, frozen where they'd been shot. They were men like him, though mostly younger, frozen forever in time.

Despite his determination to approach the investigation with the dispassion of his lawyer's training, what he saw near Malmedy had a profound effect on him. He'd still not recovered from the shock when he was sent to Honsfeld, where Peiper's men had murdered more US prisoners, these from the 394th Infantry Regiment. And before he'd had time to start investigating there, he was dispatched to Wereth, where eleven black soldiers from a field artillery battalion had been murdered by troops from the 1st SS Panzer Division. That wasn't the end of the murder of American prisoners of war: there were incidents across the Ardennes, though those were the only ones Major Fine was involved in investigating.

He was still at Wereth when he received orders to return to the 7th Armored Division, which was now dug down in the woods around St Vith and preparing to recapture the town. Almost as an afterthought, he was told to stop on the way at Stavelot, a village a few miles north of St Vith. He'd heard rumours of Belgian villagers being killed throughout the

Ardennes, but never for a moment did he imagine it being anything on the same scale and as cold-blooded as the way he'd seen his American comrades treated. After all, the local population were non-combatants, and this was a German-speaking part of Belgium.

Nothing had prepared him for what he saw when he entered Stavelot. His orders – more of a suggestion than a command – had come in a radio message distorted by static as his driver prepared their jeep for the short journey.

Some civilians may have been killed in the fighting.

His first indication of how serious the situation was came when his jeep was stopped at an American military police roadblock. The sergeant who came over glanced at Fine's papers. He was a tough-looking New Yorker in his forties but he seemed on edge, his hands trembling, and Fine noticed that his eyes were red.

'It's terrible, sir. They're animals. Head to the abbey, it's the road to the left.'

In the grounds of the abbey, American soldiers and locals were digging graves. Some of the graves were already full, each with a dozen or so bodies in them, wrapped in stained blankets. Laid on the grass were dozens more. Major Fine took out his notebook and gripped his pencil tightly as he wrote down what he saw, making a note of how many victims there were. Most of those on the ground were also covered in blankets or coats, but in an effort to conceal their faces, whoever had covered them had left their legs visible.

That was how he knew that there were children – dozens of them, some seemingly under ten. There was a boy with his legs crossed; his shoes looked just like those worn by Fine's own son, the laces neatly tied. More women than men, some with stockings still looking smart, other with bare legs, bloodstained. A local gendarme was walking with a priest and two American officers. Major Fine went to join them. A captain looked at him as if he were an intruder.

'We've got this, Major, you're all right.'

'I was told to investigate.'

The captain stared at him for a while before drawing him aside, away from the others.

'There's nothing to investigate. We're getting the names of all those killed and we're taking down eyewitness reports.'

'How many?'

'Maybe a hundred: we're still finding bodies.'

'What happened?'

'Heavy fighting in the town on the nineteenth of December – house-to-house. We think our guys caused them more casualties than they were expecting as we pulled out. The locals were mostly hiding in their cellars so the Germans decided to take it out on them. From what we can gather, they lined them up against hedges and shot them. You heard what they did to our guys at Malmedy?'

'Sure, I've been there – and at other places. Hundreds of our prisoners shot.'

The captain handed Fine his lit cigarette. 'Look, sir, I'm sorry I snapped at you. War is one thing, but this…' he turned, his hand sweeping across the field of bodies, 'this is just a massacre.'

Major Mark B. Fine made a number of decisions on the short journey from Stavelot to the woods outside St Vith. When he finally got home to Chicago, he'd quit his job as a lawyer with the bank and stop working such ridiculous hours. He'd find a job with a smaller law practice, perhaps one that defended people with limited means. And hopefully he'd be able to spend more time with his wife and his two kids, whom he hadn't seen for three years. He'd even try and make sure to visit his folks in Florida. He'd be less worried about money. He'd go for walks in the country. He'd stop smoking and cut down on his drinking, especially during the week. He'd read more books.

–

The quiet of the morning of Tuesday 23 January was broken an hour after dawn by the cacophony of outgoing artillery fire as the 7th Armored Division prepared their assault on St Vith. There was little if anything in the way of response from the Germans, and some of Major Fine's colleagues in Headquarters Company speculated that the town might be undefended.

'That's not what our intelligence says,' said Fine.

'Ever thought your intelligence could be wrong?' It was the voice of an infantry officer, who then ordered his units to advance on the town.

'I think we need to wait, send in more artillery first, perhaps.'

'Look, Major: the air force has bombed the hell out of them and there's no need for us to wait. If we listened to you guys in intelligence, we'd still be deciding whether to land in Normandy. We're going in.'

Although Headquarters Company was meant to follow in from the rear, Major Fine found himself in charge of a convoy making unexpected progress on a track across a field. When they finally stopped, they were on the outskirts of the town and his radio operator told him they were closer to it than any other unit.

'Apparently we're the front line, sir. They say well done and we're to secure that crossroads ahead of us so our heavy armour can come through.'

'Ask them if we shouldn't wait for infantry support? The 23rd should be nearby.'

'They say to move in now, sir.'

Major Fine positioned himself in a ditch and looked at the area through his binoculars. As far as he could tell, there were no Germans around. A Belgian sheepdog with a coat the colour of polished wood watched them from the other side of the road, its head cocked. It was a breed he'd grown fond of since they'd been in the country. That would be something else he'd do: get a dog. The kids had always wanted one. It could accompany him on his walks in the country.

'I'll go over and have a look.'

'I'd wait, Major: it could be a trap. Maybe we should call in air support.'

Major Fine nodded, but the idea of him being the man responsible for capturing St Vith was beginning to look quite attractive. It would certainly put a stop to those in Divisional Headquarters who took the view that intelligence officers weren't proper soldiers.

'I'll nip across the road and see what's going on.'

He had half an eye on the dog as he climbed out of the ditch, somehow oblivious to the shouts behind him to get down, somehow unaware of the grey shapes rising above the low brick wall behind the grass verge the Belgian shepherd was stretched out on.

The first bullets flew past him and only then did he realise that he had indeed run into a trap. To his left was a hedge and he made to dive into it. As he did so, a volley of fire was returned from the ditch he'd just climbed from.

When they found his body a few minutes later, he was slumped against the hedge, the same fate that had befallen the people of Stavelot.

Chapter 14

After two years in Ravensbrück, Hanne Jakobsen had come to appreciate how much news from the world outside the camp could sustain you. They certainly couldn't rely on the food for that.

Early the previous September, rumours had begun to circulate that Paris had been liberated a week or so earlier. The effect on morale had been dramatic. The news had been confirmed one morning when an inmate found a copy of the previous day's *Völkischer Beobachter* in a rubbish bin behind the administration block. An article on an inside page referred to the German forces' 'tactical withdrawal' from Paris and the need to 'step up defence of the Fatherland'. The prisoners knew what that meant.

Hanne was so thrilled at the news she wept with joy. She'd never been to Paris, but there was something iconic about the city regarded as the most beautiful in Europe, arguably its cultural heart. If it had been prised from the Nazis' grasp, then surely the war would end soon. Of course at Ravensbrück the celebrations – as muted as they were – didn't last long. That evening an SS guard heard two French prisoners humming 'La Marseillaise'. All the inmates from the women's barracks were ordered to assemble in Roll Call Square, the assembly area between the barracks and the administration block.

Hanne recognised the two women: young resistance fighters from Arras. They were standing on stools with thin ropes around their necks attached to a scaffold. The other prisoners were shepherded around them. Hanne had done her best to ensure she was as far back as possible, and could only just make out what the commandant was saying: something about how the women were going to regret singing 'that cursed song'. Then he ordered everyone to look up: Hanne, like many of the other prisoners, had been averting her gaze. As she glanced up, a guard kicked the stool from under one of the girls. The drop was not enough to break her neck, and the noose ensured she struggled in agony for a couple of minutes before expiring. All that time the other girl had her eyes tight shut, as if that were a way to avoid hearing as well as seeing what was happening. The commandant grinned as he waited a good five minutes before her stool was kicked away.

In common with the others in her hut, Hanne didn't have an appetite that evening.

–

By January 1945, the rumours that helped nourish them said that some of the camps in the east – the terrible death camps they'd heard about – were being evacuated as the Red Army approached. In Hanne's hut, a young Belgian prisoner confided that another Belgian in another hut had been told by a guard that Ravensbrück was about to be evacuated. She seemed so convinced it was true that Hanne felt it would be cruel to disabuse her. There was certainly no sign of it. Ravensbrück had turned into a vast industrial complex. More prisoners were arriving each day, and the rumours – not the kind of rumours that fed you – were that there were now more than fifty thousand inmates.

Where would we be evacuated to? The coast?

In the middle of January came the news that the Red Army had finally liberated Warsaw. There wasn't much of a celebration among the few Polish prisoners remaining in the camp. They'd learnt their lesson from the fate of the French prisoners, and in any case, they were aware that after the failed uprising there wasn't much left of Warsaw to liberate.

But the mood of the guards and the camp officials changed after that. They became increasingly edgy, even nervous, as if looking over their shoulders.

In the last week of January, Hanne was summoned to the Gestapo area. She was taken to the upper floor of a building between the commandant's office and the SS headquarters. The guard who'd escorted her led her into a room with views over the Schwedtsee, the winter sun glinting off the lake. The woods reached up to its shores and the town of Fürstenberg was visible in the distance. It was a scene of such normality that she found herself less anxious than she'd normally be in the circumstances, a feeling that didn't change when a thin man, perhaps in his late fifties, entered the office and told the guard he should remove the prisoner's handcuffs and leave them alone. The guard asked if he was sure.

'Of course I'm sure, you fool. And bring the prisoner some water.'

He told her his name was Mohr. He was still wearing his coat as he sat down at the desk between them, a thick pullover visible beneath it. He looked more like an overworked clerk than a Gestapo officer. He had a grey pallor and a hacking cough, and wiped his brow with a handkerchief.

'How are you?' he asked.

She'd had plenty of experience of the Gestapo, both from being forced to work alongside them as a police officer in Copenhagen and then as a prisoner. She knew enough not to be fooled by any suggestion of kindness. She replied that she was well enough: there was no point in saying otherwise, and she resisted the temptation to say she was better than he seemed to be.

'I've read your file.' He patted a folder in front of him and nodded as if talking about a good book. He stopped for another bout of coughing. 'It is very interesting. Do you have anything to say, perhaps?'

'About what?'

'This file tells me you are the only member of the spy ring operating in Copenhagen and Berlin who is in our hands. The businessman from Copenhagen – Knudsen – is dead. Those traitors in Berlin, Kampmann and Bergmann, they're dead too. That just leaves you and that Peter Rasmussen. Have you heard from him?'

She stared incredulously at him. He didn't look like an unintelligent man and certainly not as inept as the fool who'd interrogated her in Berlin, but the idea that Peter Rasmussen could have been in touch with her, and that if he had she'd tell him, was beyond ridiculous.

'No, I'm afraid not. I don't get much post here.'

He coughed so much his grey skin turned briefly red. 'You want to be very careful how you speak to me. Just because I'm being civil doesn't entitle you to take that tone, understand? I asked if you've heard from Rasmussen.'

'No, sir.'

'Obviously I don't imagine he sent you a postcard from a spa resort in Bavaria, but I'm not stupid: there are prisoners coming into this place all the time, many of them mixed up in the kind of criminal activities you and Rasmussen were involved in – trying to destabilise the Reich, pass on secrets to the enemy. Someone may have come across him and given a message to you.'

'No, sir.'

'You probably think that as long as he's at liberty you're safe, but let me tell you this: that may soon no longer be the case. Saying nothing and refusing to cooperate with us may not be as clever as you think. Some people in Berlin' – Mohr made a gesture with his arm as if to indicate this didn't apply to him, of course – 'take the view that because events are not going Germany's way, we should be less patient with a prisoner such as you. I'd think about that if I was you. Perhaps something has occurred to you about where Rasmussen may be – some clue from when you knew him that you have suddenly remembered?'

She shook her head.

Mohr closed the file and gave the impression their meeting was drawing to a close. Behind him she could see what looked like a pleasure boat moving quite fast across the lake. What did its passengers think when they looked towards the camp? Did they ever wonder what went on there: did they not spot the crematorium and its chimney?

'How long have you been at the brickworks, Jakobsen?'

She shrugged. 'I'm not too sure – maybe since October.'

'And you were at Siemens before that, in an office?'

She nodded.

'And now you're outside making bricks for the Reich. Very well: you're being moved to work in the Texled workshops, but don't be fooled. The next time someone comes and asks you about Rasmussen, they won't be as easy-going as me.'

—

A prisoner didn't ask to be sent to work in Texled – that was one way of guaranteeing you'd never get there. You just had to hope you were in the right place at the right time when they had a rush on and a sudden need for more workers. Texled was a business run by the SS, an abbreviation of The Company for Textile and Leather Utilisation, and the rumours were that it was one of the only businesses run by the SS that actually made a profit.

The hours were long and the work monotonous but the tailoring workshops did have the advantage of being warm, and at least you could sit down if you were operating the sewing machines. It hadn't always been like that: when the workshops had started, the guards had done their best to ensure the prisoners working in them weren't too comfortable. But then the managers complained. If the windows and doors were kept open then the uniforms and clothes they were making would get damp, and as for prisoners standing, well, that meant they were less efficient. And the less efficient they were, the less money the SS made.

Now the workshops were producing a new range of uniforms and Hanne was put to work sewing buttons onto jackets. Next to her was a taciturn Norwegian woman she'd met before in the Siemens factory and hadn't exactly warmed to: she couldn't even remember her name. Conversations between prisoners were forbidden, but it was hard for the guards to police it above the cacophony of machinery.

'Have you noticed anything about these uniforms?' the Norwegian asked.

'They're for the Wehrmacht?'

'You don't say! I mean anything unusual about them.'

Hanne pushed her chair back and held the jacket up in front of her, as if admiring her handiwork. 'I'm not sure what you mean.'

'Do you have children?'

'No.'

'Look at the size of it. It's for a boy not more than fourteen or fifteen. I'm surprised you can't tell: I thought you were smart.'

They stopped speaking as a guard strolled past, a truncheon in her hand, eager for any excuse to use it. Hanne and the Norwegian woman – she remembered her name now, Gudrun – bowed their heads and concentrated hard on their sewing for a while.

'I'll tell you what it means. The Germans are calling up children into their army. Once they do that, even they know they've lost the war.'

Chapter 15

'I wouldn't take odds of five hundred to one.'

'Yes, Lance, but then this isn't Ascot, is it? In any case, I don't think one should look at it like that. Once we've established which office the information has come from, we can then see who may have been responsible. Still, quite a tall order to have something by the end of the month: just three bloody weeks. What do you think, Prince?'

Harper, King and Prince had returned to the mews house in Mayfair after the meeting with the Americans at the Home Office. The two MI5 officers looked expectantly at Prince.

'If someone wanted to look at the map, would they be expected to sign for it?'

'That's a good question, but I suspect it varies from office to office. I suppose strictly speaking all offices ought to have a sign-out system for restricted documents, but I know from experience it won't be like that. We may well find offices where they've been rigorous in that respect and can provide us with a comprehensive list, but in other places it will have been a free-for-all.'

'In that case it will be like looking for the proverbial needle in a haystack. But even if we find that each of the thirty-eight offices that received the map had diligently compiled registers of who'd seen them, surely digging around like that will alert Milton. We don't want him – assuming it's a man – knowing we're on to him.'

'That's true, Prince. What do you propose?'

'I think we should approach the investigation the other way round. In other words, rather than seeing who had access to the Ardennes map, we ought to see if there are other ways of finding Milton.'

'And Arnhem,' said Lance King. 'Don't forget that whoever betrayed the Allies over the Ardennes also betrayed us over Arnhem.'

'I'm glad you're thinking the way you are, Prince,' said Harper. 'There's a reason why we've brought you on board for this case. We needed an outsider, someone not known within MI5, someone with a proven track record. While Lance handles the map side of this business, as discreetly as possible, of course, I want you to go undercover for a month or so. We'll find you a place in London and from now on that will be your base. The fewer people who know about you the better. We need to somehow infiltrate you into a world we only suspect exists: when you return to London, you'll be introduced to someone who knows more about that than anyone else.'

He glanced at his watch. 'I need to get a move on, but there's one other matter I need to raise with Prince: Lance, perhaps you could give us a moment?'

They waited until the other man had left the room. Harper moved to a chair opposite Prince and leaned forward, his arms on his thighs.

'My hunch is that Milton is British. For what it's worth, my feeling is that Byron is too – remember what the Polish chap said just before he died about two Englishmen. If they were foreign, I think someone would have caught wind of them by now. They're probably perfectly integrated. What we've given you today and yesterday is more than anything else the background to the case: the evidence about Milton and Byron and the radio transmissions, the arrival of Donne, the fact that everything is pointing to some kind of betrayal over Arnhem and the Ardennes – and most importantly, of course, the concern that our plans to cross the Rhine could also be betrayed. But there's something we've not told you yet. Come a bit closer.'

Prince looked around, puzzled as to how much closer he could come in the small office. He edged forward in his chair.

'We told you yesterday about the German transmissions we were intercepting and decoding, and you quite rightly asked how we were able to do this. We've developed an ingenious and complex system for breaking the Germans' most secret and highly encrypted coded radio transmissions. We call this system Ultra – the name indicates that it's even more secret than the top-security classification we previously used, "most secret".

'The Germans use a number of machines on which to send their encrypted messages – the one most used is called Enigma, but they have others, including the Lorenz. I cannot stress to you how secret this is, Prince. You must never breathe a word of it to anyone. We pass on the intelligence we decrypt to many people in the armed forces, the intelligence services and government, but very few of them are aware of the source.'

'Don't the Germans suspect we've broken their codes?'

'Good question. We've gone to considerable lengths to try and cover Ultra up, mainly by giving the impression the intelligence has been gleaned by our agents rather than through signals intelligence.'

'I appreciate you telling me this, sir, but may I ask why I'm being told if it's so confidential?'

Harper leaned back and fiddled with the knot of his tie.

'You're probably more trusted than almost anyone else: you've operated for considerable lengths of time in enemy territory and been arrested by the Gestapo, yet we know you've been utterly loyal. Very few people on our side have been tested to anything like that extent. There's another reason: you're quite possibly going to be very exposed, operating undercover in what may be quite trying circumstances. We took the view that you'd work more effectively if you had absolute confidence that what you're being asked to investigate is based on solid bona fide information rather than a wing and a prayer.'

Harper stood up and tightened his tie. 'You'd better be heading back to Lincoln to sort matters out. Lance will call you tomorrow night with the address of the safe house we'll get for you. We'll meet you there Thursday evening.'

'I've had this place up my sleeve for a while, Prince, it will be ideal for you. Don't worry about the smell; once the windows have been open for a while, that will soon go. It's been thoroughly checked over and done up – new doors, windows, locks, you name it. Lance, how about you show Prince round?'

They were in a basement flat in Granville Square, a slightly shabby area about ten minutes' walk south of King's Cross. The square itself seemed to be used as a rubbish dump, with piles of rubble from what Prince assumed were bombed buildings. There were two or three gaps on each side where houses had been destroyed. He wouldn't have thought it was the kind of place that merited much of a guided tour. He followed King into a small sitting room.

'Through here, Prince... mind that wire, there we are. This is the normal telephone – on the sideboard, where one would expect it. However, over in this cupboard – behind those books – there's this other phone. You lift up the receiver and hold that button down – the one concealed at the back, that's it – and then dial zero. That will connect through to the secure MI5 exchange. They'll know the call is on a top-priority line linked with one of my operations. The person at the exchange will say you're through to the Mirage Hotel and you're to ask for Alf in housekeeping. When they ask your name, say George. They'll know then to patch you through to me. If I'm unavailable, they'll get a message to me. If it is urgent – really urgent – then ask if you can speak with Mary. Don't worry, we'll go through it all again in a moment. Come with me.'

He followed King into the kitchen.

'You see the two light switches there? The second one is in fact an alarm: it will ring at Farringdon police station, which is just around the corner. Only to be used in an absolute emergency. Any questions?'

'Good heavens, Lance, you'll have poor old Richard here packing his bags and heading back to Lincoln on the next train, and I can't say I'd blame him! These are merely precautions, Prince, just to assure you you'll be safe here. The most important precautions of course are the ones you take yourself to make sure no one knows about the place.'

'It does rather make me feel as if I'm back in Nazi Germany, sir.'

Harper and King chuckled, glancing anxiously at each other in case it hadn't been meant as a joke. Harper took Prince into the lounge, where spread on the surface of a small table was an array of documents.

'Study all these very carefully; it's an identity to use when you go undercover: George Nicholson. These are your cards and ration book, and in this folder is your story, which you'll study and memorise. In a nutshell, though, George, you're an utter disgrace!' Harper laughed loudly as he slapped Prince on the shoulder. 'An utter disgrace indeed... dishonourable discharge from the army.'

Prince had just picked up the file when the doorbell rang. He heard King open the door and then call him into the lounge. Standing next to him was a tall woman, perhaps in her late fifties, wearing a dark blue raincoat belted tightly at the waist. It was raining, and when she removed a scarf wrapped round her head, she gently shook her hair: steel-grey hair, flecked with white streaks, hanging over her shoulders. She looked Prince up and down in a manner he had become used to.

So that's who you are.

'Audrey, this is Richard Prince, who I was telling you about. Prince, this is the one other person who'll know about you. Audrey and I worked together for many years, but I'll let her tell you her story. Shall we sit down? Lance, did you get in any whisky as I asked?'

There was a delay as Lance King fussed over the whisky, Audrey remonstrating with him for giving her such a small glass and Prince not even being asked if he wanted any as a glass was placed in front of him. Audrey sat on the edge of the sofa, her legs crossed at the ankles and holding her whisky glass on her lap with both hands. She looked shy – almost nervous – but when she spoke, it was in a confident voice.

'Hugh is very kind when he says we worked together; in fact I was very much his subordinate – indeed, I was most people's subordinate. Unlike so many others of his seniority, though, he was always most kind and proper with me. He was one of the few who managed to avoid treating me as a mere clerk.'

'I'm afraid Audrey no longer works for MI5 as such.'

'Well I don't work for them at all, Hugh – there's no "as such" about it. I wish I did. It's only because of your kindness that I'm still able to be indirectly involved in this work.'

'Perhaps if you give Prince some background…?'

Audrey sat back on the sofa, taking care to place her handbag by the side of it, and then took a sip of her whisky, nodding approvingly and declining Harper's offer of a cigarette.

'I started working for MI5 before it was MI5. In 1909 I was a teenage typist at the Home Office and was sent on second-ment to a new organisation called the Secret Service Bureau. Its role was to coordinate counter-espionage in this country, and in particular what was perceived even then as the threat of Germany. My secondment became a permanent post and I was promoted to secretary and then office manager. At the start of the Great War the organisation became a section of the Directorate of Military Intelligence within the War Office. It was designated as Section 5, hence becoming known by the name MI5. Lance, would you care to give me a drop more whisky? There's no need to be mean.

'By the 1920s – especially towards the end of that decade – our filing and records system was an utter shambles and I was asked to sort it out. In doing so I developed an unrivalled knowledge of people in this country who had come to MI5's attention and the organisations they belonged to. During the 1930s I was especially interested in the growth of support for fascism: not just Mosley's miserable outfit but also organisations even more extreme and secretive than his – and then there were the people who never belonged to any organisation but who were sympathetic to varying degrees to Nazi Germany.

'During this period I began to clash with some of my superiors who I felt devoted far too much attention to what they perceived as a communist threat and didn't take the threat of fascism in this country seriously enough. Mosley's British Union of Fascists had somewhere in the region of fifty thousand members at one point, but I felt there were too many people in MI5 who were too ready to dismiss this as a law-and-order issue rather than a serious fascist political challenge. Hugh, I ought to say, was most certainly not one of these people, and nor were you, Lance, though I think you joined MI5 a bit later?'

King nodded. 'A year before the war.'

'I felt my superiors were ignoring those in this country sympathising with Nazi Germany. They wanted to concentrate what limited resources we had on what I call the foot soldiers of fascism – people who certainly should not be ignored but who were not that important in the great scheme of things. I understand you were involved in that case in Lincolnshire in 1942, Mr Prince?'

'That's correct – Lillian Abbott, former member of the British Union of Fascists, harbouring a Nazi spy.'

'I wrote a report in early 1939 pointing out that there were three levels of fascist threat in this country. The first level was the most high-profile but, in my opinion, the least dangerous – that was the ordinary rank-and-file members of the British Union of Fascists. The majority of these people were gullible fools who once the war started would fall into line. The next level comprised people like Lillian Abbott: more dangerous, motivated by ideology and perhaps less easy to identify. The most dangerous level was made up of the people who perhaps avoided joining organisations and whose involvement in pro-fascist and indeed pro-Nazi activities was clandestine in nature. I wrote that there were a number of characteristics common to members of this group: virulent anti-Semitism and anti-communism; individuals were difficult to identify, often using assumed names; and finally they were more likely to be upper middles class or even upper class, with a number of members of the aristocracy being associated with it.'

Hugh Harper patted Audrey's knee as he interrupted her. 'I can tell you that Audrey's report was not well received in MI5. By then I was in charge of the section dealing with foreign espionage in this country, so I was not directly involved. The decision was made to keep the report in the pending tray, where it stayed until September '39. When the war started, dear Audrey rather rattled a few cages with a characteristically blunt "I told you so" memo. The powers-that-be didn't like it one bit; they took it all rather personally. Audrey has an admirable but very direct style to her writing, and I'm afraid that accusing senior officers of negligence was not going to win her many friends.'

'But I wasn't looking for friends, Hugh: I was concerned about enemies.'

The others in the room chuckled as Lance King poured more drinks.

'In any case, I didn't outright accuse people of negligence: I merely implied it. But thereafter it was a classic case of blaming the messenger. They moved me to the section that liaised with police forces outside London, and then I was hauled before an internal tribunal where they wondered whether I was a communist sympathiser – this was based on nothing other than the fact that I'd volunteered the information that I'd voted Labour in the 1935 general election. Then they questioned me about my best friend – a Jewish girl I was at school with. I'm afraid I rather lost my temper and told them they were following a line of questioning more common in Nazi Germany.'

'Oh Audrey… Audrey…' Hugh Harper patted her knee once more and lounged back on the sofa. 'I offered to bring her into my section, but they weren't having any of it. The most I could do was to persuade them not to sack her.'

'They arranged for me to be transferred to the Department of Transport. It's a tedious job: at MI5 I used to work late into the night and at weekends. Now at least I have time to assist Mr Harper. You see, what he didn't know at the time was that I was concerned during 1939 that my warnings would be ignored, so between my report coming out and my being moved to Transport, I compiled a long list of all the people I felt fell into the third category I mentioned. This was quite improper, of course; most certainly a dismissible offence. I justified it by telling myself it was in the national interest. This folder took many months to put together – I'd type the details onto flimsy sheets of A4 and remove a sheet at a time in the lining of my handbag.'

'I bumped into Audrey in Whitehall in 1942, I think it was, and told her I was in trouble on a case, and she was able to help me more or less immediately. She has since been of invaluable assistance – not least in consulting the file she kept. I told her earlier this week about you, Prince: that we'd need you to go undercover, to infiltrate you into a world where you might find some lead to Milton. She will help you with that.'

Audrey stood up and placed her empty glass on the table, walking over to the window to draw the curtains even tighter then turning round to face the room like a teacher in front of a blackboard. She asked Lance King to pass her handbag and removed something from it, holding it to her chest like a love letter.

'In May 1939, I investigated a small group that met once every few weeks in the private dining room of a hotel in Pimlico, not far from the Houses of Parliament. There was an

Italian waiter there – a refugee from Mussolini – and he claimed he'd overheard the diners toasting Hitler. I arranged for a watch on the place the next time the group met: there were just eight of them, plus a guest speaker who told them he worked for the Treasury and who spoke about how the Jews controlled the banks and the money supply in this country. I discovered he did indeed work for the Treasury: in fact he was a senior civil servant by the name of Arthur Chapman-Collins. I searched his office one night and discovered locked in a drawer the most shocking material: notebooks filled with nonsense about Jews, lists of names of people he claimed were secret Jews conspiring to control the country. The Treasury rather reluctantly agreed they had no other option but to discipline him, but I was furious when I discovered they'd allowed him to submit his resignation before the hearing. I desperately wanted to get my hands on him – he was, after all, very much the kind of person I described as being in the third category: upper middle class and not a member of any organisation, unknown to us before.

'I did get to question him, but he refused to cooperate. At one stage I even considered trying to have him arrested, but then we received a letter from his solicitor informing us he'd died: he blamed us for harassing him and had apparently gone to Ireland to get away from it all, and he died there of what we were told was stress. He was buried in some village cemetery in the middle of nowhere.'

'When did you receive this letter?'

'I think it would have been July – possibly late June – 1939. I'll need to check my notes. Certainly it was around two months before the war began, and then of course I was moved on and left MI5. Here's a photo of Chapman-Collins.'

She passed round the photograph of a nondescript man probably in his forties, with a receding hairline, a pale complexion and light-coloured eyes that looked as if they were moving. His mouth was slightly open, as if in mid speech. The reverse of the photograph was stamped 'HM Treasury'.

'Early last November, I was on my way into work on the 29 bus. I was sitting on the top deck as usual, from where I spotted Arthur Chapman-Collins.'

She paused and moved back to the sofa.

'You're certain it was him?' Prince was looking at the photograph as he spoke. 'He doesn't look terribly distinctive.'

'But remember I'd met him in real life, Mr Prince, and I'm utterly convinced that he was the man I saw in Charing Cross Road. He was standing in the entrance of a bookshop and the bus had come to a halt, so I was able to get a good look at him. I know he was meant to be buried in an Irish cemetery, but I also know I saw him: I was only a few feet from him, but as I stood up to get off, the bus set off again. The next stop was Trafalgar Square, and by the time I walked back to where I'd seen him, he'd vanished. I spent two hours in the area looking for him, but with no luck.

'To be frank with you, I'd always felt I'd mishandled the Chapman-Collins case. I should have been much firmer and insisted on him being arrested at the outset rather than let the Treasury deal with it as an internal disciplinary matter. I had a niggling feeling he might be a more significant character on the far right than I originally thought: he was after all a senior civil servant and was risking an awful lot. And now I'm convinced that he is alive, and that someone has gone to an effort to fake his death, which would prove how important he is. I was so convinced I came to see you, Hugh, didn't I?'

'You did, Audrey, and you asked me to do you a big favour.'

'I don't know what your view is on informers, Mr Prince, but I've always been rather sceptical about them.'

'I know how you feel; I've always had mixed feelings about them myself. I feel they tell you what they think you want to hear.'

'Before the war I'd occasionally used an informer called Curtis, first name Vince. I always believed Curtis was far closer to the pro-German wing of the British far right than he was to Mosley's lot, and I remember he once mentioned that he knew British people who recruited for the Germans, though he wouldn't be drawn on that. I'd heard that he was one of the fascists detained under Defence Regulation18B at Brixton Prison, and Hugh arranged for me to go and visit him. I think he agreed to see me out of curiosity. When I showed him this photograph of Arthur Chapman-Collins, he said, "Oh, that's Arthur Walker. He's one of those who was helping recruit for the Germans." Those were his exact words; I wrote them down straight after we met. But when I asked him to elaborate, he clammed up, as if he regretted saying it and ended our meeting there and then.

'When Hugh got in touch to ask my advice over Milton, I straight away thought of Chapman-Collins. If he is indeed alive – and I am convinced he is – then I believe he could be the link to Milton. I think it's more than possible he recruited him. Find Chapman-Collins and you may well find Milton.'

'And how would you suggest Prince goes about finding him?'

'I've been told you're a highly regarded police officer, Mr Prince – a detective, no less! Treat Chapman-Collins as a missing person; maybe ask around where he lived. Lance has given you a file which contains what details I have on him, last known address, et cetera. I have one further piece of information that may be of help: do listen carefully.

'I thought I had some notes relating to the group that gathered in the hotel in Pimlico – the one that invited Chapman-Collins to speak – but was damned if I could find them. However, the other night I finally managed to unearth something. Apparently the meetings seemed to be organised by a man called Fenton, initial L – he booked and paid for everything and the Italian waiter confirmed at the time that he appeared to be the organiser. I don't think he was ever investigated: once Chapman-Collins was questioned, the group stopped meeting. That was an omission, but we were very busy and our resources limited. Had L. Fenton been a communist, I've little doubt we'd have looked into him.'

'Is he still alive?'

'That, Mr Prince, is for you to find out, is it not?'

Chapter 16

London and Buckinghamshire, January 1945

When the others left his basement flat later that evening, Richard Prince pulled the armchair closer to the gas fire and carefully read through the neatly typed biography. There was little doubt that George Nicholson was, in Hugh Harper's words, an utter disgrace.

Prince's new persona had been born a year after him, in 1909. His birth date was the same as Prince's father, to make it easy for him to remember, and like Prince himself he'd spent his early years in Nottinghamshire. Unlike Prince he'd left school at the earliest opportunity and had spent the next period of his life drifting around the East Midlands. It was an entirely unremarkable life, moving from job to job, town to town, with the occasional minor brush with the law. He'd been a supporter of Mosley's fascists but never a formal member of the party. That was important, the document had emphasised: if he claimed to have been a member it would be possible to check that. The document gave the dates and venues of Mosley's rallies he'd been to in Birmingham and Nottingham, but the biography emphasised that he should be vague about George Nicholson's life and certainly not volunteer too much information about it.

The key event, the one that would be the basis of his cover story and would establish his credibility, had taken place in 1941. George Nicholson had been conscripted in late 1940, joining the 12th Battalion of the Nottinghamshire and Derbyshire Regiment, which was known as the Sherwood Foresters, based at their main barracks in Derby. In 1942, the battalion had been sent to India, but Nicholson – who'd predictably never risen above the rank of private – was not with them. He had spent part of 1941 and the first half of 1942 in the Glasshouse, the notorious military prison in Aldershot. Attached to his biography was an extract from his file kept in the regimental headquarters.

On Sunday 25 May 1941, Private George Nicholson reported late for guard duty at the Normanton Barracks, Derby. Upon being reprimanded, he was observed to spit in the direction of the sergeant and was then taken to the duty officer, Captain Marks. Private Nicholson refused to offer an explanation for his behaviour other than to say it was a Sunday and he intended it to be his day of rest. Captain Marks asked him if he'd been drinking and Nicholson's response was that it was none of his business and anyway he didn't see why a Jew should be giving him orders. He said he was a proud Englishman, 'unlike that traitor Churchill'. Captain Marks ordered his immediate arrest, whereupon the private put up some resistance.

At his subsequent court martial, Nicholson was found guilty of being drunk on duty and insubordination to superior officers and was sentenced to one year's imprisonment. He was released from the Aldershot military prison on 7 June 1942 and instructed to report to his regimental barracks to attend a further disciplinary hearing, with a view to being given a dishonourable discharge. However, he failed to attend the barracks, since when he had been assumed to be absent without leave and a warrant had been issued for his arrest.

The biography made clear that anyone checking the records at both the regimental headquarters and the military prison in Aldershot would find Nicholson's service record and the account of his arrest and subsequent imprisonment. Lance King had pencilled a note at the bottom of a page: *It is more than possible – indeed quite likely – that there are fascist sympathisers at either Derby or Aldershot or both and they may have ways of checking your records at those places. You're also on police records as being AWOL and therefore liable to arrest and being handed over to the Military Police.*

Since his release from prison in June 1942 and subsequent disappearance, Nicholson had mostly done poorly paid labouring jobs – *do remember to be vague about this, don't commit to dates and places* – and had been in London since early December.

–

Before leaving that night, Audrey had promised to stop by in the morning with more information. 'It will be early, though,' she warned.

Despite this, he'd not expected the doorbell to ring just after six o'clock. He was still wearing his dressing gown when she marched in. She told him to get dressed. When he joined her in the sitting room, she was at the table, two cups of tea waiting and half a dozen sheets of paper neatly arranged.

'Do come and sit next to me; I doubt you have the ability to read upside down. I didn't put any sugar in your tea – the bowl's there. Now then, Mr Arthur Chapman-Collins: not as much detail as I'd hoped. Lance tells me his main files have gone to Registry and probably to one of their storage places out of London. However, I do have here this sheet of paper that I think I must have typed up after he was allowed to resign from the Treasury – date of birth, date joined the civil service, that kind of basic information. This is his address in Gerrards Cross; have you heard of it?'

'No, I can't say I have.'

'It's a small town to the west of London, actually in Buckinghamshire. It's very pleasant, with a decent train service into London. It's his family home: he lived there with his mother until she died in 1937 and then remained there on his own. He never married.'

'Was the house sold after he supposedly died?'

'Lance did check that out and says apparently not.'

'Is there any other family who may live there?'

'We only know of a younger brother, but his registered address is an apartment in Kensington.'

'I should go and see him then.'

'Not without some considerable difficulty: he's a prisoner of the Japanese.'

'I did have a thought last night – about Chapman-Collins.'

'Go on.'

'You said his solicitor wrote to say he'd died in Ireland and is buried in a village cemetery out there.'

'Correct.'

'What if we were to find the grave and—'

'And disinter him?'

'Well, ask a few questions certainly.'

'I don't think you realise quite how hostile the Irish authorities are to us. I believe it would be counter-productive were we to start enquiring about where he's buried. We don't want to alert people that we're looking for him.'

'Fair enough. You also mentioned this chap Fenton – the one who organised the dinner?'

'I was about to come on to him – in fact the notes I have are more extensive than I thought. I'd forgotten that as well as Fenton's name we also managed to obtain the names of the other diners. Have a look at this.' She passed him a handwritten sheet of paper.

> Meeting at Abbey Hotel (St George's Road, Pimlico, London SW1)
>
> Speaker: Arthur Chapman-Collins (Treasury?)
>
> Organiser: L. Fenton (Rotherhithe?)
>
> Other participants: Bannister; Spencer; Davies; Philips; Cummings; Carver; Kemp

'Not too much in the way of clues, eh?'

'No, there's not. But I'm told that if anyone can make something of this, it's you. Not for me to tell you your job, of course, but were this up to me I think I'd start in—'

'Gerrards Cross?'

'Indeed. I'm glad we're of similar mind. Happy hunting: trains for Gerrards Cross leave from Marylebone station, by the way.'

Before Prince left, he made one telephone call on the line connecting him to the MI5 exchange, telling the operator it was George calling for Alf. Within moments he was speaking with Lance King. He explained what he wanted.

'When would you like this information, Richard – and please don't say within an hour or something unreasonable like that. With the local police we need to approach with caution: doesn't do to make too much of a fuss.'

Prince replied that the following morning would be fine. Meanwhile he was off to Buckinghamshire.

–

When Prince arrived in Gerrards Cross, he found a very agreeable town where everything was neat and in its place. In marked contrast to most other parts of the country, it didn't seem to be unduly troubled or indeed changed by the war. It struck him it wasn't the kind of place where George Nicholson would fit in.

His first stop was the parish church of St James, an ornate building that reminded him of some of the churches he'd seen on the Continent. Inside he explained to a confused-looking verger that he was trying to find the grave of an old family friend.

'Mrs Chapman-Collins, she died in 1937; she was at school with my grandmother.'

The verger fussed around the dusty ledger for a good deal longer than Prince considered necessary, taking off his glasses then mislaying them before putting them on again. When

Prince suggested that maybe he should look himself, the verger regarded him as if he'd suggested offering a prayer to Satan.

'There is no record of a burial for a Mrs Chapman-Collins in 1937. You say you can't remember her first name?'

'It's on the tip of my tongue, but—'

'However we do have a record of the burial of a Mrs Chapman that year. If you give me a moment, I can show you the grave.'

Muriel Margaret Chapman

3 May 1860–8 June 1937

Dearly loved wife of the late William Chapman

Much loved mother of

Arthur Chapman-Collins and Charles Chapman

The verger hung around, rubbing his hands together either in anticipation of something or to ward off the cold. Prince was unsure whether to tip him or not but decided against it. He told him he was terribly grateful but would appreciate a few minutes on his own.

Early in his career he'd been taught the value of gravestones. 'They tend to be the one place where people can be relied on to tell the truth,' a colleague had told him, and over the years he'd learnt they could be sources of valuable information. This gravestone was no exception. Most importantly it told him that Arthur had no siblings other than Charles, and it also gave him the parents' first names. The grave told him one further bit of information: Arthur had bestowed on himself a double-barrelled surname, one neither his parents nor his brother shared. It said something about the man that he felt the need to aggrandise himself in such a manner.

From the church it was a pleasant walk to the Austenwood area in the north of the town. The address for Arthur Chapman-Collins was a turning just off Bull Lane, the kind of residential area found in every affluent English town: well-kept Edwardian houses spaced far enough apart from their neighbours to ensure maximum privacy, long driveways and immaculate front gardens looking as if they were in competition with the ones next door.

Given that no one apparently had lived in the house for years, he was surprised it didn't look more abandoned. There was no hint of dereliction. The garden was not as perfect as other ones he'd passed on his way there, but it was neat enough, certainly well tended.

It was approaching 1.30 when he arrived, and for ten minutes he stood in the shadow of an enormous oak tree with a good view of the house from the other side of the road. During that time no vehicle or pedestrian passed him, and the only sounds were those of the countryside, the cries of birds and a tractor somewhere in the distance. The position he'd chosen also gave him a good view of the front of the house: it was a two-storey detached building, with the ground and first floors dominated by large bay windows with smaller windows on either side of them. The downstairs windows were all shuttered; the upstairs ones had curtains tightly drawn across them.

He crossed the road and climbed over the padlocked driveway gate, allowing himself another minute or two with his back to a hedge, watching the house, alert to any sounds or clues that it might be inhabited. He felt his heart quicken, not through any exertion but because of the thrill of the chase; the same sense of exhilaration he'd experienced in Nazi Europe but now not mixed with the fear that wrapped its arms around his shoulders.

He walked quickly down the gravel path, noting the absence of weeds, and crouched down to peer through the letter box, remaining mindful that the front of the house was quite open. The gate to the left was locked, but he was able to pick the lock quite easily and make his way along the side of the house. It was dark, but there was something about it, something he couldn't put his finger on. It felt cold and empty, though not in a way he'd have expected it to be if no one lived there. There was a neatness and order about the place: the side door appeared to have been recently painted and the brass handle newly polished. He took out his lock picks again, but it was no use: the door was firmly bolted from the inside. He decided to go round and have a look at the back of the house: he glanced at his watch and reckoned he had an hour before it would begin to get dark.

From towards the front of the house came the brief sound of falling glass. It was hard to describe, but it was as if the noise had ended early, before the glass had time to shatter – like a suppressed shout. He couldn't be sure if it had come from the front of the house or beyond it. He couldn't be sure what he'd heard.

The lawn was covered in leaves and all the windows looking out onto it had their curtains drawn. He tried the lock on the French windows, but like the side door they were firmly bolted from the inside. He paused as he thought he heard a sound, maybe a slight creak, and at the same time the starlings in a nearby tree fled noisily. He was used to the silences outside a busy town or city, when small sounds become magnified. He crouched down on the terrace that ran the width of the house. It was free of debris and appeared to have been swept recently. He thought about sitting on the wooden bench and enjoying a cigarette. But time was pressing and he turned to go back to the side gate.

'Who are you?'

It took him a while to make out the person who'd spoken to him. She was standing at the end of the dark alley against the side gate, dressed in black, the same colour as the wood behind her. They were about twelve feet apart from each other.

'I asked who you are, what are you doing trespassing here?'

The woman stepped forward, some light now falling on a pretty face with an angry expression on it. Prince glanced behind him to check no one else was there and tried to peer beyond her to see if she was alone, even though the gate was almost shut. He was as good as trapped and knew he'd need to make a decent fist of talking himself out of it.

'I'm terribly sorry; I'm an old friend of Arthur's – Arthur Chapman-Collins. We worked together at the Treasury and were great chums and then I was posted to India in… what, '36 it must have been. We kept in touch, exchanged Christmas cards as one does, and then of course the damn war started and we lost touch altogether.' He paused to catch his breath, aware that he was rambling and probably sounded nervous, which was no bad thing. Bumbling fools didn't appear sinister.

'And what are you doing here now?'

'I'm back home for the first time in many years and I thought I'd look dear Arthur up. I couldn't find a telephone number for him and I've got all the time in the world, so I thought I'd come out to Gerrards Cross and see him.'

'Did you not think of trying the Treasury?'

'No, I rather had a falling-out with them, you see.'

'So you came up here in the middle of the day, a weekday…'

'I do realise that. I take it he's not here?'

'Arthur died a few years ago. I'm most surprised you didn't know.'

'Good heavens – poor Arthur! Whatever happened?' He held his hand to his forehead in shock.

She'd moved a step closer to him, her arms crossed angrily in front of her, looking him up and down.

'He passed away suddenly while on holiday in Ireland.'

'Goodness gracious, that's appalling. When was that?'

'Five years ago. I can't quite believe you hadn't heard; you did say you were great chums.' There was a sceptical tone to her voice.

Prince shook his head. 'I know, and I suppose it's times like this that one so regrets not having kept in touch.'

'What did you say your name is?'

He paused for longer than he meant to. 'George, George Nicholson.' He held out his hand to shake hers but she took a step back. 'Are you a neighbour, may I ask?'

'I keep an eye on the house.'

'Does anyone live here?'

'His brother Charles, but he's away in the forces now.'

'Of course.'

'This gate was locked, Mr Nicholson.'

'I can assure you I found it open.'

The woman had now opened the side gate and moved aside, indicating he should leave. Once they were on the gravel drive, he turned to face her. 'I hope you don't mind me mentioning this – one doesn't want to be indiscreet – but I had heard Arthur had left the Treasury rather suddenly. I don't know if you know anything about that?'

'I really wouldn't know.'

Above him a tiny movement caught his eye. He glanced up at the house but saw nothing, though something didn't seem right. A large crow had settled on the ridge of the roof and appeared to be staring at him. As he watched, another half-dozen crows landed on the ridge, all adopting the same inquisitive pose.

'I think perhaps I'd better leave now...'

'I think you better had, Mr Nicholson.'

He stepped out onto the pavement, then turned back to the woman. 'I'm terribly grateful for your help. May I ask your name?'

She shot him a look that made it clear she wasn't going to answer. 'If you don't mind, I'll lock the front gate now.'

As she bent down to fasten the padlock, he scanned the house. Something definitely wasn't right.

'There we are. You'll be wanting to get on your way now. Is there anything you'd wish me to say to Charles when I next write to him?'

'Only to please pass on my condolences.'

'Perhaps you'd like to give me your address and telephone number?'

'I'm afraid I'm waiting to sort out my accommodation – you know how it is. I tell you what, when I find somewhere, I'll drop Charles a line here. May I ask, had poor Arthur had been unwell?'

'He'd been under a lot of stress, Mr Nicholson.'

He'd hoped to watch where the woman went after he left. He walked slowly down the lane back towards the town centre, glancing round every so often, but she remained standing outside the front gate like a sentry, her arms firmly folded, watching him to make sure he was on his way. He had no doubt that she'd remain there for some time to come.

On the train journey back to London, he reflected on what had been a largely unsatisfactory visit. He'd learnt little more than he already knew, and his cover story hadn't been good enough: it wouldn't stand up to much scrutiny if the woman was anything more than a nosy neighbour. But back at the basement flat near King's Cross, his unease remained. There was something about the house in Gerrards Cross that bothered him. He'd seen or heard something other than the sound of the falling glass; it had caught his attention but he couldn't put his finger on what it was.

He put in a call to Lance King through the MI5 exchange.

'How was your trip to Buckinghamshire?'

'Not wholly satisfactory, if I'm honest. Something's not right.'

'In what respect?'

'That's what I'm not sure about. Did you have any luck with the request I made this morning?'

'I thought you said tomorrow would be fine?'

'I did, but I just thought maybe...'

167

'As it happens, you're in luck. Apparently we have a very good man at the police station in Rotherhithe – an inspector.'

'And?'

'There is a Lenny Fenton in their manor, as they call it, who fits the bill: career as a rather unsuccessful house burglar, convictions for violence, a few spells in prison and known to be active on the far right before the war.'

'How old is he?'

'Fifty-six.'

'Too old to be conscripted then. And do they know what he's up to these days?'

'No, our contact at the local police station says that in the past couple of years Fenton's been quiet. He's not been arrested since 1940, and even that was bothering you?'

'No, Lance, there was something else. If only I could put my bloody finger on it.'

Chapter 17

Prince was in Bermondsey, heading for one of the pubs Lenny Fenton was known to frequent.

'I wouldn't go to both of them on the same evening,' the inspector had warned. 'It'll look suspicious.'

'I realise that. Which of the two would you recommend?'

'Ha! I wouldn't recommend either of them: the Duke of York can be quiet on a weekend night, so I'd suggest the Tower Tavern on Jamaica Road. Have you ever been to Bermondsey?'

'No.'

The inspector frowned, as if wondering whether to let Prince in on a confidence. 'Always feels to me that that area gets dark an hour earlier than the rest of London and gets light an hour later. It's like another city, not part of this country. Best be on your guard. The Tower's main entrance is on Jamaica Road, but I'd suggest you use the side entrance on Drummond Road.'

Prince had walked the mile or so from London Bridge station with the aim of getting a feel for the place and the best routes away from the pub should he need them. It was the poorest area he'd ever seen in England, at times reminding him of bomb-ravaged parts of Nazi Europe. The atmosphere was reminiscent of scenes from a Hogarth painting: it was eight o'clock in the evening, but young children were gathered on street corners and he picked up the sounds of shouting and arguing as he walked along. On almost every block he was asked for money, the demands more pressing and pointed as he reached Jamaica Road. He could begin to see what the inspector meant. Even though he'd dressed in shabby clothes to befit the hapless George Nicholson, he still felt self-conscious. He was beginning to feel as exposed as he'd felt in occupied Europe.

By this stage of the war the strict blackout had been replaced by what the newspapers were calling the 'dim-out', where lighting was permitted as long as it was no brighter than the moonlight. Some of the houses he passed seemed to disregard this, and as he neared the pub, a bright light shone out from a window with its curtains open. There was a loud shout and then the curtains opened at the window next to it, jolting his memory. He now realised what it was that had so troubled him as he'd left the house in Gerrards Cross.

When he'd first approached the house, the downstairs windows had all been shuttered, and those on the first floor – the bay window and two smaller ones either side of it – had had curtains tightly drawn against them. But when he'd looked up at the house as the woman locked the gate, something had registered in his mind that only now did he recall: the curtains in one of the upstairs rooms had been opened.

And that jogged another memory. When he'd arrived at the house there'd been an empty milk bottle on the doorstep. It was such a commonplace sight he'd not consciously thought it odd that an empty house would have a milk bottle. But now in his memory he pictured the front of the house when he'd left: the bottle wasn't there, which could account for the sound of falling glass he'd heard when he was in the garden.

As he replayed this in his mind, he paused, and a boy took this as a cue to ask for money. Prince handed him a threepenny bit and carried on walking towards the pub, looking up at the windows in the hope that they might tell him more. By the time he reached Drummond Road, he was certain of what he'd seen. When he'd approached the Chapman-Collins home, the house was firmly locked and bolted and all the windows were covered either by shutters or curtains. When he'd left, one curtain had been opened. And a milk bottle had disappeared.

Someone had been in the house.

–

He'd expected the pub to fall silent when he entered it, for a roomful of heads to turn towards him, eyes to remain fixed on him as people whispered into their companions' ears. He was familiar with the atmosphere of suspicion that greeted the police in places where they weren't wanted, and this sense had been heightened many times over entering bars and cafés in occupied Europe, where his life depended on him not standing out.

One or two people glanced at him, but most seemed anxious not to lose their place at the crowded bar. A couple of prostitutes eyed him up as a potential client: one of them said something to the other and they both laughed loudly. Prince smiled weakly in their direction and looked round for a friendly face, someone he could say good evening to and remark on the weather: 'nice and warm in here!'

He always made a point of doing this, striking up some kind of conversation – ideally a brief one. It helped if anyone was watching him; they would hopefully think he knew people – that he wasn't a stranger. That was the worst thing you could be if you didn't want to arouse suspicion: a stranger.

A gap opened at the bar and he slipped in and ordered a pint of bitter, telling the barmaid to keep any change. The pub was L-shaped and the part he was in – by the side door – was the smaller part. The front of the bar was a much larger room, and he edged his way round into it.

By the time he got there, he was aware that people were looking at him; not many, but a few men certainly, and one group in particular: half a dozen men in their forties and fifties standing together at the far end of the bar, a cloud of greyish-brown cigarette smoke hanging over them. Along the wall near them was a silent piano, and Prince walked over to it, placing his pint glass on top and getting out a packet of cigarettes. It was too hot and smoky in the pub for him to really fancy one, but the process of taking it out and lighting it gave him an opportunity to look round the room. He reckoned nine out of ten customers were men, quite a few of what he reckoned would be military age. On a Saturday night he'd have expected to see more women. This was probably the kind of place where men didn't take their wives.

He moved over to the bar to pick up an ashtray and found himself alongside the group of men who'd been watching him since he came in. As he reached for the ashtray one of them pushed it beyond his reach. It was a deliberately provocative act, the kind designed to start a fight, and Prince's instinct was to ignore it and walk away.

'People usually ask if they want to borrow an ashtray.'

The man was leaning back, like a boxer moving away from the reach of a punch. He could have been anything from his mid forties to his late sixties, two or three days' growth of beard, the complexion of someone who worked outdoors and bright blue eyes filled with menace.

Never be too polite… Don't appear to be too reasonable or under-standing… Standing your ground arouses less suspicion than walking away with your tail between your legs…

'Didn't realise it was your ashtray.' The accent: dropping the 'I', the 'was' sounding more like 'wuh'.

'Not seen you in here before.' It was a voice at the back of the group.

Six pairs of eyes were now trained on Prince, all daring him to say something.

'No, you wouldn't have done 'cos I've not been in here before, have I?' He sounded matter-of-fact rather than aggressive.

The man who'd first spoken to him – the one who'd pushed the ashtray away – bent towards him.

'You're not from round here, are you?'

Prince shook his head, wondering if now was the time to offer them cigarettes. *Not yet.*

'Don't say a lot, do you?'

He was aware that two of the group had now moved round behind him and he was surrounded.

'Less said the better.'

'Mister smart-fucking-arse, eh?'

He kept his head slightly bowed, avoiding eye contact, and noticed they all wore steel-capped boots. He reckoned he'd be able to push his way away from the group but doubted he'd get as far as the main entrance.

'No, I'm just minding my business and trying to smoke a fucking cigarette.'

The men glanced at each other, as if deciding what to do.

'Look, I'm sorry; I didn't mean to be rude. I'm knackered, I've been walking around all day and all week trying to find a job. Here...' He looked around furtively as he took out his cigarettes. 'I nicked these the other day. Help yourselves.'

They all helped themselves. 'You got any more packets you want to get rid of?'

'Not on me.'

It seemed to help. One of them brought Prince's pint over from the piano.

'You not in the forces, then?'

Prince laughed sarcastically and stared into his pint. *Angry.* 'I was, and I can tell you they were the worst three fucking years of my life, and there's some competition for that, believe me.'

'What happened?'

He looked round and edged closer to the men, dropping his voice as they crowded round him.

'A fucking Jew officer tried to tell me what to do: so I told *him* what to do!'

The men laughed, a couple of them slapping him hard on the back.

'What happened? You deserve a bloody medal for that!'

'I hoped I'd get slung out, but they threw the book at me. You heard of the Glasshouse in Aldershot?'

The group all grimaced and one of them pointed at a man at the back of the group. 'Sid's been in there, haven't you?'

The man called Sid nodded and stepped forward. 'Worst fucking prison I've ever been in, and I've been in a few. I was on the fourth floor: what floor were you on?'

'Second – but there are only three floors at the Glasshouse.'

'Course, mate, I get my prisons mixed up!'

The others nodded, and one of them asked, 'What happened after that? You get thrown out of the army?'

Prince turned round to check no one was listening in, then moved even closer to his new friends. 'I didn't wait around to find out... I thought they might send me to one of those labour battalions – too much like hard work for me. So I disappeared. They're still looking for me.'

'How long ago was that?'

'Two and a half years back. At least I'm my own man, but now I've had enough. I thought it might be easier to find work if I came to London, but no luck so far.'

'Where you living?'

'Some doss house up near King's Cross.'

'Long way from here.'

'I know, you don't need to tell me. I thought I'd come down to this part of London to see what the docks are like – I'd heard you can get hired for a day, no questions asked.'

'Not on a Saturday night you can't.'

'I thought I'd look around first, work out where to go before I come back next week.'

'What did you say your name is?'

'It's George.'

'Just George?'

'Nicholson, George Nicholson.'

'We may be able to help you out, George. Come back here Monday evening and—'

'Nah, best make it Tuesday, Sid.'

'Roy's right, come back here seven o'clock Tuesday evening. And don't say anything to anyone before then.'

Prince finished his pint and muttered something about needing to get back. He'd see them on Tuesday.

'And you could bring some of those cigarettes you said you nicked.'

He turned to leave but had only taken a couple of steps when he heard 'Come back here!' He felt himself go cold and wondered if he was close enough to the door to make a run for it. He turned round slowly. It was one of the men who hadn't spoken before. He had a pencil in his hand and a piece of paper in front of him on the bar. 'What regiment was it you said you were in, George?'

—

They gathered in his basement flat on the Sunday afternoon: Lance King, Audrey and the police inspector from Rotherhithe police station. Prince carefully recounted every detail he could recall.

'So none of them looked like this man?' The police inspector was showing him a mugshot of Fenton. He'd already apologised for not bringing it on the Friday.

'Definitely not.'

'I think the one you said was called Sid – darkish complexion, blue eyes – that's probably Sid McConnell, a known associate of Fenton's. I wouldn't be surprised if Lenny's there when you go back on Tuesday.'

'I imagine they'll wait until then to check you out,' said Audrey. 'That's a promising sign.'

'Don't forget I promised them some packets of the cigarettes I said I'd nicked.'

'I'll get you a carton, don't worry,' said King. 'What brand was it?'

'Player's Medium Navy Cut – packets of ten.'

'Twelves packets in a carton: give them nine, looks more plausible.'

'I could try and get someone in the pub if you want – to keep an eye on you?' The inspector seemed keen to help.

Prince was about to say that was a good idea, but King said there was no need.

'And you're certain no one followed you back here last night?'

'I'm certain of it.'

'Very well. Spend Monday wandering around the docks – the ones on the south bank, where Fenton's most likely to hear about you: Greenland, Quebec, Canada, Albion and Lady – go to all of them and ask if there's any work. Make sure you give your name.'

'What if I get offered something?'

'Doubt you will, but in any case they'd usually start you the following day.'

–

From King's Cross Lance King went straight to his office in Mayfair. He was still wearing his overcoat as he stood at his desk and picked up the telephone.

'Bartholomew? You'd better come to see me first thing in the morning: I have a job for you on Tuesday night.

–

Prince timed his entry into the Tower Tavern for ten past seven: any earlier felt like he was being too eager, but arriving too late wouldn't do either. The collar of his thin and stained raincoat was turned up and he was wearing a cloth cap against the drizzle. Twice on the walk from London Bridge station he'd taken detours around the side streets off Jamaica Road to make sure he wasn't being followed. He was sure he wasn't, but as he approached the pub, he noticed a man leaning against a lamp post opposite the main entrance: the man kept his eyes on him, carefully tracking his movements. There was no doubt he was watching him. Prince was used to more subtlety. He was sure he could see another man in Drummond Street, watching the entrance there.

When he entered the pub, he paused, looking around, unable to see anyone from the group he'd met on Saturday. The main bar was quiet but the sand-strewn wooden floor was already damp and the room smelled of rain and sweat. A barmaid caught his eye and waved him over.

'You're George, aren't you?'

He nodded and said he was when he last looked, and she smiled as if it was the first time she'd heard that, revealing a set of yellow teeth stained with dark red lipstick. 'See that door over there, at the end of the bar? Go through there and up the stairs. Here's a pint to take with you.'

Sid met him at the top of the stairs and said he was sure George would understand if he searched him. Prince said he did and took out the opened carton of cigarettes he'd been keeping under his coat. Sid took them, saying nothing as he showed him into a narrow room lit by a bare yellow bulb. The wood-panelled walls were unevenly stained with what looked like dark paint. A couple of tables had been pushed together and a man was sitting behind them in the gloom beyond the light. Sid pointed to a chair opposite him and then pulled up a chair behind Prince.

He felt uncomfortable. There was an uneasy atmosphere in the room and he wasn't sure how to break it. He took a sip from his beer. 'I brought you the cigarettes.' The man behind the table nodded, his face still concealed by shadow. After a while, he noisily scraped his chair forward and his face became visible. It was unquestionably Lenny Fenton. His mugshot hadn't done full justice to a scar that ran in an almost perfectly straight line from his nostril to his jaw, giving him a permanent sneer. The photograph hadn't managed to capture the scar's redness and how disfiguring it was. Fenton said nothing as he gazed at Prince, the familiar look of someone sizing him up.

'They tell me you're a deserter, George Nicholson. I want you to tell me your story.' He hadn't introduced himself.

Prince started talking about the incident on guard duty in May 1941, but Fenton stopped him. 'Start at the beginning. I want your life story. I like hearing about other people's lives: it's a hobby of mine.'

Remembering to be vague about dates and places, he talked about his miserable childhood and leaving home, he mentioned the Mosley rallies (*no, I'm no good with dates*), how he'd been conscripted, his reluctance to be in the army and his doubts about the war, the boredom and rigour of army training, the injustices meted out to him, the nightmare year spent at the Glasshouse in Aldershot and then his desertion and the past two and a half years on the run.

'I don't understand why you didn't go to that hearing after you were released,' Fenton said. 'Why turn yourself into a fugitive when they'd have thrown you out the army?'

It was a good question and he replied with a long rant about how Jews and communists had taken over the country and he didn't trust anyone and couldn't be sure they wouldn't throw him in a labour battalion, or worse still send him back to the Glasshouse, and if they did he'd have topped himself and… He was aware he'd raised his voice and was sounding angry and unsettled.

'If they were gonna do that they wouldn't have released you, would they?'

'I see that now, of course, but at the time… I think the year I spent there turned my mind, to be honest: I wasn't behaving normally.'

'And since then?'

'Moving around looking for work… thieving here and there. Found a woman in Norfolk whose husband was in the Far East and stayed there for a while until her neighbours became suspicious. But it was getting harder so I came down to London before Christmas: got some portering work at King's Cross and then Euston but then lost that 'cos they said I nicked a coat, and now I'm desperate to be honest with you. Sorry, do you mind if I ask your name?'

Fenton looked affronted and shrugged. 'What is it you want, George?'

'I've had enough of being a fugitive. When I met Sid and his mates on Saturday I got the impression they might be able to help. I need new papers and maybe somewhere safe to stay for a while.'

Fenton leaned back in his chair until it was balancing on two legs. His arms were folded high on his chest and his gaze was unrelenting.

'What do you make of this war?'

'I'm not sure what you mean.'

Fenton sounded exasperated. 'Now that it looks like this country's going to win it – what do you make of that?'

Prince drank his beer: it wouldn't do to come across as too clever. 'I don't know, I'm no politician… I just wonder whether the right side's won, if you know what I mean… Well, not so much whether the right side's won but whether the wrong side lost.'

It sounded far too clever.

'Don't understand.'

'The fucking Russians will rule Europe now, won't they – them and the Jews, or what's left of them.' Behind him he could hear Sid chuckling, but Fenton's expression remained unchanged. Prince wondered if it was something to do with his scar.

'Come with me.'

Fenton stood up and turned round, and as he did so, a door behind him Prince hadn't spotted in the gloom opened. On the

179

other side of it was a fire escape, and Fenton paused for Prince to catch up. Sid was behind them. The fire escape seemed to lead down to the rear of the pub. The drizzle had now turned to heavy rain, making the metal steps quite precarious.

'Where are we going?'

There was no reply. Sid was so close to him he could feel his body pushing against him. At the foot of the fire escape was the yard behind the pub, piles of beer barrels and crates of empty bottles, a wall behind which would be the alley. As far as Prince could make out, one of the double gates in it was ajar, with the figure of a man just visible in the dark. Sid guided him by the elbow under the fire escape until they were standing by the closed back door to the pub.

No one said a word for a while. He was aware that at least one other man had joined them in the dark. The only sounds were of the heavy rain and the pinging noise it made as it bounced off the fire escape. There was also the sound of the men breathing: heavy and maybe slightly nervous. Prince was sure they'd hear the sound of his heart beating. He caught Sid's eye; Sid smiled, and what little light there was caught the glint of a gold tooth.

'What you staring at?'

Prince said he wasn't staring at anything.

'You Catholic?'

He said he wasn't.

'So you won't be needing the last rites then, will you?' Sid gave a throaty laugh until Fenton told him to shut up.

'Stand here.' Sid had turned him round so he was facing the closed door. Fenton knocked on it. Prince heard someone open the door and Fenton said, 'It's me, get her.'

They stood in the rain, the mesh cover of the fire escape giving the effect of standing in a shower. Since entering the pub there'd been an air of menace and hostility, but now he realised how dangerous his predicament was.

He heard footsteps approaching the door from inside the pub, and as they came closer, Sid took out a torch and shone a powerful light in his face. He could hardly keep his eyes open.

'Stand still, don't move.'

The door opened and he was aware of two or three more people in front of him but couldn't make out any features. Fenton was holding him tightly by the shoulder and at least one other man had moved behind him, his body pressing against his.

'Is this the man calling himself George Nicholson?'

'I think so, but I'll need to hear him say something.' It was a woman's voice and there was something very familiar about it.

Fenton tightened his grip on his shoulder. 'Go on, speak; say who you are and what you're doing here… Go on.'

The light moved closer to his face and he could feel its warmth. 'George… George Nicholson and I'm here at the pub…'

'Keep going.'

'Well it's a Tuesday night and it's raining and I'm really not sure what the hell this is all about all…'

'It's him.'

'You certain?'

'Of course I'm certain: that's definitely the same George Nicholson from the other day – the one who said he was Arthur's friend.'

'That's enough,' said Fenton harshly. 'In you go now.'

Sid moved slightly, enough for the beam of the torch to leave Prince's face for a couple of seconds, and in that time he caught a glimpse of the woman, lit by the light from inside the pub.

He knew who she was now.

And he knew he was in trouble.

–

Four men surrounded him: Fenton and Sid, another who'd appeared behind them and had pinned his hands behind him, and one of the men who'd come out of the pub. He'd been shoved from under the fire escape so that now he was in the open yard, where there was more light. He could see the group exchanging glances, as if unsure what to do next. They appeared to defer to Len Fenton, who said nothing, his hands thrust deep in his pockets, shoulders hunched and watching Prince like a fighter.

'Look,' said Prince, his voice shaking, 'I don't know what the hell's going on, but you don't seem to believe me and I promise you I'm just someone who came to you for help. I mean, who was that woman? I only need—'

'Shut up!' Fenton growled. 'I hate people like you... scum, traitors to their people.' He nodded at Sid, who removed something from a pocket and held it close to Prince's face. As he did so, there was a clicking sound and the blade of his flick knife flew open.

Fenton had moved closer, the red scar on his face pulsating.

'By the time we've finished with you, we'll have found out who the hell you are. You told Sid here you wanted a job in the docks, eh? Well I tell you what, George Nicholson or whoever the hell you are, you're certainly going to get your wish and end up in the docks.'

For the first time, Fenton smiled.

Prince's first thought was that he'd managed to escape from the Gestapo in Berlin so he ought to be able to do the same with some overweight thugs in the East End, but as he looked around, it was clear he was trapped. The yard at the rear of the pub had a high wall and the gate was now shut. Sid was waving the flick knife in front of his face, allowing its cold tip to touch him just under the eye. He could smell the wet metal as the blade moved down the bridge of his nose.

'I honestly don't know what the hell you're talking about. I think you've mixed me up with someone else: my name is George Nicholson and I'm a deserter from the army; check it out if you want.'

'We did.'

'Well there we are then – so what's this all about?'

'Oh yes, we found out a man called George Nicholson was in the Nottinghamshire and Derbyshire Regiment and was jailed in 1941 and released from the Glasshouse in 1942 and then deserted. But we don't think you're really George Nicholson.'

'I'm telling you—'

One of them punched him hard in the stomach, and as he doubled up, the man behind him grabbed him by the hair and yanked his head back.

'No, *I'm* telling *you* – just you listen. I don't give a fuck whatever clever identity Special Branch or MI5 or the Jews have thought up for you... I don't buy it. All I know is that you turned up at a house in Gerrards Cross last Friday and were asking questions about an associate of mine. The lady who identified you just now, she found you there, didn't she? Like a fool, you used the same name and spun her some nonsense about being an old friend who'd come to renew your acquaintance after all these years. Of course I heard all about it and couldn't believe my luck when you came down to my manor using the same name. I reckon you were after me too.'

'I don't even know who you are.'

'You know full well I'm Lenny Fenton.'

'I've never heard of you... I promise you I—'

Another punch, this one to his groin and much harder, and as he sank to his knees he felt a knee jammed hard into his kidneys. He thought he was about to pass out. It appeared they thought so too, because they allowed him to stay on his knees as he struggled to regain his breath. Between two of the men's legs he could just make out a stack of boxes against one of the side walls. It was perhaps his best chance, though a slim one. He was hauled to his feet once more.

'I want you to tell me everything: your real name, who you're working for, what your mission is and what you know about me and the person you were looking for in Gerrards Cross. If you mess me around, I promise you you'll suffer – we know which parts of you to cut off first.'

'I don't believe you.'

Fenton looked genuinely puzzled, as if this was the reaction he was least expecting. He himself threw a punch that connected hard with Prince's jaw, then at least two of the others laid into him. They only stopped when Prince writhed on the ground in agony. He knew he had just seconds to act. He groaned and made sure his breathing sounded pained.

'Leave him a minute. We still need him to tell us who he is and who he works for. Let him come round.'

Prince remained as still as he could and thought of his unarmed combat training in a cold barn in Derbyshire, the trainer impressing on him how to take advantage of someone standing over you.

They'll be off balance.

Use gravity.

Pull them down.

Sid bent down to pick him up, and as he did so, Prince sat up, barging his shoulder into the other man's knees, causing him to fall over. He leapt to his feet, knowing any advantage he had would last no more than two or three seconds, and sprinted towards the side wall, grabbing an empty bottle from a crate then pushing the box into the path of those following him. Fenton was closest, and Prince spun round, swinging the empty beer bottle into his face. Fenton screamed and staggered back but the other two were closing in on him and Prince realised there was a searing pain down his left-hand side. He clambered onto the pile of boxes, his hands managing to grasp the top of the wall, and was about to pull himself over it when he felt his ankles being grabbed and heard the ominous sound of a revolver being cocked.

He managed to kick away the hand holding one ankle, but at that moment he heard a shot and the noise of a bullet thudding into the wall next to him, shards of brick spitting out. They had hold of both of his ankles again and were pulling him down. He was dragged along the ground and ended up sprawled next to Fenton, who was kneeling, blood streaming from his face.

'You had to use a fucking gun and alert the whole of fucking London, didn't you? Finish the bastard off and let's get the fuck out of here. Quick...'

Prince looked up to see a gun inches from his face. The man holding it was using two hands to keep it steady, a look of keen concentration on his face, his tongue poking out of his mouth. And then came the bullet.

He was surprised to feel nothing at first, and then there was an enormous weight on him, as if he was being forced through the wet concrete deep into the earth. Darkness enveloped him, and as he drifted slowly away, the only feeling he had was that at least he wasn't in too much pain. The last thing he was aware of was the sound of more bullets, which struck him as excessive.

Chapter 18

London, January 1945

'Are you a religious man, George?'

The room he was in was so bright it took a while for him to focus. The comfortable bed with crisp white sheets, the equipment around him and the presence of a nurse smiling sweetly at him from the end of the bed suggested he was in a hospital. The person repeated the question and he realised it was Lance King. A man in a raincoat stood next to him. He looked like a travelling salesman.

'I asked if you're religious?'

Prince said he wasn't, not really, and tried to sit up, but there was a sharp pain in his left side and the nurse patted his foot and told him to keep still, they were going to give him some medicine in a minute.

'Will it make him drowsy, Nurse?'

'For a couple of hours certainly.'

'Perhaps you could leave it for a while? I'll call you back in when we're finished and then you can do what you need with him.' He winked at Prince.

'This is Bartholomew,' King said when the nurse left the room. He slapped the travelling salesman on the back. 'He works for us. I arranged for him to have a team at the Tower Tavern tonight; last thing I wanted was for the local police to get involved. I thought if Fenton did show up you might end up in a bit of a scrape. Good job he was there. That's why I asked if you're religious.'

'I'm not sure what you mean.'

'If I remember correctly from Sunday school, the original Bartholomew was associated with miracles. Our modern-day Bartholomew certainly performed a miracle tonight.'

'What happened?'

Bartholomew undid his raincoat and pulled up a chair. 'I put in a team of four, including myself. Two watching outside, two of us inside: ideally I'd have had another two and been able to cover more of the perimeter, but we're a bit stretched at the moment. I was concerned when you went upstairs so thought I'd give it ten minutes and then go and have a look. When I saw you weren't there, we went round to the back of the pub and got there just in time to see a man standing over you with a gun. We shot him and then piled in. One of my chaps threw himself on top of you. There was a bit of a scuffle and Fenton was shot.'

'Dead?'

'Afraid so, yes, along with the chap who was about to shoot you.'

'Obviously Bartholomew and his men did a first-class job.' There was a slightly disappointed look on Lance King's face. 'Ideally we would have wanted Fenton alive, but there we are. On balance, better he's dead than you are, eh?'

Prince said he agreed and wondered how long it would be before he was allowed to have the pain relief he'd been promised.

'Soon, very soon. The two we have in custody are Sid McConnell and another thug called Carter. They're not talking, but I'd be surprised if they know anything. The one we really needed was Fenton. You'd better tell us what happened.'

Prince did his best to recount the events of the evening: being taken to the upstairs room, the search, the questions from Fenton and then going outside and the woman.

'What woman?'

'It was the woman who caught me at Chapman-Collins's house in Gerrards Cross last week. They'd brought her along to identify me. Once I realised it was her, I knew the game was up. It was a bad mistake to have the same identity – using George Nicholson in both places. Did you catch her?'

'It's the first we've heard about her: you're sure it was the same woman?'

'Absolutely certain – no question about it.'

'Did you get her name when you met her last week?'

'No – she said she was keeping an eye on the house for Arthur's brother Charles.'

'Who actually has a home in London and is a prisoner of the Japs. Bartholomew, we need to send a team to Gerrards Cross to check this out. What time is it?'

'Eleven o'clock, sir.'

'Send in a couple of chaps to keep a watch on the house until the morning, and then I can sort out the local police and get a warrant to go in and have a look at the place. You're bloody lucky, Prince: doctors say you've got away with some nasty bruising and probably a cracked rib or two, but nothing that's going to warrant an off-games slip. A night here and we should have you back in action tomorrow.'

'I'd like to see my son.'

'I think that's probably—'

'What day is it?'

'Well it's almost Wednesday, but—'

'Get a car to take me to Lincoln in the morning and bring me back Thursday morning and I'll be as right as rain. By then you may have found out what on earth's going on in Gerrards Cross. Now if it's all right with you, Lance, I would like some of that painkiller.'

'Of course, just as soon as you've given us a detailed description of the woman.'

–

Prince was picked up from his home in Lincoln on the Thursday morning and driven straight to the centre of London.

He had no idea where he was, other than that they passed Holborn station shortly before pulling into an underground garage. The driver escorted him in a lift to an upper floor and he was shown into a musty-smelling room with its blinds down and four people round a table. Hugh Harper and Lance King were there along with Audrey and Bartholomew.

'I'm afraid you've arrived later than we'd thought – the tea's cold. There's plenty of good news, though, not least that I went to see Sir Roland yesterday and he kindly arranged for Audrey to be seconded to his office for a few weeks. It's a technicality, of course; means she can work for me without colleagues in MI5 realising.'

'The other good news is that Bartholomew had a most productive trip to Gerrards Cross.' King gestured towards Bartholomew for him to continue. Prince noticed he was still wearing his raincoat.

'First of all, the woman who identified you at the pub: one of my chaps does recall seeing a woman matching her description leave just before we went looking for you. Says she appeared to be in a hurry but not so much that it alerted him, if you know what I mean. We asked around in Gerrards Cross: there are twenty-two houses on that road including the Chapman-Collins one, and none of the people we spoke to was able to identify a woman matching that description. None of the women living in that street look anything like her.

'It's a very private area, as you know – high hedges, long drives – the kind of place where neighbours don't have a lot of opportunity to see what's going on in other houses however much they may want to. The only neighbour who was able to be of any assistance was an elderly gentleman who lives next door who says he was friendly with the late Mrs Chapman. According to him, he received a letter a few years ago from Charles Chapman to say he was keeping the house going and would arrange for a cleaner to visit every so often. He says he does very occasionally see a woman go in or out but he couldn't give a decent description: I fear his eyesight isn't terribly good and nor is his memory, to be honest.

'However,' Bartholomew leaned back, sounding more animated, 'I am convinced someone has been living there recently.' He smiled and folded his arms, bowing his head to indicate that the others should appreciate the significance of what he'd said. 'The place rather reminded me of Goldilocks and the Three Bears, and all of my team who went in came to the same conclusion that someone had been there. Of course there was nothing as blatant as an unmade bed or porridge in the kitchen, but the house wasn't cold in the way houses are when they've had no heating in years, there was little dust and there was just a very clear sense that someone had been around. There were towels in the bathroom, for instance, and a bar of soap by the sink that looked as if it had been used recently.'

'The cleaning lady perhaps?'

'Perhaps, but there's something else: in the kitchen we found half a dozen glasses and two mugs by the sink, and—'

'Fingerprints?'

'Indeed. We also found two bottles in the lounge, on a side table by an armchair: one whisky and one cognac. I had a fingerprint chappie with us and managed to lift Arthur Chapman-Collins's prints from both bottles, both of the mugs and two of the glasses.'

Audrey leaned forward. 'What you ought to know is that in 1939 I had gone to the trouble of obtaining the Chapman-Collins's fingerprints. It was quite irregular, of course, but then so was much of what we were up to. We lifted them from a glass he used from when he was being questioned.'

Harper clapped his hands in celebration. 'Well there we are then – the bastard's alive!'

'I don't wish to pour cold water on this, but I thought fingerprints can last an awfully long time?' Lance King looked apologetic.

'They can, but our fingerprint expert assures me these prints were less than a year old, and quite possibly from the past month.'

'Chapman-Collins could well have been in the house last week,' said Prince. 'It would explain the open curtain on the upstairs window but doesn't explain why, if he's meant to be dead, he'd be hiding somewhere as obvious as the family home.'

'Who knows, but I imagine until last week he didn't think we suspected he was still alive,' said Harper. 'You turning up like that alerted him, and when you went looking for Fenton in Rotherhithe, the alarm bells really started ringing.'

'Christ knows where he's gone to ground. Is there anything in the house that could give us a clue as to where he is?'

'Not yet, Lance: we're searching it thoroughly but I'd be surprised if we turn anything up.'

'I'm not sure what we do now,' said Prince. 'If we can't find Chapman-Collins then we need another way of finding Milton.'

'And Byron and Donne too… either one of those will lead us to Milton.'

'Could Fenton have been either Byron or Donne – or the woman, or indeed any of the others on that list of people at the Pimlico hotel?'

'Not sure, Hugh. As far as I understand, there are just… what, seven more names on that list? Seven surnames, no first names or even initials, and no locations: is that correct, Audrey?'

She looked down at a folder in front of her and nodded before reading out the names: 'Bannister, Spencer, Davies, Philips, Cummings, Carver, Kemp: all fairly common names. It would be impossible to know where to start.'

'From what we've gathered about Fenton, it's not him. We found the bedsit he lived in and there was nothing there. Everything we know about him indicates he had neither the discretion nor the intelligence to be an undercover agent.'

'I wonder if we've been barking up the wrong tree all along.' Prince looked quite miserable.

'Possibly, but we have one last card to play.' Audrey looked up at him, a hint of a smile on her face. 'I think we should send you to prison.'

–

Prince was familiar enough with prisons to know that each had its own unique soundtrack. At Brixton Prison in south London he was struck by unidentifiable mechanical sounds, desperate shouts, lengthy echoes, the occasional scream followed by moments of total silence.

They were in the governor's office, a man with the appearance of a funeral director. He was being difficult: it was early evening and he'd made it clear he'd hoped to be home by now. A telephone call from the Home Office had told him to stay put. *Two men from one of our sections are on the way: ask them as few questions as possible and do what you can to help.*

'But what if Curtis refuses to see you?' he asked now.

'You'll need to persuade him, won't you?'

'It's not as easy as that.'

'This is a prison, isn't it?' As Lance King leaned forward, the governor nervously sat back. 'I thought you could force prisoners to do things?'

The governor shook his head.

'He's held under Defence Regulation 18B, isn't he?'

'Yes, we have a number of prisoners held here under that law and all are damn difficult. They think they're political prisoners and ought to be treated accordingly. Curtis is held because of what is termed "hostile association".'

'And does he have the right to challenge his detention?'

'They attempt to challenge their imprisonment all the time.'

'Tell him it's in connection with that then,' said Prince. 'Tell him two men from the Home Office have come to see him regarding his possible release. Don't look so worried, Governor: we'll deal with any consequences.'

Vince Curtis stared at the two men he'd been told were from the Home Office as if they were mad.

'What do you mean, you're here in connection with my release: what release?'

'You applied to be released from your 18B detention.'

'I applied when I was first arrested five years ago. I've appealed and hired a lawyer but haven't heard a thing for two years now, so what's all this suddenly about?'

'Don't you want to be released, Curtis?'

'I didn't catch your names.'

'We told you we're from the Home Office and I asked you whether you wanted to be released.'

'Of course I want to be bloody released: I've been kept in prison because of my political views. I've done nothing wrong.'

'Other than visit Nazi Germany on numerous occasions prior to the war, meet with officials of that country and be involved with individuals and movements hostile to the interests of the United Kingdom, thereby making yourself liable for detention under Section 1A of the Defence Regulation but not excluding,' Prince paused and looked up from the sheet he was reading from, 'liabilities under other sections of the Regulation.'

Vince Curtis shrugged. 'That was all before the war. I was entitled to my opinion. I still don't get why you've turned up now. Are you anything to do with that woman?'

'What woman?'

'The one who came at the end of last year. She shoved a photograph under my nose and wanted me to tell her who it was and give his address, weight, height and shoe size.'

King started to speak but felt Prince tap him on the thigh. *Wait.*

Neither of them said a word for a while, during which time Curtis's demeanour slowly changed from cocky to shifty and uncomfortable.

'You said you recognised the man as Arthur Walker.'

He looked around, hesitating. 'I said it *could* be him. I wasn't sure.'

'Let's cut to the chase, shall we, Curtis?' King pulled his chair forward. 'The distinct impression my colleague got was that you recognised the man and knew more about him than you were willing to say. I'm authorised to make you a promise here and now: if you supply us with information that leads us to this man, not a soul will know you were involved and furthermore you will be released from detention. An order from the Home Secretary can have you out of here within hours.'

The two men watched Vince Curtis think. They could almost read his tortured mind as he weighed the pros and cons: the price of freedom against the cost of betraying a comrade. Then he had to think about whether to believe them, whether they would take the information only to deny any knowledge of a deal.

Sweat started to glisten on the prisoner's brow and he ran his fingers through his hair and shifted in his seat. For a while he looked down and bit his lip; when he eventually glanced up, his eyes were watery and his voice uncertain.

'The war's nearly over, they say.'

'What does that have to do with it?'

'Means I'll be released soon anyway, won't I?'

Prince moved his chair close to the iron table separating them. 'It would be a mistake to assume that, Curtis. You'll be seriously underestimating our capacity for malice.'

Curtis raised his eyebrow, surprised. 'I've thought about it and realise I was mistaken. I don't know the man, no idea about him or his shoe size. I thought it could be an Arthur Walker, but I was wrong. Five years inside does things to your mind.'

Once the warder had taken Curtis back to his cell, Prince and King remained in the interview room. Both men looked surprisingly relaxed, even quite cheerful.

'I think that went rather well, don't you?'

'Indeed. How long do you think it will take?'

'No more than ten to fifteen minutes, I'd have thought.'

'You all right, Vince?'

Curtis looked round. It was just him and Len, the warder he most trusted. Len was more of a friend than anything else – in fact, he was a comrade.

'You know, Len... bastards wanting me to spill on comrades again. I remembered what you told me, stick to our principles and stick to our story and our cause will triumph.'

'It will indeed, Vince, as long as you don't allow yourself to be tricked by those commies and Jew-lovers. Come on, there's a nice meat pie waiting for you in my office.'

Curtis laughed and his paced quickened. Len was a true comrade who looked after him. He'd come to trust him.

The warder's office was cosy and warm and the meat pie excellent. Len locked the door and passed Curtis a hip flask. He knew Curtis could hold his drink but not his tongue.

'That was a treat, thanks, Len.'

'Well, with what patriots like you have to put up with, you deserve it. What were they after this time?'

'Arthur Walker again... they're obviously desperate to find him.' He leaned forward, so close the warder could see the thin red veins in his eyes. 'His name is actually Arthur Chapman-Collins and he's the real deal, Len. About as important as you can get – direct links with our friends in Germany.'

'So what happened to him?'

'Shouldn't be telling you this, but I know I can trust you. They were on to him just before the war but for some reason let him slip away and he then managed to fake his own death. He's still involved with... you know... our friends. I heard he spends some of his time at his old house somewhere in Buckinghamshire but most of it here in London, right under their noses!'

Vince laughed, whisky fumes catching the warder. Len laughed too, shaking his head in admiration, then patted Vince on his forearm. 'I don't know, clever bastard, eh? We need more like him. Whereabouts, Vince?'

'Whereabouts what?'

'You said he's right under their noses – I was wondering whereabouts that was.' He expected Vince to clam up again, but the prisoner shifted his chair closer and beckoned him forward.

'He's staying with the King and Queen, isn't he... in the palace!' He laughed almost manically but stopped suddenly when there was a knock at the door. By the time Len had assured a fellow warder that all was fine, Vince had decided it would be best if he went back to his cell.

–

'That's all he said?'

'Christ, sir, that's enough, isn't it? He seemed to know enough about Arthur Chapman-Collins and even said he's living in London.'

'Right under their noses apparently?' Prince had written everything down and was checking his notes.

'Yes, sir.'

'And you asked him where, and he replied...'

'Staying with the King and Queen – in the palace.'

Prince glanced at Lance King, who shook his head. 'He didn't say any more?'

'No, I told you: someone knocked on the door, but I think by then he'd said all he was going to say anyway.'

King nodded in agreement. 'Yes, I suppose you're right. Thank you Len – as helpful as ever.'

Prince closed his notebook. He was very pleased with how things had gone.

Chapter 19

Berlin, February 1945

By the start of February, Franz Rauter felt he was possibly the only person working for the regime in Berlin with cause to feel upbeat. He knew full well there were probably a few thousand people in the city who'd be glad to see a German defeat, and he was also well aware of the rumours that hundreds of Jews were still hiding there.

But for everyone else the pall of gloom that had descended since Stalingrad had now turned to despair. Everyone he knew was pessimistic and depressed, and although no one would admit it, most were frightened of what defeat would mean. He'd had one or two nervous conversations with some of the very few people he could confide in about when the Red Army would reach Berlin and what that would mean.

And on the morning of Tuesday 6 February it was clear that that was an even more likely prospect. The news had come through the previous day that the Red Army had crossed the River Oder. Soon they'd hear their artillery. There'd been an episode of gallows humour at work the previous week when they'd heard that Ecuador had declared war on Germany. This led to an amusing session with colleagues in Tirpitzufer as they studied a map of South America to check exactly where Ecuador was and then planned sophisticated espionage operations against it that would necessitate their being dispatched to the area immediately.

But that mood hadn't lasted long. On the Saturday night there'd been a massive air raid on Berlin. Schöneberg had been quite badly hit, although fortunately not around the Bayerisches Viertel, where Rauter lived. As a consequence of the air raid he'd spent much of the Sunday going over his plans: he'd wait until the Red Army was close to the city and then assume the civilian identity he'd been nurturing for the past few months. With luck it would get him away from the Russians and to some kind of safety.

But that wasn't the reason why he was feeling so upbeat. Since he had activated Milton, the agent in London had been producing first-class intelligence. The army High Command was delighted with what he had passed on about Arnhem, and while the intelligence about the Ardennes offensive had been more mixed, there was no question Milton was regarded as an excellent source. And now they were relying on him to provide information on the Allied plans for crossing the Rhine.

SS-Brigadeführer Walter Schellenberg was thrilled, of course. He was naturally claiming full credit for Agent Milton's intelligence, but privately, within the RSHA, he did have the grace to acknowledge Rauter's role in it. Indeed, on more than one occasion he'd told Rauter that his patience before activating Milton and the way he'd put in place Agent Byron as the radio operator and Agent Donne as the contact between the two was a perfect example of a well-run intelligence operation.

You should write it up in a textbook on espionage, Franz! If only we'd had more operations like this then we wouldn't be facing the… difficulties the Reich is going through at present.

So trusted was he that Schellenberg had allowed him to move back to his old office in Tirpitzufer from Prinz-Albrecht-Strasse. Rauter knew he wasn't in any danger – other than from RAF bombs and the encroaching Red Army. In Tirpitzufer, colleagues looked at him admiringly and not without a little envy. *Franz Rauter, our number one spy master – who'd have thought it!* Some of them had been sent to join front-line units in the east, their age and lack of combat experience deemed irrelevant.

And along with the kudos, he found he was enjoying running such a successful and well-regarded operation. It was undeniably exciting.

But by the afternoon of 6 February his mood had become more downbeat. A message had been received at Cuxhaven from Agent Byron and it was not good news. Word had reached Byron that MI5 seemed to have discovered that a man known as Chiltern was alive and were on to him. He wanted to know what he should do. Franz Rauter hadn't come across the name Chiltern before. He locked the door of his office and removed one of Otto Prager's notebooks from his safe. It took him a while to find what he was looking for among the pages of small, densely packed writing, some of it written horizontally, some vertically.

Chiltern, he discovered, was a man called Arthur Chapman-Collins, a Nazi sympathiser and the man who'd first identified Milton as a potential agent back in 1933, as well as various other agents – including Agent Byron himself. Chapman-Collins had been suspected by MI5 in 1939 and the Abwehr had helped him fake his death. As far as Franz Rauter could tell, he had been told to vanish, but now it appeared he'd failed to do that. He'd obviously been careless; they all were in the end.

Despite the chill of the afternoon, Rauter opened his office window and lit a cigar. He needed to think. If the British tracked down Chiltern, that could lead to Milton and Byron and the end of Rauter's spy ring. He shivered at the very thought of it: the inquiry he'd face, the fall from grace, and only if he was very fortunate would he be spared a criminal investigation, which meant becoming a guest of the Gestapo. He'd probably end his days hiding in the ruins of a building on the outskirts of Berlin alongside old men and young boys as they tried to hold up the Red Army with weapons from the Great War.

It didn't take him long to decide what to do – he realised he didn't have much choice. This was about his own survival as much as that of Milton, Byron and Donne. He remained by the open window long enough to finish his cigar, then closed it and turned back to his desk. He wrote four drafts of the message to Agent Byron. When he finally had one he was satisfied with, he put in a call: the senior cypher clerk was to report to him immediately.

'Encode it, Manfred, and have it sent from Cuxhaven tonight. Have them repeat the transmission tomorrow. Do you understand?'

Manfred said he did, but as he prepared to leave the room, Franz Rauter said he wanted one final look at the message. He read it through carefully, then nodded slowly and handed it back to the clerk. He was satisfied, but he'd wanted to be sure.

He had, after all, just signed a man's death warrant.

Chapter 20

London, February 1945

Hugh Harper lay dying in one of the guest bedrooms of the extensive Georgian country house in Hampshire that had been home to his family for half a dozen generations. The distant New Forest was just visible in the fading light.

The journey to his impending death was not nearly as painful as he'd spent a lifetime imagining it would be, but it was accompanied by regrets, as he'd always feared. He felt like he'd been asleep for days and slightly resented his wife having moved him during that time into a spare bedroom for his final days on earth. He could, however, see her point and was determined not to make a fuss; he didn't want to die with any rancour – there'd been enough of that in his life. He very much regretted his indiscretion in Paris a few years ago but felt now was not the time to raise it. He resolved to be as serene and dignified as he could manage. He'd spent the past hour thinking about his obituary in *The Times*. It would inevitably be somewhat sparse; they invariably were for people from his world.

Senior civil servant… Home Office… service to his country…

He hoped people would see through the code. He glanced at the wall, photographs of various animals hanging on the floral wallpaper. His eyes fell on Shooter, a red setter he'd got when they first married that had lived for fifteen wonderful years, quite the most outstanding dog he'd ever had. He felt tears fill his eyes and begin to trickle down his face and he wiped them away, annoyed at this display of emotion. With some effort he hauled himself up in bed and stared out at the willow tree in the middle of the lawn, its magnificent branches reminding him of a dancer frozen in motion. His grandfather had told him that his own grandfather had planted that tree and made him promise to care for it. Each year he waited for it to turn green once more, and when it did so, he'd be relieved he'd fulfilled his familial obligation. He felt his eyes fill with tears once more, at which moment his wife came into the bedroom more noisily than he thought was appropriate in the circumstances.

He told her how he felt, reaching out for her hand.

'Don't be ridiculous, Hugh: you have a nasty bout of influenza, and had you taken to your bed when you were first advised, you'd have probably been better by now. Instead you're lying here feeling sorry for yourself. I imagine you think you're dying as usual?'

He tried to argue, insisting she was relying on the diagnosis of one doctor, a man well past retirement age. Perhaps a glass of whisky would aid his recovery...

'You'll take the tablets he gave you and drink honey, glycerine and lemon.'

'But I heard him say I should drink.'

'He didn't mean alcohol, Hugh. Now come on, sit up and take these tablets.'

Later that evening he felt slightly better, well enough in fact to leave his bed. Once he was satisfied his wife was asleep, he crept downstairs and found an unopened bottle of single malt where he hid them from her in the boot room. An hour later, he was in a strange world, brought about he assumed by a combination of his illness, the medication and the whisky. He felt detached from reality and realised his mind had a strange clarity to it, for once not dealing with multiple worries at the same time but instead able to concentrate on one subject.

And as he lay there in the dark, the moon ahead of him broken up by the ghostly branches of the willow, his mind settled on the troubled search for the elusive Agent Milton.

Richard Prince had come highly recommended, but it was probably no fault of his that no progress had been made. Harper had set King and Prince a deadline of the end of January to find Milton, and that deadline had passed a week ago.

And now he had the generals on his back, insisting that the Allied plans for crossing the Rhine were being held up by his – *his* – failure to find the traitor.

He was convinced that Prince's instinct was correct, that their best way of finding Milton was through Arthur Chapman-Collins and the other attendees at the Pimlico hotel dinners. They'd made some progress – or so he'd thought – when they went to visit the chap at Brixton Prison. He played over and over in his mind what he'd said about Chapman-Collins; how he was living in London, right under their noses, staying with the King and Queen in the palace.

Harper was convinced the answer to the riddle lay in those three words: 'in the palace' – so much so that it had led to a major row with the royal household that had probably put paid to any slim chance he'd had of a knighthood. Harper's brother-in-law had been at Marlborough with Tommy Lascelles, the King's private secretary, and he'd hoped an informal approach would clear up the very remote possibility that Chapman-Collins could somehow indeed be at the palace with the King and Queen.

But Lascelles said he was too busy and was in any case spending most of his time at Windsor, so Harper had been palmed off with a nervous assistant private secretary, who completely overreacted – panicked would probably be a better word – and assumed MI5 believed there was a German spy at Buckingham Palace. It would be fair to say that all hell broke loose. The King heard about it and asked Churchill what the hell was going on, as a result of which even more hell broke loose and it required what Harper had to acknowledge was the admirably calm intervention of Sir Roland Pearson before the whole business was sorted out. One fortunate consequence was that at least the nervous assistant private secretary did have every single member of the household checked out and it was established that Arthur Chapman-Collins was not posing as a footman or a lady of the bedchamber, which Harper had always thought was only an outside chance of at best.

Somewhere around midnight, he began to think on different lines. They'd taken the phrase too literally. What if 'in the palace' didn't actually mean Buckingham Palace itself, or indeed any other royal palace, but another type of palace? His mind drifted as he walked through that area around Buckingham Palace and St James's, an area he knew well: it was where his mother's parents had lived and where he himself often walked on his way to his own town apartment. The pale green luminous hands on his bedside clock told him it was one o'clock as he strolled down Buckingham Gate and decided to turn left into Wilfred Street, and almost immediately saw the pub on the corner of Catherine Place.

It was the small hours of Thursday – 8 February – when Hugh Harper had his revelation about the Palace Arms, a pub where he'd drunk a few times. He set his alarm for six o'clock. He'd call Lance King first thing.

–

Early the same morning, Jim Maslin was woken by the sound of a key turning in the main door of his small flat in Shepherd's Bush. He was confused at first and glanced at his wristwatch on the bedside table: it was seven o'clock. By the time he reached for the knife he kept under the bed, the figure of a man was silhouetted in the doorway of the bedroom, leaning casually against it, his hat at a rakish angle and the lit end of his cigarette glowing orange-red in the gloom.

'Having a lie-in, Agent Donne?'

'Jesus Christ, Byron, I could have stabbed you.'

'Well you were certainly taking your time about it. Get dressed quickly and come into the lounge. I'll put the kettle on.'

Fifteen minutes later, Agent Donne was sitting next to Agent Byron at the small table, staring at the map Byron had sketched. His tea had turned cold in its cup, an unpleasant film shining on its surface. He no longer felt like drinking it but was already on his third cigarette, the remains of the other two stubbed out in the saucer.

'What time did you say your shift is today?' Byron asked.

'I told you, twelve noon to eight o'clock, but there's always overtime on that shift. Last night I didn't leave till eleven. I had to walk all the way back here.'

Byron held his wrist high, the dial catching the gloomy light of the tiny room. 'It's nearly half seven now. Let's go through it once more. Mornings are the best time to catch him anyway, and you can travel into town during the rush hour. You'll need to be away by a quarter past eleven to be sure of being at work by twelve.'

'And when did you say you were told about this?'

'Last night, but as I said, no more questions. They stressed that it's urgent. The number 11 bus will take you straight to Victoria Street. To get back to the hospital, pick up the 36 in Grosvenor Place... there, see it?'

Agent Donne lit another cigarette, a mixture of nerves and excitement causing his hand to tremble slightly. 'I'd better get a move on, hadn't I?'

'You better had. And whatever you do, not a word about this to Milton, you understand? He doesn't need to know.'

Maslin nodded.

'That knife you were going to wave at me...'

'What about it?'

'Let's have a look.'

Agent Byron studied the knife like an expert valuing a piece of rare ivory, running his finger along the blade. 'It's not good enough. Here – take this.' He placed a flick knife on the map.

'I've got to be at work myself later and I won't finish till late. Whatever you do, don't take any overtime tonight. Make sure you're back here by nine. I'll call you then – I'll have to let them know what happened. I'll ask if you saw Mother today, and assuming all goes well, you say yes and that she was a bit off colour.'

'And if it didn't go well?'

Agent Byron said nothing, but his expression made his feelings about that quite clear.

—

It was 9.30 when Hugh Harper woke up. For the first time in days he felt better. His temperature had subsided, he was no longer bathed in perspiration and the aches and pains had largely gone. When he sat up in bed, it was no longer with difficulty. He gazed out over the lawn. The willow tree appeared to have grown more leaves overnight and now had a green hue to it. It was only then that he realised he'd slept through his alarm clock. He'd meant to call Lance King three and a half hours earlier. He hurried downstairs and straight to his study.

'By the sounds of it you're better, sir?'

'Never mind that, Lance. I think I know what palace Curtis could have been referring to.'

'Go on, sir.'

'There's a pub on the corner of Wilfred Street and Catherine Place: the Palace Arms. It is, as Curtis said, right under our noses.'

There was silence at the other end of the line before Hugh Harper heard what sounded like a suppressed cough followed by King's reply. 'Oh my God, sir... you're right!'

—

The woman had been very clear.

They're on to you but you're not to panic.

206

Which was easy enough for her to say, but who in his situation wouldn't at least worry — be scared to death, to be honest?

They know nothing about this place. They only know about Gerrards Cross. They'll have no idea you're using the name Rodney Bird.

Somehow that didn't sound particularly reassuring.

Stay in this apartment. Don't leave it. Don't let anyone in. The landlord will keep an eye on you and bring you food. If you stay put and don't do anything stupid, you should be all right. We'll sort something out. Do you understand?

He said nothing and she repeated the question; he said yes, he did understand. She was very firm and clear. He regarded her as excessively bossy and he didn't like being told what to do by a woman, but he did realise he had no choice. He'd stay in the attic flat above the pub — as cramped and stuffy as it was — and hope it didn't take them too long to sort something out. He wasn't a fool, though; she had a cheek to warn him not to do anything stupid.

—

Agent Donne had studied Byron's hand-drawn map one more time before he was satisfied he'd committed it to memory. He tore it into shreds and burnt them in the sink, using the cup of untouched tea to flush them down the plughole. He pushed the few remaining scraps through with the end of a teaspoon.

The journey took a bit longer than he'd anticipated, and it was just before nine o'clock when he got off at Victoria Street and walked up Palace Street and from there into Catherine Place. The Palace Arms was a handsome four-storey corner building at the end of a residential street. He walked past it into Wilfred Street, where he found a narrow alley giving access to the rear of the building and an outside staircase leading up to the fourth-floor attic.

Before leaving his flat in Shepherd's Bush, he'd worked out his story in case he was stopped. He'd prepared the knapsack he took to work with him: it usually contained his vacuum flask, sandwiches and a spare pullover. He'd found a screwdriver and a hammer in the flat and had packed them along with his brown work coat. He'd left out the flask to create some space. At the bottom of the staircase he put on the work coat and checked that the flick knife was still in his trouser pocket.

The door to the attic apartment opened directly onto the staircase. There was no reply to his knock at first, and when he knocked again, there was a hollow echo as if the place was deserted. After a while, though, he became aware of a floral curtain twitching in the small window next to the door. He knocked once more.

'Good morning, sir, I'm sorry to bother you, but it's about the electricity – the landlord asked me to check it.' He held up the screwdriver as proof of his innocent purpose. The door had opened on a chain, with the face of a man just visible behind it.

'What did you say?'

He goes under the name of Bird: looks like one too, apparently.

'I said I'm here from the landlord to fix the electricity, Mr Bird.'

Inside the attic, Rodney Bird hesitated. The woman had said not to let anyone in, but this didn't sound like it was just anyone. This was someone sent by the landlord, who they trusted, and only the previous day he'd told the landlord about the cupboard.

'Ah, so you're the maintenance man, are you?'

'Yes sir.'

Rodney Bird's hand froze on the chain. Don't do anything stupid, the woman had told him, and he hoped this didn't count as stupid. He could always telephone the landlord; he was only a few floors below him.

'I am in a bit of a hurry, Mr Bird, sir.'

He heard the chain move and the door opened fully.

'I must say, I'm very impressed. I told the landlord about the cupboard door only yesterday morning and he said he'd get someone round to fix it. Normally that will take at the very least a week, and now you turn up the next day!' He was a well-spoken man, almost the nervous type, but Donne wasn't in a mood to get to know him too well.

'Yes, sir: he wants me to fix the cupboard and then check the electricity. You know there've been some problems.'

'You don't need to tell me.'

'Let's have a look at that cupboard first, shall we?'

The door of the kitchen cupboard had come off its hinges and he assured Mr Bird it would be no problem. In fact, if he'd be so good as to stand in front of it and hold it in place – just like that, thank you, sir – then it would be fixed in no time.

He removed the knife from his pocket and the man half turned as the blade flicked open. 'Keep facing the cupboard, please, sir, otherwise it will be wonky, and we don't want that, do we?'

Bird was still chuckling when Donne plunged the knife into the base of his neck. He struck him once more before the man staggered back making what was now a choking noise. He was still on his feet, his hand desperately reaching out for the back of his neck. Donne thrust the knife deep into his side, and only now did he collapse to the ground. He pushed him onto his back and knelt on top of him. The man was mouthing something: eyes that had hitherto been unremarkable and even lifeless blazed now that his life was ebbing away. Donne plunged the knife deep into where he thought his heart was and twisted it. The man choked for a bit longer and a stream of dark blood poured from his mouth. He waited a minute or so, catching his own breath as the man gasped his last one. He noticed Bird was wearing an expensive-looking wristwatch, the dial now speckled with blood. It wasn't yet 9.30.

He thought about taking the wristwatch but realised it could be a bit too distinctive, but he did open the man's wallet and remove a few notes from it: apart from anything else, robbery would be seen as an innocent motive. The thought made him smile. Maybe he should take the wristwatch after all. He cleaned himself up as best he could. There was blood on the work coat, but that could go straight into the laundry at the hospital. His black shoes had blood on them too, but he wiped it off with a wet towel. He looked round: he was as certain as he could be that he'd not left his fingerprints anywhere other than on the wallet, so he wiped that too, and then all the door handles just in case. Then he went into the bathroom and washed his hands and face, and used the man's comb to tidy his hair. Back in the kitchen, he leaned on the side to compose himself. He was now quite peckish and helped himself to some digestive biscuits, eating them as he looked down at the body.

He was pleased: it had gone very well and he'd even quite enjoyed it. Not for the first time, he reflected on how fulfilling his new life was. The way things had turned out was quite unexpected, but all for the better.

He was tempted to stay in the man's apartment for a while longer: it felt cosy with the morning light streaming in and he was worried that if he left now he'd arrive too early at the hospital. Then he noticed the man's face: it had turned an odd blue-grey colour and his tongue appeared to be swollen and sticking out, as if he wanted to say something. Perhaps it would be best to leave now. He'd treat himself to a fry-up at the café in Praed Street before going in to work.

–

Agent Donne was in Grosvenor Place by a quarter to ten and a 36 bus was waiting at the stop as if he'd ordered it. The day really had gone very well. He sat in the front seat on the top deck and enjoyed his journey to Paddington, a slightly smug grin settled on his face.

Had he remained in the attic apartment for even another ten minutes it would have been a close call. Had he remained there until ten o'clock, he would have been in danger of being caught red-handed.

Lance King had called Prince and Bartholomew into his office after his telephone call with Hugh Harper. *Get as many men as you can and cars to take us to Catherine Place.*

By five to ten, they were questioning a confused and frightened-looking landlord in the doorway of his basement flat under the Palace Arms. He was barefoot, with a stained dressing gown wrapped around him.

'Do you recognise this man?' King thrust the photograph of Arthur Chapman-Collins under the landlord's face, which quickly turned pale.

'I'm not sure.' He looked terrified.

It was the most unconvincing 'I'm not sure' Prince had heard in his career, and placing his hand on the man's shoulder, he more or less pushed him into his basement. King followed. 'You either recognise him or you don't, but if we find out this man has anything to do with this place and you have been less than totally cooperative, then losing your licence will be the least of your problems: understand?'

The man said he understood perfectly well, and perhaps if he could have another look at the photograph…? He nodded. 'It's much clearer in this light. Of course, it's Mr Bird – he rents the attic flat. I don't see him from one week to the next, keeps himself to himself.'

Ten minutes later, it was a scene of utter chaos in the small attic apartment. The body was sprawled across the kitchen floor on a surface of sticky blood, and the landlord was propped against the doorway, the front of his dressing gown stained with vomit. He was refusing to come any closer to identify the victim and Lance King was losing his patience.

'Unless you have a proper look at the body and tell us whether this is the man you knew as Mr Bird, then we will have to arrest you.'

'It looks like him from here.'

'You can't see his face from here.' Prince took the landlord by the elbow and guided him over to the body. The man clasped his hand over his mouth and confirmed in a muffled voice that it was indeed Rodney Bird.

–

The following Tuesday, they gathered in Hugh Harper's office in an uneasy silence, nervous coughs only adding to the tension. Richard Prince couldn't recall a grimmer atmosphere at work, with no one making an effort to appear upbeat or look on the bright side.

Harper had been summoned to Downing Street and had instructed the other four to be waiting for him on his return. As well as Prince, Lance King was there, together with Audrey and Bartholomew. When Harper arrived back, he was accompanied by an army officer, which gave the fleeting impression he was under arrest. The two sat down next to each other.

'I think it fair to say I've never seen Sir Roland in such a foul and unforgiving mood.' Harper slammed his hands down on the table and kept them there, palms down and pressing on the surface as if to keep it still. 'And I can hardly say I blame him. Needless to say, news of this traitor Milton and our failure to find him reached Winston. It also appears that according to protocol we ought to have involved the Metropolitan Police before we entered Chapman-Collins's place above the Palace Arms, though I have to say, knowing what those chaps are like, I think you were quite justified going in when you did, Lance. Thankfully Sir Roland took the heat from Winston and assured him he'd sort it – an honour he's now passed on to me.'

He glanced round the table but none of the others looked back at him. 'I am sorry, I should have introduced Lieutenant General Cunningham...'

'Cunnington.'

'Apologies. Lieutenant General Cunnington is from the army General Staff and he shares with me the honour of sorting this mess out. General, perhaps you...'

'I'm sure I don't need to convey to you the very serious concern of the General Staff at the fact that a traitor apparently has access to key intelligence relating to our operations in western Europe. The fact that this also affects the United States only exacerbates matters.' He spoke with a Northern Irish accent and smiled as he mentioned the United States. 'I understand the US embassy believes this intelligence is coming from one of thirty-eight offices in London – and how many people was it you said had access to it, Hugh?'

'We believe possibly in the region of five hundred.'

The general shook his head, appalled at the number. 'I can quite see why it is unfeasible that every one of those is investigated. I understand you had hoped to identify this Milton through another angle...'

'Which I'll come on to in a moment, General.'

'Very well, Hugh. But I wanted to let you know where the General Staff stands on this. Having seen off the enemy's Ardennes offensive, the last remaining obstacle between our forces and the invasion of Germany itself is the River Rhine. Crossing the Rhine is a matter of urgency, but we can't afford to launch the operation if our plans and deployments are known by the Germans thanks to some traitor here in London.'

Lance King began to say something but the general stopped him.

'Hold on, please... We have discussed this matter in some detail and I told Sir Roland Pearson exactly where we stand. We are asking for all maps and intelligence reports relating to our current and future operations in western Europe to be withdrawn from the circulation list of people and departments that currently receive them.'

'Won't that be—'

'What – inconvenient? Absolutely, no question about that: it will cause resentment and confusion. But we feel it is the only

213

way to minimise, if not eliminate, the possibility of our plans ending up in enemy hands.'

There was a long silence as his words sunk in.

'In the meantime, we carry on looking for Agent Milton.' Hugh Harper looked embarrassed at the failure of his operation being laid bare for the army to pick over. 'Perhaps if we—'

'I hope you don't mind if I make a suggestion, sir?'

All heads turned to face Richard Prince.

'What if we were to doctor the maps – produce thirty-eight maps that to all intents and purposes are identical, but with each having something unique on it, something that would become apparent if the enemy were to react specifically to it?'

Harper leaned over to the general and muttered something along the lines of this being the chap from the police he was telling him about.

'For example, if one map was doctored to show we were planning to cross the Rhine at a point say ten miles to the north of Cologne and we saw that German forces were moved there to defend the area, then we'd have good reason to suspect that was the source of the German intelligence. It would narrow the search down considerably.'

The general nodded approvingly. 'There is some merit in what you say, but I doubt we have the time. It's the thirteenth of February today: we need to cross the Rhine in the next two or three weeks. All our operations are working towards that. In any case, I doubt we'd be distributing a map with an X marking the exact point at which we plan to cross the Rhine. We're likely to cross at a number of places more or less simultaneously and the location of those places will depend on how the operation goes. The maps tend to show deployments – very useful for the enemy to have nonetheless. Do try and organise some kind of alert, though: we need to know if anyone pushes for maps relating to the Rhine crossing. Maybe put out something along the lines of wanting all such requests in writing.'

Harper thanked the general and asked King to show him out. When he returned, he looked tense.

'Anything from Chapman-Collins's flat?'

'Nothing, sir: no incriminating paperwork, no fingerprints, no clue as to who might have killed him. We're still going through everything.'

'For what it's worth, sir, I think there is a promising aspect to this.' It was Prince again.

'Please tell us: we could do with some cheering up.'

'I think you said, sir, that you thought the list of attendees at the hotel in Pimlico could provide the answer. I believe the murder of Chapman-Collins shows you're right, especially now we've established the involvement of Fenton. I think we need to concentrate on that list. I realise the names remaining on it are fairly common, but if we cross-reference them with those on MI5 and police files, we may find something.'

Harper said he agreed. They had little choice but to get on with it. As the others left the room, he called Prince back.

'How are you getting on, Prince?'

'Pretty down about the whole thing actually, sir. I feel as if the failure to catch Milton is my fault. I wonder if working as an agent in this country means I'm just not as sharp as I had to be when I was on the Continent. I feel I made an error the way I went to Gerrards Cross without getting my story straight, and then using the George Nicholson name again... I'm sorry, sir.'

'That's the nature of counter-espionage, Prince. It's a long game compared to spying. I always say we're playing a cricket test match whereas MI6 are playing rugger. Events happen more quickly with espionage, it's much more black and white: you either succeed or you fail. This is a much more gradual business. You need patience, though God knows that's hard at times and it can certainly grind you down. I understand you went home to see your boy at the weekend. I hope that cheered you up?'

'It was splendid, thank you, sir, cheered me up no end – and him too.'

—

Agent Milton knew nothing of the fate of Arthur Chapman-Collins. Agent Byron was determined he should remain oblivious to it; he was concerned that if he found out he might panic, or at least lose focus on the task in hand. Every transmission from Germany was pushing him on the need for details of the Allied plans to cross the Rhine.

Exactly one week after the murder of Chapman-Collins, Milton met with Agent Donne, who made it clear: it was urgent. It sounded like a threat.

He waited until the Monday, 19 February, and wandered into the MI4 map room. He allowed Holt to talk to him at length about the stamps of South America, which he was currently showing a keen interest in. He waited until Holt had finished before asking for two or three maps unrelated to the Rhine.

'Anything else, sir?'

Milton said a packet of ten Woodbine would be splendid and Holt laughed.

'Oh yes… just one more thing: the latest map on the Rhine deployments. Shouldn't there have been a new one issued by now?'

Holt stopped laughing and looked more businesslike. 'The Rhine, you say, sir? Apparently those maps are now on special request only. Would you believe, you have to make a request in writing to get hold of one, setting out why you need it, et cetera. Once you let me have that, then I can get you the map. Seems odd for them to go to such lengths, especially at this stage of the war, but there we are.'

'Is that the case with all maps?'

'The Rhine ones only as I understand it, sir.'

'Any idea why?'

Holt lowered his voice and took a step closer. 'Between you and me, sir, I understand it's something to do with a security flap.'

Milton felt his stomach churn and his heart race. He'd never heard of such a thing before and he knew it wasn't right. For restrictions like this to be imposed now suggested that someone suspected something. He regretted having used so many maps. If he was questioned, Holt was bound to say he was one of his best customers. He told Holt not to bother; it was only an afterthought – really not important at all.

He found it hard to concentrate all day, and when he returned to his apartment in St John's Wood that evening, he didn't bother with a meal, instead spending the evening pacing around the flat and smoking, finally thinking about a subject he'd long known he'd have to address sooner or later but had avoided until now.

He'd always known that one day the net would begin to close in on him. He'd also known that he'd realise that had begun possibly before the authorities were on to him. This was, he decided, a warning he'd be foolish not to heed. He just hoped it wasn't too late.

He needed to make plans.

Chapter 21

Germany, March 1945

Lieutenant Nate Markham from Minneapolis remembered little from officer training school: it had been a necessarily rushed course and felt too academic – too much about the theory of war, nothing to prepare you for being face down in a filthy ditch in sub-zero temperatures with your radio barely working, or explaining to your men why they'd run out of ammunition, or worst of all, holding the hand of a dying comrade, unable to assure him that all would be fine.

But one thing he did remember was a talk from a visiting general, who'd thought for a while before replying to a question about what battles were really like. 'Plan for everything, plan for nothing,' he'd eventually said, and from the moment the 9th Armored Division had landed in Normandy the previous September, Nate Markham had realised how true that was.

The Phantom Division, as the 9th was known, had fought hard in the Ardennes offensive and had been at the forefront of the Allied advance to the western banks of the Rhine. Now the river stretched before them as if daring them to even think about it. They knew the Germans had already destroyed more than forty bridges and had rigged the few that remained intact with enough explosive to ensure the noise would be heard back in Michigan.

It reminded Markham of summers in Iowa when he and his twin brother had stayed with their grandparents and played for hours in the nearby woods, walking along the bank of the stream until they could find a point narrow enough for them to leap across. But he and every other man of the 9th Armored knew that the only way across the Rhine would be by boat and pontoon bridges. It would be a long and bloody battle: the river would run with blood and the end of the war was still a long way off.

On the morning of Wednesday 7 March, Lieutenant Nate Markham was part of a force heading for Remagen, a small town on the west bank of the Rhine. The force was a mixture of units, mostly from the 27th Armored Infantry Battalion, plus three tank companies and a platoon from the 9th Armored Engineer Battalion. Relying as ever on the principle of planning for everything and planning for nothing, Markham had no idea what to expect. This was such a fast-moving battle that intelligence tended to become out of date very quickly. It was possible the town of around five thousand residents would be heavily defended, and equally possible that they could enter it unopposed.

Markham commanded a platoon of the 89th Reconnaissance Squadron, which meant they were one of the first units to approach Remagen. At one o'clock, his armoured car came to a halt on a hill just south of Mehlem, overlooking the town. Determined to lead from the front, he was first out of the vehicle; within moments, the other two armoured cars had pulled up. He ordered the drivers to turn the cars round and remain in them with their engines running, and placed other men to guard the perimeter. Then he took his radio operator and a sergeant and crawled to the brow of the hill, the wet grass soaking his tunic. As he reached the edge, he lay low and put his binoculars to his eyes.

In those first few seconds he knew his life was about to change for ever.

His radio operator was an Italian American from Pittsburgh who must have sensed something, because he asked if everything was all right and put his hand on the lieutenant's shoulder when he didn't reply. When Markham took the binoculars away, his hands were shaking. 'Paul, give me the map.'

'Here, sir: what's the problem. What does the town look like?'

'The same as any other fucking German town.'

'You appeared shocked.'

'There's a fucking bridge down there, Paul. Sergeant, take these – over there, see it?'

'Not the first bridge we've seen, sir, with respect.'

'This bridge,' said a breathless Lieutenant Markham, 'is called the Ludendorff Bridge.'

'I'm glad to know that sir.'

'The Germans are meant to have blown up all their fucking bridges. But the Ludendorff Bridge is intact. Paul, get me head-quarters, now!'

–

It wasn't until the Friday morning that Franz Rauter was summoned to Prinz-Albrecht-Strasse. He was astonished he'd not been called there sooner. The rumours about the Rhine being crossed had reached Berlin the previous morning, and by lunchtime it was all anyone was talking about at Tirpitzufer, the usual whispered conversations with people you could trust, with everyone looking over each other's shoulder.

A bridge just south of Bonn – intact! Of course they were meant to blow it up!

Someone must have forgotten to press the button... or something went wrong.

They've crossed the Rhine now... they'll be here soon.

Brigadeführer Schellenberg's aide Hauptsturmführer Böhme had summoned Rauter in person, marching into his office without so much as a knock on the door and speaking in a loud, high-pitched voice so everyone else on the corridor would hear.

'The Brigadeführer wants to see you, now!'

He'd struggled to keep up with the younger man as they hurried over to Prinz-Albrecht-Strasse. Schellenberg was standing with his back to a map when Rauter entered. Without turning round, he told him to come and stand next to him.

'I assume that as a competent intelligence officer you've heard the news, Rauter.'

'About the bridge you mean, sir?'

Schellenberg nodded his head. Rauter was relieved the general was calm, but doubted that would remain the case for long.

'The American 9th Armored Division found the bridge here – at Remagen – intact and crossed it on Wednesday afternoon. They are now streaming over in their thousands and with all their equipment too. It's a disaster!'

The word 'disaster' had been shouted and Schellenberg swung round to face him. 'So my question is, Rauter: your agent Milton, why didn't he tell us about this?'

Rauter hesitated. It was such a ridiculous question, it could only be a trap.

'I'm sorry, sir, but I'm not sure I understand.'

'This Milton – the agent so well placed you waited years before using him – surely he should have known about this?' Schellenberg had shouted the word 'years'.

'With respect, sir, I'm not sure Agent Milton would have known that the bridge at Remagen would be left intact. He wasn't to know it wouldn't be blown up. Was it not rigged with explosives, sir?'

Schellenberg looked at Rauter in a manner suggesting he was trying to detect even a small hint of sarcasm. He took a deep breath before replying. 'I'm not a fool, Rauter, of course I wouldn't have expected Milton to know the bridge was intact, and of course it was rigged with explosives, enough to blow out the few remaining windows in Cologne, I understand. What I meant was that the intelligence – though that's clearly not the right word – we've been receiving from Milton on the Allies' plans to cross the Rhine has been poor: sparse and poor. Even Field Marshal Keitel has remarked on it.'

'But I—'

'He didn't tell us about the 9th Armored Division being in the area, did he? What *has* he told us in recent days? First of all we heard nothing from him for weeks, and then the messages we've received have been vague and largely inaccurate. Is it possible he's been compromised?'

'According to Agents Byron and Donne, no, he hasn't. I can assume he didn't have the same degree of fortune as he had with Arnhem, sir, and to a lesser extent with the Ardennes.'

'You're defending him, Rauter.'

'It's my job to defend my agents, sir. They operate under extraordinary pressure and can't always deliver what we want them to. Maybe the British have tightened up their security in London, who knows? I agree that we've heard very little from Milton recently.'

'Why do you think that is?'

Rauter shrugged. 'Who knows, sir? It's possible he hasn't come across much intelligence, maybe as the war...' He paused, searching for a form of words that wouldn't incriminate him. 'What I'm trying to say, sir, is that as the Allied campaign moves to a new phase, it is possible procedures have changed in London that make it harder for Milton to access intelligence. Nor should we rule out the possibility that after Arnhem and the Ardennes they tightened things up: I wouldn't be at all surprised if he needed to be more careful. This could account for why we've not heard from him in a while.'

Schellenberg walked towards the door and it was clear he was seeing Rauter out. 'There will be questions as to whether he has been turned. You can redeem yourself and him by seeing if he can come up with something of the calibre of what he provided over Arnhem. Understand?'

Rauter said he did.

'Do understand, Rauter, that I'm defending you here – for the time being at least.'

Franz Rauter was so shaken by the encounter at Prinz-Albrecht-Strasse that he decided to go straight back to Schöneberg. One block from his apartment on Speyerer Strasse, he noticed that a small basement bar on Luther Strasse was open. It had been closed for weeks, like so many other places in the city; he'd assumed the elderly owner had been conscripted.

But he was there and nodded at Rauter as he entered and took his usual place at the end of the bar. It was as if he'd never closed and Herr Rauter had been in most days. Without saying a word, he pushed a glass of schnapps in front of him. Rauter noticed that the glass was filthy and the counter dusty but said nothing.

It hardly mattered.

I'm defending you here – for the time being at least.

The problem as Rauter saw it was that the war was as good as over. It had been lost for months, but with the Allies crossing the Rhine and the Red Army closing in on Berlin, it was now just a matter of time. He thought of poor Helmut Krüger being moved into the side room at the Charité knowing his life had reached its final phase. That was how it felt in Berlin now, and he imagined Milton would be feeling the same too. He couldn't conceive of any intelligence the agent could get that would stop Germany losing the war.

The one thing the Nazis were getting better at was finding scapegoats, and Rauter was sure he was in danger of becoming one. He allowed himself just one more schnapps before heading back to his apartment. Tomorrow he'd start to gradually remove evidence of his existence at Tirpitzufer.

Once back in his apartment, he pushed his bed away from the wall and carefully prised away the skirting board. His papers were still safely in place. They weren't complete yet, but it was reassuring to know they were there.

Chapter 22

She hadn't intended to escape.

She hadn't intended not to escape either; it was just that having been in the concentration camp for more than three years, she'd become resigned to her fate and doubted whether she would have either the physical or mental energy to escape – or the opportunity.

When they'd heard the news of the D-Day landings, the prisoners had assumed the war would be over in a matter of weeks – certainly by the end of the year. Her closest friend in the camp was a Danish woman, Hanne Jakobsen, who'd been in there far longer than her and who had no doubt as a result adopted a far more pessimistic view of the world. Hanne would insist she was realistic rather than pessimistic and warned her that despite the Allies' successes in northern France the end of the war was still a long way off. 'Not this year, certainly,' she said, and told her and the other French prisoners in particular not to build up their hopes too much. In any case, she pointed out, Ravensbrück was in the middle of Europe; the last they'd heard, the Allies were some three hundred miles to the west, and that was the direction she'd need to go.

In recent days, the atmosphere at the camp had been especially grim. At the beginning of the week the Nazis had executed three British SOE agents: Violette Szabo, Denise Bloch and Lilian Rolfe. The rumour was that they'd been shot in the back of the neck in the presence of the camp commandant.

But she'd forgotten that life had a habit of presenting you with opportunities in the most unexpected manner, and this was what happened to her on a bitterly cold Friday morning in February. The day had begun in the usual manner: a foul-tasting lukewarm soup and a hunk of stale bread followed by roll-call in the assembly area between their huts. No one was missing or had died overnight – the first time she could remember that happening for a while – and everything seemed to be in order. Soon they'd shuffle along to the Texled workshops and another day of sewing buttons onto uniforms.

But just as she was about to set off, the row she was in was stopped by one of the guards, a foul-smelling Austrian woman with bad teeth who'd recently tried – without much success – to be more friendly with the prisoners. Eventually an officer came over and ordered eight of them to follow him. As they were led away, she spotted Hanne walking in the opposite direction, about to start work. Her Danish friend looked shocked and mouthed something at her, but she couldn't make out what she was saying.

They were marched to a lorry. Normally she'd have worried about where they were being taken, but the officer seemed to be in a good mood and amused himself by flicking cigarette butts onto the floor and watching the prisoners fight for them.

It was a short journey, and when the lorry stopped, the officer told them they were in Rheinsberg. She'd heard of it before, a small town a few miles west of the camp, where prisoners were sometimes sent to work. They were led to a building at the rear of the town hall and taken into a large room, where they were set to work painting the walls. As far as forced labour went, this could have been a lot worse. Sure, it was damp in the room and they'd be covered in paint, but at least it was indoors and not too physically demanding.

Late in the morning she was sent out to get some more paint from a hut behind the building. And that was when she saw it: a van waiting in the entrance, its engine running. She realised the driver had stopped to open the gates to the road. She didn't pause to think, to weigh up the pros and cons, the risks involved in the escape. She didn't think what Hanne would do but ran over to the van, opened the rear door and climbed in, closing it just before the driver climbed back into the cab. As far as she could tell, the load was mainly boxes of documents.

'Stop – pull over!' The driver had released the brakes and edged forward, but now she could hear someone shouting from behind the van before banging on its side to attract his attention. Someone must have spotted her climbing in. She thought about jumping out, but knew it would be hopeless. Tears started running down her face as she realised how impetuous she'd been. It was one of her faults. Hadn't Hanne always advised her to be more patient? The driver wound down his window.

'Yes, what is it?'

'This form, you've not initialled the first two pages.'

'Really, my initials are that important? Here you are then.'

For the next hour she was too busy concentrating on keeping still and quiet to think about the consequences of what she'd done. She knew the van had been positioned to turn left at the gates so assumed they'd been heading west. She had no idea how long they'd been driving for, but it must have been close to two hours when the van stopped.

She waited until the driver got out, then carefully opened the rear door. They were in the middle of countryside, and peering round the side of the van, she saw the driver relieving himself against a hedge. She ran to the other side of the road and hid in a ditch until he drove off again.

The next month was a blur: nights and days spent out in the open, a barn where she found shelter and food, and more importantly, a set of clothes she was able to steal from a washing line and some money she found in a man's jacket that got her on a bus to Magdeburg and from there an overnight train to Kassel. The city had been badly bombed, which meant she was just another homeless person picking their way through the ruins. For a few days she worked on a gang helping to clear the rubble of bombed buildings, and there she found a purse and an identity card. From Kassel she continued to move west.

She had an enormous stroke of luck, if that was the right word, on the outskirts of Marburg. She'd run out of money and lost her identity card but found a young Wehrmacht officer on his way to Bonn who said he'd take her with no questions asked if she'd spend the night with him.

As soon as they arrived in Bonn, she disappeared into the ruins of the city, which was quickly being abandoned by what remained of its population as the Allies closed in. She found a cellar to hide in until she woke one morning to hear English voices. When she emerged from the rubble, she collapsed at the feet of a group of American soldiers, tears staining her face, which was caked with thick dust. Her only thought was Hanne and how she had to do the right thing by her.

'I must speak with a British officer.'

—

'I presume if there was any news I'd have heard it by now, Prince?'

Hugh Harper appeared on edge, his upper-class relaxed confidence not as evident as it usually was. It was a Thursday morning – 15 March – and he had attempted to break the ice with a laboured joke about the Ides of March and Milton. Richard Prince smiled politely, unable to work out the joke's punchline, or even if it had one.

'Lance tells me progress is slow.'

'I think that's a polite way of saying we're not making any progress, sir.'

'Sir Roland was taking an awful lot of flak over the withdrawal of the Rhine maps, but of course since we actually crossed the bloody river so unexpectedly last week, all that has changed and it's certainly taken the pressure off us. I read in a memo this morning that nearly twenty thousand troops and an awful lot of vehicles have already crossed the bridge.'

'Let's hope it stays up, sir.'

'Indeed, but who'd have thought the Germans of all people would fail to blow it up? A catalogue of errors on their part, I understand. Between you and me, I heard on the grapevine that to blow the bridge up they needed the written permission of the officer in charge, but he'd been replaced the very morning the Americans came across it and no one knew the name of his replacement so couldn't ask him. Such is the hand of fate, eh?'

Prince agreed and both men nodded, momentarily lost in thought as they considered this miracle of bureaucracy.

'Can I just make it very clear.' Hugh Harper coughed and paused, perhaps conscious that he sounded like a schoolmaster. 'What I want to say is, the fact that we've now crossed the Rhine shouldn't mean we relax in our hunt for Milton and the other two agents. Even though the finishing line may be in sight, a traitor can still do untold damage. A delay of just a few days or giving the enemy vital information about an operation can cost hundreds if not thousands of lives. Breaking this spy ring is as important as ever and will remain so until we find the bastards.'

Prince nodded in agreement.

'And in any case, it's a question of doing the right thing. He simply can't be allowed to get away with treason just because the war's nearly over. So let's redouble our efforts. Now, I understand there've been no intercepts from Agent Byron for a few days now. Do we know if anyone put in a written request for the maps?'

'No, sir.'

'Any luck with cross-checking the names of those other attendees at the hotel in Pimlico – what was it called again?'

'The Abbey Hotel, sir, and cross-checking the names of the attendees has turned out to be a much more complicated job than we'd anticipated. There are seven names on our list, as you know: checking the MI5 and Special Branch files is one thing, but then we have to apply to every police force in the country to see if they have a record of people with those surnames having been involved with the fascist movement. I looked after that for a while in Lincolnshire, sir, and I can tell you it's a long job, but hopefully we'll get something.'

'Just a matter of when; ideally before the end of the war. There is something else, by the way, Prince.' Harper shifted uncomfortably in his seat and fiddled with the cap of his fountain pen. 'The agent with whom you worked in Denmark... the one arrested by the Gestapo...'

'Hanne! Is there some news?' Prince sat bolt upright, almost half standing.

'There is indeed some news, but you're not to get your hopes up. Apparently Hanne Jakobsen was alive on or about the eighth of February: I thought I'd better let you know that straight away. Look, I'm sending you to see a friend of mine at MI9; they're responsible for all our prisoners of war and are obviously plugged in to pretty much everything relating to Allied prisoners of the Nazis, including the concentration camps. Tom Bennet is an old chum of mine – we were at the same college – and he's high up in that section: I understand Tom Gilbey asked him to make finding out about Hanne a priority. He's expecting you this morning. Do you know the Great Central Hotel?'

'I'm afraid not.'

'It's opposite Marylebone station. MI9 has taken over part of the fourth floor. My driver will take you there – and it goes without saying I do hope you find her.'

–

On his journey to Marylebone, Prince thought about how the way you reacted when someone you loved died was a measure of that love. He had no doubt that he'd miss Hanne for the rest of his life, such was the extent of his love for her. He realised that for the past two years he'd been experiencing a kind of grief.

When Harper had said there was news, he'd been so relieved he'd allowed the tears to well up in his eyes.

Tom Bennet turned out to be a dry character, showing little in the way of emotion or manners and treating Prince as if he'd come in to clear up some confusion over a tax return. He sat behind his desk and, with a pair of reading glasses perched at the end of his nose, held a file high in front of him, obscuring his face.

'So here we are then... I've been keeping an eye open for anything to do with Hanne Jakobsen since Tom Gilbey first asked me nearly two years ago now. I understand you and she became close during your mission, eh?' He briefly moved the file down so he could see Prince and gave him a disapproving look. 'Mixing business with pleasure rarely works, but there we are. For two years we heard nothing: the best I could say to Tom was that no news could be good news, but in truth there wasn't a lot of evidence for saying that. Hopefully it made you feel better about things. Then last week we had a breakthrough. When the Americans liberated Bonn, a woman in a dreadful state crawled out of a cellar and—'

'Hanne!'

'No, I'm afraid not, Prince. This woman made a real fuss about seeing a British officer, insisting she had an important message. Fortunately there was a British liaison officer nearby. The woman's name is Paulette Dubois and she was a French resistance fighter who'd been held at a concentration camp called Ravensbrück for some three years. She'd managed to escape a month earlier and had headed west. Her closest friend in Ravensbrück was Hanne Jakobsen, and they had a pact: whichever one escaped or was liberated first would pass on a message for the other. Jakobsen's message was to ask someone in authority in London to tell a Peter Rasmussen where she was. I understand you are that Peter Rasmussen?'

'It was an identity I used in Denmark, yes. Did this French-woman say how she was?'

'As far as I can gather, she was alive when Paulette Dubois escaped around the eighth of February. That's all we can say.'

'Can't we rescue her?'

'In due course, I'm sure that will happen.'

'But I could go and—'

'Prince, you must realise Ravensbrück is hundreds of miles from where the western Allies are at the moment. It's fifty miles due north of Berlin. Even the Red Army aren't near it yet. You have to be patient. We know a bit about that camp because some SOE agents have been held there. It's mainly for women prisoners and is also a work camp, and at the moment we understand it's very busy, which I suppose is a good sign.'

Prince sat still, quite unsure of how to take the news.

'I promise you as soon as we hear any more we'll let you know, but hopefully the place will be liberated in a matter of weeks.'

Prince said he was very grateful, and if there was any chance of him being there when that happened, he'd very much like to be considered. He was by the door, his raincoat over his arm, when he noticed that Bennet had stopped in the middle of the room, a finger on his lips and deep in thought.

'Tom and Hugh speak very highly of you.'

'Thank you, sir.'

'Are you in a rush, Prince – do you have a few minutes?'

Prince said he wasn't in a hurry.

The man from MI9 paused, still deep in thought. 'I wonder... I came across an odd tale the other day: do you mind if I run it past you?'

He led Prince over to a table and sat opposite him.

'A couple of weeks ago, a young flying officer by the name of Ted Palmer made it here on a home run: he'd escaped from Dulag Luft in Germany and managed to reach our forces in France. I did his debrief myself and he told me a most strange story that I just can't work out.

'Last July, Palmer was shot down over Flanders, not far from the town of Aalst. Fortunately for him he was rescued by the resistance and they got him to Brussels, where the plan was for him to lie low and wait for us to turn up, but he ended up being caught and was taken to the Hotel Metropole, which is the headquarters of the Luftwaffe. He was questioned there by one of their intelligence chaps, all pretty standard really. They even told him he was about to be sent off to one of their special camps for Allied aircrew. Then for no reason – and evidently to the surprise of the Luftwaffe officer – he was hauled off to the local Gestapo headquarters in Avenue Louise.

'According to his account, he was questioned there at length, and he got the impression they were far more interested in his identity than in his mission and how he was rescued. Do you speak any German, Prince?'

'Some.'

'Palmer understands some German but never let on, and he overheard them say *Berlin kann es sortieren.*'

'Berlin can sort it.'

'Indeed. The next day a man arrived from Berlin who Palmer said was jolly decent. He made sure he was patched up and allowed him to have a shower and something to eat. Palmer says that after a medical and a few questions – mainly to do with his age – this chap didn't seem terribly interested in him. The doctor insisted he could be no more than twenty-five – in fact he's twenty – and the man from Berlin told the local Gestapo chaps it had all been a waste of his time and then used the phrase "anyone can see how old he is". They were almost apologetic, and young Palmer said it was as if they thought he was someone else. Odd, don't you think?'

'It is rather. I presume this doesn't normally happen?'

'I have to say I've never heard of such a thing before. Luftwaffe intelligence and the Gestapo don't get on. The former see it as their role and theirs alone to interrogate RAF aircrew. What do you make of it?'

Prince shook his head. 'As Palmer implied, perhaps a case of mistaken identity?'

'Sounds like it, but who on earth did they think the poor chap was? He looks like a schoolboy – they all do.'

'And you say they brought a chap from Berlin to interrogate him?'

'Yes, a Herr Rauter, according to Palmer. That's what's particularly odd about it: if the local Gestapo had made a mistake and roughed him up a bit before letting him go, that would be one thing, but bringing someone obviously quite important over from Berlin doesn't make an awful lot of sense. Mind you, so little does these days.'

Chapter 23

London, April 1945

'Are you drunk, Jim?'

'Nope.' Agent Donne scowled at Milton with a 'what's it to you?' expression, then looked away hoping that would signal it was the end of the discussion.

'Are you sure?'

'Of course I'm bloody sure – in any case, it's none of your bloody business.'

'I can smell it on your breath.'

The two Nazi agents were huddled under a tree in Regent's Park, sheltering from what was turning out to be a particularly persistent April shower.

'I've been drinking but I'm not drunk: a man with your education ought to know the difference.' Donne removed a half-finished roll-up cigarette from a tin and relit it.

'You don't know anything about my education. In fact...' Milton stopped himself, immediately regretting what he'd said. The last thing he needed was to get into an argument with Agent Donne or divulge anything personal. But he still didn't like the idea of him drinking.

'I reckon by the way you speak you—'

'I'm sorry, Jim, let's forget it – it's my fault. We're all tense, aren't we? We mustn't let things get to us.' He was aware he was stammering again and proffered a hand to Jim, who briefly shook it, all the time staring ahead, the lit end of his cigarette now perilously close to his lips.

Things.

It was clear to even the most fanatical Nazi that the end of the war was in sight. It was 19 April – a Thursday – and that afternoon Milton had seen the latest briefings. The Allies were closing in on Berlin. The western Allies were on the banks of the River Elbe, the last remaining land obstacle before Berlin. The previous day the Americans had entered Magdeburg. The Red Army was even closer to the German capital: as far as he could tell from looking at the map, the Soviets could already be in some of Berlin's outer suburbs.

He'd just been told by Agent Donne that there was a message from Berlin demanding to know why they'd not heard from him in a while. He'd have thought it was obvious: there was nothing to tell them they didn't already know. He was surprised that anyone in Berlin was taking an interest in him. In any event, what was he to say – the Americans are getting close? And the British, the Canadians, the Soviets? He had a feeling they must be aware of all that already.

'It's Thursday today, isn't it, Jim?'

'All day apparently.'

'Let's meet next Tuesday, same time, same place. Tell Byron to tell Berlin that I'll have something for them by then – all right?'

Agent Donne flicked the stub of his cigarette in front of him like he was tossing a coin and watched it fizz briefly on the wet grass. 'You think it's a good idea to meet in the same place?'

'We've only met here once before. It'll be the last time we use it. I'll think of somewhere else after that.' He made to leave, but Donne remained where he was.

'Hang on a bit. I want to ask you a question.'

'Go on.'

'What do we do when this is all over?'

'You mean the war?'

'I didn't mean the rain.' Donne glanced at him briefly, a scowl still fixed on his face.

'I imagine we just get on with our lives and hope no one connects us with anything. No reason why they should; we've been so careful, haven't we? Maybe when the war's over they won't bother anyway. As long as neither you nor I nor Agent Byron makes a mistake, we ought to be all right. They'll never know we existed.'

'What will I do for money?'

'Don't you have any? I thought you were working?'

'They gave me some when I came over, but I've spent that, and as soon as the war's over I'm going to have to give up my job and move on. I've got to get out of London.'

'Why's that?'

'I need to get away from all this – you, Byron, everything. Also, I didn't tell you this before, but there's another reason I don't want to hang around here.'

The tone of his voice had changed. He sounded frightened, and Milton noticed that his hand was shaking as he held his cigarette in front of his mouth.

'What is it, Jim?'

'Byron said not to say a word about this, especially to you. Christ, I can't believe what I'm involved in; I didn't sign up for this, I can promise you.'

'You'd better tell me, Jim. Maybe I can help?'

Jim sneered and gave a brief sarcastic laugh. 'I'm sure you can. Byron ordered me to kill a man.'

'And did you?'

'Did I what?'

'Kill him, Jim – did you kill this man?'

Agent Donne nodded briefly.

'When was this? Tell me what happened.'

'It was in February. A man called Bird – Rodney Bird. He lived above a pub near Victoria.'

'Go on.'

'I got the impression they didn't trust him any more: Byron said the guy had become a liability. It was easy, actually. I did a good job.'

'What did you say his name was again?'

'Rodney Bird.'

'Can you describe him?'

There was no question Jim was describing Arthur Chapman-Collins, the man he'd first encountered in Cambridge nearly twelve years previously: the man who'd got him involved in this nightmare in the first place. The rain was now torrential, much as it had been on that fateful night in Cambridge. If Arthur Chapman-Collins had become a liability, that meant he himself was in danger. And no one had warned him. He was aware of water seeping into his shoes and Jim angrily asking him why he wasn't saying anything.

'I'm sorry. Why didn't you mention it to me at the time?'

'Because Byron said not to.'

If Chapman-Collins had been compromised, then the trail could lead to him: he was surprised it hadn't done so already. He felt quite sick and fumbled in his jacket pocket for a cigarette, which he lit with trembling hands. 'I've never heard of him,' he said. He was trying to sound as matter-of-fact as possible, but he was aware that he was stammering badly, so he told Jim he'd see him on Tuesday and hurried off.

He'd always been very careful to ensure that Agent Donne left any meeting point before him, and if they left it together, he made a point of letting the other man get on a bus or go to an Underground station before he did. He'd even set off in a completely different direction to where he needed to go: the last thing he wanted was for Donne to have any idea where he lived.

But he was so absorbed with the news that Jim had been ordered to kill Arthur Chapman-Collins that he dropped his guard. He headed west through the park, round the Outer Circle, hunched against the driving rain and not bothering to turn round or go back on himself or use any other very basic moves he'd normally employ to check he wasn't being followed.

He turned into Hanover Gate and wondered about waiting for a bus, but there was no sign of one so he carried on walking,

237

past Lord's cricket ground and eventually into Abbey Road. The rain was even worse now, bouncing off the slippery surface of the pavement, and he hadn't once bothered to so much as even glance round.

The only time he turned round was as he entered his mansion block, at which point he noticed a man standing still on the other side of the road, apparently watching him. It was only a glimpse and he couldn't be sure, but once inside the entrance he was able to get a better look. Despite the condensation on the windows, it certainly looked like Jim. Milton was furious with himself for allowing the other man to follow him, but his anger only lasted until he got into his apartment. Once there, he knew what he had to do and concentrated on that.

He'd known for a while it would come to this: the restrictions on access to the Rhine maps, the news about Chapman-Collins and his carelessness in permitting Jim to follow him had made up his mind.

Lance King had a possible breakthrough in the hunt for Agent Milton and was finding it hard to contain his excitement. He telephoned Hugh Harper and agreed they'd all meet in the morning.

The morning turned out to be nearer lunchtime because of an MI5 briefing somewhere under Whitehall that delayed Harper. He looked exhausted when he arrived in the office, nodding curtly at the others and asking King to get on with it.

'You may recall, sir, that at the end of March we decided to visit every one of the thirty-eight departments on the American embassy map distribution list? Prince and I divided them between us and it's been quite a tiresome business, making appointments and then working out how many people had access to the maps and what they'd been looking at. We weren't getting anywhere, but yesterday I had an appointment at the

War Office, specifically in the Directorate of Military Intelligence. They have a department there – MI4 – which specifically looks after maps: compiling them, distributing them, storing them and—'

'Get a move on, please, Lance. Could someone open a window?'

'The chap in charge there is called Holt and I had tried to see him last week but he was on leave. Insists on talking about stamps, but when I managed to get him onto the subject of who was requesting which maps, he mentioned a chap who works in another of their departments – MI18 – which coordinates intelligence relating to the invasion of Germany.'

'I know it – run by Johnny Oakley.'

'That's right sir, Brigadier Oakley.'

'He was on my father's staff at the Battle of Loos: came to his funeral all those years later. Decent sort.'

'According to Holt, this chap is a major on attachment from army intelligence and is in and out of there all the time; devours maps, he says.'

'Which he would do, though, wouldn't he – surely that would be part of his job?'

'Of course, Audrey, but according to Holt, just after we withdrew the Rhine maps, this major asked for one but changed his tune when Holt said he'd need to request it in writing – told him he was no longer interested. I asked him about other maps he'd looked at and he gave me a long list, including Arnhem and the Ardennes.'

'Certainly we should look into this more; it sounds promising. I'll call Johnny Oakley. Did I miss this chap's name?'

'Sorry, sir, I ought to have mentioned it earlier. It's Palmer. Major Edward Palmer. York and Lancaster Regiment... Divisional HQ intelligence... fought in Normandy, injured at Caen...'

'Please could you repeat his name, Lance?' Prince had a shocked look on his face.

'Of course, it's Edward Palmer. I say, are you all right, Prince?'

It was a while before Prince answered, and when eventually he did, there was a hint of excitement in his voice.

'It could be him, you know.'

'Who?'

'This Edward Palmer at the War Office – he could be Milton.'

'Hang on, Prince, hang on…' Harper looked surprised. 'Let's not get ahead of ourselves, eh? All we know is that a chap who had a perfectly valid reason for using these maps happened to ask about the Rhine map and then decided not to put in a written request for it. Let me have a word with Johnny: most likely there'll be an innocent explanation – the chap's a major after all.'

'I realise that, sir, but there's something else. You may remember that a month ago I went to see MI9 about Hanne, the agent I'd worked with in Denmark. Before I left, Mr Bennet told me a story about how he'd recently carried out the debrief of an RAF pilot who'd escaped from his PoW camp. According to this pilot, he was captured in Brussels and taken to be interrogated at the Luftwaffe headquarters, but the Gestapo turned up and took him to their headquarters, where he was roughed up a bit and questioned. Funny thing was, they wanted to know less about his mission and more about his identity and age. The next day a Herr Rauter from Berlin turned up to question him, but it soon became clear he wasn't terribly interested and—'

'I hope you're coming to the point, Prince.'

'I am, sir. To cut a long story short, the pilot was examined by a doctor, who told Rauter that he was no more than twenty-five years old, at which point Rauter ordered them to let him go. The pilot is convinced they thought he was someone else.'

'Like who?'

'That's the point, sir, the pilot's name is Ted Palmer – Edward Palmer.'

No one spoke for a full minute.

'Same name as our chap at the War Office.'

'Exactly, sir.'

'And how old is he?'

'He'd have been twenty when he was caught. How old is the Edward Palmer at the War Office, Lance?'

King looked through a file in front of him. 'Late thirties.'

'So it could be a case of mistaken identity, couldn't it? They thought the RAF Ted Palmer was the other Edward Palmer and only realised he wasn't because he was clearly too young.'

'But if Edward Palmer is one of their spies, why did the Gestapo pull in an RAF pilot with the same name?'

'Looks like we'll need to find this Herr Rauter and ask him.'

'Meanwhile,' said Hugh Harper, standing up, 'we'll need to have a chat with this Major Palmer, though let me give Johnny a call first.'

–

Edward Palmer had been very calm and organised that Thursday night. When he reached his apartment, he'd looked out over Abbey Road for a while and realised Jim was no longer there. For months now he'd reckoned he'd know the right moment to disappear, and the meeting with Jim had made it clear that it was now.

He typed a letter for the landlord giving up his tenancy because he'd unexpectedly been posted elsewhere and enclosing two months' rent. He checked the folder with the false identity papers along with five hundred pounds, money he'd saved over the years plus various sums passed on to him by Agent Byron. It would keep him going long enough; it amounted to almost half a year's salary. He didn't have much in the way of ration cards, but he had enough cash to be able to rely on the black market for a while.

It was harder to work out what to take with him. He reckoned one suitcase and a rucksack was as much as he should risk.

For years now he'd planned the journey he was about to take. He'd first head north by train and then keep moving, never more than two nights in one place, using buses where possible and all the time looking for somewhere to stay, somewhere it would be apparent he'd fit in. Once the war ended – it shouldn't be long now – life would be much easier.

He woke with a start at four o'clock, convinced that Jim was going to go to the police and tell them everything. Jim would have seen how shocked he'd been at the news of the murder. He didn't sleep after that, constantly watching Abbey Road in case anyone else was observing his block. He took a few bags down to the bins and then had a bath followed by breakfast. He made one telephone call, one that he hoped would buy him a few days, at least until Monday, then he checked everything again. Once he was satisfied that all was in order, he put aside a pile of anything that could identify him as Edward Palmer. He watched the papers burn to blackened embers in the small grate before leaving the apartment.

He walked to the estate agency and put the keys and letter through the door, then waited five minutes before a black cab came along. He told the driver he wanted to go to Euston station and told him he was on his way to Manchester. At Euston he waited until the taxi disappeared and then walked to King's Cross.

By the time he entered the busy concourse, he still wasn't sure where he was going. He'd study the departure board before making up his mind.

That was how his life would be now.

He felt something approaching a sense of relief, and that took him by surprise.

Chapter 24

Although it was difficult to gauge the passage of time these days, Hanne reckoned it had been at least two months since she'd been summoned to the Gestapo office in the camp. Exactly how long it was didn't seem to terribly matter.

She was sure it was towards the end of January when she'd been brought before the Gestapo officer called Mohr. Her abiding memory of him was of how ill he looked and sounded, not unlike a prisoner in the camp. He'd asked her about her Englishman, the man they only knew as Peter Rasmussen. She'd been surprised at the naïvety of his questions: had she heard from him? Had anyone tried to pass her a message from him? Did she have any clue where he might be?

She was stunned that even if she had heard from Peter or had any idea where he might be, they thought she'd tell them – not least because it was clear that it was in the interests of the Gestapo to keep her alive in case they caught him. Mohr had warned her that the next time she was visited by someone from the Gestapo they wouldn't be as easy-going as him, and she suspected that was true. And as if to show how easy-going he was, he told her she was being transferred to the Texled workshops.

There was no question that making uniforms was preferable to the brickworks. The work there had been hard, with the constant risk of injury, and she doubted she'd have survived it much longer, which was probably why Mohr had organised her transfer. It wasn't exactly pleasant in the workshops: the guards were just as cruel, the work monotonous, and it was still a concentration camp, with the ever-present threat of punishment and even death.

But the place had its advantages: it was warm, and for long periods of the day she was able to sit down. Another advantage was that she had met Paulette there.

Paulette Dubois was a French resistance fighter, and although Hanne wasn't to know her for long, their friendship quickly reached the point where they were able to confide in each other.

Paulette told Hanne she actually ran a resistance cell in Orléans but had been arrested when they discovered copies of the clandestine newspaper *Combat* on her at a checkpoint. 'They thought I was just a paper girl!' She was in her mid twenties – quite a few years younger than Hanne – but they seemed to view life in the same way, with as much of a sense of humour as it was possible to summon in the camp. They both had a kind of optimism about them, buoyed by a certainty that they'd somehow survive the hell they were in, and they were able to confide the reason for this. Both women were deeply in love, Hanne with Peter Rasmussen and Paulette with Olivier, who'd been her boyfriend since school.

The two women shared a work bench, and although conversation between prisoners was forbidden, the noise of the machinery meant it was difficult for the guards to enforce the silence. They'd speak quietly while looking at their machines, concentrating on the job in hand and keeping an eye out for the guards. Rarely did they look at each other, and this gave their conversations a strange kind of intimacy, the type that came from the detachment involved in avoiding eye contact, like lovers whispering to each other in the dark.

Paulette told Hanne how Olivier had been on the run from the Gestapo and was hiding in a village in the Sologne. Hanne confided in Paulette about Peter and how the two of them worked for the British, even hinting that Peter himself was

British. She wondered if she'd gone too far, but somehow talking about him to someone else brought him alive, and at times she felt he was alongside her, assuring her that all would be well and they'd be together soon.

She was as sure as she could be that Paulette was no Gestapo stooge. She never asked Hanne to divulge any details about Peter or where he might be. And they soon agreed a pact: if one survived the camp and the other didn't – or even in the unlikely event that one managed to escape to freedom – the other would get a message to either Peter or Olivier.

Their short-lived friendship came to an abrupt end one February morning when Paulette was one of a small group taken on a work detachment. That happened all the time and Hanne thought little of it until that evening, when a Belgian woman told her what had happed: they'd been taken to Rheinsberg to paint a hall, and Paulette had escaped.

For the next twenty-four hours, Hanne was worried sick. Perhaps Paulette really had been a Gestapo stooge: it was not unusual for them to be removed from the camp before their target was arrested. But if she wasn't a stooge, there was still danger: escapees were invariably caught within the first twenty-four hours, and the camp commandant would make sure all prisoners were aware of her fate.

But for two days there was no sign of her and no officer so much as looked in Hanne's direction. The next worry was the reprisals that would inevitably follow. The problem for the Germans was that the prisoners remaining in Ravensbrück were only there because they were fit enough to work, and their labour was now more essential than ever.

It didn't prove to be an insurmountable problem: on a morning roll-call a French woman whose name Hanne didn't know was hauled out of line. She was clearly sick – it looked as if she had typhus – and therefore now dispensable. She seemed resigned to her fate as the commandant read out a warning to the other prisoners in case they were minded to escape. The moment they tied the noose round her neck, it began to snow: a light flurry at first, but by the time her body eventually stopped twisting, it had turned into a blizzard.

Hanne was beginning to feel unwell herself, but the fact that two days on Paulette had clearly not been caught gave her enormous hope, which sustained her over the weeks to come. If Paulette had successfully escaped, then she had a chance of reaching freedom, and Hanne knew she would keep her promise.

Peter would know she was alive.

Her Englishman would come and rescue her, she had no doubt about that.

—

Friday 20 April was Hitler's fifty-sixth birthday, but there was little celebration in Berlin. The sound of Red Army artillery to the east dampened any party mood there might have been.

The same day, north of Berlin, in Ravensbrück concentration camp, the mood among the prisoners veered between despair and optimism. The despair came not just from the fact that they were still in a concentration camp but because they were terrified of how the Nazis would behave now the war was clearly about to end. The workshops and factories in the camp had ground to a halt, which meant the prisoners had now outlived any economic value they might have had. A few weeks earlier, more than twenty thousand prisoners had been sent on a death march in the direction of Mecklenburg and nothing had been heard of them since. Thousands of prisoners remained in the camp and they were dying in their hundreds.

Something strange had happened earlier in the month. The Swedish Red Cross had turned up at the camp and taken a hundred prisoners away with them. They were mostly Scandinavian and they were told they were being taken to Denmark. Hanne had only heard about this after they'd departed, but then came rumours that the Red Cross was about to return and this time take many more prisoners with them. It seemed that the Swedes had done some kind of deal with the Nazis.

Hanne Jakobsen had every reason to be optimistic that Friday morning. After all, she was Danish so was bound to be among those rescued. And it couldn't come a day too soon. She was feeling quite ill now and was beginning to have trouble walking.

After roll-call that morning she was summoned to the commandant's office, where she was shocked to find Mohr, the sickly Gestapo officer, waiting for her. She was surprised he was still alive. He still looked dreadful, but now his manner was far more menacing.

'I imagine you think you're going to be taken back to Denmark by those Swedes, don't you?'

She shrugged, unsure of how to respond. She placed a hand on the back of a chair to stop herself from falling.

'Have you heard from Peter Rasmussen?'

She shook her head, perhaps too eagerly. It made her feel dizzy and faint.

'Is there anything you want to tell me about Peter Rasmussen?'

'I don't know what to say, sir, I—'

'Any information you can give me about him?'

'There's nothing I can tell you.'

'Well let me make it clear, Hanne Jakobsen, unless you do tell me something, you'll be the last person left in this wretched place.'

Chapter 25

It was a week since they'd identified Major Edward Palmer as a probable German agent: a traitor. What they'd found out in the past seven days had turned what had been a probability into a near certainty. The meeting had now reconvened.

'Johnny Oakley's absolutely furious: incandescent – couldn't believe it.' Hugh Harper shook his head as if he couldn't believe it either. 'He recruited Palmer, said he was doing a decent job: quite liked him too. As you know, I called Johnny as soon as we'd finished our meeting last Friday and asked him where his Major Edward Palmer was and he said he'd rung the duty officer early that morning to say he was unwell and wouldn't be in that day. I went over to see him. He insisted he was a first-class chap – Cambridge and all that, well thought of in military intelligence – and wouldn't believe what I was telling him, but by then you'd called in from Palmer's place, hadn't you, Prince?'

'Yes, sir. I went straight there and had to break in: the place was abandoned. From what we can gather, he'd left early that morning. A neighbour in the opposite flat saw him make three or four trips to the rubbish bins at the back of the block, and then noticed him leaving with a suitcase. I called the local police in to secure the flat and search the bins, but there was nothing of interest in them. We tracked down the estate agency he rented the place from. He'd dropped a letter off there to say he had to give up his tenancy at short notice and enclosing two months' rent and his keys. We have no idea where he went after that, but he's not been seen since then.'

'Why would you pay two months' rent if you're going to disappear?'

'I have no idea, sir; maybe he wanted to minimise suspicion – who knows?'

'Means he's thorough: leaves nothing to chance.'

'And what do we know about his background, Prince?'

Prince thumbed through a small black notebook. 'Born in Kidderminster in 1907, making him... what, thirty-eight? His father was a bank clerk and his mother worked in a shop: both died some years ago. He's an only child and there seems to be no other close family. He went to the local grammar school, then Cambridge – double first – followed by a couple of years teaching before returning to Cambridge to study for a doctorate in medieval literature. Gave it up in 1938 when he took a short service commission. Joined the York and Lancasters, fought in Norway and after that was based at Brigade Headquarters and transferred to Brigade Intelligence. Divisional HQ next, then Normandy – injured at Caen – promoted to major and joined the War Office in September last year.'

'So he was having a good war then.' Lance King looked impressed.

'A decent enough one. Any politics that we know of, Prince?'

'Nothing, sir, no files on him anywhere – Special Branch, police in Cambridge, Metropolitan Police, MI5.'

'Friends, lovers?'

'Again, nothing we can find. A few people in Cambridge remember him, though not terribly well. Quiet and reserved were the words that cropped up, not a very sociable type, something of a loner; very bright apparently and spoke with a stammer when he was nervous. The only bit of information that may help is that he went to the Ludwig Maximilian University in Munich in the summer of 1935: seems he got the funding from Munich.'

'Could have been recruited there.'

'Who knows, sir?'

'So the trail's run dry...'

'It has, Lance, yes – we've put his name, photograph and details on the police and ports watch lists and flagged him with the highest level of urgency, but let's remember, this is a man who's been operating successfully as a German spy for at least six years if not more and managed to remain above suspicion until very recently.'

'True, and he's bound to have changed his identity: most probably his appearance too. Let's not forget we've still got to find agents Byron and Donne too. Has anything cropped up to help us with that?'

'No, Lance, nothing. I'm convinced the key to uncovering this spy ring is in Berlin.'

'Why's that?'

'Remember how I told you last week about the young RAF pilot who was obviously mistaken for Edward Palmer in Brussels? Well, you'll recall he said that this chap Rauter came from Berlin to interrogate him. He's almost certainly Abwehr or RSHA. If I can go to Berlin and track him down, he could be the key to finding them all.'

'But Berlin's still in Nazi hands.'

'Surely not for long now.'

'True, but then it will be in Soviet hands. What do you think, Hugh?'

Hugh Harper leaned back in his chair, his hands supporting his chin as though his head was weighed down in thought. 'It's possible... I went to this morning's military intelligence briefing at the War Office – Johnny Oakley was there looking somewhat shamefaced, did his best to avoid me and I can't say I blame him... Where was I?'

'The War Office sir, for a briefing.'

'Ah yes... A terribly bright chap hardly out of his teens said there are two main sections of the Red Army closing in on Berlin: Zhukov's 1st Belorussian Front and Konev's 1st

Ukrainian Front: my money would be on Zhukov, brilliant general. Half a million Red Army troops in total... can you imagine? The latest assessment is that the assault on the centre of Berlin started late yesterday. This chap said they expect the city to be under Soviet control early next week.'

'So is it feasible for Prince to go in?'

'Our nearest army is the US 9th, and they're twiddling their thumbs on the banks of the River Elbe. My understanding is that once the Soviets have control of Berlin, we can send in liaison officers. I'll pull every string I can to get you in as one of those. We'd better get you sorted out with an emergency commission, though – uniform and rank and all that.'

'We're assuming this Rauter is still alive. From what one hears, the Soviet artillery has been hitting Berlin for ten days now. There won't be much left of the place, and even if Rauter survives, how will Prince find him?'

'I very much appreciate your concern, Lance, but if I don't at least give it a try, what chance do we have?'

'You do realise how dangerous the place will still be?'

'I was there not that long ago, remember.'

'And the Soviets won't be falling over themselves to help.' Hugh Harper bowed his head slightly. 'I'm no fool, Prince, I know you'll be wanting to find this woman, this...'

'Hanne?'

'Don't blame you, and I admire the way you've been persistent about us looking for her. But I want you to be clear: finding Rauter and breaking the spy ring is the priority, no question about it. Understood?'

'Yes, sir, but—'

'Just listen: once you've done that, you have my word that you can travel back to Europe and take all the time you need to find her. Are you going up to Lincoln this weekend?'

'Yes, sir, I've not seen my son all week.'

'Be back here first thing Monday morning. By then Berlin ought to be under Soviet control. We'll have a uniform ready for you. Enjoy your weekend.'

Chapter 26

Life had never been particularly easy for the Gurevich family before that dreadful day in June 1941, but compared to how it was now, it seemed like they'd lived in paradise.

Mikhail and Yevgeniya Gurevich had a small top-floor apartment in a large tenement building on Shiroka Street, not far from the Svisloch river. They'd moved there once their children had left home. Their sons Iosif and Zelik had joined the Red Army – Iosif in particular had done well; he was now a commissar no less. He'd always been a very bright boy – his father worried he was too bright for his own good. But he'd been a committed Marxist-Leninist, which had certainly done him no harm: if only he'd meet a nice girl one day.

Their daughter Leya had married a boy called Motik – Mikhail had grown up in the same building as his father. The Gurevichs weren't particularly observant Jews but Motik was more orthodox and in Mikhail's opinion spent far too much time studying. Leya and Motik had lived on the other side of the river, close to the Jewish cemetery, not far from the railway line, with their daughter Riva and son Ilya. Earlier in 1941, Motik had been conscripted – though Mikhail couldn't imagine why any army, let alone the Red Army, would want him fighting in it.

Because Leya could no longer afford the rent, she and the children had moved in with her parents. It was cramped in the apartment but manageable. Mikhail still had his work in the tailoring workshop and Yevgeniya was probably the best seamstress on Shiroka Street, and they thoroughly enjoyed having their grandchildren with them.

But all that had changed on a Sunday morning in June, the 22nd. Mikhail's brother had woken them up early in the morning, knocking hard on the door.

Had they not heard the news? The Germans had invaded!

At that moment a nightmare began that would never end. Mikhail had hurried down to the street with his brother, but within minutes the Germans had started bombing the city. There was panic among the civilian population of Minsk, and especially among the city's Jews. They'd had very mixed feelings about the Soviet Union's pact with Nazi Germany; of course they didn't like it but they weren't in a position to express their opinion and at least it ensured the Germans were nowhere near them. They'd heard such dreadful stories about what was happening in other parts of Europe, and especially Poland.

That Sunday, some people made plans to flee east, but for most it was easier said than done. It was difficult with families, and where would they go? Mikhail and Yevgeniya prayed that somehow Iosif would be able to rescue them, and they wrote to him at the address they had in Moscow, even paying for a special stamp to get the letter there quicker.

But by the following Saturday it was too late: the Germans marched into Minsk.

The family remained in their apartment, absolutely terrified and ruing their decision not to leave the city. Shiroka Street was a mixed area and Mikhail had a non-Jewish neighbour called Ivan who was a kind and decent man. His wife had died the previous year and Mikhail and Yevgeniya had helped him considerably. Ivan's brother had a small farm south of Minsk, and he said he could smuggle Mikhail and Yevgeniya there but they'd have to leave Leya and their grandchildren behind.

Their daughter insisted they should go: after all, she said, it wasn't as if the Germans were going to harm a woman and her children. Mikhail insisted they should stay: maybe any day now they'd hear from Iosif; he'd sort something out. He couldn't sort something out if they weren't at home, could he?

In the end, though, they had no choice. By the middle of July, the Nazis had created a ghetto for the city's Jews, about half a mile away from where the Gurevichs lived. It was on the other side of the Svisloch, with everyone crammed into the streets around Jubilee Square. The family were put in a room in Chornaya Street – all five of them together, with one bed and a rough wooden floor, sharing one toilet and a tiny kitchen with a dozen other families. Mikhail was sent to work in the ghetto factory but tried not to despair. He was sure that once Iosif received their letter he'd do something. He was such a resourceful boy, and he was an officer now. Maybe he'd contact Zelik and they could rescue them together.

He even managed to get a message out to Ivan saying he'd like to go to his brother's farm after all and please could he arrange it? Once there, he'd sort something out for the rest of the family. He never received a reply.

In fact Ivan had tried to help. Twice he'd tried to get into the ghetto and had been turned back; then one Monday morning in August – it was the 18th, as if he could ever forget – he did manage to get in.

What he saw there had haunted his every waking hour since.

He actually reached Chornaya Street, only to find the road blocked off. An Einsatzgruppen unit was rounding people up, forcing women and children into waiting trucks and pushing the men aside. Ivan spotted Mikhail Gurevich arguing with a German officer, but just at that moment a local policeman came over and demanded to see his papers.

'What the hell are you doing here?'

'One of the Jews here owes me money.'

'I wouldn't hang around if I were you.'

'What's going on?'

'They're taking the women and children away. That fool is arguing with them. You see that German officer he's talking to?'

Ivan nodded and moved closer to the policeman, who clearly wanted to share gossip.

'That's Hauptsturmführer Alfred Strasser, the beast of the ghetto. He's one person you certainly don't argue with.'

But Mikhail was more than arguing now; he was remonstrating, and carried on doing so even when the officer pulled out his Mauser. He pushed Mikhail out of the way and aimed the semi-automatic at his wife, daughter and grandchildren, all cowering against the wall. He kept firing until the last of them had stopped moving.

Mikhail stood rooted to the spot, his mouth wide open and an expression of sheer horror on his face. As the full realisation of what he'd seen hit him, he looked round and for a brief moment his eyes met Ivan's. It was at that moment that the German shot him. It wasn't a clean shot, and he was allowed to moan and writhe on the ground for a while before Strasser eventually strolled nonchalantly away and told a nearby soldier to finish him off.

'You see?' The policeman was whispering. 'I told you he shouldn't have argued with Strasser. That's the problem with these Jews: smart enough, but they always argue.'

Chapter 27

Berlin, April–May 1945

On his fourteenth birthday Franz Rauter had been taken on a
rite of passage by his maternal grandfather, a strict and humour-
less Prussian whose only passion beyond his work and possibly
his family was hunting. He had treated the occasion like a
religious ritual, waking Franz before dawn and then driving
out north of Brandenburg.

They'd parked on the edge of a forest and walked through
it for perhaps an hour, Franz worrying about the flies, about
falling over and about how on earth they were going to find
their way back to the car. When they arrived at a spot that
seemed no different from the rest of the forest, his grandfather
crouched down next to him and solemnly handed him a rifle.
He spent a long time showing him how to use it: where to
point, when to breathe, when to press the trigger, not to close
his eyes, not to hesitate.

They waited another hour, Franz beginning to feel the cold
and damp eating into him and desperate to relieve himself. His
grandfather kept slapping him on the shoulder – the first time he
could recall any kind of physical affection from him – and told
him what fun it was. He even handed him a flask of schnapps
and told him to drink some. It was the only part of the day
Franz remembered with anything other than distaste.

Not long after his first schnapps, the deer came into sight: a
beautiful animal with a stunning coat glistening in the dappled
light and dark eyes glancing knowingly around the forest as its

ears pricked up. His grandfather whispered in his ear: *aim for the heart... be decisive... pull the trigger... now...*

Franz hesitated: he was unsure what to do, unclear what order he was to do things in, whether he was meant to breathe in or out as he pressed the trigger, and most of all reluctant to kill such a beautiful animal. By the time he fired, it was too late: the deer had heard something and Franz's shot hit a tree a few yards from it. The animal bolted, and his grandfather shouted that he was a fool. Franz realised he had to redeem himself: he stood and fired another shot, and somehow this one struck the fleeing animal on its hindquarters. It took them half an hour to find the deer to finish it off.

The journey back to Brandenburg was conducted in silence, his grandfather clearly disappointed. The only time he spoke was to mutter, 'You hesitated... hesitated...'

This was all Franz Rauter could think about since the Soviet artillery bombardment had begun before dawn on that dreadful Monday in the middle of April. He'd had three opportunities to leave the city and each time he'd hesitated like his frightened fourteen-year-old self in the forest. The first time had been the most likely one: on the Tuesday morning, he'd made his way to the office in Tirpitzufer, where he found his boss supervising a chaotic scene as troops loaded files into a lorry parked in the courtyard.

'They're encircling the city,' he told Rauter, as if he was letting him in on a confidence. 'But there's a gap to the north-west – between the Soviet and American armies. I'm taking these files; they're bound to let me through. Come with me.'

Rauter wasn't sure. Eventually he decided it was a good idea after all and hurried to his apartment in Schöneberg to collect some things, but by the time he returned to Tirpitzufer, it was too late: the lorry had gone.

Later that week – he couldn't for the life of him remember which day it was – a friend told him the Luftwaffe was flying out key personnel from the airfield at their staff college in Gatow, in the south-west of the city. 'You work with Schellenberg, don't you, Franz? He'll sign the papers for you.' But he hesitated again before deciding that Brigadeführer Schellenberg was more likely to sign his death warrant than papers allowing him to leave the city.

A day or so later he was conscripted into the Volkssturm, the citizens' militia, which was meant to hold back the might of the Red Army, and he assumed any chance of fleeing the city had gone. He was attached to a unit based around the Bendlerblock, the vast army headquarters where his office in Tirpitzufer was – or had been before a Soviet shell reduced it to rubble. The Bendlerblock did have the advantage of a network of excellent air-raid shelters and for a few days Rauter felt he was as safe there as he was anywhere in Berlin.

But then his unit came under the direct command of the 18th Panzergrenadier Division, which was supposedly responsible for the centre of Berlin, and he found himself being ordered around by fanatics whose behaviour veered between a state of utter panic and almost euphoria at the prospect of sacrificing their lives for the Fatherland.

His third opportunity to leave the city came on the Monday morning, the last day of April, by which time the Red Army was in the city centre. Rauter found himself waiting for them in the rubble of a building in what he thought had been Schelling Strasse. On one side of him was a man in his seventies who kept muttering that he'd always been a communist and how pleased he was the Russians were coming. The old man on his other side told him civilians were still leaving the city. 'Our best bet is through Wilmersdorf,' he said.

Rauter hesitated for an hour, and then another barrage of shells made up his mind. He pulled off his Volkssturm armband, crawled out of the rubble and headed south, planning to stop at his apartment on Speyerer Strasse and gather the papers he'd been nurturing these past few months, the ones with a new identity. Then he'd head west out of the city, through

Wilmersdorf. He managed to cross the canal and found himself in what looked like Karlsbad when he heard someone ordering him to halt.

He turned round and saw it was one of the Panzergrenadier officers.

'Where do you think you're going? You stay and fight! Traitor!' The SS officer appeared to be injured and slowly drew his pistol. Rauter drew his Mauser automatic at the same time, taking aim at the officer. He was back in the forest north of Brandenburg, unsure of where to aim or when to breathe, but he pulled the trigger anyway and watched in shock as the man crumpled to the ground.

At that moment, a Red Army unit appeared in the road. Rauter threw down his weapon and sank to his knees, his hands in the air, hoping the bullet to finish him off would be swift.

–

'Congratulations, Prince: you've joined the Royal Dragoons, one of our most prestigious cavalry regiments. My wife's uncle was a major in it.'

'I've never ridden a horse, sir, not sure I'll be much use—'

'Don't be ridiculous, Prince, there's more chance of you having high tea with Stalin than being asked to ride a bloody horse. It so happens the Royal Dragoons is our closest unit to Berlin, so it makes sense for you to be with them. Your uniform's over there; try it on. It's been a devil of a job to get this sorted so soon, I can tell you. And here are your papers: you're now Captain John Hadley. You'd better get a move on.'

Prince arrived in Berlin on the afternoon of Friday 4 May. The city had come under complete Soviet control on the Wednesday, but the Red Army insisted on waiting a couple of days before allowing in liaison officers from the British and American armies. The other British officers were aware that Prince was there on intelligence duties so left him to get on with it. It was clear he wasn't the only one with that role.

Until the Saturday morning he was in a daze, quite unable to come to terms with the destruction and chaos around him. He'd been in Berlin in December 1942, posing then as a Danish businessman. With his innate sense of direction and his good memory he thought he had a feel for the city and assumed he'd find his way around. But it was clear he might as well be in a different city if not on a different planet: the landscape reminded him of the colour paintings of the moon from books he'd read as a child.

In any case his sense of direction would have been of little advantage. The Soviets insisted that as a matter of courtesy and hospitality they couldn't possibly allow their comrades – their esteemed comrades indeed – to wander round the city on their own. It was still dangerous. Each liaison officer would be given the services of a car and a driver along with an officer to accompany them.

On the Saturday, Prince asked his driver to go to the area around Potsdamer Platz: they drove as far as the car could go and from there Prince walked first to Tirpitzufer, where the Abwehr had been based, and then to Prinz-Albrecht-Strasse, which had been the RSHA headquarters. Both had become heavily guarded mountains of rubble. It was clear that finding this Rauter was a hopeless task. He wasn't sure Hugh Harper would approve, but he told the officer with him that he urgently needed to see a senior officer. His instinct was that any matter that appeared sensitive would be handled by the commissars he'd heard so much about – the political officers who apparently had all the influence in the Red Army.

His instinct was correct. At around six o'clock that evening, Captain John Hadley of the Royal Dragoons was escorted into one of the few buildings in the centre of Berlin that could be described as intact. As far as he could tell, it was somewhere between Friedrichstrasse and Wilhelm Strasse. He was shown into an office that had boarded-up windows but was otherwise immaculate. Behind a large desk sat a man of a similar age to him, his feet on the desktop displaying a pair of highly polished knee-high boots. Also on the desk was a blue officer's cap. The man smiled and indicated the chair Prince was to sit in, then pushed an open box of cigars in his direction. Two oil paintings were propped up on the floor by the desk.

'I understand you speak German?'

Prince nodded.

'The spoils of war have been somewhat limited in Berlin, for which we only have ourselves to blame. I'm amazed they held out for so long. These cigars are very good… please.'

Prince helped himself to one and the Russian came round to snip the end off and light it. He was about Prince's height too, but his appearance was slightly darker than the Slavic or Asiatic looks so common amongst the Soviet troops he'd seen in Berlin. Prince noticed he was wearing a gold watch and there were two more on the desk.

'Your name, please?'

'Captain John Hadley of the Royal Dragoons: I'm a liaison officer with the British forces.'

'And what can I do for you, Captain John Hadley?'

Prince explained that the British forces urgently needed to interview a German intelligence officer based in Berlin called Rauter… No, we don't know his first name… Possibly former Abwehr, now most likely to be working for the RSHA – maybe running agents outside the Reich, including in Britain.

The Russian officer was making notes. 'Any photographs?'

'I'm afraid not: our information is that he's in his mid forties.'

'And you know for sure that he's in Berlin?'

'We know he was last July.'

The Russian pulled a face. 'So, just a surname, no proper description, no address and a suspicion that he worked at either Tirpitzufer or Prinz-Albrecht-Strasse – neither of which is standing.'

'So I saw.'

'Why do you need to find this man?'

In the short time he'd been in the room, Prince had worked out that the Russian officer was smart. He knew he needed to be as honest as possible. 'We believe he has information about German agents still operating in Britain.'

'And if you – we – find him, what is in it for the Soviet Union?'

Prince shrugged and coughed. The cigar was stronger than anything he'd smoked before. 'We're allies, aren't we?'

'So I'm told, Captain.' The Russian closed his eyes and put his feet back on the desk, his cigar clamped between his teeth. From outside came the sound of shouting and screams, followed by a burst of machine-gun fire. The Russian didn't even bat an eyelid. He remained in that position for a while before nodding his head in approval, a smile once again crossing his face.

'Give me one day, Captain: I'll tell your driver to bring you here tomorrow afternoon, perhaps at five o'clock.'

'Can I ask your name?'

'Iosif Leonid Gurevich – Podpolkovnik Iosif Leonid Gurevich.'

–

'From the way you describe him, I imagine he'll be NKGB. You've heard of them?'

Prince shook his head: he'd been telling a major from British Army intelligence about his encounter with the Russian.

'The People's Commissariat of State Security – they look after all aspects of security and intelligence, especially in areas they've taken over. Hard to know which Soviet organisation is what these days, but the NKGB seem to rule the roost wherever they end up. What was he like?'

'Rather pleasant, actually.'

'Not for me to ask you about your mission, of course, but you'll know to be careful. Don't trust any of these chaps as far as you can throw them. And what rank did you say he was?'

'He said Podpolkovnik; I don't know if I've pronounced that correctly.'

'Well you certainly found the right chap: a *podpolkovnik* is more or less equivalent to our lieutenant colonel rank.'

–

Prince was keen to revisit places in Berlin that Sunday from when he'd been in the city some two and a half years previously. From what he could tell, the Hotel Excelsior was in ruins. He wanted to return to the Das Bayerischer Haus restaurant on Donhoff Strasse, although he doubted there'd be much to see there. But most of all he wanted to see Sophia, the German woman who'd appeared from nowhere to rescue him and had turned out to be such a formidable ally.

He looked carefully at the few people out on the streets, those not hiding in the shadows: it was hard to catch their faces as most walked along stooped, looking at the ground. When they did glance up, they had a uniform expression of hunger and fear. Not one of them looked anything like Sophia.

What was most noticeable about Berlin was how the ubiquitous and enormous swastika flags that had draped almost every building had disappeared – but then so had most of the buildings they'd hung from. It was as if the city he'd seen before was an illusion, a stage set revealed for what it really was once the props had been removed.

The smell was noticeable too: the dust was all-pervading, seeming to choke the city, and the air was pungent with the smell of burning and explosives.

He was back at the building – which he'd worked out was on Behrenstrasse – by five o'clock, and was taken straight in to see Podpolkovnik Gurevich. The Russian seemed more on edge than the previous day, no booted legs on the table, no smile, no cigars.

'Come with me, Captain.'

He led Prince along a series of corridors and down a twisting flight of stairs until they came to what appeared to be the basement. He was searched before a series of steel doors were unlocked, and both men had to stoop as they walked down a narrow corridor. At the end, Gurevich had what sounded like a tense conversation with a guard, after which they were let through another locked door. Moments later, a cell door was opened. Crouched on the floor at the end of the tiny room next to a bucket was an unshaven middle-aged man wearing a ragged pullover and stained trousers. His shoes had no laces. He appeared gaunt and frightened and was shaking.

'Stand up.'

He stood up quickly. Prince noticed that his feet were shackled.

'Do you recognise him?' Gurevich had turned to Prince.

'No.'

The Russian took some papers from his pocket and waved them at the man. 'These are yours, yes?'

The man nodded, trying to smile but only managing to look more terrified.

'They were on you when you were caught.' He nodded again. 'Tell me your name.'

'Rauter: Franz Rauter, sir... Look, I want you to know that I—'

'Shut up and listen! I understand you were seen killing an SS officer, is that correct?'

'Yes, sir, but he—'

'That, as far as I can make out, is the only reason you're still alive. It was a wise move on your part.' Gurevich turned to Prince and smiled. 'You're lucky: fortunately Rauter's name was put on a list when he was captured, so finding him was not as difficult as I feared. He was being held in a barracks in Spandau and I had him brought here. Rauter, tell my comrade here where you worked.'

'I was a professional intelligence officer, a police officer really. I was never a Nazi. I—'

'You know, the funny thing about this city is that no one in it now was a Nazi! Please tell him exactly where you worked.'

Rauter hesitated, clearly unwilling to say anything. Gurevich waved the papers in front of him. 'Don't forget I have these – unless you want me to treat you as Gestapo, of course. I'm not sure there's much difference.'

'But there is, sir! I worked for the Abwehr until it became part of the Reich Security Office last year. I worked on purely military matters, nothing whatsoever to do with the Gestapo. In fact I—'

Prince stepped forward. 'Perhaps if I could ask—'

Gurevich cut him short. 'Not now. Hopefully you'll have an opportunity to question him soon.'

'But when?'

'That, Captain Hadley, will be up to you. He'll be kept safe until then. I'll tell the guards to give him more clothes and some food. Come with me to my office.'

The box of cigars on the desk had been joined by an oval bottle. Gurevich pushed a glass towards Prince and indicated he should fill it. 'It's cognac – Baron Otard, a particularly good one. We found two crates of it in the basement.'

Prince sipped the cognac and soon finished the glass. Gurevich refilled it for him and handed him a cigar.

'I'm very grateful you found Rauter, but I must question him, it's urgent!'

'I have a proposition for you, Captain John Hadley.' Gurevich leaned back and spent a while lighting his cigar before running his hands through his thick hair. When he looked up, his demeanour had changed: he no longer looked composed. 'I'm from Minsk: have you heard of it?'

'I think so, possibly...'

'It's in Byelorussia, west of Moscow. I left the city in 1925, when I was just seventeen. I was a committed communist and had been selected for a military academy in Moscow. I've not lived in Minsk since then. But my family, they stayed.' He paused to fill his glass and compose himself. 'My family are Jewish, and after the German invasion in June 1941...' He waved a hand in front of him and coughed, turning his chair slightly away from Prince. 'I will keep it brief because this is a difficult story for me to tell. Following on behind the German forces were what is called Einsatzgruppen – mobile death squads whose purpose was to kill as many Jews, partisans and communist party officials as they could find. I am afraid to say they were very efficient. They murdered hundreds of thousands of people – men, women and children. It is possible they killed well over one million. My parents were murdered and so was my sister and her family – her children were both under eight: aunts and uncles too – all my family. All I have left is my brother Zelik, who is also in the Red Army.

'We liberated Minsk last July and I was able to travel there to see what had happened to my family. There was a neighbour – Ivan, a non-Jew – who'd been a good friend of my father, and he told me the whole story.

'What happened to them was truly awful and since then I've not slept a night without dreadful nightmares. I wish Ivan hadn't told me in the detail he did, but then if he hadn't I wouldn't have found out the name of the man responsible for murdering my family. Have some more cognac, please... Hauptsturmführer Alfred Strasser, that's his name. I'll write it down for you. I've since discovered that in 1941, Strasser was an SS officer attached to Einsatzgruppen B, but in 1943 he joined the 17th SS Panzergrenadier Division when it was formed. You'll understand I've done my best to find out what I can about him. He has also been promoted to *Sturmbannführer* – a major. I want you to bring Alfred Strasser to me and in return I'll give you Franz Rauter. It's a fair exchange.'

'But where am I meant to find him in the whole of Europe – assuming he's still alive?'

'Oh, he's still alive all right. In fact, two days ago I found out he's in one of your prisoner-of-war camps, in Münster. Bring him here as soon as you can and Rauter's all yours.'

Prince said he'd certainly try, even though he had no idea where Münster was. 'I'll leave Berlin tomorrow morning and go and find this...'

'...Strasser: but you should leave now. I'll ensure you'll have an escort as far as your forces on the Elbe, and all the papers you need.'

Despite the cigar and the cognac, Prince now felt very clear-headed. So clear-headed, in fact, that he felt able to broach something else with Gurevich. 'May I ask you a favour?'

'Another one?'

'There's a German concentration camp just north of Berlin, a place called Ravensbrück: do you know if it's been liberated yet?'

'I will need to check, but my understanding is that our forces liberated it maybe one week ago. Why do you ask?'

Prince leaned over the desk and wrote on a sheet of paper, pushing it back to the Russian. 'Hanne Jakobsen is a friend of mine: she is Danish and a committed anti-Nazi. She was there, certainly in February. By the time I return with Strasser, can you see what you can find out about her?'

Chapter 28

Germany, May 1945

'It's completely out of the question, I'm afraid. You can forget it. Now if you don't mind, I need to—'

'But I told you, it's urgent.'

'And I told you that you simply cannot turn up here like some Johnny-come-lately demanding I hand over a prisoner to you. Prisoners of war are governed by the Geneva Convention and there are strict protocols with regard to what one can and cannot do with them. And one of the things you most certainly cannot do is hand them over to some chap who turns up unannounced. And not just any prisoner: an officer.'

'An SS officer.'

'He's still an officer, Captain…'

'Hadley: Captain John Hadley of the Royal Dragoons. I'm a liaison officer with the British forces in Berlin and it is a matter of national importance that Sturmbannführer Alfred Strasser is handed over to me now.'

'So you have told me, Captain, and more than once, but with the greatest of respect, I'd need considerably more than a verbal request from a junior officer to do that.'

'What would you need then?'

Richard Prince was at the British Army camp in Münster. He'd left Berlin on the Sunday evening and with the help of a Red Army escort made it back to the US base by nightfall. The senior British officer there had somewhat reluctantly agreed that he could have the use of a jeep and a driver the next day. They'd left the camp on the banks of the Elbe at six o'clock on the Monday morning and arrived in Münster later that afternoon. For the past hour, an increasingly red-faced major had been refusing permission for him to take Sturmbannführer Alfred Strasser back to Berlin. He'd only reluctantly admitted that the German was even being held at the camp.

'What you need to do is to fill in this form.' He pushed a sheaf of papers across his desk towards Prince. It was a questionnaire that ran to half a dozen closely typed pages.

'And then I can collect him?'

'No, no, no...' The major laughed, his face turning redder. 'Good Lord, no. Once you've completed the form, I'll submit it up the chain of command and eventually it will find its way to a committee, which will make a decision.'

'And how long might that take?'

Major Edwards shrugged and began to stand up, straightening himself in an effort to appear taller than he actually was. 'I'll mark it as urgent so it will go to the top of the pile.'

'So how long then?'

'One week, with a fair wind.'

Prince looked carefully at the major: a pompous man whom he doubted had seen active service during the war but who now clearly relished the opportunity to be as officious as possible. He realised he wasn't getting anywhere with him so didn't feel he should risk pursuing it.

'Very well then, thank you for your help. Perhaps if I could take the form and go and fill it in somewhere?'

The major directed him to the officers' mess, where it felt as if he'd gatecrashed a party: officers were slapping each other on the back and the stewards were handing out glasses of champagne. Someone thrust one into Prince's hand. A young lieutenant came over and said, 'Cheers – we did it!'

'I'm sorry, I...'

'You've not heard the news, sir? The war's over – we've only gone and won it! Apparently the German chief of staff signed an unconditional surrender a few hours ago in Reims.'

'That's marvellous news! Splendid!' Prince asked if the lieutenant could point out someone to do with communications. Five minutes later, he was in the radio room and talking to the young officer in charge. 'I need to get a message through to someone in London: it's really very urgent. Are you able to help?'

'I can get a message through to our headquarters in London and they can pass it on, though only in what they'd regard as extenuating circumstances. Write it down here and I'll see what I can do.'

Prince wrote down Hugh Harper's name and telephone number, followed by the message. *Have tracked down FR in Berlin but first need permission to collect a Sturmbannführer Alfred Strasser from British Army camp Münster. Please authorise this with Major Edwards here, with instruction for him to expedite as a matter of urgency.*

The radio officer promised to deal with it straight away and suggested Prince wait in the officers' mess and he'd find him once he had a response. Prince assumed it would take a few hours for the message to get through and for Hugh Harper to deal with it. He was dozing in an easy chair when he realised someone was standing in front of him, coughing nervously to attract his attention. It was the major. He couldn't have been more contrite.

'I had no idea quite how important this was… If only you'd said.'

'I did.'

'If I'd realised then, of course, I'd have dealt with your request immediately… Didn't know you were… Anyway, the chap's all yours. Just need you to sign this form.'

They were hurrying over to the prisoners' compound, Prince now very much in charge. 'I'll need all the paperwork you have on the prisoner, his papers, interrogation notes, everything…'

'Of course.'

'Tell me about the circumstances of his arrest.'

'As far as we can gather, back in March the 17th SS Panzer-ergrenadiers were routed by the Americans in the Pfaelzer Forest, south of here. Some of them managed to escape and headed north. When we captured Münster at the beginning of April, Strasser was in the uniform of a Wehrmacht sergeant and would probably have got away with being treated as an ordinary prisoner of war had not other Germans denounced him. Apparently they took exception to his shooting some of their wounded men, accusing them of desertion.'

Sturmbannführer Alfred Strasser was brought before him: shorter than Prince had somehow expected, and older too, perhaps in his late forties. Despite his dishevelled appearance, he strutted in with all the arrogance of an SS officer, the hint of a grin on his face masking any sense of confusion. Prince quickly realised he was someone who was used to getting his way. He told the guards to keeps Strasser's handcuffs on and asked the major to leave. He'd already ensured there was no chair in the bleak room, so the German stood awkwardly in front of the table Prince was sitting at.

'Your papers tell me you're Sturmbannführer Alfred Strasser of the 17th SS Panzergrenadier Division. According to my information, your division was formed in October 1943, so I'd be grateful if you could tell me what you did before that date.'

Strasser shrugged as if he couldn't quite remember. 'I am only obliged to give you my name, rank and serial number – isn't that correct?'

'It is indeed. I just thought you might want to tell me what you were up to before October 1943.'

He watched as an 'I'm not sure what you mean' expression crossed the German's face.

'You see, Strasser, there are allegations that you may have been involved in war crimes prior to October 1943, and I'm sure you'll realise it's in your interests to clear that up.'

'I served in the Wehrmacht, mostly in France and Belgium. I was an administrator.' Strasser spoke with an Austrian accent and Prince had to concentrate hard to understand him.

'So you never served in the east?'

The German shook his head, still managing to look confident.

'You know the war's over now, don't you, Strasser? Your General Jodl signed an unconditional surrender a few hours ago. Unconditional...'

Strasser stared straight, determined not to allow the Englishman the pleasure of a reaction.

'Despite what you say, I believe you served in Einsatzgruppen B.'

He shook his head once more, but only after a brief hesitation. His confident demeanour was now fading and he was beginning to look worried.

'I told you, I was only in France and Belgium – and Luxembourg too for a while.'

'So if someone said you were in Minsk in August 1941, it would be a case of mistaken identity?'

Strasser's mouth opened in shock and beads of perspiration appeared on his forehead. He swayed slightly and his fists clenched.

Prince closed the file in front of him. 'But we don't need to go into all that now, do we? I was just checking I have the right man. You'll be taken back to your cell and we will leave first thing in the morning.'

'To go where?'

'To Berlin, Herr Strasser, where a Red Army officer is very much looking forward to meeting you.'

They left the camp at Münster at dawn and drove through the day to Berlin. Strasser was silent for most of the journey: he looked as if he'd had no sleep and dozed off occasionally, each time woken up by the jolting of the jeep and his handcuffs pulling on the frame of the vehicle.

It was a gruelling journey but they had no trouble getting through the British and American checkpoints. Prince thought it would be trickier once they passed into territory controlled by the Red Army, but if anything it was easier: the paperwork provided by Gurevich seemed to so impress the Soviet checkpoints, Prince got the impression they'd have been able to get into the Kremlin with it.

At a checkpoint in Potsdam late that afternoon, he showed a NKVD commissar a letter Gurevich had given him. The officer said he'd call his comrade immediately to let him know they were on their way. Indeed, it would be his honour to provide an escort.

They arrived at the NKGB headquarters on Behrenstrasse early that Tuesday evening and drove straight into the courtyard where Podpolkovnik Iosif Leonid Gurevich was waiting for them impatiently. He barely acknowledged Prince as two of his men dragged Strasser from the jeep before the driver had even put the brake on. Prince watched as the German was pushed against the wall and saw for the first time real fear in his eyes. Gurevich said nothing; just moved forward until his face was an inch or two from the German's. Then he stepped back and shouted a command, and Strasser was dragged away. The NKGB man turned round and shook Prince's hand.

'Tonight I will deal with Strasser to be certain he was the man who murdered my family. Tomorrow you will get Rauter. Be here for seven o'clock. Is something the matter?'

'Do you remember I asked you to find out what you could about a Danish prisoner at Ravensbrück concentration camp – a Hanne Jakobsen?'

The Russian nodded. 'I was going to wait until tomorrow, my friend: it's not good news, I'm afraid. Don't look so worried;

it's not bad news either – it's just there's no trace of her. I was able to speak with one of our commissars up there. As far as they can tell, a few thousand prisoners were rescued by the Swedish Red Cross and taken to Denmark, but she wasn't on that list. Nor was she on the list of survivors at the camp, or listed as dead. Now that I have the commissar involved, we should get news soon.'

That evening, Prince was able to move around the city without a Soviet escort. He was desperate to see if he could find Sophia, but he had no idea where she lived and realised it would be too dangerous to give the Russians her name. He discovered the RAF had turned the Excelsior Hotel into a hollow shell. He found the Das Bayerischer Haus restaurant, the place where she'd saved him from the Gestapo. Its windows were missing and wooden boards only partially covered the gap, through which he could see the glint of a dozen eyes staring at him, but when he stepped closer and said hello, he heard the sound of children scurrying away. Nearby, on Kommandahtenstrasse, he spotted a pile of rags huddled in the doorway of what appeared to have been an elegant office building. The rags moved as he approached and a terrified face peered at him. The eyes and the once stylish hat could have belonged to Sophia, but when he called her name, the woman edged further into the doorway, holding out a hand to keep him away from her.

–

He slept little that night, the silence of the city punctuated by the occasional burst of gunfire or the rumble of Soviet tanks. But what really kept him awake was the thought of Hanne and the news – or lack of it – Gurevich had brought him. Not alive, but not dead either. And then there was a growing worry that he'd been fooled. He'd found Franz Rauter but then left Berlin without him on the word of a Red Army officer. He should have insisted on exchanging the two Germans somewhere near

Potsdam: Gurevich coming out with Rauter to meet him and Strasser.

It was, he decided, another example of him being less alert. When he'd been operating in Nazi Europe, it had been on the edge of his existence, knowing one small mistake could cost him his life. Every sense had been finely tuned. He'd survived three trips into Germany and countless other incidents. He'd evaded the Gestapo, escaped from a concentration camp and made his way back to Britain not once but twice. But he worried he'd not been nearly as sharp hunting for Milton in England, and now he felt his naïvety could keep Rauter from him. Gurevich was no fool: he knew he had someone the British wanted. He could still ask for something else in return. Prince lay on the lumpy camp bed with his jacket as a pillow, staring at the ceiling and wondering how on earth he was going to explain this to Hugh Harper.

He was back at Behrenstrasse by seven o'clock, and Gurevich met him in the entrance. He looked as if he hadn't slept all night and appeared agitated.

'Strasser confessed, eventually.'

'Good – but what about Rauter? You promised…'

The Russian stopped and placed an arm round Prince's shoulder. 'You're worried I won't let you have him, aren't you? It sounds as if you've been told not to trust the Russians, yes? Don't worry; he's all ready for you. But first, please come with me.'

He led Prince to a small courtyard at the rear of the building. One of its brick walls had collapsed and they had to step over the rubble, eventually coming to a group of men. Strasser was shoved out from the midst of them: he'd lost any vestige of the arrogance and assurance that came from being an SS officer. He looked petrified, shuffling with a limp, and his face was covered in bruises.

'Do you think I should treat him with some dignity and finish him off quickly, or do to him what he did to my family?'

'That's really not for me to say.'

'Isn't it? You're English; you're so good at rules.'

Prince shook his head.

'If you want Rauter, my friend, tell me what to do.'

'If you're asking about rules, then he is a prisoner of war and—'

'Not any more; he's now a war criminal.'

Prince looked at Strasser, hunched against the wall, dark eyes imploring him and his cuffed hands clasped together as if in prayer. He started to speak, and Prince saw that most of his teeth were missing.

'Please, I beg you to let me write one letter, that's all I ask.'

'What would you do if it was your family?' Gurevich had turned to face Prince, keenly interested in how he was going to respond. 'Give me an answer and I'll give you Rauter; if not...'

'If it was my family, I'd make him suffer in the same way.'

Gurevich's first shot hit the German in the ankle, the second one in the thigh. Prince realised he was working his way up Strasser's body, which was now writhing in agony amongst the rubble. A Red Army soldier looked anxiously at Gurevich and raised his sub-machine gun. Gurevich shook his head: *not yet*. The third shot hit Strasser in the stomach and was followed by howls of pain. Gurevich stared at him for a while, tears forming in his eyes. As they streamed down his face, he nodded at the man with the machine gun.

They stood in silence as the echo of the gunfire faded, watching a pool of blood spread around Strasser's body. As they moved away, Gurevich beckoned Prince over and pointed to a first-floor window overlooking the courtyard.

'You see that man at the window?'

'Yes.'

'I gave orders that Franz Rauter be made to watch Strasser's execution. That should ensure his cooperation with you.'

'I take it you're a British officer?'

Prince couldn't help but be impressed at Franz Rauter's demeanour. For someone who was a prisoner of the Red Army and had just watched a fellow German executed in a brutal manner, he appeared calm. He also displayed some of the characteristics Prince had noticed among intelligence officers: an ability to take control of a situation without it being obvious. Asking the first question and attempting to dictate the course of a conversation was a classic example of this.

He watched Rauter carefully, in no hurry to reply. Since learning his name in March, he'd imagined what Milton's handler in Berlin would be like. He'd built up a picture of someone who'd be hostile and difficult, an older man with the bearing of a Prussian officer and something of the fanaticism of a Nazi.

But the man opposite him was nothing like this. He came across as urbane, perhaps in his mid forties, and despite the state of his clothing and his dishevelled appearance, he seemed like someone who in other circumstances might be described as elegant. He reminded Prince of some of the solicitors he came across in Lincoln, men who exuded a certain charm and assurance – some of whom he'd become friendly with.

'I am a British officer, yes.'

'May I ask your name?' Franz Rauter held up his hands in case Prince hadn't realised he was wearing handcuffs. Prince called in a guard and indicated he should remove the cuffs, and was wondering which name he should use when he realised Rauter had subtly gained control of the questioning.

'We'll come to that. Can you confirm *your* name, please?' Prince tapped the small pile of papers he had in front of him.

'Franz Rauter.'

'And you work for…?'

'I think it would be more accurate to say *worked* for, don't you think? I'm assuming I've lost my job!' Rauter laughed: he'd switched to English, another way of controlling how things were going. 'I am a professional intelligence officer – I really have nothing to hide. I was a police officer; I joined the Abwehr in 1932 and moved to Berlin, I've been here ever since. Last year the Abwehr was merged into the RSHA because we were regarded as not Nazi enough. I was attached to Section 6B, which looks after foreign espionage. I was involved exclusively in military espionage. I had no role at all in any political activities. We are completely separate from the Gestapo. And I'm not a Nazi.'

Rauter paused. Two weeks previously, he'd burned his *Mitgliedskarte*, his Nazi Party membership card. He'd lit a celebratory cigar with it. He knew it was possible his name might still exist on a list somewhere, but he was counting on the Englishman not being aware of that.

'And as part of your work as a professional intelligence officer, have you been running agents in Britain?'

The German paused, certainly for longer than Prince was expecting. It was as if he hadn't anticipated this question. Prince concentrated on not showing he was pleased. His old inspector, who'd shown him how to interrogate suspects, would have been proud.

Keep your questions short and to the point… Ask one question at a time: that way they can't pick and choose which one to answer.

When Rauter replied, he was no longer as assured and articulate as he had been. 'My role was more… complicated. I looked after a number of operations and I—'

'My question was very specific, Herr Rauter: have you been running agents in Britain?'

'I had agents in the east, in Poland and—'

'That doesn't answer my question, but it's not a problem. If you're admitting to running agents in the east, I can hand you back to my Russian friends. As you witnessed this morning, they have a very different method of dealing with suspects than we do.'

Prince waited, the only sounds being Rauter's increasingly heavy breathing and some shouting outside. A door slammed down the corridor and in the distance came the sound of gunfire, a single rifle shot. Prince toyed with the idea of gathering up the papers and making to leave, but he knew he could only do that the once, and he didn't think the time had come yet.

'One.'

'I beg your pardon?'

'One: I ran one agent in your country. Just one – and not an important one.'

'And the name of this agent?'

Rauter shook his head. 'It was some time ago.'

'I can leave, Herr Rauter: of course I'll be disappointed, but think about this – I'll be leaving you with the Russians. If you tell me who your agent is in Britain, then I will take you with me back to England. You'll be treated fairly there, I can promise you that.'

Rauter stared at his lace-less shoes and adjusted the frayed cuffs of his dirty pullover. 'How can I believe you?'

'You'll have to take my word for it, but of course you don't know for sure. What you do know for sure, though, is how the Russians will treat you if I leave you with them. Tell me the code name of your agent in Britain.'

Rauter didn't reply, now looking up at the ceiling.

'My patience is running thin, Herr Rauter. I have to leave Berlin soon. I understand your reluctance to give me this information, but you must realise that the war is over. Who's going to thank you for your misguided loyalty? After all, you tell me you're not a Nazi. I'm giving you an opportunity to save yourself. How about if I give you the code name of the agent I believe you've been running in London.'

The very slightest of nods from the German.

'Milton.'

Rauter's eyes widened and he turned pale. He became agitated, shifting around in his chair and running a hand across his brow and through his hair.

'Is it Milton?'

'Yes.'

'And what is Milton's real name?'

'Palmer, Edward Palmer. But I didn't recruit him.'

'And the other agents that work with him – Byron and Donne: who are they?'

Rauter appeared to regain his composure. He asked for some water and drank it slowly. He was buying himself time to think.

'I promise you that when I am in England I will tell you, I'll tell you everything. But first get me away from here. Let me ask you something, though: how the hell did you know about me?'

'Edward Palmer was a suspect, but then we heard about your being brought to Brussels to interrogate an RAF pilot with the same name. I put two and two together. But now you tell me something: how come the Gestapo in Brussels thought a young RAF pilot could be one of your spies?'

'Because they're fools, that's why. When Palmer told us he was being sent to fight in Normandy, I had his name put on a watch list in case he was captured by us. I wanted him brought to me. The watch list details were clear enough: they gave his age and said he was British Army. Those idiots in Brussels... The RAF officer looked like a teenager.' He shook his head.

'Do you have any idea where Palmer is now?'

'I assumed you'd arrested him.'

Prince shook his head.

'So where is he then?'

Prince stood up and straightened his uniform. 'That, Herr Rauter, is what I very much hope you'll be able to help us with.'

Chapter 29

England, May 1945

It was a glorious afternoon, a pleasant breeze drifting in from the nearby low hills across neatly arranged and seemingly perfectly square fields and in through the open doors of the house.

Prince's state of exhaustion was all too familiar: he'd experienced it often enough on his clandestine missions in Europe, and before that as a police detective working through the day and night to solve a case. It was the kind of tiredness where one moved beyond exhaustion into an odd kind of light-headed euphoria, slightly drunk without having touched any alcohol. In occupied Europe, it had induced a degree of courage that bordered on the reckless. He'd last slept – though only fitfully – on the Tuesday night in Berlin, before going to Behrenstrasse to collect Franz Rauter on the Wednesday morning. They'd made their way to Hamburg, where the British had captured the airport intact, and left on an RAF flight early on the Thursday morning.

The whole time Franz Rauter was calm, promising Prince he'd be no trouble and had nothing to hide. His relief at being rescued from the Russians was obvious.

When they landed in England, Lance King was waiting for them at the steps of the plane, and an hour later Prince was with Hugh Harper in the lounge of a large and isolated Victorian country house somewhere in the south of England. Rauter had been taken away to be checked by a doctor.

'There's nothing wrong with him, sir.'

'That may well be the case, Prince, but let me tell you, there's been quite a flap at head office about this.'

'A flap about what, sir?'

'About bringing Rauter over here. I'm not blaming you, Prince, but you need to understand there are politics at play at the top of my organisation, and when one of my colleagues heard about this, he questioned the legality of what we'd done. Evidently it's problematic because Rauter's a non-combatant and as far as we're aware hasn't committed a crime against British subjects. In fact—'

'Surely, sir it—'

'Hang on, Prince, hang on… We've had the bloody lawyers all over this and their solution is for Rauter to sign a declaration saying he came over here of his own free will. We will acknowledge he's here as a witness and not as a suspect and that he'll be able to return to Germany once he's helped us. The form's being drawn up now and brought here by dispatch rider. The director general himself got involved and insisted Rauter had a medical, so I hope nothing untoward happened.'

'The Soviets roughed him up a bit, but I've not laid a finger on him. Pardon my naïvety, sir, but I thought that in the world of espionage and counter-intelligence rules were somewhat more relaxed. Surely bringing a German spymaster over on a critical investigation is a matter of some urgency?'

'I would agree with you, Prince, but no sooner has the war ended than some of my colleagues have reverted to their civil service mentality. Let's just hope Rauter signs the bloody form. But do let's look on the bright side: we had little other than circumstantial evidence against Edward Palmer, but now that Rauter's confirmed he is indeed Agent Milton, we have a clear-cut case against him. You've done very well, Prince.'

'I've only done well if we can find Milton – I presume there's no news?'

'No, there isn't, I'm afraid, but I'm rather hoping Rauter can assist us with that. What's he like, by the way?'

'Fine – insists he's a professional intelligence officer dealing with military matters and nothing to do with politics. Claims he's not a Nazi, but then he's hardly likely to go around quoting extracts from *Mein Kampf*, I suppose. Seems a rather agreeable chap if you want my opinion, sir, and I do think I have a reasonable instinct for knowing when someone's pulling the wool over my eyes. I think we should take him at his word and treat him accordingly. He'll be more cooperative if he realises he's a witness rather than a suspect.'

'Any idea *why* he's being quite so agreeable, as you put it?'

'To be blunt, because we're not the Russians. From what I could gather over there, all the Germans are doing their best to avoid the Red Army.'

'So I understand. I was at my club the other day and someone said the only reason Jodl agreed to an unconditional surrender was because Eisenhower told him that if he didn't, he'd stop Germans approaching Allied lines to surrender. You look exhausted, Prince. Go and have a bath and a rest: the form ought to be here soon and we can't start our chat with Rauter until then, can we?'

–

It felt more like a social occasion than an interrogation as they gathered in the dining room just after seven o'clock that Thursday evening. The two guards looking after Franz Rauter stayed in the background. Rauter had been given clean clothes to change into and appeared relaxed, helping himself to the buffet. Hugh Harper took Prince aside and told him the German had signed the form: they were free to go ahead with the interview.

They were joined by Lance King, Bartholomew and Audrey, and once they'd all eaten, they adjourned to another room where half a dozen armchairs had been arranged in a circle. Rauter said he was very grateful for how he'd been treated and had been very relieved to have it confirmed to him that he was here as a witness, nothing more than that. 'So how can I help you?' He leaned back in his armchair, crossed his legs and smiled.

Once more Prince recognised the tone: the charm and the attempt to take control of the situation. *Ask the first question.*

Hugh Harper was slightly thrown, and muttered something about the war being over but there was still a need to root out—

Prince interrupted. 'Perhaps if I kick off, sir? Herr Rauter confirmed to me in Berlin that Agent Milton is the code-name for Major Edward Palmer. We want to know as much as possible, Herr Rauter, about Milton and the other agents he's connected with, most particularly agents Byron and Donne, who we believe still to be alive. If you could start at the beginning of your involvement in this case, that would be helpful.'

Harper nodded approvingly and Rauter helped himself to a glass of water from the small table in front of them. He remained silent for a while as he seemed to gather his thoughts, a hint of a smile on his face.

'I have already made the point to your colleague here, who I had the pleasure of meeting in Berlin, that I was a police officer before joining the Abwehr, where my role was purely as a professional intelligence officer dealing with military matters. I was never involved in the regime's political activities and nor was I a Nazi. Let me state at the outset that I didn't recruit Agent Milton. As I understand it, he was first spotted by one of your countrymen in 1933, I think it was.'

'What was the name of this man – the one who recruited Milton?'

'His code name was Chiltern and I only became aware of him a few months ago. I discovered his name was Arthur Chapman-Collins.'

'Why do you say "was"?'

Rauter leaned forward in his armchair and then back again before reaching for his glass of water. For a while he didn't say anything, but then he shrugged his shoulders as if it didn't matter. 'I'm not sure what you're getting at.'

'You said "was", Herr Rauter: that is the past tense. It implies Arthur Chapman-Collins is dead.'

'You must understand my English is not very good. I didn't mean to imply anything.'

'You said you only became aware of Arthur Chapman-Collins a few months ago. Can you remember when this was?'

Rauter stared hard at Prince as if he realised he was being led into a trap. He swept his fingers through his hair and coughed, shrugging his shoulders again. 'No, I'm afraid I can't remember exactly.'

'Let me help you, Herr Rauter: was it this year?'

'I think so, yes.'

'Which month?'

'I'm really not sure.'

'You see, we too are aware of Arthur Chapman-Collins, and he was murdered in his apartment in London in February. You'll understand why we might speculate whether there's a connection between your becoming aware of him and his death.'

Rauter smiled and looked round the room. 'There appears to be a misunderstanding. When I say I became aware of this man, I simply meant I was reading some notes in the file and came across his name: his last involvement with the Abwehr would have been back in 1933 or 1934. I know nothing about his death. What happened was that a colleague of mine called Helmut Krüger came to Cambridge in the summer of 1934 and actually recruited Palmer, though I understand it was a year or two before Palmer realised he was an Abwehr agent. I'm sure you're all familiar with how that works. A series of subtle steps and by the time someone realises they are working for you as an agent, it's too late for them to get out of it.'

'Are you saying Palmer was an unwilling spy?'

'A good question. I would say that by the time he understood what had happened, he decided he needed to be professional about it. There's no doubt he was sympathetic to Germany.'

'May I ask a question, please?' It was Audrey, checking her notes. 'You say he was recruited by a Helmut Krüger: do you know where Krüger is?'

'He died in 1939, which was when Milton was handed over to me by my boss, Otto Prager – who also died, in case you want to meet him too. And before you ask, both men died of natural causes. That did happen under the Nazis.' Rauter continued: how once the war started, the idea had been for Milton to be allowed a few years to establish himself before being activated as a spy; how a series of agents had been sent over to work with him, all of whom died.

'The first one of these was code-named... perhaps you'd be so good as to tell me the code name, Herr Rauter?' Audrey spoke without looking up from her notebook.

Rauter leaned back and closed his eyes momentarily. 'Keats.'

'And did Keats ever make contact with Milton?'

'No.'

'And he was killed in a railway accident in... November 1943.'

Rauter said that was correct.

'Can you please give me the code name of the agent who replaced poor Keats, and when.'

'That was an agent code-named Shelley and he came over the following month.'

'And he was found dead in December 1943. You didn't wait long, did you? You sent over yet another agent, who died in January 1944, correct?'

'I think you'll find it was the March, actually.'

'And his name? The name he was using here?'

'Dabrowski, Jan Dabrowski.'

'Code name?'

'Dryden.'

'Three agents,' said Prince, 'all dead within weeks if not days of arriving here. Rather a run of bad luck, wouldn't you say?'

Rauter shrugged. 'The first three agents, they weren't recruited by me. But tell me, how do you know their code names?'

Prince leaned over towards him. 'I think you'll find that the way this works is we ask questions and you answer them, if that's all right with you. So you've confirmed that Keats, Shelley and Dryden were your agents. We understand that last August or September, I think it was, you sent over yet another agent.'

Rauter half nodded, frowning at the same time.

'And his code name, please.'

'Donne. May I ask, is he still alive?'

Prince ignored the question. 'You said you didn't recruit the first three agents who came over. Presumably that means you did recruit Donne?'

Rauter said nothing.

'What can you tell me about him?'

'Tell me first – is he alive, and if so, is he in captivity?'

Prince looked at Hugh Harper, who nodded. 'We believe he is still alive, and no, he isn't in custody.'

'Really? In that case, he's done well to have survived so long. Agent Donne is a British prisoner of war called John Morton. There was a crazy scheme to recruit a British unit of the SS from among your prisoners of war. They called it the British Free Corps but never managed to recruit more than fifty men, and most of them were fairly pathetic cases. I visited them and thought Morton was a good prospect – the only one who was.'

'Do you remember any details about him – rank, regiment?'

Rauter dropped his head back, deep in thought. 'Had I known you'd be asking all these questions, I'd have stopped by my office in Tirpitzufer and collected his file!' He laughed and looked round the room. 'That was a joke: all my files will now no doubt be ashes. John Morton, let me see... I remember he was only a private and had been taken prisoner at Dunkirk in May 1940. As for his regiment, I did check it out, just to be sure he had indeed been at Dunkirk. The Middlesex Regiment – could that be correct?'

Lance King said there was such a regiment.

'I presume you gave him another identity?'

'Of course.'

'And are you going to tell us that identity?'

Rauter hesitated and leaned back in the armchair.

'You see, so far, Herr Rauter, you've not told us anything we don't already know. You've served some purpose in confirming those facts, but for this to be helpful to us – within the terms of the agreement we've signed – then we need you to tell us more of what we *don't* already know, if you catch my drift.'

'You agreed that I'm a witness and here in a voluntary capacity.'

'Indeed.'

'And that I can return to Germany when I'm finished?'

'We'll determine when we've finished, Herr Rauter, and where in Germany we're obliged to return you to is yet to be decided.'

'Now look, I—' Rauter looked furious.

'Hang on,' said Prince, shooting an angry glance at King. 'I asked Herr Rauter for the identity Agent Donne is using, and I'm sure he's about to give it to us.'

Rauter shook his head. 'The identity we furnished him with is Jim Maslin.' He leaned forward, his arms resting on his thighs and his head bowed.

'And do you know where he may be?'

'No. The system we used was for the contact agent – Donne in this case – to be the go-between, linking Milton with the radio operator.'

'Agent Byron?'

'Correct. It was – is – Byron's job to look after Donne. He would find him somewhere to stay and use him to pass our messages on to Milton, and vice versa. That way we could ensure Byron and Milton didn't need to meet in person, thereby ensuring their safety.'

'So Byron is the key man in all this?'

288

'Indeed.'

'And you're now about to tell us *his* name, aren't you, Herr Rauter?'

'Before you start threatening me again, let me tell you this. I expect I don't need to lecture you on how espionage works. You'll know that even someone coordinating an espionage operation as I was in this case won't be aware of every single detail about every person involved. Sometimes an agent is only ever known by their code name. After all, the more you know, the more security can be compromised. That was the case with Agent Byron. He'd been recruited some years before the war started and was already in place as a radio operator when I took Milton over, so I didn't recruit him, I inherited him. I knew his code name and our radio operators knew how to contact him. I would write messages to him, which would be encoded and then transmitted, and likewise his messages to us. I'm afraid I can't tell you his name. I realise it would be easier for me if I could. I just know he's in London, and so is Donne.'

'Any idea where in London?'

'Who, Byron or Donne?'

'Both of them.'

'I've no idea where Donne will be; that would have been organised by Byron – I've already told you that.'

'So do you know where Byron is?'

Rauter started to speak, then stopped himself and took his time to drink some water. 'The one person who knew about Byron was my old boss, Otto Prager. Otto was an old-fashioned intelligence officer and certainly not a Nazi. He left the Abwehr very suddenly soon after the war started, around the middle of September '39. He died a few days later, as I told you, from natural causes. He had a heart condition but I've no doubt he was under considerable stress. What you need to understand about the Nazis was that they didn't need any excuse to kill someone. Had they wanted to kill Otto they'd have taken him to Prinz-Albrecht-Strasse and done the job in the basement there

– they'd have been pleased to use it as an example for the rest of us in Tirpitzufer who they never quite trusted.'

'You suggested Otto Prager knew more about Byron.'

'Yes, but how much I'm not sure. He knew Byron was British and had been in place for a while, and that he lived in a part of London called Chelsea. Or at least he did in 1939; whether he's still there…'

'You've no idea where in Chelsea?'

'No. Whether Otto knew his identity, I'm not sure. There were handwritten notes in the file but nothing about Byron's real name. It's interesting that all three men in the spy ring are British – Palmer, Morton and Byron. Just goes to show, eh? All those fools we sent over – the Dutchmen, Germans, Poles, whatever – they were all caught. But your local traitors have prospered!'

Glances were exchanged around the room. Lance King spoke first. 'And that's all you can tell us about Byron – that he's British?'

Rauter nodded. 'And where he lived – I've told you that.'

'Milton has been missing for nearly three weeks now. You can't tell us where he is?'

'I have no idea, but maybe you should start with Agent Donne. He certainly met both Milton and Byron, and I've given you the name he'll be using.'

'Have you heard from any of them recently?'

Rauter laughed. 'Seriously, do you have any idea what it's been like in Berlin for the past month? We've had the Red Army to worry about: they rather interfered with running any kind of intelligence operation. If you want my opinion…'

He paused and looked up, his eyebrows raised, wondering whether the others did want his opinion. Harper muttered, 'Go on.'

'I think Edward Palmer is very smart and resourceful. He was an effective agent who managed to operate successfully in a very exposed position. Even maintaining his cover while he was a sleeper agent required skill and bravery. I think he suspected the game was up and disappeared. My opinion is that even if he didn't suspect anything, he certainly knew the war was over. If he had any sense, he'd have had another identity waiting to be used: I know I did. I just didn't get a chance to use mine.'

Hugh Harper said that was enough for the evening and they'd meet again in the morning. The guards took Rauter up to a secure room.

'What do we make of that?' Harper looked slightly deflated.

'Not sure it was worth going to all that effort, to be honest, Hugh. I mean, jolly well done to Prince, of course, but what did Rauter tell us that we didn't already know?'

'He told us Agent Donne's real name and the identity he's using here.'

'Assuming he's telling the truth.'

'But it's something to go on.'

'For what it's worth,' said Audrey, 'I believe him. You've done plenty of these interrogations, Hugh – you too, I daresay, Lance. I think he was telling the truth. We got him to give us the code names of all three contact agents, and when I deliberately got wrong the month of Dryden's death, he corrected me.'

'True, Audrey, and nor did he embellish his story or give us lots of extraneous detail; no long tales that we'd lap up. Plus he volunteered Byron's Chelsea connection.' Harper now looked less deflated.

Prince stood up and yawned. 'If you don't mind, I've been up for God knows how long and I need some sleep. How about tomorrow Bartholomew and I head to London and start the search for Jim Maslin? If we find him, that could lead us to Byron.'

'And who knows, Milton too.'

'Good idea: Lance you'd better go too. Audrey and I will stay here and go through Rauter's account with him with a fine-tooth comb. Annoying about Byron, though; if only we had something on him…'

Chapter 30

England, May 1945

'Christ, this had better be important.'

'I wouldn't have called you if it wasn't important: you told me only to use that code in an extreme emergency, and I think this counts as an extreme emergency.'

'Let's head over there.'

Despite being shorter than Jim Maslin and walking with some difficulty, anyone observing the pair would have discerned that the older man was the one in control, the younger man deferring to him.

'Is this really the best place for us to meet – behind a fucking prison?'

Byron shot him another angry look and the two men walked on in silence. It was early on a Thursday afternoon in the middle of May, and they were on Wormwood Scrubs, a large open stretch of land behind the prison of the same name, with Hammersmith Hospital next door to it. The ground was still wet from the downpour earlier that morning.

'I've been doing this long enough not to require your advice on where to meet, thank you very much. We've got East Acton station over there and at least two bus routes on Du Cane Road, and there's the hospital: if anyone asks, we're here to visit a sick relative. You can enter the hospital through the door at the rear and it's easy to lose anyone in all the corridors that will take you to the main entrance at the front. So please give me some credit, all right?'

'Do we still need to be so cautious – the war's over, isn't it?'

Byron shot him another angry look. 'Not for us it isn't: it will never be over for us – all these fucking street parties, idiots celebrating… Let's sit over here. Tell me what the extreme emergency is.'

The two men were on a bench, their backs to the hospital and the prison. Jim Maslin leaned forward and Byron did likewise.

'They're on to me.'

Byron sat bolt upright. 'What! Who are?'

'I dunno… the authorities. I mean for Christ's sake, I…' Jim Maslin dropped his cigarette and leaned further forward to search for it in the grass.

'Calm down and start from the beginning. Have you been drinking?'

'You would too if you were in my position.'

'I told you to cut it out. You'd better tell me what's up.'

'I was meant to be on a ten o'clock start at the hospital this morning – a ten-to-six shift. I finished at eight last night and a few of the other porters were going for a drink and asked me to come with them. It was another bloody victory party, this one at their local off the Edgware Road. I thought if I didn't go it would look off, so I went along and—'

'Got drunk?'

'I admit I had a few drinks, but how would it appear if I'd sat on my own drinking water and looking miserable? Anyway, I got talking to this woman: must have been mid forties, too much lipstick but an enormous pair of tits and—'

'Get to the point.'

'She was moaning about how now the war was over her husband would be coming home and she'd no longer be a free woman, and I asked her what she meant by that and the next thing I know she'd got her tongue down my throat and her hand down my trousers and ten minutes later we were back in her flat, which was only round the corner, and when we finished with... you know, we had a few more drinks and then carried on where we'd left off. I must've fallen asleep after that 'cos next thing I know it's ten o'clock this morning.'

'You fool.'

'Christ knows how much I must have drunk. So I got dressed and rushed out and stopped at a telephone box near the bus stop and rang the porter's office at St Mary's to tell them I'd be a few minutes late, and the girl who looks after the office – Kath – said, "Talk of the devil," and I said what do you mean and she said, "Your ears must have been burning 'cos there's been people asking about you," and I said what people and she said the police.'

'The police?'

'She said two men in plain clothes but with police identity cards had turned up at eight o'clock that morning asking for me and said it was routine or something, and she told them I wasn't due in until ten. She gave them my address in Shepherd's Bush and obviously I wasn't there, but now they were waiting outside the porter's office for me. So a good job I got drunk, isn't it? If I hadn't, I'd have walked right into a trap.'

'It's not bloody funny; I don't know why you're laughing. Did you tell her where you were?'

'Of course not, I'm not stupid. I made up a story about losing my identity card and said it was probably some misunderstanding over that and I was on my way in. Then I crossed the road and got on a bus going in the other direction and found another phone box and called you and used that code you said was for an extreme emergency, and here we are. Did I do the right thing?'

'Of course you did, Jim, you've done well. It's... what, a quarter to twelve now. I'm going to be late for work myself. Let me think, give me a minute. Wait here.'

Maslin watched as Byron stood up painfully and paced up and down in front of him.

'Goes without saying you can't return to your flat in Shepherd's Bush. You're going to need to leave town. Get as far away from London as possible but obviously steer clear of any of your old haunts.'

'Leave when?'

'Today, as soon as possible, and you'll have to get rid of your Jim Maslin identity card; you can't risk having that on you if that's who they're looking for. Get a new one wherever you end up.'

'What about if I'm stopped before then and haven't got one on me?'

'By law I think you've got up to forty-eight hours to go to a police station and show it there. Just be very contrite and say you've left it at home or something.'

'I'll need money for a new card – that will have to be a black market job.'

'You've been given enough. I suppose you've spent it all on drink?'

'It's in the flat in Shepherd's Bush.'

Byron resumed his pacing, deep in thought, glancing occasionally at Jim as if to check he was still there. 'Christ knows how they're on to you. I hope they've not got Milton. You didn't let anything slip out to anyone, did you?'

'Of course not.'

'Even when you've been drunk?'

'Nope. Look, if I'm going to be all right and not go and get myself caught, I'm going to need a fair amount of money, aren't I?'

Byron opened his wallet and took out some pound notes, folding them into Maslin's hand. 'Here's some cash.'

'Eight pounds – are you joking?'

'It's all I've got.'

'Jesus,' said Maslin, 'maybe I'd be better off turning myself in. A couple of years in prison and then I can have a new start without having to worry all the bloody time...'

'Come on, Jim, pull yourself together. You don't want to be turning yourself in. It will be a lot more than two years, I can tell you; in fact they'll probably throw the book at you.'

'They won't if I cooperate, eh?'

Byron smiled. 'I'll tell you what, Jim, I'll tell you what... hang around until tonight and I can get you more money.'

'How much?'

'How much did you have in mind?'

'It's going to need to be a hundred at least if I'm going to keep out of trouble.'

'I can get you a hundred, maybe a bit more.'

Maslin's eyes lit up.

'Look, walk north from here into Harlesden and keep to yourself. Maybe use that money to buy yourself a new hat and jacket and a bag. There are cheap boarding houses round there; get yourself a room for tonight. Some of them off the Harrow Road won't bother with asking you to register if you slip them a bit extra. Then meet me back here at nine o'clock: wait if I'm a few minutes late.'

'Nine o'clock?'

'I won't be able to get away from work before then, and anyway, I need to get the money, don't I?'

'Can I ask you a question?'

'Better hurry, Jim, I need to get a move on.'

'How did you start working for them?'

'Who?'

'You know... the Germans.'

The older man stopped and frowned in concentration as if it was a good question that required careful consideration.

'Like so many of us, I didn't start working for them, I started working for a cause, and then they came along and I suppose they became that cause, if you see what I mean. That guy you killed in February...'

'Rodney Bird?'

'Yes, he recruited me: that was his speciality, finding people to work for them. He found Milton too. Once he found you, it was too late: he reminded me of Count Dracula in that respect

– you were under his spell. It's not been a bad cause to work for, but now… who knows. I'll see you here at nine, Jim.'

–

Prince, King and Bartholomew had returned to London on the Friday morning, the day after Rauter had been brought to England. They agreed King and Bartholomew would concentrate on the search for the person going by the name Jim Maslin, while Prince would check out John Morton.

He'd headed straight to the MI9 office on the fourth floor of the Great Central Hotel and assured an annoyed secretary that although he didn't have an appointment with Tom Bennet, he needed to see him nonetheless. The MI9 man was surprised to see him.

'How did you get on with your Danish lady, the one at Ravensbrück?'

'I'm still looking for her.'

'And is your visit in connection with that?'

'No, sir: you remember you told me the tale of the RAF pilot who was arrested in Brussels, and how they'd brought someone over from Berlin to interrogate him?'

'Ted Palmer, yes, that's right. Anything come of it?'

'As it happens, it did, sir, and we're very grateful to you. My visit is indirectly connected to that. How easy is it to check on one of our prisoners of war?'

'When you say check…'

'A name has come up in the case I'm investigating – one of our prisoners of war is alleged to have been helping the Germans. We urgently need to check this out.'

'I take it he's a prisoner of the Germans then?'

Prince nodded.

'Do you have a name?' Tom Bennet had removed his jacket and placed a sheet of paper on his blotter.

'The name we have is John Morton, most probably a private with the Middlesex Regiment, captured at Dunkirk in May 1940.'

'That's it?'

'Yes, sir.'

'Well, Registry is out in Wiltshire these days.' The MI9 man was screwing the cap on his fountain pen. 'But I could telephone them if you want this now?'

'If you don't mind, yes please.'

Bennet spoke with a clerk, carefully repeating the information Prince had given him. *Yes, I'll wait.* He lit a cigarette, clamping it between his teeth at the side of his mouth and then filling his fountain pen. He was halfway through this when Prince heard him say, 'Yes… Oh really? Well, well, fancy that, eh? … Hang on, slow down, let me write this carefully.'

Prince watched him anxiously, noting a broad grin emerge on Bennet's face.

'Looks like this could well be your man: Private John Morton, the Middlesex Regiment, captured at Dunkirk in May 1940, as you say. Last heard of in Stalag IV-B, which is one of their larger prisoner-of-war camps; it's in Saxony – near the town of Mühlberg. Dates are unspecific, but it seems Private Morton was one of a very small number of our prisoners who were attracted by the idea of joining a British SS unit, would you believe. Apparently he was something of a fascist agitator at the camp. Last heard of in Berlin. I'd like to get my hands on the bastard.'

'So would I.'

–

Prince had to admit it had been easy enough to track down John Morton, though he'd have preferred Bartholomew and Lance King to have been slightly less grudging about it. They all knew he wouldn't be using that identity: the man they needed to find was Jim Maslin.

298

It was Friday afternoon, 11 May, and the three of them were sitting round a small table, Bartholomew reading from his notes. 'Rauter said agents Byron and Donne were both in London, so I suggest we work on the assumption Donne is still in the city.'

'What date was it that Edward Palmer disappeared?'

'He went missing on the twentieth of April.'

'So three weeks ago today?'

'Indeed.'

'Jim Maslin could well have gone with him.'

'It's possible,' said Prince, 'but I very much doubt it. Two of them travelling together makes them more exposed. I agree with Bartholomew: let's work on the basis that Jim Maslin is still in London. If we've not got anywhere in a week, then we can think again.'

'Christ, this is going to be a tedious job.' Lance King was now sitting by the open window, his feet on the table. 'You obviously know how it all works, don't you, Prince?'

'The National Registration Identity Cards? Of course I do... the bane of our lives in the police force. Everyone needs to be registered at their local police station, and if you move to another area and don't register, it's an offence. I doubt an agent who's been here so long would have made the basic mistake of not registering.'

'Every bloody police station in London will have a register... It'll take us forever to go through them. Perhaps if we speak to Scotland Yard we can get them to send a message round to all their stations instructing them to check for a Jim Maslin.'

'I wouldn't.'

'And why would that be, Prince?' King was busy lighting another cigarette.

'Because it's unreliable, Lance. I know how police stations work: they're undermanned and overworked and when an instruction comes in from headquarters half of them will leave it in the pending tray. If we want to do a thorough job, we need to have one of our own people – preferably a couple of them

– visiting every police station in London and looking through the records themselves.'

'I agree,' said Bartholomew.

'How many police stations are there in London?'

'I don't know exactly, but certainly in excess of two hundred.'

'We'd better get started then, hadn't we?'

-

By the Wednesday morning, they'd checked the registers at every police station in London with no sign of a Jim or James Maslin. They'd found a few Jim Martins and a James Masters and a dozen male Maslins, one of whom – a John Maslin – was in his forties. It turned out he'd been invalided out of the army and lived with his family in Leyton. They reconvened on the Wednesday morning, Lance King making it clear he'd doubted all along that Agent Donne would've registered with the police. Or he'd used another name. Or had left London.

'There is another possibility, sir.' Bartholomew had allowed King to finish.

'Go on.'

'Police stations carry separate registers for some of the places of work in their patch, usually larger ones deemed to be of some importance, such as government departments and hospitals. They're more of a list of people who work there than their identity card details: it's useful to have a record in case the place is bombed. I believe the practice began during the Blitz.'

They started with the larger central London police stations, and it was Bartholomew himself who found him just before nine o'clock that evening. Later that night, they gathered in King's office.

'Perhaps you'd like to bring Hugh up to date, Bartholomew?'

'Paddington police station has a register of all staff employed at St Mary's Hospital, sir. They have a Jim Maslin down as a porter: he started work there last September.'

'Which would fit in with Agent Donne's arrival here, would it not?'

'Yes, sir, but unfortunately there's no home address for him: that would be kept at the hospital.'

'I've just returned from the hospital.' They all turned to look at Prince. 'I found the porters' office and kept it low-key in case he's working there tonight. Turns out he's on the rota to start at ten o'clock in the morning. I think the safest approach would be to wait for him to turn up tomorrow. The woman who looks after the office gets in early and we can get his address then.'

—

It had been a disaster from the start.

In between the few hours' sleep he'd grabbed that night, Prince worried he'd made yet another error. He'd been far too cautious. They should have found the woman who looked after the porters and found out Maslin's address that night.

He and Lance King arrived at the hospital the following morning just as a woman called Kath turned up for work at the porters' office. Once they'd shown her the police warrant cards they were carrying, she gave them Jim Maslin's home address. They assured her he wasn't in any kind of trouble. *Routine.*

The two men then managed to have an argument standing in the drizzle outside the office. Lance King insisted they should immediately go to the address in Shepherd's Bush; Prince felt it would be safer to wait at the hospital. By half eight, they'd reached a compromise and called Bartholomew from a telephone box, instructing him to send a team to the flat. When they called him back half an hour later, he had bad news.

'He wasn't there.'

Prince was holding the receiver between himself and King. The two men were pressed together in the box, its windows steamed up with condensation. Outside the rain was getting heavier. King's cigarette was just an inch from Prince's face.

'Does it look like the right address?'

'You'll need to speak up.'

'I said, does it look like the right address?'

'It's certainly the right address; there's a wage slip from the hospital on the table in his name. If he was here last night, he's tidied the place up: bed's made and there's nothing dirty in the kitchen area. It's not the kind of place I'd expect a hospital porter to have.'

'What do you mean?'

'It's a very nice little flat: it has a private entrance and decent furniture and – here's an interesting one – its own telephone. How many hospital porters have a flat like that? It's just gone nine, sir; I reckon he's left for work.'

Prince and King stood in a doorway opposite the entrance to the porters' office, unable to avoid the rain soaking them and squabbling about what to do next. Overnight they'd managed to get hold of a photograph of Private John Morton from his regimental headquarters, and they studied each man who walked past. Prince said it would be better if one of them went inside in case he used another entrance.

'This is the only entrance, Prince: be patient.'

They finally went in at a quarter past ten. *No sign of Jim?*

'Don't you worry, my dear, he'll be here soon: I've just spoken to him, in fact.'

'You what?'

'He telephoned.' She patted the phone in front of her just in case they weren't sure. 'Said he was running late and I told him you were waiting to see him and he said it must be something to do with his identity card and he was on his way.'

King and Prince shot furious looks at each other.

'Did he say where he was?'

'No, but I wouldn't worry: Jim's normally a good time-keeper. Why don't you make yourselves comfortable over there? Don't look so worried – the war's over!'

Jim Maslin wasn't sure. He wasn't sure that remaining in London had been a good idea; he wasn't sure that being on the dark expanse behind the prison and the hospital was wise, and he wasn't sure about Agent Byron. He was no longer sure he trusted the man: although he was older and shorter than him and walked with that limp, there was something threatening about him he didn't like. He made him feel inferior, as if Byron had spent his life being ordered around so relished the opportunity to treat Maslin the way he had been treated by others. He felt uneasy in his company.

He crouched down by a low wall with the hospital to his left. The longer he waited, the more his doubts increased. He'd only stayed in London because Byron had offered him money, and now he worried that he'd been too greedy. He'd had twenty pounds on him anyway – he always made sure to carry a large sum just in case – and he should have relied on that. It was almost a month's wages. That and the eight pounds Byron had given him should have been fine. And there was something a bit too quick about the way the older man had promised to get a hundred pounds and then said it could be more. He wasn't sure this felt right.

He decided to leave. He'd stay overnight in the fleapit in Harlesden where he'd taken a room for the night and then leave by bus first thing in the morning.

'Are you going somewhere, Jim?'

He could barely make Byron out. It was just a voice out of the darkness.

'No, I was waiting for you.'

'You looked like you were leaving.'

'No, no… I was just wondering where you were; it's gone nine fifteen.'

'I said to wait if I was late. I have the money. We'd better go over there Jim, we're too near the hospital. Someone might see us from that car park.'

Maslin hesitated. There was a nearly full moon but it was obscured by cloud. He could just make out Byron moving further away from him, deeper into the Scrubs.

'Come on, let's get this over and done with. I got you a hundred and sixty in the end; that will sort you out fine. You'll be able to afford a new identity and have plenty left over. It'll last you months.'

Maslin hesitated. He reckoned he was closer to the hospital than Byron. If he ran off now, the older man would never catch him. On the other hand...

'Come on, Jim: look, I'm sorry I've been a bit sharp. The tension gets to me too, you know. Come and take the money and then we're done.'

Maslin made up his mind. As soon as he had the money he'd be off. He could make out Byron walking towards him now holding a bundle of notes, and stepped forward to accept it. He couldn't take his eyes off the thick wad of cash, and by the time he spotted the knife it was too late. He stood fixed to the spot as Byron lunged forward, thrusting the long blade into his stomach, then sank to the ground, still reaching out for the money.

Byron was surprised at how unresisting Jim was, still silent as he used one hand to support himself on the ground, the other, held out to take the money, moving to his stomach. He moved quickly behind him, grabbing him by the hair and yanking his head back before slicing across his throat. Then he shoved him forward, using his foot to force him face down in the long damp grass.

He crouched down and waited a while, catching his breath and watching Agent Donne's body to check it wasn't moving. Then he dragged it a few yards behind a large patch of bushes and wiped his shoes and hands on the wet grass.

Maybe I'd be better off turning myself in... if I cooperate...

It was odd, he reflected, how readily people could condemn themselves. When he stood up, his leg was aching; the shrapnel tended to do that when the weather was wet and he'd been exerting himself. It wasn't yet half nine; if he hurried, he could catch the last train into central London from East Acton. He decided against it. They'd almost certainly find the body the following day, and he didn't want some nosy parker at the station remembering the man with the limp passing through the previous night.

He'd head north across the open land until he came to Scrubs Lane.

If his memory served him right, the 626 bus would take him all the way to Chelsea.

Chapter 31

England, May 1945

'So on balance we can say the body is that of John Morton: do you agree, Prince?'

Prince breathed in as he prepared to answer Hugh Harper's question for the third time. For some reason, Harper was being obtuse. They couldn't prove the body found on Wormwood Scrubs was that of John Morton, but Prince reckoned they'd come close enough to doing so. Franz Rauter had identified it and they had the photograph of Morton supplied by his regiment. And the blood group was the same as Morton's according to his army records.

'And remember, we can prove the body is that of the man calling himself Jim Maslin, sir: we have his fingerprints all over the apartment.'

Harper finally conceded that the body was indeed that of John Morton.

'And the results of the second post-mortem Prince?'

'Same as the first one, sir – that he died as a result of significant trauma caused by a bladed instrument to both his stomach and his throat, the latter being the primary and fatal wound.'

'And time of death?'

'Both pathologists agree he was killed sometime on the evening before his body was discovered, which would be the Thursday night. The body was found at ten o'clock on Friday morning and by then full rigor mortis had set in, so it's hard to be specific about the time of death.'

'And enquiries are taking place throughout the area?'

'Naturally, sir, though they haven't turned up anything thus far.'

'And Franz Rauter... how's he getting on, Lance?'

'Rather enjoying being the lord of the manor. The guards say he's no trouble at all; spends his time in the library or the gardens. Tells anyone who'll listen that he's always been an Anglophile, and certainly acts like one.'

'If I were in his position I'd say the same too: an English country house is preferable to a Red Army prison. But can we be sure he's telling us the truth? Let's not forget, this chap's been a professional intelligence officer for twelve or thirteen years, as I'm forever being reminded. We know he's run at least one very successful agent against us, and if we believe what he tells us – that he was no Nazi – then he's been extraordinarily clever to have survived for so long, especially when the Abwehr was pretty much dismantled last year.'

Harper leaned back in his chair surveying the room and angrily pushed a file to the other side of his desk. 'So if we agree he's telling the truth, we have a spy ring that comprises three traitors. One has disappeared into thin air, another is dead, and Byron continues to be a man of mystery – even Rauter says he doesn't know his true identity. We need to redouble our efforts to find Palmer, but if we find Byron, that may well lead us to Milton.'

'With respect, sir, I don't agree that we have no clue who Byron is.'

'Go on, Prince.'

'Rauter confirmed that he's British and lives – or lived – in Chelsea. He wasn't to know we already suspected Byron had a Chelsea connection, what with the radio trackers and the taxi driver who was given the letter by Agent Dryden and obligingly posted it to—'

'An address in Chelsea, yes, I don't need reminding. Hardly narrows it down, though, does it?'

Prince flicked through his notebook, appearing distracted. He said nothing as Harper closed the meeting and ordered King and Prince to come up with a plan to find Milton.

A few minutes later, Prince knocked on Hugh Harper's door. Could he have a private word?

'I'm anticipating you're about to say that your job is done and you wish to return to Lincolnshire – am I correct, Prince?'

'Actually, no, sir, my job is far from done: it's about Byron, actually.'

'Go on.'

'Apologies if this is a bit off track, sir, but when we were talking before about Byron and Chelsea, a thought occurred to me and I checked my notebook, where I often jot down seemingly inconsequential snatches of conversation only marginally related to a case: sometimes trivia like that helps jog the memory.'

'This is to do with Byron, is it, Prince?'

'It is indeed, sir. Here's the list of the attendees from the meeting at the Abbey Hotel in Pimlico back in 1939.'

He handed over a sheet of paper.

'Of course we know all about Chapman-Collins and Fenton...' Harper nodded. 'But we didn't get anywhere with the other names on the list – Bannister, Spencer, Davies, Philips, Cummings, Carver, Kemp. We wondered if Milton was one of them.'

'Came to a dead end, I recall.'

'I accept this is speculation, sir, but I think one of these is Agent Byron.'

'Which one?' Harper frowned as he studied the list.

'When you recruited me back in January, you may recall we talked about Byron and his possible Chelsea connection, and you took me for a drive there. When Rauter told us he believed Byron lived in Chelsea, there was something at the back of my mind that was bothering me, though I couldn't be sure what it was, so I looked back over the notes I made that day. I'd written down how you'd parked the car and we went for a stroll and bumped into a chap with a slight limp. You greeted each other and later you told me he was a steward at your club.'

Harper said nothing, but he was gripping the sheet of paper, his eyes wide.

'Good Lord – Spencer!'

Christopher Spencer's world collapsed in such a dramatic manner on Tuesday 22 May that he wondered whether his attempt to kill himself had succeeded after all and he was now in some deserved version of hell.

Hugh Harper had taken some persuading at first. After his initial expression of shock, he'd looked for reasons why Spencer might not be Byron: *Spencer's a common enough name… Maybe not that unusual for him to live in Chelsea… Tens of thousands of people live there… He's a decent chap, injured in the Great War, always obliging…* 'The case against him is circumstantial at best, Prince.'

'True, but then that's the way so many cases start. We have a suspect based on what may be just circumstantial evidence but then we look for firm evidence to build up a case against them. We have someone here we can link with the area and who has the same name as one of the attendees at the hotel.'

'What do you think, Lance?'

'I know Prince and I don't always see eye to eye, but there may well be something in this. There's no harm in investigating him, is there?'

Harper agreed, though with a degree of reluctance. It would, he said bitterly, be a terrible thing for the club if it turned out one of their stewards was a German spy: he'd feel person-ally responsible. The committee would take a dim view of the matter: they'd blame him. He'd have to resign from the membership committee.

It turned out Spencer was on duty at the club that day and wasn't due to finish until much later in the evening. Three of

Bartholomew's men were sent to watch the place in case he left early.

Prince then started digging. Christopher Spencer's name didn't crop up in any files held by MI5 or Special Branch: he appeared to be beyond reproach. He'd been born in Surrey in 1891 and joined up in 1914 only to suffer appalling injuries at the Battle of the Somme in July 1916, as a result of which he was invalided out of the army. He was twenty-five and left with a limp and no job, eventually becoming a steward at Harper's club, where he'd been since 1923.

'If we could go in and have a look at his flat while he's at work, sir, then maybe we can find some evidence – after all, the chances are that's where he transmitted from.'

'We'll need something more to justify that, Lance.'

'I thought MI5 didn't need an excuse, sir?'

'Only if we clear it with the director general, and I don't want to involve him yet. Get something more concrete and I'll allow it.'

'I think we ought to be careful, sir.'

'Why's that, Prince?'

'It's possible Spencer has someone watching the flat, someone who could alert him. I think it would be risky to go in now.'

Prince spent the next few hours poring over the files, but with no luck, until he decided on a different approach – concentrating his search instead on anything connected with Spencer's address. It was three in the morning when Harper was summoned back to his office. Bartholomew and King were already waiting with Prince.

'I searched using Spencer's address and came up with a reference to a Gerald Andrews living at that address. Between 1932 and 1935, Gerald Andrews was involved in a fascist organisation called the Imperial Fascist League, which I gather was a virulently anti-Semitic and pro-Nazi outfit. There is no record of him being involved with them after that period. Andrews is shown as residing at Flat 7, 18 Ascot Terrace, SW3 – the home address of Christopher Spencer, full name Christopher Gerald Andrew Spencer. According to the National Registration records at Chelsea police station, Spencer is the only person living at that address and the electoral roll shows he moved there in 1931.'

Harper nodded, apparently satisfied.

'I took the liberty of going to have a look at the address earlier this evening, just in case we needed to go in,' said Bartholomew. 'It's an attic flat with direct access to the rooftop. It would be a perfect place to transmit from – he could erect an aerial hidden in the high chimney stacks and then take it down when he'd finished. There's a communal entrance to the building but I think Spencer could escape across the rooftops. I'd be very surprised if he'd not planned that. My advice would be to go in now, sir. We don't want to make the mistake we made with Agent Donne, do we?'

–

Christopher Spencer was such a light sleeper, he always assumed he'd hear anyone well before they reached the front door of his flat. A combination of nerves and the constant pain in his leg ensured he was awake more often than not.

But he was woken by the noise, and it came not from his front door but from the lounge. It sounded as if the door to the roof had opened, but that was followed by silence. He reached for the pistol he kept by the side of the bed and sat up. The next moment his world fell apart: the sound of the front door crashing back, shouting outside his bedroom door as it burst open, and the glare of a powerful light trained on his face.

He remembered holding the pistol towards his head and pulling the trigger as someone launched themselves at him, and after that it was a confused sequence of senses: excruciating pain, a deafening noise that wouldn't abate, and the smell and taste of blood as he was hauled from his bed before he sank into a dark void.

His next memory was of waking shackled to a hospital bed, with a thick bandage round his head and an argument going on between a doctor and someone else saying they weren't leaving the room.

Now it was sometime on the Wednesday – or so he'd been told – and he was handcuffed to an uncomfortable chair in a large, low-ceilinged basement, the bright light shining into his face making it difficult for him to make out the three men behind the table in front of him.

One of them was asking why he'd tried to shoot himself if he was innocent as he insisted he was. He realised he'd made a mistake saying he was innocent when they'd not directly accused him of anything yet. He told them he had a headache and couldn't think properly, but they ignored him.

'I thought you were intruders so I pointed my pistol at you. I didn't try to shoot myself; someone must have knocked my hand.'

The man ignored him and fired a series of questions at him.

Are you Agent Byron?

Were you a member of the Imperial Fascist League, using the name Gerald Andrews?

Did you attend dinners at the Abbey Hotel in Pimlico in 1939 using your real name?

Were you recruited as a German agent by Arthur Chapman-Collins?

Did you know Jim Maslin, also known as Agent Donne, and did you kill him on Wormwood Scrubs last week?

What can you tell us about Edward Palmer – Agent Milton – and do you know where he is?

In response to every question he gave what he thought was, in the circumstances, a reasonable display of ignorance. He either shook his head, even though that hurt what remained of his left ear, or said sorry but he had no idea what they were talking about. It was encouraging that they were asking where Milton was: it was a month now since he'd disappeared. Maybe they had no evidence on him after all. He was glad he'd got rid of the knife that he'd used to kill Jim.

'I don't know any of these people you're talking about. I'm not a political person in any way. I'm a loyal and patriotic British citizen. I was wounded at the Somme. I wonder if this is a case of mistaken identity?'

He tried to ensure he didn't sound too confident. But what happened next changed his life, or what little there was left of it. The man asking the questions said something and the lights turned on. Now he could see everything: three men at the table, one of whom was none other than the Honourable Hugh Harper from the club! Another man had removed a cloth from a smaller table and on it was displayed the radio transmitter – the aerial, the wiring, everything. He stared at it in disbelief: he'd gone to such trouble to stash it all away a few weeks previously: the aerial moved to the roof of another building and concealed in a disused chimney, the transmitter pushed on rollers under the floorboards until it would be well out of sight. Just another week: he'd already booked a few days' leave to hire a van and dispose of the equipment. There wouldn't be fingerprints; he always used gloves.

'Agent Milton – Edward Palmer – left his apartment in Abbey Road on or around the twentieth of April. Where is he?' It was the man in the middle, the one who'd asked most of the questions.

'I haven't got the faintest idea who or what you're talking about.'

'How do you begin to explain all this equipment, Spencer?'

He hesitated for far too long before muttering that he'd never seen it before. 'Maybe it was in the flat before I moved in there?'

The man in the middle waited before replying. 'Who said anything about it being found in the flat?'

Spencer's ear throbbed and he was wincing with pain. He felt sick and dizzy and asked if he could have a break, and Hugh

Harper said something about not being silly and he should be ashamed of himself. It went on for over an hour, during which time he threw up even though he couldn't recall when he'd last eaten, and then wet himself, the humiliation of which was compounded by the three men falling silent as he did so, listening to what was going on. He tried to tell himself they had no evidence against him, but now it was apparent they did. He wondered whether to tell them something close to the truth – how he'd felt abandoned after the Great War, his life ruined; how he'd fallen in with the wrong crowd, who seemed to offer a solution, and by the time he tried to get out, it was too late – but he stopped himself. It would be tantamount to a confession.

He begged them to turn off the light shining into his face, but they ignored him and continued to fire the same questions at him. He realised he was crying; at first it was tears streaming down his face, but soon it was uncontrollable sobbing. He heard himself begging for them to stop.

Tell us when you met Agent Milton…

And so they continued until, as if by a prearranged signal, they fell silent and the bright light was turned off. He was aware of Hugh Harper standing next to him and giving him a glass of water, then patting him on the shoulder and telling him not to worry.

'We know you were put up to all this, Spencer: just tell us where Milton is and you have my word you'll be treated leniently. I know you're a decent sort.'

Spencer hesitated. The only evidence they seemed to have against him was the equipment, but then he'd made sure his fingerprints weren't on it and he'd burned all the code books, so maybe they didn't have as strong a case against him as he feared. But he resolved to remain silent. When he heard his own voice, it was as if someone else was speaking for him. 'If only I knew where he was, sir, I'd tell you, but he always treated me—'

He'd stopped himself at that point, but of course it was too late. He could only think of Jim Maslin, whose words had signed his own death warrant.

And now he had done the same.

Chapter 32

Ravensbrück and northern Germany, June 1945

She was the last prisoner to leave before the Red Army arrived.

On the Sunday morning, Hanne Jakobsen stepped over half a dozen bodies before curling up in a filthy corner of an abandoned hut to allow whatever was trying to consume her to run its course. As she covered herself with a ragged blanket and closed her eyes, she had no idea whether death or sleep was about to overwhelm her. She hadn't eaten for days and no longer had the energy to care.

Ravensbrück concentration camp had been quiet for a few days now. At one stage the vast complex had housed tens of thousands of prisoners, but now just a few thousand remained, most of them too sick to be moved.

She was woken by heavy coughing and a boot prodding her ribs. She looked up, surprised she was still alive. In the gloom she couldn't make out the figure standing above her, and for a brief, optimistic moment she wondered whether it was her Englishman, but the man who bent down with a look of disgust on his face was Mohr, the Gestapo officer. He threw some clean clothes at her and told her to get dressed.

'Hurry, the Russians are almost here.' He didn't take his eyes off her as she undressed and put on the clothes he'd brought with him.

When they left the hut, the camp seemed deserted: no guards in sight and just a few prisoners moving around uncertainly in the shadows like ghosts. He pushed her along and at the main entrance she recognised Hauptsturmführer Reeder waiting by Mohr's car. He was one of the SS officers in charge of the uniform workshop.

'You can go now,' Mohr told him, pausing for a prolonged bout of coughing. 'Remember, not a word.' He shoved Hanne into the back of the car and pointed to a paper bag with bread and cheese in it. 'Eat – there's water in that flask. And here, make yourself presentable.' He chucked a hairbrush onto the seat. 'If we get stopped, you don't say a fucking word, understand? We should be all right, we're about a day ahead of the Russians, but in case you have any funny ideas...' He waved a revolver in her direction.

For much of the journey he made her lie down on the back seat, so she had little idea where they were going, although she was sure they were heading north. From her prone position she could just make out the clock on the dashboard: the journey took a little over three hours.

In between bouts of coughing, Mohr spoke from time to time, mostly about the dreadful mistake the Allies had made, how awful the Russians would be, how at least the Jews had gone – well, most of them at any rate – and how he had a plan: he'd been an accountant before the war, he told her. People like him would be fine because they'd been smart.

She spotted a sign for Rostock, and soon after that they pulled off the main road and onto a narrower one. A few miles on he slowed down at the entrance to a narrow track and threw a blanket at her, telling her to put it over her head and keep it there until she was told otherwise. The next mile or so was over rough ground, the car bumping up and down and lurching from side to side, the undercarriage occasionally scraping the surface. When they eventually stopped, Mohr sat in silence as the engine died down and breathed a sigh of relief, followed by a cough, which sounded as bad as ever.

'Here at last. You're part of the preparations I was telling you about, by the way: you're going to be my insurance policy.'

'One week, Prince, I'll allow you one week over there and then I want you back here.'

'I'm not sure a week will be enough, sir.'

Hugh Harper looked at Prince in a manner suggesting he regarded the last remark as impertinent.

'You promised me I'd have an opportunity to return to Germany to find Hanne, sir. I've come to a dead end: MI9 have no more information on her and nor has the Danish government or the Swedish Red Cross. If I don't go soon—'

'I said you'd be able to go and look for her once we'd solved this case, which we haven't done yet. Until we find Edward Palmer, then...' Harper's voice trailed off as he gently shook his head at the thought of not finding Milton.

'Then what, sir?'

'Then I've still got Sir Roland Pearson and Downing Street on my back, not to mention the vultures in MI5 waiting to pick over my corpse. Palmer's a traitor: an officer who worked in the War Office. He can't be allowed just to vanish as if he never existed.'

'There is still my suggestion, sir: it could be our best chance of flushing him out.'

'I doubt I'll get approval for it. I've already run it past the Metropolitan Police: the commissioner won't have it. He doesn't think it's even legal.'

'What about if the request came from Downing Street?'

WANTED FOR MURDER

EDWARD PALMER (born 1907)

The Metropolitan Police Force urgently wishes to trace a (Major) Edward Palmer in connection with the murder of a seven-year-old girl in the Camden

Town NW1 area of London on or about Thursday 19 April 1945.

Palmer was last seen in the Abbey Road NW8 area on the morning of Friday 20 April. The suspect is formerly of the York and Lancaster Regiment but is not believed to be in uniform. Palmer is approximately six foot tall and speaks with an English accent and an occasional stammer.

A REWARD OF £250 WILL BE PAID FOR INFORMATION LEADING TO HIS ARREST

Hugh Harper studied the poster carefully and then turned it round so Prince and Lance King could see it too.

'Three photographs?'

'Different angles, sir.'

'Well let's hope this flushes him out. Sir Roland's ordered it to be displayed across the whole country: railway stations, bus stops.'

'And he was all right with the ethics of it, sir? After all, there was no murder, no seven-year-old girl...'

'One can never predict Sir Roland; he can be so enigmatic. As it happens, Prince, it rather appealed to his cunning nature. He asked whose idea it was and sounded very approving when I told him it was you. Wish I'd claimed the credit for it now. Of course the press will want to know all about the little girl, but hopefully we can deal with that.'

'The reward should help. Shame it couldn't be a bit more.'

'More? Hang on, Lance, that's coming from my budget as it is!'

–

Richard Prince arrived in Berlin on Friday 1 June with no intention of returning home until he'd found out what had happened to Hanne.

When he arrived at Behrenstrasse, Podpolkovnik Iosif Leonid Gurevich greeted him like an old friend. The Russian had a new box of much larger cigars and a crate of Italian wine they'd found in a basement.

'Now that I've had my revenge, I sleep a bit better at night. I don't have my family, but I have some... satisfaction. The German – Rauter – was he helpful to you?'

Prince said he was, thank you very much.

'Have some wine: I think Italian white wine is better than French white wine. I'm becoming a connoisseur! So you've returned to Berlin just to see how I am?'

'You remember I asked you to find out about a prisoner at Ravensbrück concentration camp – a Hanne Jakobsen?'

Gurevich nodded behind a thick cloud of cigar smoke.

'I know there was no news then, but I'd like to go there myself to try and trace her. Would you be able to help with any papers I'll need, and maybe transport?'

The Russian had swung his booted legs onto the desk and was toying with the end of his cigar. He watched Prince for a while. 'Do you love her?'

'How do you...?'

'I loved a woman in Moscow, before the war: Frida. She worked at the Foreign Ministry as a translator and was arrested on some nonsense charge – reading the foreign press, which was part of her job. To my everlasting shame I didn't intervene, which I could have done. When I was questioned about her, I admitted she was someone I slept with occasionally but said I found her too bourgeois. She was sent to Siberia; I've no idea if she's still alive. I could probably have saved her if I'd vouched for her, but that would have had a detrimental effect on my career. I've regretted it ever since: she was the love of my life and I behaved so badly. That is why I ask if you love this Hanne.'

'Of course I do.'

'Then I shall come with you!'

The commissar in charge at Ravensbrück was Boris Novikov, a fat NKVD major with an enormous head and a face raddled by drink and battle. He was considerably older than Gurevich and barely managed to conceal his resentment of him.

'The prisoners have all gone, Comrade Podpolkovnik: there were only around three and a half thousand when we liberated the camp on May Day. Some of those have since died; the others have been repatriated by now.'

'And no record of a Hanne Jakobsen?'

'I told you before: there's a record of her having been a prisoner here but no record of what happened to her.'

'Could she be dead?' It was the first time Prince had spoken. Gurevich was translating.

'There's no record of that, but then in the last few days the camp was in chaos, so it's possible.'

Novikov stepped back from them, his arms folded in front of him and a blank expression on his face, as if he had no more to say. 'My job here, Comrade, is to investigate war crimes. We captured some of the camp's SS officers. I think one of them might be able to help you.'

Hauptsturmführer Reeder was a wreck of a man, possibly over six feet but now stooped and trembling as he kept touching a face covered in cuts and bruises. He'd been dragged into Novikov's office and thrown to the floor. It took him a couple of minutes to climb painfully to his feet.

'Tell the colonel here what you told me. They understand German.'

'About the Gestapo man?'

'Get on with it.'

Reeder turned slowly to face Prince and Gurevich, a pleading look in his eyes. He held his shackled hands as if in prayer. 'I'm just a junior officer, believe me, sirs. Before the war I was a manager at a clothing factory in Leipzig, and that is how I ended up in the SS, to help run their clothing workshops.'

'So you're telling us you're just a tailor, eh? I imagine you're also going to tell us you're not a Nazi?'

Tears filled Reeder's eyes. 'I was obliged, sir: everyone was obliged. Please believe me: I have a wife and three children and I am God-fearing and—'

'He's wasting our time.' Gurevich had drawn his revolver. 'Don't you understand that saying you're God-fearing doesn't impress us?'

'Please – let me tell you what I told the other officer. I could have left the camp earlier; everyone was leaving it that weekend before your army arrived. In fact I was about to leave when a Gestapo officer arrived. He'd been here a few times before and said I was to remain until he'd finished. He wanted to know where a Danish prisoner was, Hanne Jakobsen.'

'So she was alive then?' Prince moved closer to the German, who recoiled as he approached. 'What day was this?'

'Either the Saturday or Sunday – the very end of April. She was definitely alive; we found her in a hut. She was asleep. I thought she was dead at first but he woke her, and when I saw them next they were marching to his car, where he'd told me to wait. He'd given her ordinary clothes to change into.'

'How did she look?'

Reeder shrugged. 'I'm sorry, what can I say? She was walking, if that means anything, but she'd been a prisoner here for some time. That Gestapo officer had taken a special interest in her, from what I understand. He'd been here before to question her. If it's any consolation, he had food and water in the car for her. I don't think he intended to kill her.'

'And where were they going?'

'I don't know. I tell you, I'm just a junior officer and—'

He stopped when Gurevich released the safety catch of his revolver. 'I think you know more than you're saying, Reeder.'

'I beg you, I have a family... All I know about him is that he's called Heinrich Mohr and he's deputy head of the Gestapo in Rostock – a large port maybe one hundred miles north of here.' Reeder looked nervously at Gurevich's revolver. 'And one other thing. I remember now what car he was driving: a black Mercedes-Benz, a 320 – my boss in Leipzig had the same model. That's everything I remember, please, sir, believe me.'

Gurevich nodded at the other Russian officer as he made to leave the room and beckoned for Prince to follow him. Moments later, they heard a brief cry followed by a gunshot.

–

'You want a Gestapo officer, do you, Comrade? I can do you all sorts of Gestapo officers: old, young, fat, thin, alive or dead. You have a choice.' The man laughed loudly and the half-dozen officers sitting around him obediently joined in.

He was a general from the 2nd Belorussian Front, confident that he was senior enough and with sufficient battle honours to get away with speaking like that to an officer from the NKGB. They were in the Red Army garrison in Rostock, the city looking as if the battle for it had ended that morning as opposed to a month before.

'His name's Heinrich Mohr. Apparently he was deputy head of the Gestapo here.'

'And you've brought a British officer to help you?'

'The British are our Allies, Comrade, and that British officer helped us find a war criminal, but if it's a problem for you, I can always let Moscow know that you...'

The general stared at him through narrowed eyes, chewing something noisily. 'No, no, no, Comrade: that's not necessary. Of course I can help. We're holding a dozen Gestapo officers in the prison: we've already executed two others.'

Gurevich told the general he wanted a junior Gestapo officer brought to him.

'Are you sure?'

'I do have some experience of interrogating prisoners, Comrade. A junior officer is far more likely to spill the beans about a senior one – especially if he believes that will save his life.'

The man they brought along was in his early thirties, filthy and unshaven and unsteady on his feet. His right arm was in a sling and he winced every time he moved. Gurevich told him to sit down, then nodded at Prince to ask the questions.

The German told them he wasn't even an officer in the Gestapo, no more than a senior sergeant. He looked after records and that kind of thing: he wanted to assure them he never dealt with prisoners or anything like that. Prince recognised the pleading look, the desperate protestations of innocence.

'Do you know Heinrich Mohr?'

'Of course.'

'Tell me about him.'

'He was the deputy head of the Gestapo in Rostock and indeed for much of Mecklenburg. He dealt with political issues and had good contacts in Berlin; in fact I believe he'd worked there earlier in the war.'

'Do you know where he is now?'

The prisoner shrugged: *You're asking me?* 'I've no idea. The office closed down at the end of April, when most of the staff fled west. Those of us who stayed had family in Rostock, like I did – and Mohr.'

'Really?'

'I told you, I worked in our records department, which included staff records. Mohr had an apartment in Rostock but that was destroyed during the battle for the city. I do know Mohr moved his family to his wife's family farm in Mecklenburg – my guess is he'll be there.'

The prisoner fell silent, gingerly moving his arm and shifting uncomfortably in his seat. Prince studied his papers: there was no question he was indeed as junior as he claimed to be.

'I can take you there if you want.'

They left Rostock as first light broke with none of the usual bustle that normally accompanied a city coming alive: no lights turning on in buildings, no curtains being drawn, no queues at bus stops or noise of early-morning deliveries. Instead their convoy slowly picked its way through damaged streets and along barely passable roads.

The prisoner sat in the front of a staff car alongside Gurevich, Prince in the back seat. The general had given them an NKVD platoon of thirty men. The prisoner clutched a map and told them to head south-west out of the city.

By the time they'd been driving for an hour, the Mecklenburg countryside was bathed in sunlight. The prisoner kept glancing at the map, occasionally asking them to stop so he could check the name of a village they were approaching, and then giving directions to take them on for another few miles. There was something about him that made Prince trust him. He was also smart: he realised it was in his interests to reveal details of Mohr's whereabouts bit by bit. Prince felt his own breathing quickening: he was convinced they were getting closer to Hanne.

An hour and a half out of Rostock they came to a village and the prisoner said they should stop. 'We need to ask someone now. The farm's supposed to be somewhere round here. The family's name is Brandt.'

They found the village priest and dragged the terrified man to the small convoy gathered in front of his church. *No, I'm sorry, I don't know any family of that name in this area… You must have the wrong village… Possibly one closer to Rostock?*

Five minutes later, with his family lined up against the wall of the church, he displayed a power of recall that had previously eluded him.

Now I think about it, yes, of course I know the Brandt family, good God-fearing folk. I think you must have made a mistake, though. They're just poor farmers… not involved in the war at all.

The priest guided them to the farmhouse, which was only just visible from the top of the narrow lane that led to it. Gurevich spoke with the major in charge of the troops accompanying them. Half of the men were to form a perimeter fifty yards from the building and hold its line as he moved in with the others.

A hundred yards from the farmhouse, Gurevich ordered them to stop and leave their vehicles. The platoon approached on foot. At the farmyard gate the troops took cover. The priest was ordered to go to the front door and ask for help: he was to tell them his car had broken down.

'I don't have a car.'

'Just go and tell them. You see the rifles these men are carrying? A dozen of them will be trained on you.'

There was a small ditch by the open gate and Prince dropped into it, watching the priest's tentative approach to the front door. A long wisp of smoke spiralled from a chimney and he was sure he saw someone walk past a window. Inside an open barn he spotted a black Mercedes-Benz 320.

When the door opened, there was no sign of danger: a couple perhaps in their fifties greeted the priest and appeared to invite him in. He retreated down the steps and pointed to the drive. There was still no sign of concern from inside the house. The man – who Prince guessed was Mohr – strolled into the farmyard behind the priest and followed him to the gates.

They were just feet away when Gurevich leapt up and shouted in Russian. Within moments the two men had been thrown to the ground and the rest of the NKVD platoon raced into the house. Despite Gurevich telling him to wait, Prince ran in too. Two women were on their knees in the hallway, their hands high in the air. Some of the troops had rushed upstairs, from where there came the sound of children screaming and of doors being slammed and furniture pushed over. Downstairs, other troops were moving from room to room and into the basement.

'They say there's no sign of her, sir.'

Prince ordered the women to stand up. One was middle-aged, the other much older. 'Is there another woman here?' The pair shook their heads.

'A foreign woman – from a camp? You must have seen her!'

The women began to sob but said nothing as they huddled closer together. Gurevich shouted orders in Russian and marched outside telling Prince to follow him. The man from the farmhouse was on his knees, and they were now joined by the Gestapo sergeant they'd brought from Rostock.

'Who's this?' Gurevich asked him.

The sergeant said nothing as he stepped back and looked away from the man on the ground.

'Come on, you'd better not be wasting our time.'

'That's Heinrich Mohr.'

Mohr shot a furious look at his former colleague and then looked down at the ground. He coughed violently and spat a mixture of blood and phlegm and a couple of teeth onto the ground.

Prince bent down to him. 'Look, Mohr, we know you were at Ravensbrück the day before the Red Army arrived there, and that you took away a Danish prisoner called Hanne Jakobsen in a black Mercedes-Benz 320, just like the one parked over there. I want to know where she is.'

Mohr said nothing; blood trickled from his mouth. A bruise was forming on his temple and one of his eyes was swollen. Prince leaned closer. 'Let me tell you this: I'm a British officer. I've been sent to find this woman. All the others are Russians and they have a very different approach to prisoners, so I think it would be in your interests and those of your family to tell me where she is.'

Mohr coughed again and his face turned red. Gurevich was shouting in Russian; moments later, three children were dragged out of the house and lined up in front of Mohr: two teenage girls and a younger boy.

Prince whispered into the Russian's ear. 'Not the children, Iosif, please.'

'Don't you want to find your woman?' Gurevich turned to Mohr. 'You: I'll give you one chance to answer his question. Where's the Danish woman you collected from the camp?'

Mohr looked up as the Russian trained his revolver on the three children.

'But I rescued her – I let her go! I was driving back to Rostock from Berlin and stopped off at the camp: she'd helped me with an investigation and I wanted to help her in return. I dropped her off at a crossroads just outside Malchow. I even gave her money to escape.'

'Ha! Who needs the Red Cross when we have the Gestapo?' Gurevich took aim with his revolver. 'I don't believe you!'

'No, Father, please… I beg you to tell them where she is!' It was his son, looking terrified.

'Shut up, Hans!'

'She's in the barn!' The boy was crying. 'I've seen him go there: there's a trap door underneath the car. Please spare us!'

Mohr looked up at Prince, a look of terror on his face as his body hunched into a pleading position. 'Please, you must believe me. I knew this woman was important to the Allies; that's why I took her from Ravensbrück. I hoped saving her would save me. I thought if I was ever questioned, I'd be spared because I'd rescued her. But I had no idea she was so ill. It's a miracle I kept her alive so long! I swear to you I was going to get a doctor for her, that's the honest truth – I swear on my children's lives. When I checked her last night she was very poorly. I pray she hasn't died overnight, but if she has, it's not my fault, I tell you… How was I to know she was so ill?'

—

They brought her out and laid her on the floor of the lounge in the farmhouse. Prince was in a state of profound shock. The woman stretched out on the floor didn't appear to be alive: her chest wasn't moving and her eyes were glazed. Nor did she look like Hanne, her skin taut and deathly white, her hair filthy and matted.

But he hadn't counted on the battle-hardened medics of the NKVD platoon, more skilled than many doctors, and now two of them worked on Hanne with an intensity that appeared like an act of religious devotion. At first it seemed a hopeless cause as they urgently gave her chest compressions and mouth-to-mouth resuscitation. Her eyes had now closed. One of the medics spoke to Gurevich, who called Prince out of the room.

'You can see how ill she is, my friend.' He gripped Prince's arm as he spoke.

'I realise.'

'They say she may have typhus or another disease and her heart is in trouble. They fear she may not have long. You need to prepare yourself.'

Prince felt the hallway swirl around him and he leaned against the wall. Gurevich's grip tightened.

'They're going to try one more procedure. They say really a doctor should do it, but there's nothing to lose.'

A medical bag was rushed in from their truck and Prince watched from the doorway as they appeared to inject her around the heart. He moved into the room: he wasn't sure if it was his imagination, but he thought he saw her eyelids flicker and she appeared to be breathing on her own, though the breaths were shallow and with long gaps between them. One of the medics – a boy who looked hardly out of his teens but with the knowing eyes of an old man – gestured for Prince to come closer and gently lifted her hand and put it in his.

'He says she may be able to hear, my friend. They say to talk to her.'

Prince lay on the floor next to her, still gripping her hand and whispering into her ear. He told her who he was and how much he loved her and how he'd always known he'd find her and she must be strong and hold on. They gave her another injection, this time in her neck, and her lips briefly moved. One of the medics shouted out *Voda! Voda!* and a flask of water was produced and pressed to her lips. The younger medic gently raised her head and gave more urgent instructions. Someone passed him a bottle of brandy and he spooned a tiny amount into her mouth as if he was feeding a baby. Some colour briefly returned to her face before she turned deathly white again and her breathing became even shallower.

She seemed to be slipping away, and Prince held her hand as if to stop her falling.

'The medics say to wait. If the injections are to work, then maybe...'

Prince stroked her face and gently kissed her cheeks. One of the medics felt for the pulse in her neck and shook his head, and Prince tried to scream but couldn't make a sound. But then came the most remarkable few moments of his life, and he wouldn't have believed it had happened had Gurevich not confirmed it later.

Hanne's eyes opened. Not in the gradual way they do when someone emerges from a long sleep; rather they shot open and she stared ahead of her as if unfocused. Prince remembered being told that people often did this at the moment of death, and feared this was what was happening, and he screamed, 'Hanne!'

Her head tilted in his direction and her eyes now appeared less glassy, and he could have sworn she recognised him. She closed her eyes again slowly, but the faintest of smiles had appeared on her lips and he could feel her hand gripping his, weakly at first, but soon quite firmly.

As they carried her stretcher to the ambulance in the farm-yard, Prince noticed the troops from the NKVD platoon come to attention, including those about to hang Heinrich Mohr from the beams of the barn.

Chapter 33

Germany and England, June–August 1945

The day the war ended in the middle of August also happened – by coincidence – to be the day Edward Palmer's new life began.

He had fled London four months before and done his best to stick to his plan: head north and keep moving, never more than two nights in one place, use buses where possible and wait for the war to end.

By early June he was in Manchester, and he felt it would be safe to stay there for a while. It was a busy city still recovering from heavy bombing and no one appeared to have much time for anyone else. He found a bedsit in Salford, and when he realised the landlord was never around, he decided to stay there for a month.

He was outside Oxford Road station in the city centre when he first saw the horrific poster: WANTED FOR MURDER: EDWARD PALMER. He hurried to find a bus back to Salford and spotted another poster outside a police station. He didn't leave the bedsit for a week, lying on the bed or pacing round the room, feeling like he really had murdered a child and waiting for the door to burst open. By the time he ventured out, he'd begun to grow a beard, and although his first outing was tense, no one gave him so much as a second look. At a busy market he bought a bottle of black hair dye and a second-hand pair of thick-framed spectacles, which were weak enough to make them quite wearable. Within a fortnight he had trouble recognising himself in the mirror.

Before leaving Manchester, he took a gamble he'd always planned: buying a new identity card on the black market because he reckoned any false identity had a limited shelf life. It took him the best part of a week to arrange: finding someone in a pub, money changing hands, arranging to meet someone else in a different pub the following night, more money, the process repeating itself and depleting his wallet further until one Thursday night, when it was raining so hard he feared the dye from his hair would be running down his face, he knocked on the door of a dark basement within sight of Old Trafford.

But the man he'd been told to meet was charming and reminded him of his grandfather. He sat Palmer down with a cup of tea and a plate of biscuits and said to call him Michael, and fussed over him just like his grandfather used to, saying this would be no problem at all, sir, and everyone had a reason for needing new papers, and of course it was none of his business, this was his job after all, and there was no one out there who didn't have a little secret or two, and we're nearly done, sir, and I hope you understand, sir, but there will have to be a surcharge of ten pounds, but I think you'll find the quality is second to none.

Palmer was conscious of his stammer but insisted that for the extra ten pounds Michael must hand over the negatives and the roll of film. He had to admit his new papers were very good. He immediately felt comfortable as Harold Hamilton: he'd ask people to call him Harry.

He'd had plenty of time to think where to go next: anywhere near his home town of Kidderminster, or Cambridge where he'd lived for so long, was out of the question, as was London, of course. He'd read something in the paper about how farms were desperate for people to help with the harvest, so he headed to south Lincolnshire and found work on a farm just north of Boston, where the fields backed onto the River Witham and the elderly farmer and his wife were grateful to have him and were more than happy to leave him to get on with the job.

He had his own room in an outbuilding, and although it was gruelling work, by the middle of August he'd lost more than a stone in weight and developed a tan, making him look even less like the child killer Edward Palmer.

He almost relaxed at the farm: it was as if time was suspended while he was there. He never left the premises and could just be Harry, a quiet man who was happy to work hard in return for cash and his meals and being left alone. But he knew he'd soon have to move on and find somewhere more permanent.

One evening in the second week of August, the farmer's wife asked him to help out in their garden. She followed him around, giving her opinion on the bombs that had just destroyed two Japanese cities and asking him why they couldn't have done the same to Berlin, and he said he had no idea and do you want me to cut this shrub back?

No, she replied, I like to keep it as it is: it's a myrtle. And without thinking, he replied that was nice because he had a friend called Myrtle.

Thereafter he was consumed by two thoughts: how on earth had he forgotten about Myrtle, and how could he find her?

He'd met Myrtle through Arthur, the man who twelve years previously had found him one rainy night in Cambridge and begun the process of recruiting him as a German spy, though he'd not realised it at the time.

After that, he'd hear from Arthur two or three times a year: a handwritten letter telling him where they were to meet a fortnight or so later. A generous cheque was always enclosed to cover his expenses.

They tended to be soulless meetings: he had little in common with Arthur and didn't terribly like the man; indeed he resented him for having inveigled him in the first place into something he knew he was unable to extricate himself from. He had the impression the purpose of these encounters was for Arthur to check he hadn't gone off the rails.

The last time they'd met had been in early December 1938 – a largely silent lunch in a stuffy restaurant on Jermyn Street. As it came to a merciful close, Arthur said there was someone he'd like him to meet, and within moments a woman he introduced as Mary had joined them at their table.

She was a good ten years older than Palmer, possibly even in her mid forties, but with a very pretty face and an air of sophistication that completely charmed him – so much so that after half an hour he realised Arthur had slipped away and he hadn't noticed. She told him she had rooms nearby and he was to join her, which he did as if in a trance.

It wasn't his first time with a woman, though it might as well have been. She persuaded him to stay that night and for much of the following day, and had she allowed him to, he doubted he'd ever have left. But in the middle of the following afternoon, she told him it was time to go. When he'd dressed, she was waiting for him in the tiny kitchen with two large sherries.

'I want you to know I'm aware what you do for the cause.'

He was about to reply that he really wasn't sure what she meant, but she hushed him and continued.

'I want you to know how much I admire you: if only there were more men like you.' She paused as if unsure whether to continue, and then pointed to the bedroom. 'That was… work, you know, they wanted to be sure there wasn't anything… untoward about you, nothing they'd need to be concerned about. There isn't.'

She finished her sherry before he'd begun his and moved close to him, her hand stroking his face before resting on his shoulder. 'I'm not supposed to see you again, but I want you to know that if you ever need me – really need me, I mean as a matter of life or death – my real name is Myrtle. Not far from here – in Cork Street – is an art gallery called Bourne and Sons Fine Art. Bourne is spelt B-O-U-R-N-E. You'll need to visit it in person and ask for either a Mr Bourne or a Mr Ridgeway, and enquire if they have any works by an artist called Myrtle. If they say no and inform you they no longer sell her works, you must leave immediately and never return. But otherwise they'll ask your name. Give me one you'll remember.'

He looked around the room and spotted the bottle of sherry. 'Mr Harvey.'

–

It had been touch and go for a while. They'd taken Hanne to the Red Army field hospital in Rostock, where her condition deteriorated. The doctors explained that her body was overwhelmed by typhus. On her second night there a doctor took Prince aside and said he should follow her outside, where she lit a cigarette and leaned against a wall.

'She needs to be in a specialist hospital in your country. She requires drugs we don't have. You need to arrange it as soon as possible.'

By the end of the week, Hanne was stronger. Prince had heard that the British 6th Airborne Division was based just thirty miles to the west, in Wismar, and she was taken there by ambulance and then flown to Britain. A week after being rescued from the farmhouse in Germany, she was in hospital in London. Her condition worsened again, and apart from a brief visit to Lincoln to see his son, Prince spent every waking moment at her bedside. After a few days she regained consciousness and seemed much better. That evening he bumped into her elderly doctor in the corridor.

'It was touch and go: I've no idea how she managed to survive.'

Prince felt tears forming in his eyes. Would she recover fully?

'Oh, I expect so: women are far more resilient than we are. I understand,' the doctor dropped his voice and looked round, 'your wife operated behind enemy lines for us?'

Prince replied that that was right, but she wasn't actually his wife.

'Really? I've never met a couple more obviously suited. You'd better get on with it, hadn't you?'

He left the farm in Lincolnshire in the middle of August and travelled down to London. He knew he was taking an enormous risk. He'd met Myrtle almost seven years previously and anything could have happened to her in that time, nor could he be sure the art gallery would still be there, and even if it was, whether Mr Bourne or Mr Ridgeway would still be around.

He'd travelled to the capital on VJ Day and people were even more euphoric than they'd been on VE Day. The whole country seemed to be partying and no one paid any attention to him.

Bourne and Sons Fine Art was a small gallery with a dark painting in an ornate frame in the window and a musky smell inside. It appeared deserted until an elderly man in a three-piece suit emerged from the back and asked how he could help. Prince asked whether a Mr Bourne or a Mr Ridgeway was there. He sounded hesitant: he wasn't certain he'd remembered the last name correctly. His stammer must have sounded quite pronounced. The man said he was Mr Ridgeway and how could he help?

'Do you sell any works by an artist called Myrtle?'

The man had been shuffling around and wringing his hands but now stood quite still. For a while he said nothing, looking at the man in front of him in disbelief, then beyond him into the street. Without saying a word, he went to the door and locked it, turned the 'Open' sign to 'Closed' and pulled down a blind. 'And may I ask your name, please, sir?'

'Mr Harvey.'

He was told to return at eight the following morning. When he did so, an anxious Mr Ridgeway hurried him in and took him to a cluttered office at the back.

'We've heard all about you and seen those dreadful posters. We wondered what had happened to you. We can't have you hanging round London, though, can we?'

Edward Palmer agreed.

'Myrtle will look after you. She said she was wondering when you'd be in touch.'

'Thank you, I—'

'Please don't thank us. We ought to thank you. Now, we don't want to write this down, do we, so you'd better listen. I'll let you out the back and then you should walk to Marylebone station. We are sure they don't know anything about us, but you can never be too careful. Are you all right for money?'

Edward Palmer said he was fine.

'Purchase a return ticket – always looks less suspicious, I'm told. You probably know that kind of thing better than I do. When you arrive at your destination, leave the station and keep walking. Don't look for Myrtle – she'll find you.'

'Where am I going?'

'I am sorry, I ought to have told you that first. Your destination is Gerrards Cross.'

Aftermath

Justice was meted out to Christopher Gerald Andrew Spencer with what in more normal times would have been described as improper haste. Agent Byron had been caught in May, and with the end of the war in sight, Hugh Harper worried that could mean the end of emergency regulations, which permitted treason trials to be held behind closed doors and with any publicity kept to a minimum. Spencer went on trial at the Old Bailey on the first Monday in July, and by the Thursday afternoon he had been found guilty. He was sentenced to death the following morning and his appeal and plea for clemency were disposed of by the end of the month.

On the evening of Thursday 2 August, Spencer was visited in his death cell at Pentonville by Prince and Lance King. Since his first interview he had given nothing away, remaining largely silent other than occasional protestations of innocence or ignorance. No, he told them, he had absolutely no idea where Edward Palmer could be. 'I'm terrified: don't you think if I could tell you I would?'

He was executed at nine o'clock the following morning.

–

MI5 was satisfied that Franz Rauter had told the truth and provided them with invaluable information. Indeed, the former Abwehr officer had so impressed Hugh Harper that he had a word with Tom Gilbey, and Prince was deputed to broach with Rauter the possibility of him working for the British.

The German was surprisingly amenable to the idea, and in September he returned to Germany with a new identity.

–

Iosif Leonid Gurevich's combination of cunning, intelligence and competence, along with his relative sobriety, marked him out in Soviet-occupied Berlin, so much so that within months he'd been promoted from *podpolkovnik* to a one-star commissar.

Author's Note

Ring of Spies is a work of fiction, so any similarities between characters in the book and real people are unintended and should be regarded as purely coincidental.

There are references to obviously non-fictional characters such as Winston Churchill and Hitler, and in Chapter 7 (and elsewhere) real people such as Schellenberg and Keitel are featured in the context of the German High Command, but otherwise none of the book's characters existed in real life.

The spy ring at the core of the plot – Milton, Byron, Donne et al. – is fictional, but *Ring of Spies* is factually based on the Second World War, so many of the locations and events mentioned in the book are genuine.

In particular the central plot of the story is built around three important military engagements: Arnhem (September 1944); the Battle of the Bulge (December 1944–January 1945) and the crossing of the Rhine at Remagen (March 1945).

There is no evidence that the failure of the British airborne assault on Arnhem was due to espionage. However, it is a fact that Field Marshal Model's Army Group B intelligence officers had predicted an airborne assault in that area, and Model had chosen to base himself there, along with the 9th and 10th Panzer divisions.

Much of the detail relating to the Battle of the Bulge is based on fact, including the various massacres carried out by the German forces – most notably the murder of more than eighty US Army prisoners of war at Malmedy by units of Lieutenant Colonel Joachim Peiper's 6th SS Panzer Army.

The unexpected capture of the bridge over the Rhine at Remagen by units of the US Army's 9th Armored Division is based on fact. Capturing a bridge of this size intact probably shortened the war by a matter of weeks.

In Chapter 5, references to the resistance in Belgium are based on real organisations, in particular the Armée Secrète and the communist Milices Patriotiques. Schaerbeek was a stronghold for the communist resistance. The Luftwaffe was based at the Hotel Metropole and the Gestapo in Avenue Louise.

There was indeed a Directorate of Military Intelligence at the War Office, and it did include sections such as MI4, MI5, MI6 and MI9. However, the section where Major Edward Palmer was based – MI18 – is fictional.

Ultra is the now well-known British system to break top-secret German codes at Bletchley Park. Knowledge of it during the war (and for many years afterwards) was highly restricted.

Latchmere House in south London and Huntercombe in Oxfordshire (chapters 3 and 4) were both MI5 interrogation centres during the war.

The following regiments referred to in *Ring of Spies* were all part of the British Army in the Second World War: the Nottinghamshire and Derbyshire Regiment, the Royal Dragoons, the York and Lancaster Regiment and the Middlesex Regiment.

As remarkable as it may seem, the Germans did indeed establish a British Free Corps, which was intended to be a British unit within the SS. They recruited from among British prisoners of war but were notably unsuccessful: at its height, the Free Corps had fewer than one hundred members and never saw action. Most of its members – known as renegades – were prosecuted after the war but treated surprisingly leniently.

And talking of fascists… the Imperial Fascist League, with which Spencer is linked (Chapter 31), did exist during the 1930s (as did Mosley's British Union of Fascists, which is also referred to). It was dissolved when the war started. Many British fascists were held in detention during the war under Defence Regulation Section 18B – as is the case with Vince Curtis in Chapter 18. Many of these prisoners were held at Brixton as he was.

Franz Rauter worked for the Abwehr, the German military intelligence organisation. The Abwehr long pre-dated the Nazis and was regarded as a professional and successful operation. However, it was increasingly distrusted by the regime (its heads, Admiral Canaris and General Oster, were not party members) and was abolished in February 1944 with its functions being taken over by the RSHA.

I've endeavoured to be as accurate as possible about Ravensbrück. This Nazi concentration camp was primarily for women, and it is estimated that it held about 130,000 prisoners during the war, of whom around 90,000 were murdered there. The British SOE agents Violette Szabo, Denise Bloch and Lilian Rolfe were murdered at Ravensbrück on 5 February 1945. The camp was also an important industrial complex for the Nazis. There was a death march involving around 25,000 prisoners towards Mecklenburg in March 1945, and the following month hundreds of prisoners were rescued by the Swedish Red Cross and taken to Denmark. The camp was liberated by the Red Army on 30 April.

The Palace Arms, where Arthur Chapman-Collins was killed (Chapter 20), did exist during the war in that exact location, though as is the case with so many pubs, it is now a residential block.

In *Ring of Spies* there are references to sums of money in pounds sterling. I used the Bank of England website to estimate the value of those sums today: £5 in 1945 would be worth in 2019 (the latest date they have) £217, which equates to approximately €243 or US $275.

I'd like to express my sincere thanks and appreciation to the many people who've helped bring about the publication of this book, not least my agent Gordon Wise at Curtis Brown who has been enormously supportive over a number of years. My publishers Canelo have done a fantastic job with the *Prince* series and also in re-publishing my *Spy Masters* novels. Their enthusiasm and drive have been impressive and motivating not least because I began writing *Ring of Spies* in the middle of March, days before the COVID-19 lockdown began in the UK but Michael Bhaskar and Kit Nevile and the whole team at Canelo remained utterly professional and helpful throughout. Thanks too to Jane Shelley for her skilful copy-edit and to the many people who helped me with aspects of the book and answered seemingly odd questions as I was writing it.

And finally to my family – especially my wife Sonia, my daughters and their partners and my grandsons – for their encouragement, understanding and love.

Alex Gerlis
London, August 2020